Rodney Stone joined Government service after the RAF and Cambridge University. He has held senior posts in five Government departments and was the recipient of a Nuffield Fellowship. He has travelled extensively on various official assignments. He has now resigned to write full-time.

He is married and lives with his wife and their two children in London.

By the same author

The Dark Side of the Hill

RODNEY STONE

Cries in the Night

HarperCollinsPublishersLtd

A hardcover edition of this book was published by
HarperCollins Publishers in Great Britain: 1991

First HarperCollins Publishers Ltd paperback edition: 1992

Canadian Cataloguing in Publication Data

Stone, Rodney, 1932-
   Cries in the night

ISBN 0-00-647395-4

I. Title.

PR6069.T66C74 1992   823'.914   C92-094501-5

92 93 94 95 96 97 98 99 HC 10 9 8 7 6 5 4 3 2 1

Printed in Great Britain by
HarperCollinsManufacturing Glasgow

CRIES IN THE NIGHT

Prologue

I dreamed that I was back in France last night. A road shining in the dusk, a donkey's head over the fence. Back at the house with the shadows closing in. Trees. Oak and ash and walnut trees, waving under the storm wind. A litany of trees.

Shadows in the wood. Long shadows, late shadows, after a hot day when the sun lay thick as butter on the country-side. Fantastic shadows under the swaying branches, dancing round a clearing, where the woodcutters had left their coppicing. And my children's voices, clear in the evening air, like bells, shouting and calling. But dark. Too dark for me to see their faces. One, two, three, four children, shrieking round a palisade of logs. Bang bang, you're dead. A kind of catch-me game, and two of them making a fortress, a timber stockade. Some of the voices are French, French children with the accents of the south, but I can hear them in English.

'Come on, you're my prisoner.'

A scream of fear. The knowledge that it's happening again. A rumble of distant thunder like the premonition of rain.

The evening shadows are darker, deeper, and the game becomes more excited, more hysterical. A child is running away into the trees, trying to escape, but they are chasing him, the others, boy and girl, manically pleased to be catching, to be holding, to be tying him.

'Got you!'

Another shout as they hit him. The fourth figure disappears, but these three, they are real. Brother and sister, calling, 'Come on, it's only a game.'

The wood is darkest now, the sun submerged in storm clouds. Why don't they go home? Why, why why? I ask myself, seeing these children run, the great trees full of leaf, the crackling undergrowth dry with the drought of summer.

'Come back!'

The figures have closed together, pushing the other child with them, into the timber palisade in the middle of the silent woods.

A prisoner. His hands and feet are tied and he is shut in the prison, the fortress, the log house that they have made in the clearing.

'Leave me alone. Please.' I can hear him.

'Shut up,' the bigger boy says, but I cannot see their faces, only hear them. If only I could stop them, then it would be all right . . . but they are forcing him inside the little structure made of sticks and lumber, with a roof of dried grass.

'That's enough,' the girl says. 'We've done enough.'

The bigger boy ignores her. I can hear his laughter, shrieking round the captive.

'Let him go,' she says.

'Fe, fi, fo, fum, I smell the blood of an Englishman.'

My children, my trees, my summer. Why should they say such things? But the children have joined hands again, the boy and girl, and now they are running and jumping, barricading the door of the hut.

I seem to be there and not there. Stateless, bodiless, lost. I try to speak and say nothing, but I see the trees bending down as night comes on.

'Let's burn it,' the bigger boy says.

The girl shakes her head, urges him to come away. They sit in the grass, almost hidden, and stare at the hut they have made, this bastille in the secret clearing.

And suddenly there are matches.

'No,' she begs. 'No. No. No.'

But the boy is shouting again, seeing how easily it lights, this tinder of the hot summer, leaves and sticks and peelings in the clearing.

'It's burning, it's burning.'

'No. No. No. He's still inside.'

But he piles dried grasses on the already flickering pyramid of bark and branches, from which there is flame, then smoke, then flame again, fierce yellow-blue flames.

'Put it out,' she screams. 'Stamp on it.' But a furnace of wind as the thunder rolls nearer catches the flames even before he can shout, and blows them crackling and swooping like a tidal wave over the hut.

'The boy has gone,' he says. 'I let him out. Let it burn and burn.'

'No. No. Are you sure?'

He grins like a maniac, waves his arms in excitement. 'Burn down the traitor's palace.'

She shouts at him. Then he is gone, inside the wall of flame, the acrid smoke of burning grass.

'Come back! *Come back!*'

Dancing figures now. How many are there, how many? One, two, three. In and out of the flames, engulfing the wooden hut, scorching the grass at their feet.

She runs inside the fire.

Flames go higher and higher. The children have disappeared now, but then I hear the screams. A scream of torment, and fear and torture and death. Unforgettable, scored on the mind.

I hear them, I see them, they've gone. The donkey brays like doom.

I wake up shouting, time after time, remembering that summer. The bed is wet with sweat and Emma is holding me.

1

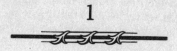

I didn't have those dreams before. In hot weather, such as that midsummer, we used to sleep easily, Emma and I, under the high ceilings of the London house, while I thought about us.

A house. A family. A home. The kids snug in their bedrooms. And break my back to keep it so, I told myself. Every day of the week.

Emma stirred beside me, half opened one eye. 'Where have you been?'

'Honey. Working. You know that.' She remembered I'd come back late, after she had drifted to sleep.

She moved. I liked to see the curves of her body, the blonde hair and the soft limbs.

'Martin broke the Buddha's head.'

It was bad medicine. I treasured that souvenir, and gave a groan of displeasure.

'Jim. The boy is sorry. It was only china.'

'What the hell was he doing playing around with it? Jesus Christ. Kids.'

'Leave him alone,' she said.

She rolled over on to her back. I saw her face in profile against the window with the chimney pots along the roof, a skyline out of *Peter Pan*. The old house lay still. A moon like a fingernail clipping in a luminous sky. This was Richmond, London, Georgian Richmond of handmade bricks, and cast-iron lamp-posts that masqueraded as genuine. I loved it as an adopted country, but a man in another country is like a man without a memory, not sure who he is. I wasn't quite in that position – I was a US architect married for fourteen years to an English girl – but somehow we were growing apart. I wasn't identifying with Emma, and she knew it.

I was there, in the marital bed, and all I could do was curse about a piece of broken china, bought in goddam Calcutta, when we remodelled the airport there five years back. Emma just shifted away from me as if I was infected.

'Honey?'

'What?'

'Kids OK?'

'Yes.'

I put out a hand to feel her thigh and knew she didn't want me.

'It's late.'

'It's only one o'clock, darling.'

'For God's sake, I'm shattered. Aren't you even tired?'

'Guess I'm kind of tired. Been working my butt off on that lousy Bristol job.'

'Uh . . . huh.'

OK, she didn't understand. I suspected she had no idea of the pressures on me, on earning a living. One minor problem with marriage was wives who thought they should be up there on a pedestal, while Joe Soap hunted the cash. But maybe that was unfair. I mulled things over beside her, sensing her displeasure. If she could only realize how much I sweated to please her, how vulnerable I still was about being accepted.

I had learned as a kid in the States that what counted was getting things right. Mom always said that. What had counted with me was marrying Emma and all that classy history that somehow she embodied. Making it in another country. Why couldn't she see what I was striving for, the house, the family, the job, the success we had gathered around us?

There would be no joy that night, and I wanted some shuteye. Visions of the landscape that I had chosen. Jesus, could I ever explain how much I liked it, and them, the community, the countryside, the oldness, everything stopping for tea. It was for her sake that I was grafting in Dorcas Freeling, but recently it seemed that the more the business flourished the more we failed to connect, Emma and I.

What the hell was it, I worried. She had two kids, she knew that I loved her. But there was something missing. I guessed it wasn't something sexual, or even personal. It was as if we had grown stale, married past the sell-by date, as if we needed a challenge, a shake-up, that neither of us found easy in the years of commitment, of striving for the bread and butter.

The kids came down to breakfast early, long before Emma stirred. I had looked at her face on the pillow and kissed her as I slipped out of bed, but she murmured and wriggled away. I had showered and dressed aiming for a quick get-away but suddenly Martin was there, in the kitchen door. Maybe he just smelt coffee: Emma preferred tea in the morning, but I had to have my fix of Brazilian blend.

'Hi,' I said, the percolator bubbling away.

'Hullo.' Martin, first-year boy at King's, Wimbledon, usually dug himself in till ten or eleven in the morning on Saturdays like this. Now he slipped into the kitchen fresh-faced, round-eyed, sleepy but looking determined.

'You going back to the office?'

'Sure.'

'Dad. I'm sorry. About breaking that Buddha thing.'

I guess I sounded choked off.

'Martin. What the hell were you doing there?' I had my curios, a little private collection lined up along the book-cases in the big living room. Nothing so grand as a library, but plenty of books, and the odd spaces given over to some glass and ceramics, among them the precious head, a copy of the Sarnath Buddha, fifth century AD. Somehow to me that contented, erotic face with the tight curls of hair and the self-satisfied smile on the lips of the young prophet, almond-eyed and sensuous, had symbolized inner peace, a glimpse of the state of perfection. Not that I was a Buddhist. I wasn't anything – Emma had more religion in her little finger – but it reminded me of life's mysteries. And it was smashed.

'I'm sorry, Dad,' he said again. 'Susie and I were just playing.'

'Horsing about. Grow up, kiddo. How many times you been told not to play ball inside?' The kids were twelve and ten, and Martin as the elder ought to have had more sense. Then, to my amazement, I heard Susanna's footsteps as well, coming downstairs. The clock on the kitchen wall showed it was five past eight. They were ambushing me.

A mop of unruly hair, already darker than Emma's, and the shining features of someone born to be married; or so we told each other, Emma and I. But there was a look on her face similar to that on Martin's, a kind of subdued worry. Something was biting the kids, that was for sure.

'Hey, sugar, what's up?'

She seemed almost scared.

'Susie. Come on,' I said. 'What's cooking?' They didn't rise at dawn unless it was Christmas morning.

She sat down at the table with Martin, opposite me. I pushed across the orange juice. Outside the sun was rising on an English summer's day: sunshine and cold showers. I could hear the birds in the garden and see the overnight rain dying out on the flagstones. The irises were in full bloom, mauve-blue and yellow. Dog-roses from over the wall rambled across the brickwork. How I loved that back yard, the roots I had put down. Pittsburgh just didn't have that kind of atmosphere, stretching back generations in the inherited fabric, the very buildings. History. Where I grew up and cut my teeth in Pennsylvania nothing was really old. OK, you could start a career, you could make money, you could buy a fancy apartment in Pleasant Hills, but you couldn't grow real history. Real ambience. Not to my satisfaction. In the end I just quit.

When Pa got bored he had sold the trucking business and searched for another woman. It had ended in tears, the usual divorce, and none of us – the three children – saw much of him after that. So I guess I was Mom's boy, and when she knew I was set on leaving she gave me some homespun advice. Marry a lady but make sure the lady loves you. Never fear the unknown. Work hard and settle your debts. Well, maybe I had and maybe she did. I was just beginning to wonder.

The kids were looking at me now with those round, owlish faces.

'OK. Don't worry about the Buddha,' I said. 'It's nothing. Really nothing. Maybe one day I'll find another one. How about some cornflakes?' With Emma not there I was tempted to offer coffee, knowing she didn't approve. Emma said it was bad for them.

Susanna shook her head.

I was forced to confront them, these young, uncertain mutants of myself. The muesli suddenly tasted like birdseed. Outside through the french windows leading to the patio I remember seeing a robin, drinking from the birdbath that Martin had fixed. An interloper on our disquiet.

'Somebody tell me. What's going on?'

Long pause. Martin was munching Honey Crunch like an automaton. It was Susanna who said, 'Dad . . .'

'Yeah?'

'Mom isn't so happy.'

I stared at them. It had never occurred to me, until that moment, that Emma might have set them off. We were a shell, a family sticking together as far as I was concerned.

'Susie, give over. What do you mean?'

Susanna drew a deep breath. 'When we broke the Buddha she cried a lot.'

I waved it away. 'Aw, come on. Is that all? Sugar, that's just one of those things. An accident. Forget it.' Families with kids, you take the small disasters, even the loss of cherished possessions, in your stride. They were treating it like some omen out of *Nightmare on Elm Street*.

'No, Dad. It wasn't just that,' Martin retorted, his voice strangely muted. He leaned across the table, head cupped in his hands, his blue eyes alarmed.

'What then?' Fourteen years, and I still didn't get the message, maybe because it was that long. It was as if they didn't want to tell me, until Susanna said:

'Mom cried because she said you cared more about your work, and your collection, and the Buddha's head . . . than her.'

'But that's ridiculous, Susie.' Emma must be going

bananas. I wondered what the hell had got into her. I couldn't believe it, even though I had been flat out ever since Dorcas Freeling picked up the Bristol contract. Hospital redesign. Months and months of work to deadlines.

The robin flew into the bushes, as if he had witnessed enough. It was unreal, being taken to task by the kids for things I hadn't even noticed.

'It's not true. You know that.'

'She says you're always away. And when you come home you're not there.'

I should have realized. That part at least was true. I was often away, all over the country, on those hospital jobs, and though I phoned every night it was somehow false sentiments along a length of wire. Too wrapped up in my problems, in my damned career. And when I came back I was too often tired, just like last night.

'Dad. Is everything . . . really all right between you and Mom?' Susanna whispered hesitantly. I understood then why they had come down early for this private session. They must have discussed it between them, alarmed by some childish fear. Christ knows, there were enough divorces among their schoolfriends' parents.

I still tried to brush the problem aside. No way would that happen to me. For if it did my adopted life would be shattered, my country of residence soured. I would be up shit creek. And that would be Pittsburgh here I come. No way.

'Kids, I love your mother very much,' I said. 'That's why I married her.' It wasn't just because she was English, and I liked the way of life, I told myself. No, I loved Em. 'Come on. Make me some toast.'

Susanna seemed to relax. Martin was relieved it was over. I could see they had delivered a set piece. I reached across and held their hands, one in each of my own. Outside the sun was bursting through the trees and the robin was back. I looked at them and made a resolution to forget the job and the office and the lousy Health Service. To concentrate on the family.

'You know something. We need a vacation,' I said.

*

16

It was easier said than done. It was panic time in the partnership and I left home early only to come back late. Bob Dorcas had been away, and the whole damned design team was in my hands. I liked Bob, but he was a bastard about taking time off. Too much work chasing too few people, so that I was tied to the chair, trying to get fifteen drawings revised before the client went mad. Apart from a beer and a sandwich that one of the girls brought in we were at it non-stop until 10.30 that night. I rolled home to Richmond as bushed as before.

Emma had washed her hair. She was sitting there in the upstairs front room, looking over the green in the twilight. The curtains were undrawn, her hair was a wet straggle, like twists of dark honey. The kids were in their bedrooms but I could hear Martin's computer game blipping and buzzing.

'Have you had a meal?' Emma asked almost suspiciously.

I hadn't really thought about it, we'd been too busy chasing our tails.

I kissed her. Her lips were resistant, even though the evening was warm, one of those soft dusks, the long sunsets of late June when the children never want to settle.

'No. Doesn't matter, darling. I'm not hungry.'

I saw she had been drinking a gin and lemon, and I went across to the sideboard for a slug of Jack Daniels. Emma swivelled round and stared at me. She was small and smart as a model, dressed in a scalloped white top and washed-denim blue skirt. She was the girl I had wanted and to me she was a million bucks. Now here she was accusing me.

'Jim.' A disbelieving head-shake. 'You don't remember, do you? You don't have time to remember.'

'Remember what?' I was beginning to panic, the alarm bells ringing, fearful that I had forgotten a birthday, an anniversary, some other pledged commitment.

'We were supposed to be going to the Macombers. For dinner. Tonight.'

'Oh Christ, Em. Why the hell didn't you remind me?'

'You went out before I was awake.'

'Shit, honey. Why didn't you ring me at the office?'

She slipped off the settee and ignored me, fingers clasping

the glass that she was holding, her back towards me as if she found the twilight more appealing. I walked across the room and stood beside her.

'I cancelled it,' she said, 'because I knew you would be too damned busy.' She paused. 'Jim, it can't go on. It can't go on like this.' Her voice faltered with dismay. 'We hardly ever see you as a family man. You're either at the office or away . . .'

'Emma. It's commitments . . .' I began. 'Contracts. You know that.'

'Bugger the contracts.' She stamped her foot. 'I don't care what you say. It can't go on. Either you stop or I do.'

'Stop?' Even then I didn't understand. I put my arm out to touch her and she drew back. She drained the glass and slammed it down, lucky not to break it. Then she faced me. I could see that her eyes were puffy as if she had been crying. With the wet hair and her pale face in the half-light she looked bedraggled. And my heart bled for her unhappiness.

Emma said fiercely, 'It's got to stop, Jim. The children see nothing of you. I see you hardly at all. You're either at that bloody office somewhere or away, the whole damned time. There's more to life than that.'

'You have to take the work when it's there, honey. This hospital job is a hassle . . .'

'I don't care. How do I know where you go to? You have your private world, a professional life. I'm stuck here, at home. Do you ever think about that?'

This was an old resentment that had troubled us before, resentment that she had sacrificed her own career and was ending up at forty with nothing. No jobs for rusty lecturers.

'Emma, I love you. It's all for you. You know that.'

She had been drinking, I saw, to kill some of the aggro. It had made her morose. She stood there swaying slightly. 'No. Don't start handling me. I'm not your goods.'

'Darling, come on,' I said. 'I'm tired. You're tired. Let's go to bed.'

Emma snapped back. She was like an outraged lioness. 'Listen to me. I mean it. Unless things change, Jim, I tell you this marriage won't last.' The challenge was flung down.

'Don't be crazy.' I hardly believed her even then. It was absurd. But there was more to come as she stormed at me.

'Marvellous, isn't it? You wander off to the office and then you come back like a zombie. Too bloody tired to ask what kind of time I've had, left here with the kids. Too bloody late to make love. Do you realize that you've been working six, seven days a week? We never even get a day out.'

'It won't last . . .'

'Jim. It's got to stop now.' She flung back her head. I could see the veins in her throat. 'Else I won't wait for you.'

'Oh Christ, honey. Be reasonable. I promise you . . .'

She spun away, breathing fumes. 'And another thing. When you're not here . . . how do I know what you're doing? How do I know you're not running round with . . . some other woman?'

It brought me up with a jolt. So that was it. Suspicion. I swore to her that I hadn't time to run an affair, even if I had wanted one. I laughed, and the laugh sounded hollow. How is it the truth is so difficult to make convincing?

'Emma, darling. Don't be stupid.'

'Don't call me stupid.'

'For Christ's sake, Em. It's ridiculous.' We were quarrelling like two schoolkids.

'The children are worried.'

So that was it too. The reason for the morning's démarche, which all came back to me now. She didn't really suspect me of infidelity, but the frustrations had boiled over, and she had set up the kids.

'You're telling me the office is more important than me and the family—'

'Hell, no. I never said that.'

'All right.' She stood there breathing defiance. 'Then prove it.'

The answer came into my head ready-made. I remembered what I had said to Susanna early in the morning, in response to a similar worry, and I repeated it then.

19

'Listen, honey. Darling. I've got a proposition. We'll go away together,' I said. My marriage was not going down the tube. No sir. 'I'm going to fix us a great vacation. Straight up. A surprise vacation. And fuck the work.' I knew that we had cracked the job: a few more days and I could leave them to it, now Bob Dorcas was back. 'Two weeks in the sun,' I said. 'How about that? We'll just take the car and go.'

She snapped, 'We can't. The kids are still at school.'

'OK. As soon as term ends.'

Emma began to calm down. 'Where?'

I shrugged, reached an instant decision. 'Any place warm and sunny.' Where was the nearest one that guaranteed the weather? 'What about the South of France?'

I saw a look of disbelief, then of relief, then the first flush of happiness come into her face.

'OK. I'll tell 'em tomorrow. We'll hire a place away from it all. No telephones, nothing. Just sunshine and country inns where we can sit and relax. Some place like Provence.' The half-remembered France that had first captivated me, as a youngster in Europe, five years before I met Emma.

'Rural France? The kids won't like it. They want the beach,' she said.

'Honey, the kids can lump it.' I put my hands around her at last. 'I need you,' I said. 'And I want you to be happy.'

The tiredness seemed to flow away. Emma was smiling. 'Do you mean it?'

'Sure thing. I mean it. Monday, I'll find us a travel agent. Make an immediate reservation. Just as soon as he can find the right spot.' I visualized it as we spoke. 'Somewhere with vines, and a patio and windows looking over the fields, as remote as hell.'

She kissed me. 'Where we can sit and drink . . .'

'And then make love,' I said.

I had a few problems with Bob, but in the end he bought it. Bob Dorcas was one of those English guys who seem to think you owe them a lifetime.

'Christ, old man,' he said. 'I've only just got back. From

Glasgow. There's another job there, a big one, Jim, and I think we've got it landed. They liked the Bristol ideas and want us to develop them. Us, Jim, and that means you.'

'It'll keep for a couple of weeks.'

'A couple of weeks is important, Jim. They could be crucial.' Time was always so goddam important, important for me as well. We were in the inner office and I could see the others looking at us through the glass, wondering what was going on.

Bob lowered his voice. 'Look. I don't want to be unreasonable . . .'

'That's great. I've been working my ass off, the Bristol job is sewn up. I tell you I want a vacation.'

'Of course, old boy, of course. But surely not now. If you could only leave it a few more weeks I'm sure we could work something out . . .'

I shook my head. I had nightmares of Em packing a bag, even if it was only to that hill in Hampshire where her parents holed up, and the kids hating my guts. I knew what was more important. Something had to give.

'Nope, Bob. I'm worked out, and Emma's pretty damn frayed. She's on edge, Bob, and I got to do something about it. Now, not later.'

He looked at me bemused, as if the idea of a holiday without nine months in gestation was beyond his comprehension. 'What do you mean by now? I was hoping to put up some ideas to the Regional Health Board—'

'Stuff the Board, Bob. They'll keep for a couple of weeks. I just want to get away.'

'But you can't—'

'I can. I can walk out,' I said.

I was bluffing and he knew it, but something ate into his heart. He rubbed the back of his neck: maybe he'd been bending over too many drawings as well. A crafty old bugger in tweeds in the middle of summer, with horn-rimmed specs and a polished pink head. No family, a worka-holic, and hoping to make me one too if I waited to inherit the practice. He put his hand on my shoulder.

'All right, Jim. I get the message. You want to have a break . . .'

21

'Right on the nail, Bob. Two weeks,' I said.

His blue eyes were puzzling out how anyone could go away without appropriate preparation. Anticipation, planning, insurance, I could see them flash through his mind.

'When exactly, Jim?'

'As soon as my travel agent comes up with a suitable reservation. In a week or two. The kids have almost finished school. We can take them away. Then I'll come back for Glasgow . . .'

Bob Dorcas blew out his cheeks. Somebody tapped at the door of the inner sanctuary. 'Hang on,' he called. 'Jim, where are you thinking of going?'

And just as I had promised Emma, I told him then. 'Somewhere down into France, taking Emma and the children.' Down to the roots of the memory, to the first small slow villages that I had ever stayed in, when I had come to Europe at twenty-one. The vanished summers of youth.

Bob was looking at me strangely. 'Are you all right, old boy?'

'Sure. I'm fine. But I just want to get away and look after my family.'

2

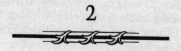

The sea at night seems swollen. Expectation, I guess. I remember watching the lights of Weymouth harbour slide gently away as the Channel ferry pulled out. Emma was by my side with her hair swept back in a band, the kids bubbling with anticipation. There were fishermen on the end of the jetty, waving goodbye. It was a sultry evening, the second week in July, and the children had skipped the last three days of the summer term. I had the feeling that things were on the mend, from the moment that I had told Emma about the *gîte* in Aveyron. Someone who knew someone had contacted the rural agency in the *département*, and they had confirmed by telephone. A long drive south in the sun, and the children wound up with excitement at the journey to come. As we hung over the rail watching the ship's wake it seemed that we were sailing into warmer and calmer waters.

Martin ran off with Susanna to explore the boat, now that its sounds and smells created a living thing, and I put my arm through Emma's. It was only two weeks since my promise.

'Honey, we did it.'

She gave me an upturned smile. 'You know, I didn't believe you would dare leave that job for so long. I thought you were married to it.'

'Come on, darling.'

She put her arms up and kissed me there on the boat deck.

People were more important than paper, Mom always said. We had a long way still to go, never take things for granted, I told myself. Get it right. In a way we had become

23

accommodated to a godawful complacency: the house in Richmond, the kids at private schools, a partnership in Dorcas Freeling, Emma giving part-time service to War on Want. Things that I had not questioned but assumed would continue. A comfortable rut, a water-bed. Forget about accident, illness, death, until it blocks out the light, and we are locked in the dark.

The shoreline dwindled to a necklace of lights and we followed the children below. Night boats are suspended in time, ploughing between fixed points, and we had four hours to kill. The smell of warm oil from the open hatchways as we stood on deck had made us hungry, and we wandered down to the half-empty restaurant.

I told the kids they ought to sleep but they were too worked up. We would be driving through Cherbourg at half past four in the morning.

'Will there be a beach?' Martin said. 'I want a rubber dinghy.'

I said again that there would be a river – the Loup, according to the map – but I'd picked rural France, beyond the back of nowhere. Maybe there would be a *plage*, a strand of sand in the river, perhaps a *piscine*, and a camping place with canoes, but this would be unspoiled France, the nearest village Chenoncey, the nearest town St Maxime le Grand, in the south central mountains. No, not beaches like the ones they had played on before in Spain, Corfu and Italy, when they were small. Now they were growing up I wanted to show them the France that I remembered, the France of tiny auberges, and steaks grilled over vinewood fires, washed down with sweet Sauterne.

Long before I met Emma, smiling at me now.

'What are you thinking about?'

How can you say 'happiness'? The kids were into burgers and chips. I poured a glass of Sealink plonk. It tasted as tepid as blood.

'Us . . . urgh.'

'What?'

I said the wine was lousy. We were on a British ferry, and not yet into France. Emma said the children must rest,

24

as soon as the meal was over. Outside through the dark windows we saw the white tops of the waves.

'Jim. Are you sure that you can spare the time from the Bristol job, just like that?' She was moving towards me, beginning to register my pressures and settle down. The restaurant was emptying and the *Earl Marshal* ploughed across a lonely sea.

'Sure. No sweat. Bob can finish things off, now that he's back.' Bob Dorcas, the senior partner. Bob had built up the practice, made it his life's work, and that was going to be his problem. Now he was back he would cope, and I'd told him I would vacation or else. If he'd yelped I might have postponed things but in the end he had swallowed and said 'OK. You get going, Jim.' He'd seen my face.

Jesus, it was good to be there, heading south again, and I clinked glasses with Emma.

'Here's to a great trip.'

'Here's to us,' she said.

A voice like a Polish refugee over the loudspeaker reminded us the purser's office was open. We made our way slowly back along the saloon deck, where people were sprawled like dummies, scattered derelicts hit by some virus, trying to sleep.

Emma grabbed at my arm as if she was suddenly nervous, looking at the pallid faces turned upwards in repose.

'They look as if they've died,' she whispered.

To land in France at dawn was stepping through a gateway into my own youth. At five o'clock in the morning, the mist just lifting off the docks, the seagulls swooping for scraps, we drove the family Sierra through the deserted streets of Cherbourg and headed out on the N13. The clouds hung over the road, like curtains being pulled back, as the sun warmed up. The Garde Mobile were starting a patrol, someone was already unstacking crates in a cellarage, then we were through the empty town and heading into the country.

The kids were still bouncing about, after the thrill of arrival. Martin as usual was hungry and I promised we would stop for breakfast at a roadside café, when we had made some time. To me it was going like a dream but Emma, sitting beside me, still seemed less sure. She broke open a bar of chocolate. 'Rations,' she said. We unrolled the kilometres with the radio on, a babble of French voices and platitudinous pop tunes. I felt that we had made it again, recrossed into each other's domains, as if neither of us had changed, or ever would. Yet looking at Emma I saw that flicker of unease.

We swept through the uncurling villages and pulled up in a small town where someone was unpeeling a blind at one of those faded and tasteless tabacs that decorate the edge of French squares, next to the war memorial. There was a smell of fresh bread, croissants and coffee appeared, and we sat with blue-jowled locals who were drinking from bowls. A sound of shutters released, the squawking of ducks in a crate as the market trucks pulled in, a black-clad matron slowly wiping the table and offering a grudging 'Bonjour'.

I smiled at Emma and hoped. There was still a small tremor of something: anxiety or tiredness, or plain resentment, I could not quite define it. What was she seeing in me? I wondered, as she sipped the hot coffee. A husband, a friend, or an alien from another planet? We were so close yet different, naturalized Europeans, the cautious, solid American and the English rose. Her parents never quite approved, but we had made our own space. They were retired now, with a cottage in the New Forest, and they worshipped the kids. I had brought Mom over to visit them just before she died. That had been a good deal, but I was thankful they'd never met the old man.

'Are you OK, Em?'

'I expect so,' Emma mused.

Martin was exploring the shops, as they stacked up for the day: ironmongery, cheeses, vegetables, the strange sights in the charcuterie. Lean cats slunk into alleys where they disturbed the dogs, the sun began to warm the marble tops of the tables where we were sitting. A guy in blue overalls nodded. 'Bon appétit.'

I wished I had more of the language, for Emma started showing off, asking directions in French, unnecessary direc-

26

tions since I was clear from the map, but once she hooked into a conversation she left me stranded. Deliberately asserting herself. I had to hang on, trying to remember a few high-school phrases. Her facility was in language and music, mine was in line and form, spatial dimensions. OK, so we made a team, but no need to rub it in.

Emma suggested we returned to the car. 'Sure, honey. When you want.' She was one of those people who always had to move on, round the next corner, where the view would often be worse. That's why I knew two weeks in any one place was enough. I reckoned I was tuned to her moods as I called to the kids to come back. Susanna came running up, carrying a kitten she'd found, a scrap of black and white fur, glaring with impotence in her arms. I could see the tiny claws waving in the pink pads.

'Put it down,' Emma said. 'It might have rabies.'

'It's gorgeous.'

'Sugar, we can't take it with us. It would miss its mother,' I told her.

Reluctantly she released it and we watched it skid back inside.

Martin was looking at beach balls, inflatable dinghies, plastic rackets and skittles hopefully hung out in the middle of an inland town on the Cotentin peninsula. 'I want to go canoeing,' he said. My kids, my wife, my France. I pulled Emma close and kissed her there in the square with the young workmen watching. 'How about it?' I whispered. One did these things in France.

'I don't know,' she said.

We travelled south, the weather getting steadily hotter – memories of that journey are like fading photographs – the hill town of Domfront where we stopped for drinks, the crawl through the dreary hinterland of Le Mans, the first glimpse of the Loire at Tours, so low on its gravel bed that it seemed we could have waded across. We picnicked on tomatoes and cheese, then pushed on to Poitiers and Limoges, heading towards Brive. A long hot drive on a long hot day with the kids getting wild with fatigue.

'Wrap it up,' I shouted, ratty, losing my temper.

'Jim. We've got to stop,' Emma said. 'They're overtired.'

'OK, OK.' I bellowed at them to be quiet, to rest up in the back while we looked for a place. The sun was scouring the sky, even the road seemed dustier, the men on bicycles more patched and parched. The soft red tiles of the roofs heralded the south, and the windscreen was splashed with crushed midges. 'For Christ's sake belt up,' I told them, 'before I lose my cool. I've had enough from you.'

The boy was punching the girl. 'Martin, you are a turd.'

'We need a hotel,' Emma said. 'Somewhere soon.' Emma always liked things planned, bases organized in advance, but I had fixed up so late that we had no booking for the overnight stop.

And then we found the inn. The auberge Le Chapeau Rouge. It seemed too good to be true, this peeling cream façade with the green shutters and the bright red sunshades. Vines grew over the door and there was that deep brown of old memories in the interior that said 'yes' to my youthful impressions, 'you were right to remember'. A timeless, shadowy place where the *patron* had rooms to spare and the dining room was quietly full. Not excessive but right, so right I could have hugged Emma there and then. And she knew it. What you look for in people you love are the little human signs, the twitches, the itches, the tired smiles of 'I understand'. Emma was all that and more. On that first evening she had an endearing weariness. She had called me to order, told me I worked too hard, and drove too hard, and here we were, with time to relax together. I felt that we had it made.

We ate that evening like lords, tearing in to a great *pot au feu* ladled by the hotel waiter as if we were chosen guests. Half drunk on Macon rouge. The kids were bushed, but they gobbled it too, and followed it with an ice-cream that might have been made by the gods. Around us people were chatting, a murmur of conversation over the scraping of forks, but for me it was as if the years had suddenly rolled away. This was time-honoured Europe, the civilization that had captured me when I was twenty-one. Now I had a family to share it, a job that could support it. Maybe I was on a high or just plain happy, but I recall Emma's sweet stare as we clinked glasses and linked our little fingers, promising each other the future.

'I'll sleep like a log,' she said.

The children were in two small rooms right next door to ours, and as we settled them down I could see they were nearly asleep. Emma was washing as I tucked them up and switched off the light.

I went back to our room, a bedroom with an attic window looking down to an ancient yard. I could imagine the horses once stabled below, under the hay-loft that now made a rambling garage. Travellers for hundreds of years, going home, retreating from wars, setting out to make fortunes, hoping to marry some girl, all of them would have been there before us in the little room. They had breathed the same air.

I shut the window and turned.

Emma was already in bed, an old-fashioned wooden bedstead with a white coverlet, and as I came across she raised her arms and slipped off the nightdress. The summers of youth pass like holidays in childhood, but she was beckoning me back into the days of flame.

A car with those yellow French headlights manoeuvred into the yard and just for a moment illuminated the room: the stark little wardrobe and blue-painted chest of drawers, Emma in bed waiting.

We had ground to make up, in the marriage, in ourselves.

I remember tightening the curtains and slipping into bed beside her. It was a long time since we had felt like this, a mutuality. Something had been going wrong, behind the chores with the kids, and my professional anxieties and Emma's growing resentment. Work and suspicions, guaranteed to fade the charm. I kissed her face and body and felt like whispering 'sorry'.

There, in the little bedroom, with the sounds of cars revving outside, we began to make love, a kind of illicit, temporary, stolen love as if it would be the last, savouring every moment, lingering on the sensations, postponing the pleasure—

Until Martin burst in.

'Dad! It's spooky next door.'

29

I levered away from Emma, furious and half ashamed. How can you make nooky with your kid snooping in the doorway. Emma was huddled in a blanket, I was sitting up yelling.

'Get out. Get out.' Jesus Christ, what had he seen? 'Get back to your own room.'.

But the kid was scared. He clung on inside the door, frozen, uncertain and frightened, waiting for me to calm down.

'But Dad—'

I managed to regain control. 'For God's sake what's the matter with you?' I could see Susanna behind him, pale-faced in the passage at the top of the house, disturbed by his shouting.

'There's noises in my room,' he said.

Emma was covering up, as if our time was finished.

'Grow up. Don't be stupid, Martin.'

'I'm not . . . you come and listen.'

I was angry and naked, but simmering down. 'All right. Wait outside.'

They hung around in the well at the top of the stairs while I grabbed my pyjamas and followed them to Martin's room. It was a tiny box, sandwiched between Susanna's and ours, and I saw the pipes running through from a water tank up in the roof. Poor old Martin. After the long drive and the food and the wine, he must have lain in the dark and half woken to the noises, tapping and murmuring and dripping. The unknown had scared him enough to make him run shivering into our room, something he would never do at home, not without calling out first. I put my arm around him, and tried to explain.

'I'm sorry, but I'm not sleeping in there,' he said, panicking. I could see he was out on his feet, swaying and ashen-faced.

Emma had slipped on the nightgown and was standing beside me. 'Don't worry, Martin. It doesn't matter.' She understood.

'The room's OK. Just some noise in the pipes,' I sought to reassure him.

'No way,' he said, shaking, tears close to his eyes.

'Let's put him in the room with Susie,' Emma said. 'There's a camp bed in there. We can make it up.'

'Yes. Please,' Martin whispered.

We went into Susanna's room and saw the bed stacked by the wall. They had offered two rooms because the kids slept apart but we could put them together. Martin was already humping in his bedding and we opened the camp bed out, fitting it next to his sister's.

The boy was happy now. Even though Susie was younger she was the resolute one, competent and domestic. I watched her smoothing the pillows. Emma said, 'You'll be all right now.'

Once it was settled, he was too tired to care, and almost disappeared inside the blankets.

'Do you want the light out?' I said. But he was already asleep.

Emma and I kissed Susanna and went back to our room, but the spell had been broken. 'Jesus, you can't even fuck with kids around.'

She gave me a sinful smile. 'Plenty of time,' she said.

'I could have killed him,' I told her.

3

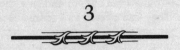

On the second day, in the evening, we came to the place in Aveyron. Lemon-yellow France in mid-July, canary fields of sunflowers, sunshine and burnt grass and ripening grapes on the hills as we headed off the Route Nationale along the local black-tops, following the Michelin map. We had an address at the village – Chenoncey – which turned out to be a crossroads leading to nowhere much. A church, a small and closed-up restaurant, the general store, the bakery, also closed by the time we arrived, somebody selling *brocante*, the relics from ancient farms.

Following the directions from the agency, the Relais Départemental des Gîtes de France, we branched left at the crossroads and down a narrowing lane. The overgrown fences were stiffened with barbed wire, a grey donkey stood in a field, some goats were tethered to an abandoned plough, otherwise the only life was an old man hoeing potatoes.

Emma of course must speak to him, asking how near we were. The old guy straightened his back, kicked the potatoes aside and shuffled slowly towards us, a pensioner in blue fatigues and heavy-duty sandals. At first he did not understand and Emma repeated the question like he was some dumb idiot.

'*Connaissez-vous le gîte Mimosas?*'

He shook his head.

'Mim-o-sas,' she said.

At last the message got through. His walnut face cracked open and he gabbled in a kind of patois, pointing further down the road. Within a couple of kilometres we had arrived.

The place – I cannot bring myself to call it more – the gîte, the house, was attractive enough. It lay close to the road, a bendy road wandering for miles along the one-horse valley. Emma called it a bungalow, in a plain country style which featured an external stone chimney, a red-tiled roof and two steps up to the door, in front of which was a patio with wrought-iron chairs. It had an unused appearance, as if keeping secrets inside. A white-walled, discreet building no more than forty years old, set behind unclipped hedges and an iron gate which opened on to a gravel path. You went up the path, the gravel loose underfoot, across an unkempt lawn, lumpy with molehills. Here and there a nondescript bush struggled to survive, and outside the main doorway were two acacias. Bougainvillaea grew against the walls, trained up on trellises, flowering mauve and purplish-red; the windows were recessed, with flyscreens, and the shutters – old-fashioned, white-painted louvres – pulled close against the heat. Walking round the exterior we found an earth trench for plants, mostly shrivelled by the sun: ice plants and marigolds and indeterminate pinks. The windows on the eastern side looked out across empty fields, all of them abandoned to grass. Those fronting the road, where the kitchen and living room stood on either side of the hallway, had a view of some cows and beyond them more fields, then a wood. On the western side was the garage, joined to the hall by a passage with a connecting door, and on the other side of the passage the three main bedrooms overlooked a yard at the rear. The garage had been used as storage for spare pieces of furniture, sunbeds, oildrums, the mower, and had an up-and-over door at the front of the house. As we explored we found at the rear of the yard a little thicket of birches where somebody had built a barbecue. That somebody had even left charcoal.

This then was the place we came to on that July night, after the second day's travelling. We had chosen the minor roads, winding into the hills, and we were tired. And deep in the heart of France.

The place was unlocked, just as the instructions said, and we opened the doors and shutters, seeking a breeze. The evening light flooded in, the air was as warm as a steam bath, sticky and brooding, threatening rain from the hills that we saw in the distance, hemming in the valley with violet clouds. On the other side of the road, the cows moved slowly in unison searching for sweeter grass and we watched them shuffling away towards the big woods beyond as the shadows lengthened.

'Well, let's get unpacked,' I said.

Emma just stood and looked.

'Honey. How do you like it?' I put my arm round her. This was my answer to pressure, the bolt-hole, the escape, the search for a lost innocence. It mattered very much to me that Emma enjoyed it too.

'I don't know,' she replied, standing there in the evening light, a neat figure in a sundress, her fair skin already reddening. 'It's very quiet.'

Martin inevitably said, 'Boring.' I told him to wait. There were excursions I'd planned, fishing along the river, maybe canoeing as well if we could hire some boats, and scrambling up in the mountains, exploring the ruined castles left over from Merovingian kings. And I promised we would drive to the coast and have a night on the Med, perhaps camping under the stars.

Susanna was jumping about, testing the springs on the beds as if they were trampolines. 'It's comfortable.'

We began to offload, planning the next two weeks, wondering if we could find a restaurant that would be open nearer than St Maxime, the closest town. In the end, Emma made do. The kitchen was polished and trim, with a Totalgaz stove and an electric fridge. None of us wanted to move, we were all bushed from the journey, and we sat down to some cold chicken and opened a bottle of wine.

'Perhaps it will grow on me,' she said.

When we had finished, feeling a little better, I remember saying, 'Let's explore.' The kids ran off to unwind in the grass yard outside and we emptied the rest of the car. Emma was unnervingly silent and I knew something caused her disquiet. The place was clean as a pin; it had all the necessary virtues right down to soap in the bathroom and aired linen on the beds. In our own room was a large double bed with modern brass headrail, some wall-fitted sliding closets, a table, two easy chairs. I watched her as she tried it for dust, then wiped her hands on her dress: a girlish figure and face à la Claire Bloom. She stared at the double bed on which our cases were piled then gingerly sat on the side.

'Well . . .'

'It's great,' I said. It wasn't quite the ancient farmhouse that I had hoped for but we had to take what was going and it was well appointed.

'It's all right.'

I knew better than to labour the point. It was as if she could not tell me her fears, as if she wanted to say 'I'm not being unreasonable, I know you wanted to come here . . . but . . . but . . . but . . .' and couldn't because she was uncertain.

'Do you think the children . . . will find enough to do for two weeks?' she asked.

'Sure. Once they get into things.' I mentioned the plans I had, the strange places we would prospect.

She looked at me for reassurance. I was unlocking the secret boxes of my own mind, hoping that she would share the formative years of my youth when it all seemed so rich and crazy and wonderful just being in country like this. But I couldn't explain, and I went out again to the car.

As I was checking it over for the last pieces of junk – Martin's snorkelling kit – Emma came out to join me. It was growing dark, the light was on over the porch and great moths were swooping around it as the sun went down.

'Listen,' she said.

I thought she could hear their wings.

'Don't be stupid,' she replied. 'That murmuring. There must be a stream nearby, a brook somewhere.'

'We'll look in the morning,' I said. 'I think it's going to rain.' We could see flashes like explosions over the far-off hills. 'Let's get sorted out first.'

But she went on searching for the elusive stream. Around us the ground was dry, parched almost, the road we had come on was empty, the cattle on the far side had merged into the trees. But she still said she heard noises, bubbling and murmuring somewhere, although I could not be sure it wasn't a wind through the air, the sigh of the impending storm.

Emma had disappeared, round the side of the house.

'Where are you?'

'Looking for the children,' she said.

We found them playing with the barbecue, a substantial brick affair dating from the time of the house, designed for parties long gone: the birch trees had grown up around it.

'Hey. Come inside and settle down, kids. You've had a long day.'

'How's it going?' I asked Martin.

He shrugged. Susanna said it was 'cool'. I could see Emma's face, tense and perspiring in the mirror on the wall in the hall. Behind her Susanna was frowning. Well, family life was like that, I told myself, someone was always different, you couldn't please 'em all the time. Emma would soon calm down and sense the peace of the place. But she kept coming back to the noises that she thought she had heard.

'There is no stream,' the kids said, 'we've been all round. The ground is as dry as a bone.'

'It must be in your head, honey,' I suggested.

Emma's lips tightened. When the children had gone, unpacking in their rooms, she suddenly whispered, 'It frightens me . . .'

'What? This place? Why, for God's sake?'

She shook her head. 'I don't know . . . It's strange.'

'Aw, come on.' I wiped my brow. 'It's hot. We're all pooped.' It was now eleven o'clock and we needed to settle the children. Martin bagged the room next to ours, and Susie was next to the garage, with the bathroom in between them. 'They're both the same,' I argued. Neat, square rooms with single beds and chests of drawers.

'Dad, I want to be next to you,' the boy said, as if still scared by the spooks of the night before. Susanna said she didn't mind. She would always be OK.

We tucked them up and left them. Emma's big eyes were

wide with unarticulated concerns. 'It's your choice,' she said.

'Look darling. It's going to be fine. Just relax,' I told her. 'We need the time away together, some place quiet like this. To make space for each other.' The petty squabbles in London already seemed a long way away. I breathed in the air deeply, and we wandered through to the kitchen. The last third of our bottle of wine was still on the table there.

'Tomorrow will be great, Em.' I poured two glasses and raised them. 'Here's to us—'

'But those noises in the air . . .' she said. 'There can't be a stream round here. It's miles from the river, and there's no sign of water.'

'It's going to rain. We got a big storm coming. It's a kind of advance warning.' There was more lightning over the hills.

'Don't give me that.' She smiled uneasily. 'You know damned well . . .'

'Well, maybe it's some kind of drain—'

Emma put down the glass. 'It's more like a sound in the earth' was what she said. 'Something trapped there.'

In the end we went to bed, in the room next to Martin's. I was planning tomorrow, when we would drive into St Maxime and stock up with gear, food, toiletries, ice-cream, drinks, all the things that were missing. See if we could hire bikes, and buy a badminton set for the yard. All the things you think of so irresistibly at the start of a break, the first real chance, I realized, that we had had in years not to be pressurized and packaged. That terrible impulse to work, the thought that it all mattered, slaving to deadlines, delivering ideas on time, was all behind me at last. We had finished the rest of the wine.

Emma was in a nightdress, a flimsy new shift of lace-work, feminine and pretty, but she had covered up, in that stifling room.

I stripped to my underpants and stared. 'You surely don't need that on.' The heat dripped down from the roof and sweat ran between my shoulder blades. The rainstorm was coming nearer and we could see the lightning dancing in and out of the dark.

'What do you mean? Don't you like it?'

'Sure thing. Of course. But, you know . . .'

'I'm cold,' she said.

'Cold?'

'Inside.'

I knew better than to argue. At night we are the products of our parents again. My childhood was a broken marriage with Dad in the walk-on part, way back in Pennsylvania, while Mom kept the junior Freelings – two boys and a girl – on the straight and narrow by grinding away in Finance in Dimant's Stores. Emma was an only child, introspective, wrapped up in her parents' love and safe and secure in Hampshire, England, when the Colonel came out of the army.

'Jim boy, Jim boy, Jim boy,' I could hear Mom cautioning, though she'd been dead two years, 'always give way to a lady. It don't matter what they say, don't argue with 'em, son. You got that, Jim?' And when I nodded she hugged me.

So I found some pyjamas too, and sweated in bed beside my beautiful wife.

Emma threw off the quilt and lay there under the sheet. The bedroom was unbearably stuffy with the windows open but the flyscreens and shutters drawn. The lightning flashed through the slats.

'I'll open the blinds,' I said.

'No. Please. I want them closed.' It was as if she was scared that someone would be looking in. We had had that experience once, in a hotel in Corfu, when we were fooling in bed and saw a guy in the shadows, a Peeping Tom on a bank outside.

'OK.' We lay in bed side by side listening to the rumble of thunder, the storm playing round in the hills. I put out my hand to reassure her and tried to kiss her. She gave me a nervous peck.

'Not tonight,' she signalled. 'I'm too nervous, with that storm.'

38

'What's the matter?' I asked again. 'Why don't you like this place?'

'I don't know,' was all that she would say.

'Honey. Let's get some sleep,' I whispered. 'It will all seem different tomorrow.'

The distant lightning flickered and sparked, the air was as hot as steam. We must have been exhausted, too tired to complain, after the long drive south: Le Mans, Tours, Poitiers, Limoges, Pontauban, the road signs slipped through my brain as we lay in the dark. I wanted to explain so much, to tell her how much I needed her.

'Emma?'

But she had rolled on her side and was already switched off.

I began to think about the morning: fresh bread from the village, a drive to the river somewhere, the feeling of freedom, the sense of release between us, warm sunshine after the rain, the reasons why we had come, as I drifted to sleep.

4

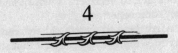

The cry came at three in the morning. Rain on the roof
after thunder drummed me awake. Dark, and black as hell.
The wooden shutters were creaking. I remember sitting up,
at the beginning.

'Emma!'

But Emma was dead with sleep, physically exhausted.
She stirred but did not wake and I was reluctant to touch
her.

Yet there had been a noise in the night, outside, a cry
like an animal in trouble. I could have sworn it.

I knew where the hell I was now. In the place in Aveyron,
the house in the fields. Sheet lightning briefly illuminated
the bedroom through cracks in the shutters. Then black as
pitch again, as I reached for the bedside lamp.

My fingers searched for the light switch. It did not work.

Another crash of thunder, following sheet lightning, left
me wondering what I had heard. I groped for the edge of
the bed, swung my legs over, blundered my way to the
door. The room switch was just inside, on the wall.

Nothing. The storm must have cut the supply. Sod it. I
knew there was a torch somewhere: in the glove pocket of
the car, which we had been too tired to manoeuvre into
the cluttered garage. I was surprised not to find the kids
running in as the thunder cracked overhead, crashing along
the valley. They must be worn out, beyond caring, after
two days on the road. I stood confused in the dark, remembering the tunnels of trees, the swishes of sound through
car windows, the stalls selling melons and apricots. Yesterday.

The air had cooled only a little. Treacle-dark. Which edge

of the door was the handle? I found it and stumbled into the passage. The door to Martin's room was ajar and I thought I saw his shape in the bed as I felt my way through to the hall. The key was still in the front door, and I unlocked it, heading for the Ford Sierra. Jesus Christ, it was pissing down. Forked lightning, overhead, ripped open the sky, and the Sierra seemed to be in a car-wash. As I hesitated, a wall of water from the eaves, suddenly blown towards me, saturated my pyjamas.

'Jesus.' I shut the door and retreated, soaked.

I was back in the hall now, lost, navigating in the blackness, wet and shaken. I stumbled back into the bedroom.

'Jim? Where are you? Where have you been?' Emma was alert in the bed, woken by the noise at last.

'Darling, I'm here. It's one hell of a storm.'

She reached out and touched my jacket, then ran her hands down to my waist. 'What's happened? You're wet through. Your pyjamas . . . ?'

'I went to get a torch,' I said. 'The lights are down.'

'Down?'

'Electrical storm. Must have cut a power line somewhere.'

'What about the kids?'

'They'll be OK. They're asleep.'

'But they don't sleep through thunderstorms. Not ones as big as this.' The lightning flashed again and I saw her face, sculpted like a Medusa. 'Why did you go outside?'

'Honey, I didn't. I only got as far as the door. I wanted a torch.'

'A torch?'

'We've got one in the car.'

'Forget it,' she said. 'Wait till this thing is over.'

I remembered why I had tried. 'I thought I heard a cry.'

Even in that darkness, I sensed Emma's concern. 'Jim. Go and check on them.' I felt her shivering.

'I have. I looked into Martin's room.'

'What did he say?'

'Nothing. He was flat out.'

I heard her voice fill with alarm. 'He never sleeps through storms like this. You know that.'

Another explosive rumbling, a crack of doom. More flashes, forked this time, and the pissing rain again, harder than ever. We could hear it swilling across the patio. The house, the holiday gîte that we had rented, was under water and shaking.

'Jim, I'm frightened,' she said. 'And so will they be. I don't like storms.'

'Don't worry. They'll be all right . . .'

'Then where are they? Why aren't they here?' She sounded really scared.

'They're OK. Calm down, honey.'

'Go and see.'

I took off my wet pyjama jacket and mopped the moisture from my body. I called out, 'Martin! Susie!' in the dark.

'Go and see.'

'Sure.' I had no sense of foreboding, unlike Emma. Martin was twelve now and Susanna ten. Old enough not to be frightened by storms in the night.

'Christ!'

'What?'

'Stubbed my toe on the goddam chair.'

I had to find the door again, which had swung closed behind me.

'It's over there,' Emma said, standing beside me. Her hand felt for mine. She had moved from the bed, and I noticed that she was trembling.

'Go back to bed and keep warm. No need for you to come.'

'Of course I will.'

I heard her knock over the chair. 'Bugger.'

'Mind the end of the bed.'

Hand in hand, we picked our way across the room.

A flash of lightning showed where the door was. I knew the geography now, standing in the passage between the bedrooms, the tiled floor underfoot. We sensed rather than saw the doorway to Martin's room.

'Martin? Susie? You OK, kids?'

Thunder. Silence. I could hear Emma's breathing. I felt across Martin's bed and found it empty.

'Go on, try Susanna,' she urged.

42

'Yeah. I'm going. Just let me find the door.'

Exploring the passage, cupboards jutting out, loose matting, we shuffled on.

Next room the bathroom, then Susie's.

Susie's door was shut. That was why they couldn't hear: both of them must be in there. Fuck this darkness, why had the damned lights failed?

Found the handle, opened the door.

'Susie. Martin? Are you all right?'

Single bed across the room. I groped for the edge, the sheets. No smell of sleep. Grabbed at the covers, felt again. Empty.

'Hell. They must be hiding, somewhere in the house,' I said, the panic beginning.

Emma beside me. 'Hurry up.'

'Honey, I'm hurrying.'

Banged my head getting back to the first door. More thunder, rolling round the hills. Hosepipes and buckets of rain.

We navigated round the boy's room. Even probed under the bed.

'Where in God's name have they gone?' Emma was ahead of me now, checking the kitchen, the living room, the bathroom.

'Martin! Susanna!'

It was like calling into a cellar.

'Susie? Martin? Come on, kids, where are you?'

My heart began to lurch with fear.

Emma called desperately, 'Jim. Jim. Oh my God, Jim! They aren't in the house.'

Terror knocked at our hearts, in the dark, alone.

'They must be, Emma. They must be hiding. They've run off somewhere.'

'Oh Jim! They wouldn't do that. You know that. They'd come running to us.'

'Well, maybe they're playing some kind of trick.'

An explosion of thunder right on top of the gîte; Emma clutched at my arm as it shook us. 'Jim. I'm so scared.'

43

They must be somewhere around. Can't have gone far on a night like this, we thought.

Our hands collided across the simple wooden bed in which we had tucked up Susanna. 'The sheets are pulled back. And cold,' Emma said slowly. 'She must have been gone some time.'

A crack as a chair fell over, by the bed. Another flicker of lightning outside the shutters just for a second showed Emma distraught. 'Jim. All her clothes are here. I've got her dress.'

'Look in the cupboard.' We searched in the empty spaces. I started to go back to Martin's room.

'Jim . . . Don't leave me alone. I'm terrified.'

Over the thunder I shouted, 'It's nothing to be frightened of. There must be an explanation.'

But Martin's room was empty as hell. A boy of twelve and a girl of ten had disappeared. Jesus, I thought, it can't be. It can't be. It can't happen to us. We loved each other, we were a family together. Kids were a complication, but not a problem, so far as we were concerned. It had been fun setting out. I was going to show them. Life was going to be good. We began to call. Desperately, hopelessly, in the darkness.

'Martin. Susie. Where are you? Come on out. No kidding.'

Silence.

We knew that they weren't there, and were shit-scared.

'For God's sake, let's get some light.'

We hadn't even got a torch. The car was outside, but Emma begged me stay there, close to her.

I remember opening the shutters, waiting for more lightning. No moon; the air as black and warm as velvet, the steady rain. An eerie feeling that we were the only ones living. The storm seemed to cut us off.

Sheet lightning round the valley showed that the car was still safe on the drive. Emma began to sob.

'Don't be silly. We'll find them. There must be a candle somewhere . . .'

'Where? Where?'

I tried the lights again, feeling stupid.

'The gas. Light the gas cooker,' she said.

I couldn't even find the matches, knocked them on to the floor, spilled the box. Scrabbled on the floor, retrieved them, got it going with a hiss and a plop.

The blue flames were at least alive, and gave us a faint comfort. We looked at ourselves like strangers.

'They must have wandered off, before the storm, and be sheltering somewhere . . .' I didn't even believe it, but it was necessary to say something, however bird-brained. Mad ideas filled our heads.

'They've been taken. Kidnapped. Or killed.'

'That's crazy talk, honey.'

'No it's not. Jim, I'm frightened. Terrified. Why aren't they here?'

'I don't know. I don't know. Shut up.' I tried to keep the panic from my voice. Even began to look for a weapon, in the dim light of the gas ring, in case we were attacked. We stayed where we were, the gas at least was on our side, a comforting blue halo.

'What do you think has happened?' Emma whispered.

'How the hell do I know?'

'I hate this place,' she said. 'Why did you have to bring me? You read about things in these parts. People murdered and raped. Never heard of again.'

'Aw. Come on. Don't be ridiculous.'

It can never happen to you, can it? Except when it begins to, and you start praying. Please God, keep them safe. They're all we've got. We love them dearly. Help us, wherever you are.

Emma put her arms around me. 'Hold me, Jim.' She was shaking. I was numb. 'Telephone the police,' she said.

'Where from?' The place had no phone of its own. We were three kilometres from Chenoncey village, and the nearest house.

'Take the car.'

'OK. Let me get dressed—' A fresh crash of thunder, jagged razors of light, stopped us in our tracks.

'That was right on top of us. What if—'

'Emma. It doesn't help. Keep buttoned up.' I tried to rally

45

her Britishness, one of the fallbacks. I wanted to yell. Fuck you, kids. What the hell are you doing?

We groped back to our bedrooms and found some clothes; I left the wet pyjamas in a corner and struggled into trousers and shirt and slip-on shoes. The car keys had a reassuring firmness.

'Where are you going?'

'Up to the village to telephone.'

'Don't leave me here,' she screamed.

'Then come with me.'

'Jim. Someone must stay here. What if the children come back . . . ?' she sobbed in the dark.

We crawled back into the kitchen. My watch said 3.20. In a couple of hours it would be daylight.

'Let's try and hang on till then.'

What do you do in a strange house, in a foreign country, without even a light, in the middle of a thunderstorm when your children go missing?

We weren't prepared. We didn't know. During the flashes of lightning we clung to each other and hoped. Slowly found courage to explore the dark places room by room, two blind people, feeling for we didn't know what. Soft things, hard things, dead things. The living room, the closets, the corners. Under the beds. Bathroom, broom cupboard.

'The attic,' Emma said. 'Under the roof.'

'They can't have got up there. I don't even know how to get in.'

We huddled against each other. 'If only this bloody storm would stop . . .'

But it went on reverberating round and round the hills, as if it had it in for us. We had to wait, in the dark.

We had never faced, never had to cope with a thing like this. The rain hammered on the roof tiles as we listened for every strange noise, every smack of the shutters, every whistle of the wind. Each flicker of lightning grew monsters on the walls, giant heads in the night.

'Oh God Jim...' she cried. 'There's something awful here...'

'Don't be stupid,' I said. 'There must be an explanation.'

'Jim. Oh Jim... How can there be... unless someone has taken them?'

'Emma. Stop it. Stop it. We've got to keep our heads.' I took hold of her shoulders and shook her. 'Em. Sit down.' I found a chair in the kitchen, then filled a saucepan with water. The fridge had stopped humming, but there was fresh milk inside that we had bought on the journey. In the lulls of the storm the only sound was the hiss of the gas, as we contemplated the options lurking in the shadows.

'We've got to get help. The police,' I said.

She stared at me. 'You went outside. You went outside,' she kept on repeating.

'Honey, I tell you I didn't make it. I got soaked instead, when I tried to get to the car.' That fucking torch. I could go and dig it out now.

'No.' We had the flame from the gas stove. 'Let's have a cup of tea first.'

That was more the old Emma. I stroked her arm while we waited for the water to boil. 'Honey, it will be OK.'

Somehow it was a help, just to be doing something. We sat and drank the tea slowly, listening to the thunder climb out of the valley, the lightning distance itself, the rain diminish, the country wrap itself up and go to sleep. We waited for the night to end, each of us consumed by dread. A barrier forming between us.

Perhaps they would come back, if we just sat and hoped, as if it was some kind of joke.

Time seemed to have stopped. The dimly lit numerals flicking around on my watch did not bring the dawn any quicker. I decided to find the torch and then to search outside, but Emma screamed at me. 'No. Jim. No. Don't go out there. Not until it's lighter. Don't leave me alone.' She was shivering again, and I found a blanket for her. Emma was going berserk.

Dark, dark, dark, they all go into the dark. I couldn't remember the rest, but the thought chilled me. I put the heaviest saucepan close at hand, in case.

47

In case of something I did not understand. For fear of things.

We had never been far apart, Emma, me and the kids. Until the job got on top of me, the marriage had been good. We had enjoyed each other, we had our shared friends and interests. No ghosts intervened in Richmond. Why in the name of Christ had something gone wrong here, in this godforsaken valley? I began to hate it now, smelling of nerves, my armpits sour.

Jesus Christ. Suppose they were dead, their throats cut in a ditch; molested; raped; dumped bound and gagged in the river? Or just taken away, driven off in the night, flown abroad to Arabia, South America, never to be heard of again? My old man had walked out one day, leaving three children behind, just like that, to live with another woman, steamy and messy. But at least it was known, he had been traced. There were dreadful stories of lost children never seen, locked up in Bluebeard's Castle. Oh my Christ.

I found Emma's hand seeking mine. 'Look. It's growing lighter, over there.'

I opened the shutter wider, peering out. The last notes of the thunder were replaced by a bird chirping.

'It's over.'

But in my heart I felt it was only beginning. And I had brought her here. I could have wept.

The dawn was starting to break. Gradually, I made out the shape of the car, a hedge, and a stark line of trees.

It had stopped raining. I dashed out and found the torch inside the glove box. Its pencil of light showed only the sodden gravel and dripping leaves . . . Nothing moved. The light came up quickly now: it was nearly half-past four.

We knew that they wouldn't come now.

'I'm going down to the village.'

'I'll come with you,' Emma said.

We left the front door open, stood by the unlocked car and looked at each other.

No sign of a struggle, no sign, no message, no hope. The gates to the house were open, as we had left them, but any tyre prints had been washed out by the rain.

We loved them, between us we loved those children, and they had gone.

'That thing. That thing in the field. What is it?' she shouted.

Against the emergent skyline I scanned the field across the road, and saw a black lump in the middle. 'I don't know. Let's go. We must find the gendarmerie.'

'But what in God's name is that?'

I could see better now, the black hump in the opposite field, like some primeval rock.

Holding the torch, I walked through the gate and crossed the road to look. Perhaps the thing held a clue, or was a plastic cover underneath which ... they ... could be ... sleeping.

The grass squelched over my shoes, the saturated cattle, brown and black, with worried, bloodshot eyes, trudged away.

The thing lay on the field, as dead and black as a curse.

I paddled through the pools of water, under the leaden sky, the cottage behind me, the children on my mind. The air was heavy with threat.

The thing loomed up like a tomb; a marker or a black altar.

It was a cow. Dead. The lightning had singed its head and there was a smell of burning.

5

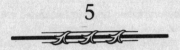

The village was a collection of houses at the crossroads of the D183 and the road to Albi. Pure chance that we had come there, through the agency that booked the gîte. In the early morning it had the washed-out colour of a litho-graph: the grey stone church on the corner, the shuttered stone houses, tiles glistening wetly, the ugly criss-cross of electricity cables. We could see that the lights were on: the power failure hadn't been general. There was the *alimentation*, shut. The *boulangerie*, shut. The garage, the Total-gaz store, the place selling *brocante*. And that was it.

Emma's jaw was set firm, but I knew she was weeping to herself as we drove in. The donkey, maybe a mule, loomed over a barbed-wire fence. A few chickens clucked in a run. Otherwise it was dead. The parked cars seemed almost abandoned, no one stirred in the houses as we splashed through the puddles. A strange mist covered the hills and seemed to drip off the buildings. We were totally alone: a couple that no one had heard of reporting the loss of two children that no one had ever seen.

'They must be around somewhere,' I said to calm my fears.

'They haven't run away on their own. I know that,' Emma muttered tersely. Her mouth was a thin line in a face that had gone white and hard as a stone wall.

My stomach was sick. Sick with the same despair I had felt on the death of my mother, as if another tie had been irrevocably broken. All I wanted, at any price, was the knowledge that they were alive. Alive. Somewhere, any-where, so long as there was hope. Instead we had only the message of those two empty beds. Their faces haunted

50

me: Susanna, brunette and chubby, always smiling, our domestic and sensible daughter; Martin, into computers and sports, accident-prone, coming home with gashed knees, or half a front tooth knocked out. Oh Jesus Christ. Oh God, please not now, not to me. Send me a sign, some word.

'Suppose they went the other way . . . down the valley,' Emma mused.

'Who? The kids? They didn't go anywhere.'

'How do you know?' I felt the edge of suspicion. 'What do you mean?'

'I don't know what I mean. For Christ's sake shut up.'

We stopped the car at the crossroads and huddled together. 'Well. What do we do?' I said.

'Find the police.'

'Honey, there won't be a cop in a village this size.'

'Then we go to the nearest town. St Maxime le Grand. It's only ten miles down the road.'

'OK, OK.' I pulled back on to the main drag.

Then Emma said, 'But what if they come back? Somebody must be there in case.'

'Honey, do you want to go back to the house? To wait there on your own?'

Her face was waxen, drained of colour. 'Someone must stay,' she said. 'In case they reappear.' I saw the desperate hope.

I moved to reassure her. 'Drop me back there,' I said. 'You go find the cops. The gendarmes in St Maxime. Honey, you know how to explain things. You go in and report.'

She shook her head. 'I can't . . . I can't leave here while there is still . . . a chance. You go. I'll stay. I want to stay.'

'Emma. My lousy rotten French won't stand it . . .'

'Of course it will. Explain in English. They'll take more notice of you. Anyway your French can cope. Go on,' she urged. 'But for God's sake get back as soon as you can.'

I hesitated. 'We could knock up somebody here, ask them to go back with you.' It was 5.17 a.m.

She shook her head. 'They wouldn't understand. And we'd be losing time. Whoever it was took the children, they weren't after us. They could have cut our throats.

51

They won't come back during daylight. None of them will come back.'

The awfulness of what she said echoed like a dirge between us. Someone had taken the children. Someone, persons unknown, who could have stabbed us to death in the dark. But they wanted the kids, not us. Now we could only pin our hopes on some kind of police dragnet.

Tyres hitting the kerb, I turned the car round and shot back to the house.

It loomed up across the hedgerows, red-roofed, cheerful, bougainvillaea round the door, the white chairs on the patio already beginning to steam as the sun rose. Our holiday retreat. As we drove up we hoped against hope that somehow they would have shown up, grinning at completing some kind of big crazy joke. But the house was empty and dead. It broke my heart as I tried to rally Emma along.

'Don't worry, honey. It's going to be OK. I'm sure it's some sort of trick.'

I took her inside. Told her to make some breakfast and lock the doors. Her eyes never left my face, until I went back to the car.

When I returned through the deserted village one of the doors at the end, by the sign saying Chenoncey with a red line through it, was already open.

I braked and knocked. An old man in a blue shirt was getting ready for work. His leathery face was frosted with silver stubble and his hands were as dry as jerked beef. When I tried to explain, he grinned dumbly, confused, and muttered in that hopeless patois. His eyes seemed narrow with cunning and I sensed a wall of indifference. We inhabited different planets. How could he understand this guy from outer space, gabbling in half-forgotten high-school French? He shrugged his shoulders, began to shuffle back inside. My white mask must have been frightening.

I mumbled something about the gîte down the road, pointed, shouted, 'Gendarmerie?' He shrugged his shoulders.

'Fuck you,' I said, and drove on.

It started to rain again, a thin drizzle this time, a curtain to the heat of the day. The road sign said St Maxime 14; I could be there in ten minutes.

We centred round the children, Emma and I. She was a smart girl, great with the kids, and sometimes almost eerily clairvoyant. I understood all too well how terrified she now was, not for herself but for them. Terrified by the premonition that something was horribly wrong. She feared the worst. I tried to rationalize, thinking up other explanations. Some kind of adventure, or sleepwalking, or hiding and getting lost and going to sleep. But none of them added up in my mind. The kids had now been gone three hours or more, in the middle of that godawful storm. Wasn't the worst more likely; why shouldn't it be?

St Maxime. Five thousand people. Big enough for a gendarmerie, and people already moving. I shouted at a truck driver and he pointed down the road. I found that my hands were trembling and my shirt was sticking to my back.

The old town was built on a hill with the market-square on top, and cheapjack stallholders were already setting out pitches. The road curved downhill and narrowed over a bridge, where traffic queued along a file of cones. Halfway down the hill a tricolour flew from a pole and a blue, white and red sign said 'Gendarmerie'. A gendarme on the gate, in his summer khaki uniform, waved me in.

I slammed the car to a halt inside a courtyard and ran up the steps of what had once been a mansion. Grey double doors opened into a lobby where a middle-aged cop in shirt-sleeves sat behind the reception counter drinking coffee. He looked up in surprise as I tried to explain in fractured French. English, tourists, two children missing. Do something, for Christ's sake.

He scratched his head. There was nobody available. He was waiting to be relieved. It was too early.

'Jesus wept. I need police help now.' I hammered the desk top.

The noise opened a door and another guy appeared, pulling on his tunic.

I tried again, conscious of time draining away. Two

children. Missing in the night. English passports. American father.

He listened patiently. 'We will have to send for the sergeant.'

'Listen, you dumbbells. They are my children,' I shouted. 'My kids have gone missing. *Je ne pas trouver mes enfants. Comprenez*? Lost. *Disparus. Deux enfants. Mes enfants.* Can't you understand, for God's sake? They could be in great danger. *Grand danger.* Kidnapped *peut-être.*'

'*Oui.* I understand,' he said in English. 'Please sit down.' I was an episode in the duty book.

I calmed down. Told him slowly in English.

'If they have disappeared, we will arrange to search,' he said politely.

'For Christ's sake, I want a search now. Every moment could be vital.'

Would I have some coffee, and wait?

What the hell could I do? I couldn't tear down the structure of French provincial policing and set out on my own. I couldn't force him to get the detective squad out of bed in Albi or Pontauban or wherever. I couldn't complain to the Commissaire de Police. I wanted to kick him and shake him, hit his head against the wall until his sleepy dark eyes rattled in their sockets. But it was useless. The electric clock on the wall clicked on regardless. He forced me to sit and wait, said that he would telephone the Chief Inspector as soon as it was feasible, in an hour or so. The Chief Inspector had had a late night, he added, on account of the storm.

By now I was in shock. I wanted to go back to Emma and see if anything had changed. I had an awful, incomprehensible fear that she might have vanished too. They must have seen me panicking.

Screaming that I would be back, I ran down the steps, and out into the yard, and in twelve minutes I was back at the gîte. Emma was hovering in the doorway, dressed in a T-shirt and slacks. She ran towards me.

'Thank God. Are you OK?' I asked.

'They haven't come back,' she said.

I told her about the police. We stood there holding hands,

waiting, praying, pictures before our eyes of our two children strangled or shot or left for dead. Unthinkable, unbearable. It could not happen to the kids we had held in our arms, and carried on our backs, and watched in the school concert, and played hide-and-seek with in the Surrey woods.

'Honey, come back and help me explain to these dimwit country cops. Leave all the doors unlocked. Just leave a note for the kids, in case they turn up.'

She looked at me strangely. 'In case . . . What do you mean? They *will* come back.'

'But not without help. We've got to get help.'

This time she agreed with me.

We abandoned the house, the holiday cottage that seemed to have destroyed us, and I drove her back, overtaking like a madman, to the gendarmerie. We dared not speak, frightened of what we might say.

Places were coming alive. We were dying. I looked at Emma, whose face seemed skinned: the bones suddenly showing. What did the marriage mean now? It could be we loved the kids more than we needed each other. We were unable to focus, we could not trust our emotions.

Waiting. Waiting. Wondering.

'Get me a drink,' she said.

I bought cognac and coffee at the café in the square while we waited for the gendarmerie to summon help. Regulars dropped in on their way to work, buying cigarettes. One of them played with the pinball machine. I could have throttled him.

But in Emma now, after the brandy, there was an unnatural calmness, almost an acceptance, a flush of something unreal. I found myself praying.

I drank a second brandy. Dutch courage.

We touched each other for comfort. They had told us to come back at eight. The duty gendarme assured me that orders had already been relayed: the area would be sealed and roadside searches would begin. Chief Inspector le Brève of the departmental CID and the Garde Mobile would be arriving in person from Pontauban to take charge.

We toyed with croissants and jam. More coffee but

unable to eat. Emma by now was trembling with fatigue, but I felt stronger, cold sober.

Hand in hand we walked down the cobbled street, into the forecourt of the gendarmerie where I had parked the car. They knew me now. I was one of the events.

We found ourselves still waiting, sitting on cane-bottomed chairs that slid on a linoleum floor in one of the inner offices. A frosted-glass door, regulation furniture, some filing cabinets, a pinboard on which was spread a large-scale map of the district. On the right-hand side our gîte had been flagged, in the middle of the valley, in the middle of Aveyron, in the middle of France.

Dear God, help us now. Visions of Martin and Susie as we used to know them, coming home at the end of the term, excited at the start of the holiday.

There was time to remember, while preoccupied men looked sympathetic, bustling in and leaving with papers.

Eight o'clock came and went.

'I'm sorry, he's late.'

'Why can't you do something?' Emma said.

'We are doing all we can, madame. Please, you must wait for the Chief Inspector. He is in control of everything. If necessary he will inform the investigating magistrate.'

The Inspector, the Inspector. Why was he so bloody wonderful?

It was 8.27 before we heard the car screech up somewhere outside. A girl poked her head round the door, as if to make sure that we were still kicking our heels there. We listened to feet in the corridor, an urgent murmuring, a babble of briefing, before he came in.

Someone opened the door. 'Chief Inspector le Brève,' they announced.

He swept in quickly, small, light on his feet, a grey shock of hair, eyes like buttons in old chairs, grey suit, Italian shoes. A snappy striped shirt with white collar and cuffs, a small trimmed moustache on a round face smelling faintly of aftershave.

Chief Inspector le Brève was black.

*

56

OK. So he was black. So what? He seemed a self-confident guy as he walked across to us, his hand outstretched, speaking immaculate English, immediately offering hope.

'My dear sir. I am most deeply disturbed. You understand? This is a most unusual thing.'

We nodded, groping for his sympathy. He flattered with his attentions, quick and birdlike, and began to ask a series of questions, taking us through that dreadful night, hour by hour. I realized here at last was a professional who knew his business.

'I assure you we will find them,' he said. 'I know this area. I have lived here all my life.'

'But . . . they can't have . . . just gone,' Emma said.

'Madame. Have faith. It is my duty to find them. Please. Come with me.' He bowed us towards his car, a bright blue Citroën, and whisked us back in convoy to Chenoncey and the gîte. Again we had that brief hope that somehow they would have returned, but the cottage stood empty in its plot of rank grass.

Emma by now was distraught. 'You've got to find them. You've got to.'

'I understand, madame. Perfectly.' He touched her hand. His brown eyes flicked restlessly over the fields. I could see some men with a tractor roping the dead cow to pull it on to a trailer.

He waved towards them, a gold ring flashing in the morning light. 'Everything is in hand,' he said in English.

But nothing could convince me that they were doing enough. I wanted to pin them down, to ask how many men they had, if they had sealed off the roads, and where they were going to search. I wanted the whole damned police force helping us.

'What's in hand? What are you actually doing, as of now?'

He stared at me coolly. 'I have the area ringed. We will look high and low. We will find them.'

'Hell, man. What does that mean?'

'House to house and barn to barn. In every ditch,' he said.

Emma looked so ill that I was worried for her mind. We had arrived in three cars, with a posse of Garde Mobile

57

bikers. The noise from their machines seemed to drill through Emma's head. Le Brève suggested a doctor, but she refused to move. Her hands twisted together. The Inspector would strut off to give orders and then come back to ask how she was, begging her at least to lie down.

She tensed back at him, her voice anguished. 'Please tell me the truth. What do you think has happened?'

'Happened? Happened?' He looked away across the fields. 'Who knows, madame? In France many things simply occur. My job is to try and explain, try and explain.' He gave instructions for the house to be searched for anything strange or suspicious. Then he beckoned to me. 'Monsieur. Please come inside. On your own.'

For the next hour he grilled me. Plain-clothes men tramped through taking photographs and measurements as I sat with le Brève in the kitchen. He sighed and shrugged.

'So far we have found nothing. But who knows?' He leaned towards me. 'Now. Your wife said you heard a noise?'

'Sure.' I explained about the cry that I thought I had heard, and the attempt to find my torch.

'So you went outside?'

'No way. It was too damned wet.'

'Ah. What sort of cry?' he pressed.

I had been thinking about that moment for a long time, and the more that I tried to remember, the less clear I became.

'I can't be sure. It might have been an animal, or even my imagination. The storm woke me up. I wasn't expecting anything.'

Le Brève peered at me as if I was lying. He had found my discarded pyjamas, which were still damp. 'Why are these clothes wet?'

'I told you, I was going outside.'

'But you said you did not go.'

'Look. The rain caught me in the doorway. That's all. For God's sake—'

'I understand.' He smiled and changed the subject. I could see he only half believed me.

58

'So. You say that you locked the front door before going to bed? And bolted the kitchen one, even in the country?'

'That's right.' It was second nature.

'But it was open when we arrived?'

'Of course. We left it for the kids. I left it like that when they vanished.'

He had closely examined the keys and the locks. 'What about the garage?'

The garage? I had parked our car outside. The place was full of junk. I had not even pulled up the shutter, but had glanced in through the side door. Le Brève called me to it, showed it had never been secured, triumphantly. There was no lock on that door.

'You see. They could have gone this way . . . eh?'

'Gone where?'

'Ah. That is the question, as your Shakespeare said.' He seemed to imply it was my fault he could not answer it.

Pacing through the house, he went methodically from room to room, identifying the contents. 'This is yours?' He held up Susie's cuddly dog.

'My daughter's. She calls it Chocolate Dog.'

'She takes it to bed with her? At ten years old?'

'Yes.'

He examined the stuffed toy, her much-loved and travel-stained pooch, and made it seem almost obscene, against the empty bed with its rumpled sheets.

'So she would have taken it with her, if she had the chance?' He spoke in a mixture of French and English, often repeating the words, just to make sure.

'Sure thing.'

'I see.' He laid it carefully on the little bedside locker and put on gold-rimmed glasses, examining the books and the papers in the living room.

'Monsieur. These gloves in the drawer, they are yours?' Some gardening gloves, unused.

'No. They must belong to the house.'

'But why are they left here, monsieur, in this buffet?'

'How the hell do I know?' It was for him to tell me but he put them away again, and instead confronted me, his dark eyes glinting.

'You say you had no lights at all?'

'That's right. The electricity failed. You can see it's still off.'

Le Brève smiled thinly. 'There is – how you say – a switch in the garage that shuts off things. Maybe the system overloaded, or it was affected by the electrical storm—'

'A trip-switch?'

'Exactly. Or it was just switched off . . . by someone . . . even by you.'

'Listen,' I said. 'I've told you the truth, so help me God.'

'Come with me, please.'

He took me through to the junction boxes high up in a corner, professing surprise that as an architect I had not inspected them. He scratched his head as he looked at the switches.

'That lever has not been touched?'

'Hell no. I've not even seen it before. It must have flipped down in the night for some reason.'

He returned it to 'on' and the garage lights blazed.

'Are you sure that you have not tampered with it? When you got wet?'

I was angry, and it showed. 'Jesus Christ, Inspector. I never even came in here. I wanted the lights back on, I couldn't see a goddam thing. I had gotten soaked trying to reach the car.'

'The car? Why the car?'

'I told you. There was a torch inside it, man . . .'

He shrugged again, and motioned to one of his men to photograph the switches. We were standing outside on the wet gravel and he noticed that Emma, who had reappeared, was shivering in her thin shirt and pants. Suddenly he was solicitous.

'Madame, you are trembling. You will catch cold.'

'I'm all right.'

'No. Please, you must find a coat. And rest. I am concerned for you.'

He took her by the elbow, round to the front door. 'Go into the house and sit down. Madame, please. Leave the worrying to me.' His neat little figure was bouncing along beside her. 'Cheer up. Cheer up.'

Finally he succeeded in coaxing her indoors, staring at nothing. I had the distinct impression that he was anxious to tackle me further.

Standing in the hall he pulled me aside, so close that I could smell his breath.

'You are American passport?'

'Yes.'

'And your wife is British?'

I nodded.

'So it is a love-match, eh?'

Again, I was annoyed. 'What the hell are you implying?'

He stared at me. 'I ask you bluntly, monsieur. You have had no quarrel with your wife?'

'No.'

Le Brève paused, as if he only half believed me. 'All right. So you sleep with her?'

'Yes,' I found myself saying. 'I love her.'

The corners of his mouth turned down.

When Emma was settled he left one police car in front of the house, ordered the second one down the road towards Chenoncey and pushed me inside the third. His big blue Citroën. There was a gate into the field opposite where they had been roping the electrocuted cow, and the Citroën turned inside it. We drove a short distance, bumping along a rough track at the side of the field until stopped by a barbed-wire fence. Beyond lay the belt of woodland that Emma and I had seen when we arrived, oak and ash and walnut which loomed up dark and silent. He slammed the car doors, told the driver to wait.

We unhooked a makeshift gate and went inside the woods. The great trees were like people suspicious of our intrusion. Water still dripped from the leaves.

'Please—'

A cold fear ran through my bones. Why should he bring me here? Supposing that they had been found, Martin and Susanna, here, their bodies discovered under a pile of bran-

61

ches, in a shallow grave, and that le Brève wanted to show me . . .

He must have understood my nightmare, for he tapped my arm in one of those little gestures that were becoming familiar, a bird's movement.

'Please. I want to show you something.' He plunged off busily ahead of me, pushing aside the brambles of a scarcely recognizable path, into the woodland.

'Hey. Where are we going? This isn't a search.'

'Ah. Do not be alarmed. My men will continue the search, if your children are still . . . to be found.'

'If they are what?'

But he seemed not to have heard, and I trailed after him, with a head full of crazy prayers. At least it did not appear that he had found their bodies. Surely they must be alive, somewhere, somehow. I swore to myself that they were, that there was always hope.

Le Brève turned round to face me. 'Come on, please.'

Shit. What the hell was he playing at?

We had reached a clearing in the wood, with nothing but a tangled mound, old stones or stumps overgrown with debris and brambles. A mark in the soil. Or a grave, maybe.

'Don't worry,' he said.

I wanted to shout and shake him. What the fuck were we doing there, this little French cop and a guy like me? I had a profession, a job, an up-market house in Richmond, and Bob Dorcas wanting me back. I used to have a future. Instead of which the Garde Mobile were out there searching, road-blocking and ring-fencing, while this man, the Inspector, had to drag me to some godforsaken space in the trees.

'Monsieur, this part of the world is full of mysteries,' he muttered. He pulled out a packet of Gauloises and offered them. I shook my head, and tried to control myself while he lit one and threw the match away. His sharp eyes kept scanning my face.

'What exactly does that mean?'

He shrugged. 'Unsolved crimes. Unplanned deaths—'

'Deaths—' I forced myself to contemplate what he was

suggesting: my children's end. My kids who were tucked up in bed eight or nine hours before. 'It's not possible—'

'Who knows, monsieur?'

'Sweet Jesus. Why should anybody want my two children . . . ?' Not mine, please God, not mine.

He waved his hands. 'Why should they disappear?' He hopped on to the top of some rotting tree stumps. 'That is for us to find out.' The cigarette burnt in his hand like a wand. 'There are disappearances all the time. In France.' He gave the word a gravity, as if it was a different dimension of quality from England or the States . . . 'Perhaps you recall two cyclists disappeared, only two years ago, not fifty kilometres from here?'

My blood froze at what he was trying to say. 'No.'

'Oh yes. We found them several months later. Bound hand and foot. Shot in the head. By someone they trusted.'

I must have lurched forward.

'I'm sorry. I did not want to upset you . . . only to indicate . . . to explain that these things are very difficult. And often sad.' Le Brève lit another cigarette from the stub of the first one.

'Difficult?'

'Difficult. And they take time. We shall take time. You must not expect too much.'

I found that I was nervous. Very slowly I said, 'I want you to find them . . . alive . . . or . . . dead.'

'Of course. Of course.' He smiled at me, as if I was setting a problem. 'We shall do that.'

'I want my boy and girl back . . .'

'I understand what you say, monsieur.' He spoke softly, his eyes downcast, a faint bead of perspiration on his brow. A dark Hercule Poirot. 'Bodies usually come to the surface, in my experience.'

In a cold sweat of fear and loathing I shouted, 'What makes you so sure they are dead?'

His foot tapped on the ground. 'I do not say that, monsieur. It is your thought. But bodies have been found once . . . here. Did you know that?'

At first I did not understand. How could I know that locality? But he kept on pointing towards the little mound.

63

Some shadow lay over that site, the mound by which he was standing, the reason he had taken me there. The trees closed in like a prison.

'Jesus Christ, Inspector. Stop playing games with me. What happened here?'

The world around us seemed to be holding its breath. I was conscious of every bird, every rustle of leaf.

Le Brève jumped down from the tree stumps and swivelled round to point at the clearing. I was standing beside him, a head and shoulders taller, resisting the urge to pick him up and yell at him, and I know he understood.

'Two bodies were found here. Two children,' he said.

'Oh my God. When?' My shout seemed to echo round the trees. Surely he could not be telling me about Martin and Susie?

Le Brève stood with hands on hips, confronting me. 'Thirty-seven years ago. Almost exactly.'

'Who were they?' I asked.

'It is a private matter. Nothing to do with you.'

My mind went numb. I could not think what to say. Could not, would not, relate it, that historical happening, to my two wonderful kids. Children who had been running and laughing with us only a few hours past, hours now becoming for ever in my mind. I remember staring at him.

'What are you trying to say? Why? Are you implying . . . ?' What did he mean, what was he seeking to prove?

And le Brève refused to budge. He said the names were irrelevant. He ran his tongue over his lips. He did not trust me.

'All I am saying is that there are mysteries, monsieur. At the end of the line, whenever it comes – ' he finished the cigarette, and threw the butt on to the ground, treading it with his heel ' – at the end of the line perhaps no one understands why people do some things. Some terrible things.'

'No one understands what? For God's sake. What happened here?'

He bowed, slightly, wearily. 'Monsieur. There are sometimes happenings that we just have to accept. Motives we do not comprehend.' His voice was harsh and dry. 'I found two bodies here, thirty-seven years ago.'

He let that sink in.

Thirty-seven years ago. Le Brève must have been in his early twenties. I put him at sixty now, though it was difficult to tell. His skin was smooth and unwrinkled. Had he been a young gendarme, in this area, all those years ago?

He saw my implied question and nodded. 'In France, we are a local people. We stick to the country we know.'

I felt cold, in spite of the sunshine breaking through the foliage. His face was a non-committal blank, neither friendly nor opposed, just expressing a fact, a fact of death there in the woods. Knowing my children were missing.

Le Brève swung his hand around, pointing at the full-leafed trees.

'Look at these. All of them living. Healthy.' He paused as if considering. 'Suddenly a leaf falls. And who knows why?'

6

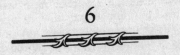

It was then that the processes of France took over. I shuttled backwards and forwards between the gîte, where Emma was mostly sleeping, sedated and exhausted, St Maxime and Pontauban, as the search was extended. The local gendarmerie in St Maxime seemed overwhelmed by the detective branch under le Brève, and paramilitary police swarmed on the roads like gnats, checking every car. The Chief, le Commissaire de Police, le Brève explained, had given him full powers. The investigation would be in his personal hands.

But the children had gone, as suddenly as water through sand, leaving only the marks of their presence, the holiday gear and their toys. Susie's toy dog, Chocolate Dog, sat forlornly on top of her suitcase in the empty bedroom, and Emma broke down when she saw it. Her raw eyes looked at me, sometimes groping for hope, sometimes in bleak despair . . . and at times as if she hated me.

I was clearly under suspicion: the last one who had seen them, the one who had wet pyjamas, who could have been outside the house. Hadn't I arranged the holiday, driven them down, and said that final goodnight? Had there been quarrels, threats? le Brève asked drily, pushing and probing. I wondered what Emma had told him.

He shrugged. 'Your wife? She does not commit herself.'

'What do you mean?'

'Who can say, monsieur? Only that something has happened, and like me she does not know why.'

'Are you implying . . . ?'

'I imply nothing, monsieur. I am only the investigating officer.'

But Emma's puffy face seemed to blame me. 'It's all your fault,' she said to me once, as we waited for news. 'You wanted this bloody holiday. This bloody country . . .'

I tried to reason with her. 'Honey . . . it was because of you.'

'Don't honey me,' she snapped.

Le Brève took me into Pontauban and we sat in room after room while a blank wall of despair hung in front of my eyes. The floor tiles were yellow and staring. The questions mounted. Martin and Susanna, were they sexually mature? How did I feel towards them? Could they have wanted to run away? Were their relations incestuous? Was there someone we knew who was interested in them?

No, I told him. No, no, no.

I just wanted them back. Or, failing that, to be found. As the days wore on the process became a nightmare; which preyed on both our minds, Emma's and mine, in different ways. We needed the children as much as they must need us.

Fly-blown interview rooms.

Shrieking heads.

Dismembered bodies.

Le Brève sat and interrogated me, always polite but never without the hint of suspicion, as he peered over gold-rimmed spectacles.

'Why did you pick that place? In Chenoncey?'

'Why not? We wanted peace and quiet. It was available at short notice. Less popular because it was inland. We needed a vacation.'

'A vacation?'

'I had to get away from pressures of work.'

I wondered if I ought to ring Bob and tell him what had happened, but what was the point? Maybe other people should know. The British Embassy? Emma's parents? Yet I made no move to do anything, feeling helpless and trapped. All my illusions of competence, my office, my practice, my hopes, were swept away as we sat there, le Brève and I. He continued to imply my guilt. I could not silence him.

There must be some reason, he persisted. 'It was no accident.' He glared at me with those hot eyes.

It was worse than an accident, for they were only missing. Unaccounted for, like someone lost in a war. And the loss disembowelled me.

He crowded me with his questions, sometimes swinging his face eyeball to eyeball a foot in front of me.

'Did you really love your children? Or did you threaten them at any time?'

Stupid questions, trying to insinuate, trying to help.

There was another inspector now, among the strange faces in the police headquarters in Pontauban, a pink-brick city looking down on the Tarn; a soft-spoken, dark-haired man who said that he also had a family. Inspector Clerrard.

'I appreciate how you feel, monsieur.'

We sat in a sun-shielded office of the Commissariat, the blinds drawn against the heat. Somewhere nearby outside, street traders were shouting over the traffic. But it was quiet enough to hear the ticking of the clock.

'We have to look at all the possibilities,' he said in careful English.

Those were days of sheer hell. I knew that le Brève and his people were doing what they could, but it was never enough. While they probed me for a motive I sat and despaired at them. And all the time in my mind there was the terrible feeling that in some way I had failed my family.

For Emma it was even worse, for she stayed in the gîte on her own, with a gendarme outside, as if she was under house arrest. She refused to talk about anything, and tried to shut out the pain.

Time seemed to have stopped. The days merged into each other, never so long. It was a measure of Emma's despair that she agreed to take the Valium prescribed by the police physician – normally she hated the idea of drugs. But even that was little help. She sat up and cried in the bed beside me for three long nights, until in the end he gave her a knock-out pill and she lay like a statue, clammy with exhaustion.

Day after day we waited, hoping. Day after day they said there was no news . . . yet. And either le Brève or Clerrard would begin another session, asking about my job, my background, my habits, whether I played with the children, if there were other people with whom they stayed, how long we had been married, whether the marriage was stable, why we had come to France, probing to find an excuse, a failing, a reason.

Combining with sleeplessness, they drove me close to fury. Worse, I did not trust their competence, and I felt that they knew it: something of the old ambivalence between two different cultures always seemed to hang between us. Suspicion, contempt and dread, they saw them in my eyes. I wanted them to get off their butts and move, move, move.

In the end I called Bob Dorcas, and told him the situation. 'Stay as long as it takes,' he said. I decided to keep the news from Emma's folks. There was no point in worrying them, until there was something to say, especially with le Brève monitoring every step. I glared across the table at him.

'Listen. I have a pal in London. A lawyer: John Simpson. I need to bring him in.'

'Of course, monsieur. Why not?' Le Brève waved at the telephone, watching me over his reading glasses. 'Please speak to anyone you wish.'

I did not know what I wanted to say and it took me hours to get through. When I did, Simpson said, 'Jesus Christ Almighty. Don't sign any statements without faxing them to me first.'

Statements? What was he talking about – a criminal trial? What did I expect him to say: that he would find them for me?

'Just co-operate with the police,' he advised. 'I can't do much from here but if necessary I'll come out. As soon as there's some news. Have you consulted the FCO?'

'Who?'

'The British Embassy. And the US consul. They need to know. The kids have British passports. We have a consul-general in Lyons, but I suggest you ring Paris.'

Somehow I was lost between countries, once again.

Le Brève sat there staring at me, rubbing his hands, frowning when I told him. 'Why do you not speak to the American Embassy? Are you reporting on me? Do you not trust the police?'

'It's not that. I've got to let someone know. My children hold British passports. Dual nationality.'

'I understand.' He pursed his lips as if to say what did it matter to him. 'You look tired, monsieur. It is a great strain on you.'

'I feel like my world has stopped. But I'd better do what Simpson says. Tell some of the Foreign Office guys.'

'Very good. Of course.'

Another call. Another wait. More hours grinding by, until a young blood in Paris called me back.

Names. Ages. Addresses. I staggered through it all again for the benefit of some crappy Third Secretary whose blasé voice implied he'd heard it all before, and did not want to be bothered. Drop-outs, old women, drug-freaks, students, disappearing all the time, he seemed to imply. What did a couple of kids matter more or less?

'We are very sorry, naturally. I understand your concern, Mr Freeling. The Ambassador I am sure would share it. But the French police are very competent. You can rely on them.' I thought he was going to recommend me to tuck up with a good Simenon.

'Have you warned the immediate family?'

'That's up to me.'

'Have you consulted your solicitor?'

'Yes.'

'What did he say?'

'Get in touch with you,' I shouted.

'Good. Jolly good. Well, I'm sorry that there's so little we can do. Keep us in touch of course. My advice is that you get some sleep. If I may say so, you sound pretty whacked.'

'Whacked? I'm fucking exhausted.' By him, by Simpson, le Brève, Clerrard, by Emma herself becoming more and more introspective. I tried to give comfort by holding her close, but she edged away into a private grief.

Whenever we met le Brève kept returning to the episode of the torch. Whatever the immediate issue, he would contrive to bring it up.

'Why did you try to go outside in the middle of the storm?'

'Listen. I've told you. We needed a light.'

'But there were switches in the garage?'

I would stare him down, in the interview room or over a cup of coffee in his spick and span office. 'I didn't know they were there. We had only just arrived.'

'Why didn't you put the car away?'

'Because we were tired, and there were things in the garage that would have had to be moved. Tables and chairs. The mower.'

'Humph. So you awoke in the dark?'

'There was thunder and lightning. And I thought I heard a cry.'

Le Brève made yet more notes. 'But not a human cry? Not one of your children?'

'I can't be sure now. I didn't think so then. It seemed to come from outside, more like a fox or a trapped animal.'

'Humph. Yet your wife was not woken too? Only you were awake. Is that not strange?'

'No. Emma was fast asleep.'

'I understand. Thank you.'

You bastard, I thought. Days and days of helplessness.

On the fifth day Clerrard said, 'Perhaps you should go back to England and wait there. It is the best advice that I can give. As soon as we have information we shall be in touch . . .'

But I could never have gone, even if Bob Dorcas had asked me. The job was dead to me. No pressure now: only the present counted. I shook my head.

'I'm staying right here, buddy, until there's some news.'

He sighed. 'That may take time.'

'OK. I'll wait. We have that place for two weeks. I shall stay as long as it takes.'

'You have work to return to . . . ?'

Work did not matter now. 'I don't care. All I want is to find them.'

His sallow face gloomed at me. 'It may not be possible.'

'Someone must find something.'

'You speak as if they are dead. Why do you assume that?'

I could not answer. None of us is prepared. Ever.

Clerrard shrugged. 'Inevitably, in a country the size of France ... A hitch-hiker was found near Albi, last year. Australian girl. Raped and shot. We still do not know who ...'

'And two children,' I said.

He frowned, puzzled. Sitting behind a plastic table, he placed his hands on the top and played with a perspex ruler. Clerrard had the air of a solicitor, or a family doctor, compassionate, shirtsleeved, with sad, pouchy eyes.

'I don't follow you,' he said.

I told him about le Brève's little excursion into the woods, to the overgrown clearing.

'That happened a long time ago. Before my time,' he said.

'But not so long for the Chief Inspector. He remembered at once.'

'Ah. He has a long memory. He was born in these parts.'

Le Brève born here?

Clerrard smiled. 'His father, so they say, was from Senegal. His mother came from Toulouse.'

I was curious, and Clerrard seemed ready to talk.

Had le Brève been in the local gendarmerie for nearly forty years?

'I believe so,' he said. 'He is the senior man now, in this *département*. You must trust him. A good detective. And he knows it like the back of his hand.'

But how could I trust a man who had done nothing except try to incriminate me? Who started by attempting to frighten me with that macabre precedent in the woods? If the story was true, not just a shot in the dark.

Clerrard put down the ruler. 'The Chief Inspector has a strong record. There have been very few unsolved crimes in the *département* over the years. Few regions claim as much. You must give him a chance.'

He seemed to be appealing to half-understood guidelines of Brit fair play. Did I think the French police were somehow less competent simply because they were different?

Did I trust the cops at all? That was the unspoken question in Clerrard's eyes.

Eventually I realized that they weren't able to help. Not any of them. Not really. Of course they would go through the motions, checking the stories, filtering the area with checkpoints for a few days more. A paragraph in the papers to see if it dredged something up, but in the end a hollowness, another unsolved riddle. Looking at him I read the message in his face and felt sick to the bone, physically sick as if I wanted to retch. But I stood up straight-backed in spite of the knife in me.

'You need some sleep,' he said, automatically.

Sleep wouldn't do much good, and he knew it. It might be what Emma needed, but not me. They could put the whole bloody crime squad on to my little catastrophe and still come up with no news. I tried not to see the mutilated bodies of my imagination. If anybody was going to find them it had to start with me.

I managed to nod. The atmosphere had become stifling. Inside the Commissariat I was passed from room to room, all smelling of stale cigarettes, and along grubby, unpolished corridors with curling posters tacked up. The cream-painted façade was like a barracks, set behind iron railings, a kind of prison. I had to escape and think.

I decided to go to the press. If anything was to be found I had to keep the story in the local papers, and hope that someone knew something.

The regional rag was the *Sud Journal-Express*, which had its offices in Pontauban. It occupied a concrete blockhouse in a street near the centre, and when Clerrard said he had finished I found myself walking towards it. They had asked if I was going straight back to the dreadful place in Chenoncey where Emma was still waiting, with the gendarme outside. What did they anticipate: something they wanted to protect us from, or to keep to themselves? Maybe they could give me a lift? I told them not to bother. I can't even be sure when I finally made up my mind to begin my own enquiries but I remember finding the building, a big grey slab in a side street, and going in through the green doors.

There was a desk with a woman, two telephones, some chairs and magazines. Beyond it I could see the offices, stretching away down corridors. On a pinboard beside the woman, just as in the windows outside, were photographs of recent events: weddings and dinners, fêtes and agricultural fairs, horse-ploughing teams and silos, swimming galas and veterans' reunions. Some pictures of new buildings, a renovated railway station, a house standing in a field. I looked again. The place, our place, that ghastly house near the woods. The woods where something had happened all those years before.

The woman was enquiring what I wanted, and I pointed to the photograph, stumbling over my French. She shook her head: the place was bad. I tried to explain what I wanted – the back number on a story from thirty-seven years before, but she did not understand. We stood puzzling at each other.

'Les journaux de 1953.' I wrote it down on paper for her.

She shrugged her shoulders. 'Old papers,' she said, in English.

'Right. Great. Old papers.'

She must have thought I was a nut, but she smiled and pointed along the corridor. I walked on down, and wondered what the hell the French was for back issues. What was I searching for anyway: a needle in a haystack, some madhouse clue from what le Brève had said happened there when I was in rompers?'

I saw a door marked 'Archives', and knocked gently, conscious of the woman watching me from her desk at the entrance. There was no reply, so I tried the handle and walked in. It was a room full of files, battered paper folders bulging from steel racking, set behind a long counter like some spare-parts depot. An old fellow shuffled forward, from a den at the rear. He looked as if he was coming out of a long hibernation: a blue shirt flapped outside his trousers and he badly needed a shave. As soon as I saw him I knew that it would be hopeless. I couldn't explain in French, and he had no words of English.

'Nineteen fifty-three,' I said. 'Chenoncey.'

He just grinned at me and waggled his head. No communication. I realized it was a dead duck and I suppose I would have walked away, empty-handed, but suddenly he seemed to take pity. He opened a gate in the counter and came through. Taking my arm he propelled me outside again to the corridor and through the main doors at the end. All at once I was in the newsroom where desks were scattered around, mostly empty at midday.

A man had his back to me, standing at one of the desks. 'Monsieur le rédacteur,' the old guy with me called out, and as the other man turned I saw he was talking to a woman seated at a metal desk stacked high with paper.

There must have been some problem to have brought the editor-in-chief in on the wrong side of noon, but there he was, and there the woman was, both wondering what on earth I was doing.

I found myself explaining in English, which left Giroud, the editor, frowning as he tried to follow it, so that the woman broke in. 'It's all right. I translate.'

She was not the sort of woman you studied closely at first: in early middle age, with a sheen of ash-blonde hair, almost silver, a suntanned face, and a sensitive mouth, dressed in a yellow shirt and sandy linen trousers. But she had a kind of quality that set us talking together or perhaps she saw how bad things were from the look on my face. Her name, she said, was Estelle.

I didn't know what I wanted. Some news about the loss of my kids, some crazy idea that it might have been linked, at least in Inspector le Brève's mind, to the dark events nearby nearly forty years before. Maybe somebody could tell me from the back numbers what had happened there then.

Giroud called me in to his office, and set up some cups of coffee from a Cona machine. He was a middle-aged man in his shirtsleeves, struggling with new technology, and waved rather despairingly at the keyboard and screen newly installed on his desk. Estelle, who came in with us, said it was supposed to take over from the room of old files that I'd seen. The result was they could now find nothing so far back as 1953 without mind-boggling confusion. 'These days,' she said, 'we ask people to inform us.'

'Information?' Giroud picked up the word. 'Monsieur Freeling has a real story. Le Brève is the best policeman in this part of France – ' even I understood that ' – and if he can't help . . .'

'So?' Estelle sat in a chair and crossed her legs.

'So . . .' I could see Giroud thinking, drumming his fingers on the desk. The back-room guy had shuffled off and the two of them were at it, hammer and tongs, Estelle shaking her head, Giroud pressing for action.

Estelle was turning to me. 'I must go.' She held out a hand.

She left me standing there with Giroud, in the square box of glass that cut him off from the news floor. Two or three people were entering the big room from the other side. The place was coming to life and I felt I did not fit. What the hell was I doing there?

But Giroud answered for me. He drank his coffee at a gulp and perched on the end of the desk, summoning his halting English.

'Goodbye. Thank you. Is good story,' he said. 'I syndicate in all France.'

7

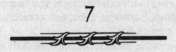

Le Brève was back at the gîte. He met me at the gate and his eyes flickered over me as Clerrard's squad car delivered me.

'Monsieur,' he murmured as he politely shook hands. 'I was paying a fleeting visit to your wife. I am afraid there is no further news. Fortunately now she is resting.'

No help from you, I thought. I was still number one suspect.

There were several police at the house again and le Brève's Citroën outside. As we stood on the drive I looked at the place with fresh eyes. So much seemed to have happened since the night of our arrival that it was hard to accept it was less than a week ago. The gîte was stone-walled, with a wood store at the gable end. The two struggling acacias had been dug into sandy pits on either side of the door, which opened on to the patio, where the duty gendarme was lounging. He scrambled to attention as we walked up and gave le Brève a quick salute.

The Chief Inspector bustled me inside, where the shuttered windows darkened the living room so much that his face almost disappeared. I could see the whites of his eyes.

'Where have you been?'

I told him: the local press.

'You were supposed to come back here. We have been waiting for you,' he added curtly. As if he half suspected that I had run away. I faced him out.

'All right. Tell me the worst. Is there any news?'

'I regret not, monsieur.' He pushed his hands together, his gold-rimmed spectacles gleaming. 'You must give us more time, monsieur.'

'For God's sake, how much more time?' I said. 'Jesus Christ, man, what have you found so far? Nothing. Nothing. How can two children – not simply one but two – be spirited away between midnight and three in the morning, in a strange house in a strange country, and no one knows what's going on?'

He sighed, a little bird bouncing. 'Ah. You tell me.'

'What about fingerprints?' I asked. 'Surely your boys have some sort of clue by now?'

The grizzled head waggled. 'Of course. We now have the lab report.'

'Don't tell me there aren't any . . .'

'Naturally there are prints, of the children, your wife, yourself. And other people. People who rented before you, people who clean the cottage. How can we tell . . .' He nodded towards the bedrooms. 'Do you wish to talk to your wife?'

'Not if she's resting.'

I could see le Brève's teeth flash. 'I understand.'

The smell of his aftershave was strong, his slight figure seemed to shimmer in the gloom. Something about the man, his disappearing presence in the shadows of the room, alarmed me. I could not pin it down. I wanted to let in air, to rip open the shutters.

But le Brève anticipated me. I saw him silhouetted for a moment against the blaze of sky as he fastened back the jalousies and flooded the room with light, dazzling us both.

Through the open window I glimpsed the trees. The big clump to which he had led me was wrapped in heat, mirage-like in the distance, chained to the horizon. I saw the unanswered question in his eyes as he came over to me.

'I must go back, monsieur. Now that I have talked to Madame Freeling.'

'I hope that you found it useful.'

'Inspector Clerrard can give you details of the extent of our operations,' he muttered.

'Do you want to see me again?'

He shrugged. 'It is of no consequence,' he said.

I wanted to run after him, to make some fresh appeal, but before I could move the door had closed. I saw him walk over the gravel and climb in the big Citroën. I could have shouted but the words would not come.

I went through to Emma's bedroom on the other side of the passage, the room in which we'd been sleeping when the storm broke. She was lying on her back under a thin white coverlet, her shoulders bare. I wondered if she was undressed, trying to avoid the humidity which was dripping from us. It was clear that she was heavily sedated; a pallor drained the colour from her skin and lips. I found myself looking at her and realizing how rarely we really study the people we know, and even less those we love. Her blonde hair was disarranged, jumbled on the pillow, and I wanted to kiss her: the sweep of the unlined brow, the small curves of her nose and nostrils, the soft peach of cheek. It had been a good marriage, fourteen years, but we had taken it for granted. What if we had been childless: if there hadn't been the Christmases and birthdays and family treats? Would it have been the same, or would we have wandered apart after other excitements? I screwed up within myself, denying the admissions as they tumbled out. Martin. Susanna. If we lost them, where would we be in another fourteen years, or ten, or two? Remaking our lives together or one more divorce statistic, if I ploughed on with the job? Emma was not yet forty: she might conceive again, but can you produce replacements when your first love has gone?

Emma stirred in the bed, half conscious of someone standing there as I bent over her. She had that musky smell of sickrooms, sweet and sharp together.

'Honey, it's only me.'

She did not seem to hear, but shifted on to her side, her arm flung out. A noise in the doorway behind me, and Clerrard was there, his finger beckoning.

'It would be better to let her sleep.'

Damn him, how did he know?

There was another officer by now in the kitchen, in khaki uniform and rubber overshoes. They had been searching the fields, and he had come back to report.

'I fear,' Clerrard said, 'that there is nothing unusual any-where. Not even a mark on the grass.'

The gîte was in an acre paddock, fenced off from the road, the nearest house 2,000 metres away, and no one strange had been seen at any time, so they said. 'Whoever abducted your children took them away efficiently,' the Inspector muttered. 'In twelve hours they could be any-where in France, or even Spain or Italy.'

I sat there helpless, feeling I wanted to rage, to cry, to punch the table, anything to release a bottled fury, corked up with anguish.

Bastards.

Clerrard said quietly. 'Everything that can be . . . will be . . .'

'Don't give me that crap again. I don't want to know about the mysteries of France,' I yelled at his complacency, as if he did not *care*.

'I'm sorry, monsieur. Perhaps there is an explanation that we have overlooked.'

'Overlooked?' I roared at him. 'For Christ's sake get out of my hair. Come back when you can help.'

I wanted to be unfair. To get my own back.

He hesitated, then rose to his feet. Minutes later he drove away.

Alone in the house, apart from the man on duty, who kept his own vigil, I stormed through my mind. In those first six days a way of life had overturned, as surely as if the kids had died. I had come face to face, not with a fact I could visualize, not with a known fate but with the worst of terrors, fear of the unknown. It had exposed the sham I was, the poseurs that we both were. Only a week before we had been a successful couple, by all the rules of the game, an architect with a bank balance and an attractive wife. I recognized the faults in the picture, the lack of any deep convictions, the differences in our background, the occasional rows, the failures in understanding, but they were the small change of a pair of decent lives. The positive side was the kids, the family, Emma's social commitment, the help I had given to people to get their habitats right. And once a year we relaxed, a short holiday somewhere, eating and sleeping and loving as if the world had stopped and put on fancy dress for our benefit. And what was wrong with that? Nothing, of course, so long as the ship held water. But when it sank in three minutes, the length of time, groping about in the dark without a torch, that it took to discover they were gone, Martin and Susie, Susie and Martin, then we were swimming in black waters.

I went to the toilet, feeling the vomit inside me, and was sick, a thin spume of alcohol and coffee kicked back from my stomach. The bowl of the toilet was stained as I hung my head over it, not just with my own bile but with the hate I had. I hated le Brève and Clerrard, who were only trying to help, I hated southern France, a twisted part of me now began to hate my own wife, and then myself. It was the sign of fear. No one seemed able to help me. This was my naked self, alone, confronting everything I'd thought I wanted, pointless now in the face of my children's disappearance.

8

The next day I decided to go back into Pontauban, to have things out with le Brève. It wasn't Clerrard who worried me, it was the Chief Inspector. He had been less than frank with me, and I wanted to know why.

Emma would not or could not tell me, but something had passed between them. I begged her to go away, to leave that house of bitterness, but she refused. I wanted to telephone her parents, who would rush out and comfort her, but Emma said no. It seemed that her grief was so personal that she wanted nobody near it: not me, not her mother, not anyone. She was alone in a nightmare.

Somehow we had lived through the days without really existing, sleeping in the same bed, next to the two empty rooms, as if the kids were still there. The Valium prescribed for Emma by the police physician made her remote; she seemed to be drifting away from me. The cottage was guarded by police, who came and went in cars, eight-hour, twelve-hour shifts, vaguely comforting but also unreal, in that they were on our side, and could not help. I found I had to get out, to get moving and meet people, but she would lie there and look at me, on the bed like a wax cast, her eyes open, unblinking, her face celery-white, and whisper from time to time, 'They've gone, Jim. They've gone for ever.'

'Aw, hell, honey. They'll come back. The cops are looking.'

But her eyes were blank, and often she said, 'Why did you bring us here? It's all your fault.'

It did not help matters to be told, to have salt rubbed in the wound. In my mind I went over and over the night of the storm, just as le Brève had done. But whoever really knows anything, certainly not in recall? Why pick on us? That was the awful question, and you wrote your own explanation, while the dumb, bored gendarmes stretching their arms in the car, or creeping in for coffee, had no more idea than we did. Language became a barrier, not a link, as I tried to understand what they said, but mostly the word was 'Non'.

The embassy guy sent a letter, a fucking letter, complaining that he couldn't call us, but adding that the details were noted. Noted. And they had spoken to the Paris police, who expressed great confidence in Inspector le Brève. We should co-operate with the authorities and give them all the help we could.

Jesus wept.

I walked out to the lawn in front of the bungalow, a place of tufty grass and cracked brown soil. The lines in the soil were already crumbling in dust as I watched the sun rise across the cow-spotted fields. Over there were the trees where le Brève had shown me the graves. I pictured the empty clearing and saw Martin and Susie in some other shallow trench, silent and cold. My body would break into sweat and I wanted to run away, anywhere out of this haunted place, and out of France. And yet ... and yet ... stubbornly I held on. Determined to find out something, to pull myself out of the pit.

But Emma was deteriorating, and when she looked at me I could feel the suspicion, a cloud in her mind that I was somehow, in some way, involved.

The doctor came again, a sallow man from Pontauban who acted as the police consultant. He had the air of a mortician, elderly, dressed in black, driving a black Mercedes. I thought of mutes and plumed horses as he inclined his head. Emma's hand lay limp on the bedspread when he took her pulse.

We stood at the bedroom window, staring at the empty countryside, as he whispered to me. The house seemed lost in the fields, far apart from Chenoncey up the road.

'She's hanging on, but her resistance is low. I have seen similar cases, after a severe shock, where the patient lives in a dream world, for weeks and weeks.' He pursed his lips and blew between his teeth. 'Sometimes they awake like princesses.'

Emma perhaps was in hearing, perhaps not. No impression flickered across her face. She seemed old, thinner, within seven days, eating scarcely at all and drinking little. The Mephistophelian doctor perched on the end of the bed and clucked his tongue, concerned about dehydration.

'Come on now, madame. We must get you better.'

She looked at me and did not seem to want to know.

I held her hand and left for Pontauban, in the Sierra, driving there across country, along the minor roads. Someone in this hot, steamy landscape had taken or murdered my kids. Person or persons unknown, in the dry, Biblical language of the English courts. But this was not England: I realized how different the two countries could be, in terms of systems and language, in their approach to things. Would any other police force have been as inconsequential as Inspectors le Brève and Clerrard, the one trying to frighten me with the ghosts of some buried past, the other a father-confessor? As I wove into a stone-walled country where dogs stretched out in the sun and chickens pecked in the road – country as dried and desolate as parts of the American West – I found myself shuddering. Secrets were shut up there, unattainable like the mistletoe hanging high in the trees. An empty landscape with shutters closed to prying eyes. The Romans had been here, and the Merovingians, and the Goths. Christianity was paper-thin: they probably worshipped the sun. Le Brève had hinted at deeds that choked in the throat and ended with similar grave mounds to the ancient tumuli that littered the fields around.

I began to see why Emma hated it, when the whole thing turned sour. What is history but the dead? I was even glad to emerge into the outskirts of Pontauban with its draggle of filling stations and furniture emporia, as I drove up the hill to the town.

I parked in the Place Nationale, the big central square used as a market and car park. Pontauban was one of those towns you drive through once and forget, a one-star entry in Michelin. Not one of the great cities or an upgraded stone village, but one of the in-betweens, with its pink-brick streets around the cathedral, its museum and shopping arcades, the medieval bridge on the river, the restaurants and *salons de thé* which lined the banks. Some fool in the middle of the square was playing a harmonica.

In the heat of midday, I was too late to find le Brève. Inside the Commissariat I blundered through my schoolboy French.

'Ou est Monsieur le Brève?'

They shrugged their shoulders and grinned, gendarmes sitting in offices marked *Réception* and *Crime*. So similar and yet so different that I yearned for the tin-star directness of American cops, let alone British politeness. Sod them, and sod them all.

I wondered about calling Bob, or John Simpson again, but what the hell could they do? I must have walked aimlessly about, buying papers I could not read and hoping they would tell me something. The *Sud Journal-Express, L'Horizon, Sud Presse*. Not even a photograph, not even the word Chenoncey. In my own mind the only thing that mattered was that Martin and Susie had gone, but I began to be scared that I was losing Emma as well. Somehow I came to an ornamental pond in a small public garden, close to the river. The moment of recall is blurred, a picture through a distorting glass.

She came and stood by the bench where I had drifted. The woman that I had seen in the *Journal-Express* offices. Estelle something.

'Hullo, monsieur.'

For a moment I scarcely noticed, except that her eyes were blue in the healthy, tanned face.

'Please . . . May I sit down?' A whisper of that ash-blonde hair strayed out of place over the still-young face, and she brushed it back impatiently, as if it didn't matter.

'I'm sorry that I have to find you.'

At first I did not understand. In front of us on the grass sparrows were hoping for breadcrumbs and children were playing and laughing. On another seat next to a flower bed two teenagers were fondling each other. The sun was burning a hole in a duck-egg-blue sky.

I even wondered if she was trying to pick me up, one of those lonely women of a certain age, finding out what she still had to offer. But she wasn't looking at me, as if the light smile was directed at the flowers in the little park.

'I followed you,' she said.

I must have been still dazed.

'Followed you,' she repeated, 'from the Commissariat.'

I heard her, and sat and waited. Numb. I had to get back to Emma, yet something in her manner stopped me.

'I'm sorry,' she said, in English. '*Je regrette.*'

'It doesn't matter.'

'No. Not for speaking,' she said. 'For having to meet you again.'

I glanced at her with more interest. A fine-boned, intelligent face, bronzed by the sun, a good figure in a loose shirt that exposed the smooth skin of her neck. White jacket, blue cotton trousers. The silver hair was anomalous, and shone like silk against the unlined forehead. She must have gone grey prematurely, and settled for ash-blonde, confident of her looks.

'What does that mean?'

Something about her manner told me that she was perturbed. Almost unhappy, as she sat alongside me.

She gestured to the young couple with a slim hand, soft, carefully manicured, and I seemed to glimpse a quality of understanding, a sympathy she somehow conveyed.

'It is very difficult for me,' she said.

'Why?'

'I have been asked to interview you. I do not wish it, but my editor insists. Monsieur Giroud. After you came to the newspaper. I say not me, but he says yes, you. One of my jobs is to pick up the police stories. I saw you today at the Commissariat. They are used to me there, in Headquarters, and the towns in the *département*, including St Maxime. One or two of them here – Sergeant Lefèvre for example, the fat one with eyes like coins – are always helpful. I am

86

a general reporter. You understand me?' She spoke very slowly in English.

'I don't want to say anything to anyone. For God's sake leave me alone.'

She nodded. 'Yes. I know. But I have been told to interview. And perhaps it is better to be seen and heard. Then maybe someone comes forward. Someone who can help.'

'And you get your story—'

She seemed upset. 'You misjudge me,' she said. 'I do not wish for this assignment, but I have my work to do. Do you have a job to do?'

A job. A past or a future one, I wondered, thinking of that office back home that had once meant so much. Another world. I buried my head in my hands.

'Perhaps I should go away,' Estelle said, seeming almost relieved. 'I tried to talk to him and failed . . .' I could see it going through her mind. And I needed help.

'Come on, I'll buy you a coffee,' I said.

We moved – I scarcely remember it – to some poky café-bar nearby where I bought two coffees in small white cups as thick as insulators, and she explained that she had worked for another of the Southern Press papers, the weekly *L'Horizon*, but recently had changed jobs. So she couldn't afford to upset Monsieur Giroud. A divorcée, with a teenage daughter who was now studying in Paris.

For all her disappointments, Estelle could smile, a smile from a warm mouth. And she was a good listener: she pumped me without seeming to try, mixing cognac and advice, fishing for my past history. She had a youthfulness about her, and unburdening myself was a comfort: the sense of her interest, the way she held her head, suggested a serious concern.

People embody their past, and as we sat at the tiny table in that bar I found that she was telling, as well as asking. About her attempts to survive, bringing up little Jeanne after her husband's desertion. Estelle Devereau knew how to win sympathy, and she was good at her job. The look in her eyes said clearly that she understood what was hitting me. That she could care.

'So you are an American, who settled in England?'

87

Why did they always want to know what goddam country you came from? I guess I was still confused.

'My wife is English,' I said.

She seemed perturbed. 'They are very different.'

'Different?'

'From us. From me.' She placed her hands under her chin. 'You have to have everything . . . just so. And now you face a mystery.'

'I'm facing hell,' I said.

Her eyes were wide and blue and innocent, full of a childlike hope. 'You must not despair,' she said. 'I believe they will be found.'

We moved out of the bar and walked along the street towards the river, which was flowing dark and green.

'I'm sorry,' she said again.

'It doesn't matter. It's just that I can't speak about the things that . . .'

'I know.' She hesitated. 'Then I will go.'

'You live near here?'

'Yes. In Pontauban. I have a small apartment.'

I found her gaze on me as if she tried to read my mind, or to console me. 'I must get back,' I said. Emma would be waiting, alone in the place at Chenoncey. 'Perhaps there will be some news.'

Estelle nodded. We watched a small boy fishing from a ledge. He was the same age as Martin, whose tackle was still at the house. She realized what I was thinking.

'Perhaps.' There was a crack in her voice as she said 'Au revoir.' I felt she did not want to leave me.

I walked away, then watched her retreating steps. The back of her head, the slim figure, stroked my nerves. Suddenly I called out, 'Wait! Please wait.'

She stopped and turned. 'Yes?'

'Can you help me?'

She stared at me, as if from a long way away, uncertain who I was. 'Help you?'

'Yes. Le Brève is concealing something. I'm sure of it. Something that happened there in the past. I need someone like you to help me. To research.'

She shook her head, as if frightened. 'I can't. It's in the

88

hands of the police ... Chief Inspector le Brève is a very good policeman. You must ask him.'

I gave a snort of derision. 'Le Brève. Shit. He's not going to do anything. Least of all tell the truth.'

'What do you mean?'

I hurled a pebble into the water and watched its rings spread outwards. 'There's something wrong. Something being covered up. I'm sure of it. Why did he take me to that place in the woods?'

Estelle was backing away. 'I must be going, please. And you have to find your wife.'

I pulled her back. 'Look, will you help me ... Please, Estelle?'

Estelle stared at me. We lingered on the road by the river with the traffic roaring past. Two women waiting for buses watched us as if we were quarrelling, a billboard offered sale prices for electrical goods, a shop sold second-hand chairs. It was her France, not mine, and I needed her to explain it.

I caught her hesitation, while we stood as if we were conspirators.

'It cannot be.'

'Why not?'

'I have my work. I'm busy.'

'But not all the time,' I said. 'Please.'

She smiled, her face upturned into mine, so close that I felt her breath. 'It would be wrong. Impossible.'

'Impossible?'

'Yes.'

I made up my mind. 'Will you meet me tomorrow?'

Even then she hesitated, and touched my arm. 'I'm not sure that—'

'Please. Help me, for God's sake.'

'Is it that important?'

'It is to me,' I said.

9

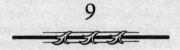

Her place was in a dark alley, crawling with cats. Carrying
a leather satchel-bag looped over one shoulder she led me
through the stony streets of the old town, where the houses
tumbled together, like building bricks placed by a child.
Estelle strode on ahead, threading a way through the crowds
of housewives, mothers with toddlers on reins, old men
gossiping slowly, vans parked on the kerbs. It seemed quite
a walk but I suppose that we were near enough to the
café-bar I have never since found, and the park that had
materialized, as these things do, on the previous day.

I followed her slim figure, aware of the rounded buttocks
under her thin linen suit.

We entered the Rue des Escaliers, which lived up to its
name, stepped and cobbled with old-fashioned iron railings.
Estelle beckoned to me, elbowed past a street stall selling
peaches and oranges and disappeared into a cool dark doorway. Inside, a sudden courtyard, with a broken fountain in
the middle and washing on a balcony.

'Four apartments,' she explained.

An ancient black-stockinged woman scuttled away like
a spider. We mounted more stairs. 'Excuse the disorder. I
hope you will forgive me.'

There were five rooms: a large high-ceilinged living
room, piled with books which had escaped from the table
and begun to colonize the floor, a tiny separate study with
an electric typewriter on a trestle table, two bedrooms and
a kitchen.

The kitchen was panelled in varnished pinewood, and
we sat down there, while she made yet more coffee. I felt
again the sympathy of her presence, not a sexual call but

a human one, as if we were two people in need, each with a grief to share.

'Will you have an apéritif?'

We carried it through to the living room, where she pushed books from the chairs, two winged armchairs not out of place in a club or a doctor's consulting room. There was no décor as such, no personal theme, as if it did not matter. A large mantelpiece over an empty fireplace was littered with postcards and invitations, some a year out of date, and three pictures of Jeanne, petite and pretty.

I sipped a Campari, while Estelle took off her jacket.

'Why do you want to see me again?'

I had been asking myself. It was not because she was attractive, or sympathetic, or simply that she spoke English. I needed help.

'I want to find out what has really happened to my kids. To establish the truth.' I almost begged her. 'You must have heard the stories about strange disappearances in country like this. I don't understand the language. The cops are no goddamn use. All I ask is your help. Please listen to me.'

'Inspector le Brève has a first-rate reputation . . .'

I swore softly. 'Jesus Christ. He's covering up for something. And I don't like the way he tries to pin a rap on me.'

'What do you mean?'

'He implied it was not just coincidence that my two kids went missing opposite those woods. Otherwise why take me there?'

'I don't know.'

'It's not some damned game.'

'Of course not.'

'Estelle. That's why I need some help. Some researches. Do you imagine it was just an accident that they were spirited away?'

She did not respond, thinking perhaps that I was half mad. I needed more drink, beginning to feel light-headed. The beading on the window rattled as a train went by somewhere. There were dark mahogany fittings in that room, the trappings of someone else's life, some previous

91

tenant's or the landlord's she rented from, as if she had no roots of her own and was, like me, an outsider.

'What do you think has happened?'

I drove myself to say, 'Kidnap or murder.'

She shook her head. 'No. Surely not. One perhaps, but not two children. Not without signs of struggle, disturbed clothing, shouts for help . . . was there any of that?'

'No.'

'Jim . . . may I call you Jim?'

'Come on, Estelle.'

'Has there been any contact, any suggestion of ransom?'

Nothing, I said. We had heard nothing, that was the hell of it.

She drew a deep breath. 'I ask myself whether for some reason they have run away?'

'Goddammit, Estelle. We loved our kids, and they loved us.'

But I remembered le Brève, his face glowing, climbing up on the log-pile. 'Children have been buried there before.'

'Did he say when and why?'

I told her what he had told me.

'I have heard as much,' she said. 'It's the official version. But there are differing accounts.'

We began to realize that we were sitting on something that was as lost and mysterious as that space in the woods. Underneath the surface the ancient fears creep out, against the dark and the unknown. For some reason le Brève had chosen to trade on them by taking me there, in case it perturbed me, disturbed the memory, shook out some kind of admission. Or because of something he knew. Estelle's face shone. I saw that she was attentive.

'What do you know of this story of two children who died?'

She shrugged. 'Not very much. Only that something happened.'

'But you can find out for me. The police will have records. So will your paper. They told me that you had archives.'

Estelle laughed. 'Of a kind,' she said.

Even so I knew that history wouldn't bring Martin and Susie back. Already, and this was the horror, some part of

92

me came to terms, while the other part shrieked. Came to terms with their disappearance in a way that put them in a picture on the wall. 'Time, like an ever-rolling stream, bears all its sons away. They fly forgotten, as a dream dies at the opening day.' The terrifying words of that old hymn, Mom's favourite, which I had sung so often and so meaninglessly as a kid, in the little Episcopalian church in Pennsylvania, hammered inside my skull. My hand was shaking as I put down the glass.

Estelle was on her feet, energetically pacing the room between the piles of books. The pink glow washed her cheeks and made her look years younger.

'Estelle, I do need help,' I pleaded. 'You've got to think of the story you might uncover.'

But Estelle was still reluctant. 'I'm sure there is nothing to discover,' she replied.

'For God's sake, see what you can find out.' I must have seemed at the end of my tether.

She sighed and shook her head. 'It will not be easy,' she said, 'but maybe I try a little.' She tipped her glass against mine. 'Now you must go home.'

She walked with me, back across the courtyard. 'Sometimes there are no explanations . . .'

She was talking like le Brève, and I wasn't having it. 'My kids didn't just run off . . .'

'You must try to put them in perspective,' she said. As if to imply that they were already lost.

'I want to know if there's a madman around. Someone who kidnaps children . . . Maybe a pattern from the past.'

'No. I'm sure it's not so.'

We stood for a moment together on the steps at the top of the street. My car wasn't far away. 'I used to love France,' I told her.

'I'm sorry. So sorry.'

'Now I hate it.'

She shot a quick glance at me. 'To hate is to misunderstand,' she said.

*

93

Le Brève came back to the gîte in the afternoon, in a different suit, accompanied by two different officers, smart young men in sharp jackets with shiny sunglasses. He gave me a progress report. So many sightings made, so many leads checked, psychics and theorists interviewed, someone arrested on suspicion, then released. A sex killer in Lyons, who could not have been here, because, you see, he was being arrested the very night they disappeared. A slow smile across the features, as he scratched his grey hair. 'It is a most puzzling case, monsieur. Most unusual circumstances. These things do not happen to tourists, as a rule.'

Then he decided to question me once again, with the insistence of a schoolboy. How much longer did we stay? Was Emma often neurotic? If we returned to England he would of course contact us as soon as there was any news.

Emma was rallying now, but woozy from the drugs. I was scared that she was taking too many, but le Brève kept pressing her to obey the doctor's instructions. Why was the man so obsessed with us? Couldn't he do his job, his hundred other jobs, without this show of concern, this artificial consolation? The more I saw, the less I trusted him.

'Please, just leave us alone.'

'Of course. But I worry about your wife's condition.'

'She'll be OK,' I said. 'We will pull through.' What we had now was each other, and I was concerned to show him.

'I love my wife,' I said.

He nodded his head and sauntered off, still suspicious, as he called for his car and drove away.

10

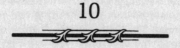

I went on long walks, trying to work things out. I explored the road to Chenoncey, and the surrounding tracks which led to remote farms with green fishponds and chained-up dogs. I found myself wondering more and more about Estelle: whether she would decide to help me and what her researches might find, but I heard no more. The sun beat down and flowers withered as they grew. A few men hoeing in the fields, children shouting from doorways, occasional cars hooting as they shot past too fast, but the country seemed to have closed over the bones, the bodies of my children.

The days went by, and still no news came through. Yet we continued to hope, Emma and I.

'No news is good news,' I mouthed.

She looked at me with contempt. 'How do you know?' she asked.

'Well, honey, it can't be all bad.'

Emma now sat by the window, hour after hour, looking out over the fields towards those terrible trees.

'Why did you bring us here?'

'For Christ's sake, Em. Nobody *knew*. How could I?'

'You went outside . . .' she whispered.

'Jesus, honey. Have you gone mad? Do you think I did it?' We couldn't afford to quarrel, a quarrel which no doubt le Brève expected.

'I didn't go any place,' I reminded her. 'I woke up and heard a cry. Or heard a cry and woke up. Found there was no goddamn power and tried to get a torch from the car. Instead I got wet through, just standing in that doorway. You know that, darling.'

But I began to wonder if even Emma believed me.

I went to Chenoncey for food, and felt the black cloud of suspicion. It was a tiny village, at the crossroads, with the restaurant on the corner, Les Trois Oranges. Just a church and a store, and a garage that seemed to have shut, plastered with out-of-date posters for wrestling and pop groups in far-off Toulouse. They knew it was all going on at the place down the road, the village natives, and they knew who I was, the foreigner in his drill trousers and brown shoes. Old women peered in their baskets or disappeared behind the racking when I entered the *alimentation*. I had the conviction that they were scared.

Out there in the main street doors shut as I appeared. Somebody called to schoolkids playing football round the trees and they shot off like startled rabbits. I thought that I was being watched from behind the upstairs shutters. Perhaps one of those men on the corner was posted there by le Brève. They were all talking about me, that was for sure. Two of them shuffled away as if something might happen to them, leaving the other two staring as I walked past. Old men with bloodshot eyes. Old men who would have memories and no doubt secrets if I could only talk to them. Old men who did not want to know me. An airlessness settled on Chenoncey, as if it was brooding on its past, under a coppery sun.

I crossed the road to the church, a dull-looking working-class building much restored, and found the doors were locked. A stone elf over the entrance seemed to be pouring a pitcher on to the sins of the world, grinning like buggery. The spire had grey slates missing, and scaffolding on one side. No one was working there, or worshipping, and nettles grew over the graves.

All I wanted was news. Not even hope or discovery, but simply to know. I sat on a stone seat in the shadow of the tower and watched the cars roar past, heading south, on the Route Nationale, holiday cars full of children and beach balls, their baggage racks on the roof. I cursed that they were so lucky.

Everyone is a stranger in a foreign country, and back in that lonely house our isolation increased. On the surface Emma's condition had returned to something like normality, yet we faced each other at mealtimes scarcely speaking, hoping that whatever prayers we ground out of ourselves might keep the show together. We knew the kids should have been there, noisy and irreverent, causing us to shout back. Instead there was this climate of fear, the gendarme outside the gate, the staring heads of the villagers.

Le Brève had appeared less frequently, but Clerrard came instead, as quietly solicitous as ever. Both urged us to go home, but Emma's stone face glared back at them.

'Not yet,' she said. As if she had a sentence to serve, the two weeks for which we had booked. But I wanted her to go now: I found her silence unnerving. I was disturbed by sitting there with her, and yet I felt guilty away. I pressed her to go home and wait.

'I've got to be sure,' she replied.

Yet we might never be sure. I told her life had to go on, that she should go back to her parents, or to our place in London. Please, darling Em. She was eaten up with despair that I could only watch, a kind of self-sickness that frightened me. To escape, I would walk. Anywhere. Long wanderings down the lanes and into the hills. Even the birds were rare, and human beings scarcely visible. It was a fearful time that seared into our minds as we tried to come to terms with our loss. The police said we must be prepared: for what they would not say. Loss was the unspoken assumption as news of the events at Chenoncey filtered back into the papers. Emma read certain paragraphs in *L'Horizon* over and over to me, stunned by their obviousness. 'Mystery disappearance of English children.' A muddy little photograph of the gîte and our two names.

I would return exhausted, to find Emma sitting there pretending to read, a book on her lap upside down in the sunshine. Life is pretence, she implied. We pretend to be happy, to be well, and wait for the blows to come which we can never prevent.

'They're dead.'

I tried to cheer her up. 'For Christ's sake, honey, that's bullshit. We've still got hope.'

'Hope for what?' she asked bitterly. 'Another family?' and her voice trailed away.

I felt her in bed beside me, tense and unyielding. When I moved she shunned me, unwilling to take comfort. The saturnine physician prescribed ever stronger pills. We crawled through a tunnel of despair, without a light at the end.

Yet it was Emma who made the first breakthrough. Day after day she had remained in the house, refusing to leave it. On bad days she sat without talking, or lay in bed sedated, however much I urged her to drive into Pontauban with me. But she clung on in the lonely house which seemed to have swallowed our hopes. The books we had brought over with us were soon exhausted, and she would not let me buy more. She turned instead to the cabinet of paperbacks and pasteboard covers that someone had left in the living room, a glass-fronted cabinet with the drawer where le Brève found the gloves. They were the usual mixture of romance and history, all of them in French, that could be found in any small bookshop in the area. Emma picked one out to look at and I heard her exclaim as something fluttered to the floor.

She bent down to pick it up. It was a series of yellowing newspaper cuttings, clipped together.

At last we had a kind of evidence, the references I had been searching for.

Emma sat back in her chair at the living-room window and began to translate the brief undated accounts, which seemed to have no common theme except a concern with fires: a hayrick here, an old barn there. Then a motor car. A wood yard. An animal pen. Cut out and carefully preserved in a volume of recollections by St Teresa of Lisieux, *Histoire d'une Ame.* 'The Story of a Soul,' Emma said. 'It's mainly about her childhood.'

'But why the cuttings?'

'I don't know,' Emma replied. 'But listen to this. It names the two detectives connected with the investigations. One of them is le Brève. The other is someone called Elorean.'

Le Brève and Elorean. Names I will never forget. The

agents de police at the time. For some reason I felt my nerves tingle, and I remember hugging Emma. We sat down and studied the cuttings, which I judged might cover two years, fragile, neatly clipped extracts from the provincial press that someone in the gîte before us had thought it important to keep in a religious book. The binding was tooled leather. Le Brève and Elorean, two young policemen who had followed up the burnings, and were mentioned several times. And le Brève was still around, elevated and successful. I found myself beginning to wonder what might have happened to Elorean, a name that stuck in the mind.

In some way I was sure that the reports must be connected with the gîte, otherwise why would they be kept there? Le Brève himself had said that two bodies had been found nearby, thirty-seven years before. The more I thought about it, the more I suspected that the fears and mysteries surrounding the place we had come to were in some way linked with those fading cuttings.

Emma was tired again; the excitement had made her headache worse, as if the effort of discovery had been too much. I helped her back into the bedroom, and begged her to lie down.

'Now don't you see that something strange happened here? I'm sure that there's a connection.'

'Then ask the Inspector,' she snapped. She was looking at me again as if she hardly trusted me. But I knew that whatever had happened, le Brève was unlikely to tell me. I was still the chief suspect. Le Brève had closed up like a clam after taking me to the woods, and he would be the last one to welcome questions running back to his youth. If so, that perhaps left Elorean, a name I turned round on my tongue.

It was by now late evening and when I had settled Emma I could not relax. A police car was parked outside with its radio on, playing pop jingles that grated on my nerves. The duty gendarme. I asked him to turn it down. This one was young and placid, drumming his fingers on the steering wheel, as if he was ready to go as soon as the chore was up. I left him and walked inside, along the passage, past the children's empty rooms, and into the garage.

It was stacked with the spare chairs and tables that had been there since we arrived. Sunbeds and parasols, the lawn mower, some oil drums, a treadle table with an old-fashioned Singer machine. And in the corner on a shelf a series of out-of-date directories, the old telephone books for the *département*. I pulled them down and dusted the covers. Most of them were twenty years old, piled one on top of the other as if someone here had once kept everything. As I checked on the Pontauban names I found there were two le Brèves and a single entry for Elorean. I made a note of the addresses.

'I'm going into Chenoncey for a minute,' I said.

'What for?' Emma's voice from the bedroom was sharp and anxious. 'At this time?'

'To make a call.'

'Who to?'

'A friend of mine.'

'A friend? What friend?'

I felt the suspicion resume, yet Estelle was the helper I needed. 'A reporter on the *Sud Journal-Express*.'

'Who?'

'It doesn't matter,' I told her. 'Just some reporter.'

I drove the three kilometres back up the lane to the crossroads, and managed to use the telephone in Les Trois Oranges.

'Listen,' I said. 'You promised to help me.'

'I can't,' Estelle replied. 'I have no information.'

'But I have.' I told her about the clippings from the local press, and the two police names. 'There must be some more information in your newspaper archives. Estelle, check for me – please. Elorean might still be around, perhaps still in the police force. Will you check that out too?'

At first she flatly refused to be drawn in any further, but in the end she agreed. I gave her Elorean's address, at a farm called St Honoré, a few miles outside Pontauban, if he was still around. I asked if she would be prepared to go there with me.

11

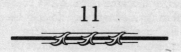

That night the thunder came back: another long, moonless night when clouds sweeping in from the ocean met the heat of the land and set up a war in the hills. An electrical storm. It came at much the same time as on that other night, and I lay in bed and watched the lightning flicker through the shutters. I could tell that Emma was awake, but when I touched her she froze.

I got up and crossed the bedroom, half opened the window. The flyscreen banged. The duty gendarme had moved in from the car to the living room, where he slept on a put-u-up. I could hear him rustling about.

I opened the door and stepped across the passage, to find him standing in the middle of the room, uniformed and alert. A flash of lightning through the shutters illuminated his figure like a cardboard sign and then left us in darkness. I noticed his white face as he turned towards me, and I could smell his body sweat.

He was probably a country boy, who had enlisted as a softer option than driving a tractor, so he should have known this lonely farmland, the big, high, threatening skies where the thunder rolled. There was no reason to panic, and he was in uniform, armed, representing authority, le Commissaire de Police. And yet he trembled. I could sense it as I called out to him, and saw the fingers clutching his gun, the wild look in his eyes.

No one had switched on the lights. Rolls of thunder, like intermittent gunfire, then rain spattered on the bungalow. It drained through the gullies and rattled the windows. For one absurd moment I thought we were reliving the past, less than two weeks ago, and wanted to go along to the children's rooms and find them there, tucked up, awake, wide-eyed.

'Are you all right?' It was the victim who asked, the gendarme who was scared in the dark.

Perhaps he was too frightened to try the lights, or the trip-switch had overridden again just as it had before. I sensed rather than saw him as neither of us made a move, and suddenly I had the feeling that there was something out there. Outside in the dark. I grabbed for the wall and felt across it for the switch, but it eluded my hand. Shit. It was on the other side and once again I smelt the fear that trickled in his armpits. I blundered past the table, seeking to avoid him, feeling for the edge of the door, the doorframe, a chair in the way. Where was the goddam switch?

Click. The room exploded in light.

'Jesus Christ.'

There was no one there.

I spun round, thinking he had slipped behind me, was playing some stupid game. I had heard him, seen him, spoken to him, in the room seconds before. My heart pumped and I picked up a bottle of wine, half expecting I don't know what, a knife in the back maybe, a sudden wire round the throat, a strangled cry.

But the room was full of light while the night outside shook with thunder. The duty cop had vanished.

I tried the shutters, which jammed. Eventually I forced them open. Hailstones danced on the window ledge and the warm, wet rain splashed into the room. I remembered how it had soaked me on that first night. There should have been a patrol car on the gravel, the gendarme's car, I had seen it there three hours before, when Emma and I went to bed. For Christ's sake, yesterday evening I'd asked him to turn down his radio.

I leaned out into the night, not caring about the rain, waiting for the revelation of the next burst of lightning. When it came it showed the driveway was empty.

The car and the gendarme were gone. I hadn't even heard him start. The tyre tracks were already washed out.

If he had ever been there. I was beginning to wonder at my own sanity: if feel and smell were not real how far

102

could I hallucinate? And then I thought, Christ Almighty, don't give me that. Anybody else maybe, but not Jim fucking Freeling. No sir. Pick some other bastard to scare the pants off. That's what they all were: scared. I had seen it in the villagers' eyes. I did not believe in ghosts. No one had spirited the kids away on a magic carpet. There was a killer about, and some of the police were frightened. Too frightened to talk, even if I could understand them. That was a different ball game.

Excitement surged through me as I gripped the top of the wine bottle. Côtes de Roussillon: shame to waste a decent drink. The events of the night stopped turning, I was getting straight. I remember shouting for Emma, but she could not or would not hear me. The yellow light beat down on the Formica table, the white of the kitchen units, and spilled out through the open window, where the sheet lightning now danced more distantly.

My pyjama jacket was soaking again. Damn. Damn. Damn.

As I began to calm down, my thinking became more rational. I knew the duty cop had been there. I had seen and spoken to him; I had also smelt his nerves. A policeman on duty, the gendarme le Brève had allocated, had been standing there in the room when I arrived. I had seen him silhouetted. Yet he had been so shit-scared, so terrified, that as I was groping for the switch he had somehow squeezed past me and out through the garage. He'd gone through the garage side door, jumped in the car and fled. I knew then, irrefutably, the route that the kids had taken – or had been taken on. That cry on the first night had come from somewhere. The garage side door was unlocked, and somebody had come to their beds and carried them outside. Person or persons unknown.

Still grasping the Côtes de Roussillon I checked the connecting door from the passage into the garage. Sure enough it was ajar, and the outer garage door was open. I peered out into the rain, trying to remember if it had been shut that night. The little gates to the front drive had been left open and the car had driven straight through, without being seen or heard. The same could have happened on that first night. I sat down in the kitchen and opened the bottle of wine but could not drink it. It tasted like vinegar.

Emma was still on the knock-out jobs, curled up like a small animal, only the top of her head showing in the bed. The quack knew how to put her out. The storm was fading as quickly as it had built up, just as it had on the night of the kids' disappearance. Automatically, I walked back to check on their rooms, half hoping, half imagining they might have returned in some miraculous way. The beds had been remade by Emma, as if she also expected that they would come back, but they were cold and empty. But their comic books and Susanna's Chocolate Dog, the soft toy pooch, which had been piled on top of Susie's locker, those had gone.

Perhaps Emma had packed them, although I did not remember it, but I could not be sure. I went back into her room and shook her by the shoulders.

'Emma. Wake up, for God's sake.'

'What do you want?' she muttered.

'Did you hear anything just now? Inside or out?'

She rubbed her eyes, rocking back from the drugs, trying to make sense of things, then buried her face in the pillow. 'Go away.'

'Emma. Listen . . . Did you pack the kids' things? Martin's books and Susie's woolly pooch?'

She groaned and rolled over. 'The storm . . .'

'It's over, honey. It's OK. But some of the kids' things are missing.'

'What?'

'Did you pack Susie's dog? Or put it anywhere? And that pile of comics? It isn't in her room.'

She was coming to now, groping to comprehend. 'What?'

'Have you packed anything?'

'I haven't touched a thing.'

'Well. OK. The stuff has gone. And so has that young duty gendarme.'

Emma struggled to sit upright, hugging her chest. 'Show me.'

I fetched a robe and draped it round her shoulders. Her legs didn't seem to move and she was swaying as she held on to my arm. 'You're wet,' she said. 'Wet through.' Her fingers trembled as she felt the pyjama top.

'Honey. I'm trying to tell you. The cop has gone. Something scared the shit out of him. When I opened the windows to look the rain just poured off the roof. Then I found the kids' things were missing.'

'You've been outside again.'

'Emma. Don't be ridiculous. You feel my pants, they're dry.'

'And you've taken their things . . .'

'Honey. That's crazy. You don't know what you're saying.'

She didn't want to hold me again, and tottered on her own two feet down the passage to Susie's room. I showed her the open door into the garage, and the one leading outside.

'Somebody came in this way, tonight, and the first time. Somebody who scared the cop. Or maybe he just got scared standing around in the dark.'

Emma was looking at me, and then at the empty locker beside Susie's bed. Her eyes travelled across the wet shirt-top of my pyjamas and then back to the bed. I saw the disbelief in them.

'I'll talk in the morning,' she said.

But when she was settled I wandered back to the kitchen, unable to sleep, and found myself making tea with the tea bags we had brought from England. Emma's beloved tea. Me drinking tea, for Christ's sake. It tasted of UHT milk, but it revived me a little. I was glad that the kids' things had gone, glad of the terrified cop, for maybe the unknown had gone too. The intense depression of the last few days began to lift, because I could sense a logic. Emma and I were not just victims of chance, we were part of a plot I did not begin to understand but which gave me in a funny way hope. Martin and Susie might not have been chosen by fate, but might after all be involved with the mysteries of this area, the story le Brève had hinted at as he stood on the mound in the woods. This compact bungalow, this holiday gîte which the travel agent had booked straight from the departmental agency, must be holding a secret.

As I sipped hot sweet tea I tried to work it out. The house was not old, built some time after the war, a few years before those first children were buried in the clearing. Built facing the woodland where their bodies had been found. A plain, sensible house, three bedrooms, kitchen, lounge, integral garage, that someone had planned to live in and no longer did.

Somebody who stole children and came back for their toys?

I retrieved our bundle of travel documents which had been pushed into the drawer of the bureau. They normally stated an owner, though the money was paid to an agent . . . but in this case the ownership was missing.

That was an interesting fact, and I made a mental note to investigate. Why should someone choose this particular spot in the middle of nowhere, along the road from the village, and build here? Who would want to own it when the story of the burials was known, a part of local folklore? What was the secret locked up in the closed faces of Chenoncey? Le Brève had led me to the graves, deliberately testing me out; much as I disliked the man, he had some theory in mind, and that made sense. There was a weird-ness in the black face of le Brève, the soft-spoken unhappi-ness of Inspector Clerrard, the spectre that had caused a country policeman to run, even in Estelle Devereau's reluc-tance to probe. It was increasingly certain that they had not told me everything yet: there might still be a reason why the children had gone, dead or alive, and why those toys had been stolen, and I was determined to find it.

I went back to the bedroom and slipped in beside Emma, feeling completely drained but in a way elated. I had no fear of the dark now, for the dark could be frightened of me. For the first time since it happened I slept like a log.

12

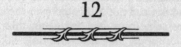

On the following morning we cleared up after the storm and waited for another visit from le Brève or Clerrard. Emma sat opposite me over the kitchen table as we nibbled at a kind of breakfast of stale baguettes and coffee. I did not dare go to the village for fresh bread.

'What happened?' Emma looked ill.

'I told you. I woke up to find that young cop was chicken-shit scared. Something he'd seen or heard. When I asked what the hell, he fled. By the time that I'd worked that one out I'd got another soaking. Then I found the kids' stuff gone.'

'This place is terrifying,' she said. Her face was a chalky white as she struggled against the pills. She swallowed another one then, and stared at me.

'Em, darling. Knock them off. It's not any good,' I said.

'Shut up. I know what I'm doing.'

'Honey. Calm down. You really ought to go home,' I urged. 'It's no good hanging on here.'

'I'll think about it,' she said, and turned back again to the subject of the toys. 'How do I know you haven't taken them?' Deeply hostile. I feared she was joining le Brève in thinking I must be involved.

'For God's sake, honey. I'm not here playing games.'

We had searched every room, and knew that they weren't in the house. The kids' things had disappeared.

Emma could not believe it. 'They must be some-where . . .'

'Somebody came in for them. It's as easy as that. Some-body who knew there was no lock on the garage door. Somebody who knew the house.'

'Then there would be footprints,' she said.

It ought to have occurred to me before. Anybody coming in during that storm would have left a wet track, along the corridor and on the bedroom floor. But I had put all the lights on and noticed nothing. Moreover the cop had been there, before something had frightened him. Something sufficiently cautious, and also terrifying. Like a noise in the night, or a figure he'd half glimpsed, before the rain started.

I tried to explain to Emma.

'I think some guy came in earlier, after we went to sleep but before the storm. I guess that the gendarme heard noises, and suddenly he panicked.'

'Policemen don't scare,' she cried.

'Well, that one did, honey.'

She shook her head, ran her fingers through the unbrushed hair. 'I don't believe you,' she said.

'For Christ's sake, Emma. I didn't take the kids. Honey, you must know that.'

'Maybe you know who did . . .'

'Oh, Jesus wept. That's sick. You've got to go home, Em. Go home and stay with your folks, while I look around here. Until there's some real news.'

'I wonder what you're looking for . . .'

'Emma. Believe me. I haven't taken anything!'

Her lips were a hard line.

'We'll see what the police say first.'

But that morning they seemed to be late; or maybe they thought the gendarme was still on duty.

Emma went to the bedroom to dress. The day was already hot and vapour steamed off the soil. I hung around in the kitchen, unable to concentrate, thinking the whole time of why someone wanted those toys. At first it had given me fresh hope, hope that the kids were alive, yet I could not be sure. It could equally be some sadist returning to the scene of the crime, or some voyeur who wanted a souvenir. Like my precious Buddha's head. Crazy. That way lay madness. Or maybe that frightened gendarme had taken them himself: couldn't that explain his panic when he found me watching him? The more that I puzzled and worried the less sure I became. For once I wanted le Brève, or the melancholy Clerrard, in spite of what Emma might say, so that when I heard the car I ran to the door with relief.

It was a green sardine tin with the canvas roof rolled back. Estelle had a 2CV Citroën, and she'd taken me at my word.

'Emma!' I called to the bedroom.

'Is that the Chief Inspector?'

'No.' I wondered what she'd make of Estelle, whether I'd been wise to ask another woman for help, but it was too late now. I remembered Estelle had said she wanted to visit the gîte and see the place at first hand.

'Who is that?' Emma enquired from inside.

'A reporter from the *Journal-Express*. I met her in Pontauban.'

'The one you telephoned?'

'Right.'

I watched Estelle step out of the little car, more smartly dressed than before: an orange costume that showed off her legs, her hair newly washed and shining.

And Emma did not like her. I could feel my wife bridle, although she was the younger woman. The unspoken question was what Estelle wanted me for, and why I had asked her to help. Emma was like that. In a territorial way she fought for me and possessed me, and Estelle was an intruder, trying to share our grief. But so far as I was concerned, disturbed by the night that had passed, I clutched at any straw.

'Emma, this is Estelle Devereau. She works on the *Sud Journal-Express*.'

Emma gave a cautious nod, and I saw the other woman smile. We were standing outside on the patio.

'You had a bad storm last night . . .'

'It was more than that,' I said. 'Somebody came to the house, and took the kids' things.'

Estelle gasped in astonishment. 'No. It's not possible.'

'That's what he says,' Emma added.

'I don't understand.' Her blue eyes were full of concern

and a crease line appeared on her forehead. 'What about the gendarme on duty here?' She looked round at the white house behind us as if expecting him to appear. 'Where is he now?'

As I told her what had happened her eyes widened in disbelief. 'Why should someone want their toys?'

'You tell me,' Emma said, and she was staring at me.

'Of course, you must tell the police.'

'OK,' I said. 'Next time I see the Inspector.' I didn't particularly want to report on the poor bastard who'd run.

Estelle hovered outside the house. The frown line had come back again between her eyes. Emma seemed disinclined to invite her much further in.

'It's difficult,' she said to Emma. 'Your husband asked me to help him and I was going to take him into Pontauban . . . But now he must tell the police . . .'

'What's in Pontauban?' Emma queried, interested in that city for the first time. Her face was coming alive as if Estelle was a challenge.

Estelle glanced at me and shrugged. 'Another link with the past . . .'

And Emma shuddered. 'Oh God.'

If Estelle noticed, she kept it out of her eyes, simply saying, 'Let me take you both there, and show madame the city.' I recognized a slight deception, in front of my wife. Of course we were both invited, but she perhaps assumed that Emma would refuse to come. Instead Emma tried to stop me.

'Jim. I don't want you to go,' she said.

But Estelle had signalled me. 'I think I must,' I replied.

'Then I'm not staying here on my own.' Emma's eyes never left Estelle: she was coming out of her shell.

'Please,' Estelle said. 'Let us forget it. I do not wish – how do you say – to intrude. It was only that Monsieur Freeling asked me. We find out about an old policeman, and I translate for your husband.'

'I don't want to know,' Emma responded tersely.

'But you should see the city.' Estelle even suggested that we should take both cars, the Sierra and the Deux Chevaux, so that I could drive back. Emma could visit the shops, try the museum of art, while we looked up this guy Elorean.

'Honey, do you feel strong enough?'

'Of course I do,' Emma snapped.

At that moment Clerrard arrived, with a second police car, containing the missing gendarme, or rather his replacement. We stood outside in the sunshine, in the middle of that empty landscape, arguing about what had happened when the other guy ran.

'He says that he heard a noise,' Clerrard said.

'Too right. Some bastard in the house.'

'And that he followed a car, until he lost it, many miles in the country.'

'A car?'

'He thinks it was a big Peugeot.'

'He thinks?'

'It was in a storm, monsieur.'

'So?'

'So when he lost it he decided to report to Pontauban.'

'Leaving us isolated.'

'It was a mistake, monsieur, which I regret. But it gave rise to no harm.'

I wondered if the gendarme was lying, remembering his terrified face, but did not say so: trouble enough straightening them out about the thief in the night.

'Are you sure?' Clerrard asked.

'Man, I'm sure. Nobody else wanted soft toys.'

Clerrard confronted Emma. 'You say these things have gone?'

'I didn't touch them,' she said.

'You check it out with le Brève. He asked about the toy dog.' It sounded so mad. Chocolate Dog.

Clerrard rubbed the pouches of his eyes as if the theft in the night was another piece of evidence that they would hold against me: a decoy, a false trail.

'We have a contents list,' he said. He began to gabble in French, giving the usual instructions for searches and fingerprints, but I knew it would be useless. They only half believed me, Clerrard and Estelle, and even my own wife.

Estelle glanced at her wristwatch, a gold band against

tanned skin. 'I think if we go . . . I must . . . I have some work,' she said.

It was Emma who decided. 'We'll all go,' she said. 'There will be time enough.'

We left Clerrard standing there.

Emma insisted we leave her in the Place Nationale where I had parked before, close to the market and shops. She looked tired but composed and assured us she would be all right. She gave us a couple of hours, Estelle and me, before we met up for lunch.

Once we were on our own Estelle revved the little 2CV until it shuddered, and then screeched out of the town on a road heading north, into the range of hills that trapped the evening storms. She slipped off the costume jacket, and I could not miss her breasts pressed against an embroidered shirt.

'Where are we going?'

She smiled a little grimly. 'You were right about Elorean. He is still living here. A witness to what happened all those years ago. Perhaps I ask questions for you, then you set your mind at rest.'

'Holy cow.'

Things were beginning to click, and I shouted aloud, but I saw that she was serious. Her face was tight as she looked at me. Then we were smiling together, understanding each other. The Citroën left the road and began to bounce like a jelly up an unmade-up track, curving past fields of corn which petered out towards the hills.

'What is all this about?'

'I show you,' she said.

I had asked for her help, and now she was giving it. In the same way that I distrusted le Brève, in some intuitive way I trusted her. I also began to realize that she wanted to please me.

We came to a white stone wall, with a house beyond it, one of those ancient places swamped in trellis and vines, with an espaliered pear tree clawing up one side. The building had an air of prosperity, built up over years. It was more than a farmhouse, more like a retirement villa: the old frontage, two-storeyed with a central door and cerulean shutters, concealed substantial extensions at the rear, set in a long walled garden. The soil had been pricked out with bushes: myrtle and bougainvillaea, in flower around a well-watered lawn. This richness was in stark contrast to the bare hills behind where scrubby little trees and heathers scratched for a living.

Estelle stopped the car, all her actions now intense, and directed at me.

'Do you want to go on?'

'Yes.'

'Look at the house.'

'So what? A nice little pad.'

'Monsieur Elorean.'

'The cop who investigated those fires?'

She opened the gate and led me up the path, between the scented bushes. 'Ex-policeman,' she said. 'Leave him to me.'

I don't know what I expected: someone wealthy, perhaps, retired, well heeled, one of those very French professionals, a doctor or lawyer, living in some seclusion. I felt unsure of myself, aware that I was in her hands.

I noticed Estelle was tense.

The man who came to the door was elderly and large and stupid-looking, a pug-nose on a beefy face framed by the remnants of curly hair, now a dishevelled white. Bemused is the only word for his expression, as he stood there gawping. He might have been the jobbing gardener, except that the clothes were good, well cut and expensive.

I glimpsed a lavish interior, dark and cool behind him. He was standing in carpet slippers.

Estelle held out her journalist's card. 'Monsieur Elorean? May we come in? I am from *Sud Journal-Express*.'

He began to shake his head dumbly, like a large old dog, but she was too brisk. She would not let him think, she smiled and flattered him. Elorean shuffled his feet, denying responsibility, large feet in hand-stitched moccasins.

Then we were inside, whether he liked it or not. No

impression of authority was left in the big fellow, he was like a derelict house.

Another shock. The place was not merely big, but sumptuously appointed. Room emptied into room, across a floor of patterned tiles, a setting for elaborate furnishings. Luxurious Islamic carpets, large suites in damask, at least two long-case clocks, a welter of chinoiserie, carvings and dishes in glass-fronted cases. It jumped at you in confusion. Against this nouveau-riche décor, the owner's taste in the fine arts ran to a range of nude women, on the walls like some Turkish harem.

'Please sit,' Elorean said, in a gruff voice.

I was conscious of another person, a woman who had flitted away after our arrival, and was hovering in the background.

He ran a hand over his skull, a long, laborious process, like an enlarged Mr Magoo. A pekinese dog, biscuit-coloured, jumped out of a chair.

I watched Estelle make the right noises before she began the questions. What a lovely garden it was, and such a beautiful house! That furniture and those pictures! She crossed her legs as she looked. Elorean shuffled slightly, quite lost, then settled down opposite, feet on a Persian carpet. How lucky he was to live there, with so many nice things.

'Yes.' Grudgingly.

Estelle began to translate for me. Was it not true that he'd once been in the police . . . at St Maxime?

A silly, slow smile mooned over his face. He nodded. Quite a long time ago.

'Ask him how long,' I said.

A noise from the next room, and I realized his wife was listening, shunted out of the way, out of the sunlight. Maybe she lived indoors, in one of this series of boxes.

'Why?'

'I want to know when he retired.'

Elorean counted up on his porky hand. 'Oh, a long time . . . over thirty years.'

Really, and what had he done since then?

'Nothing much.'

'Ask him how high up the tree he got, to retire in such style. Commissioner, or Chief Inspector, at the least?'

'I don't see the point,' she said; but she enquired.

'No. Not very far,' he muttered.

Then what was he when he retired?

He had been on the beat. Nothing more or less.

I persuaded her to lead him on. He must have come into money, to enable him to leave so young.

'No.' Very emphatic. But would we like a drink?

'A glass of wine, perhaps,' she indicated.

He shouted something to his wife, not bothering to introduce her. He was a clown, a goon, wealthy without style.

Then how had he got this far, if his career in the police had not been that spectacular?

Was he in business later?

Mr Magoo shrugged. 'No.'

I established he had been retired for some thirty-five years. 'That would make him, I guess, no more than twenty-nine when he gave up the police?'

'Look,' she said. 'This is stupid.'

I intervened. 'Ask him what made it worth his while.' I tried out my French on him to make sure he got the message.

Elorean at first seemed not to understand. His wife, an elderly woman in a silk dress, came in with glasses of wine on a japanned tray, and he drank his greedily, wiping his lips on the back of his hand.

'What do you mean?'

I launched an attack. 'Oh, come on. We weren't born yesterday.' He was a bent copper, and somebody had paid him off.

Estelle said, 'I can't say that.'

The old man climbed to his feet. 'I think you'd better go,' he mumbled.

'Jog his memory,' I said. 'There was a major scandal, wasn't there? Concerning the death of two children . . . ?' I pushed in front of his nose the press clippings about the arson outbreaks that Emma had found.

'I don't know what you mean.' But his potato face was not so sure.

Suddenly Estelle saw the point. She began to take him through his past, translating sentence by sentence. I could have hugged her. In that glossy room, looking at their two heads, his shining pate, Estelle's ash-blonde hair, I heard the full story. She had pushed on a pair of glasses and was testing him like a schoolmarm.

'There was a fire,' she said. 'A series of fires, at the time he was working with le Brève.' She turned to him. 'Fires on the local farms, you say?'

He nodded his head, a dumb ox of a man.

'Ask him about the deaths. The deaths of two children, in case he's forgotten. Ask him what was the connection with the fires.'

Magoo's eyes were like popcorn, yellow and knobbly.

'I can't remember . . .'

I wanted to kick his memory.

'I think he can. I'm sure he can. First of all he investigated some fires, and then the bodies of two kids were found in the woods. Doesn't he recall that?'

Estelle leaned forward expectantly. Again he shook his head, his eyes bewildered as if trying to disinter something he had long buried, old bones in the ground.

'He doesn't know . . . can't remember.'

'All right. What about the burnings then? Getting more and more serious.' Estelle relayed the questions. 'Rick fires and old barns. An empty house and a motorcar. Who was responsible?' I paused. 'Who were they?'

'I don't know.'

I laughed in his face, a tight little clenched-teeth laugh. 'Oh yes, you do. Weren't they the two kids that were found at Chenoncey? Were they killed or burned to death?'

He stirred, then got to his feet, looked over his shoulder to the shadows where his wife listened, and said slowly, 'They set themselves alight.'

'Ah.' I felt a long thrill of satisfaction. A fact at last. An accident, not a murder. But who were they? Would he like to tell me that?

'I don't know,' he muttered again.

'Le Brève knows,' I said to Estelle. 'There's some reason why he won't tell me.'

Elorean was looking puzzled, and I explained. 'Two more children have disappeared, at the same age, close to the same spot. Why?'

'Why don't you ask the Chief Inspector?' he said.

'I have, but he shuts up like a door.'

I looked from Estelle to Elorean. 'Ask him where he gets his money.'

'What money?' Elorean loomed over her, and for a moment I thought he would raise one of those awkward hams.

I pointed round the room, calculating the cost of the décor. 'All this doesn't come from the police force at twenty-nine. Enough to keep you in luxury.'

Whether or not Estelle told him, he understood. 'Get out.'

I had to come between them with Estelle now on her feet.

'Get out.'

'We have to go,' she said, her face tight.

'Go—'

He had knocked over a small table standing close to the armchairs, as he lunged to get at her, and I intervened. Christ knows what would have happened if she had been alone, for I caught a blow like a sledgehammer on my forearm, then swept her out through the door. It slammed behind us, leaving us blinking in the sunshine.

She relaxed for the first time. 'Well. You seem to head for trouble.'

We heard him shouting inside, as we walked back to the car, between the neat bushes and the painted lawn, where sprinklers were swishing round. 'I know I'm right,' I said, 'about those fires.'

'What do you mean?'

'There must be some connection – those fires, the two deaths, the disappearance of my children.'

We crammed back into the car, and she looked at her watch, then at me. 'We've got half an hour left.'

She made it sound like a prison visit, a last wish. As we fled down the track, the dust billowing behind us, I sensed she was in turmoil.

'Jim . . .' she said. 'Oh, Jim.'

'What is it?'

'Jim . . . you shouldn't have asked me.'

We were on the narrow road leading back to the highway, then into Pontauban, and something had happened between us. There were gullies where little sidetracks ran off, and suddenly she swung right, skidding the car to a stop beside some trees and a stream where water jumped over boulders. A hot, shadowy place.

I knew then that she wanted loving, or wanted something. I had asked for her help. I had lost what I loved, and Emma had rolled over in bed. Estelle was touching me.

'What is this all about?'

Her hand was on mine, our heads as close as two people can get.

'I'm so sorry for you,' she said. Her presence was all pervading. I held her tight against me, back against the door of the car, neither of us understanding what we were doing. What was she seeking, I wondered, led on by compassion or sorrow, anguished, her hands on my face?

Estelle's arms enfolded me and there were tears in her eyes. What did she know, I managed to ask, what had she found out?

'Don't. Don't,' she pleaded.

'You know something. You must tell me.'

Estelle was crying. 'There is a terrible story. About the original children, and the place where le Brève took you. It is too painful.'

We were so close in the car, as close as in bed. 'Please,' I said, 'I must know.'

'I have found the press reports,' she whispered. 'Le Brève was there when they discovered the bodies. He was named at the inquest. The second policeman was Elorean.'

'I know. I know.' Emma had found that much out. 'But why were the names concealed? Whose kids were they?'

The moment of intimacy had come and gone. She pulled away from me. 'We should not be doing this. Your wife does not like me.'

'Estelle, just tell me.' My mind started functioning again. This was a working relationship. Those cuttings preserved in the book. Elorean had struck it rich. Somehow they were connected.

'Who bought him off? Who put him in the money?'

'They were important children.'

'Who? Who?'

'The son and daughter of Marcel Soult. Spoiled brats,' she said.

She relived the past as she told me. There had been a series of pyromaniac fires, thirty-seven years before. Going through the newspaper archives she had pieced the picture together. Then suddenly they stopped. After two children were found burned to death in the woods. A sensational story: two rich and spoilt brats, the older a boy, the younger a girl, the pair of them the only offspring of Marcel Soult, head of the Soult-France Aviation Company, the son of the man who had built up French aviation before the war, with two great factories at Toulouse and Marseilles.

'What happened?'

'I am trying to find out. It was officially denied that the Soult children had started the fires. Remember that this part of France guards its secrets well, and the Soults were powerful. Apparently the Soult children were playing in some kind of hut when it accidentally caught fire. The boy, Henri, tried to rescue his sister but they were both overcome . . . There was a big funeral. Monsieur Soult himself was already dead and it was said that it was the end of the dynasty. His widow became a recluse.'

'What about the fires after that?'

'I did not find any more reports.'

'So they really died there? Those two kids?'

'Yes.'

I took my hands away from her, imagining Martin and Susie exploring the woods, coming across that clearing. We could have been picnicking there. But of course they had not seen it: we had only just arrived.

'I'm sorry,' Estelle murmured again. 'It is a dreadful story.'

I felt squeamish, as I visualized the fire and the screaming, all those years before. But it didn't help me. None of it could help me. How could it explain why my own two children had disappeared, missing and probably dead? How could there be any connection? Estelle was crying again.

She understood me. 'The house where you are staying was rebuilt to face the scene of the fire. That's why he took you there.'

'Jesus wept.'

'In those days it was all part of the Soult estate.'

My heart raced. The book about St Teresa was tooled leather and expensive, and had probably survived from that time.

'Who owns it now?'

Estelle wiped her face. 'I don't know. It doesn't matter.'

But in my mind it did. Supposing that my children had not been just casually selected, but picked on by other forces, deeper and crueller ones? I clung to a tiny hope that in this treacherous web, with no bodies found, Martin and Susie might just still be alive. But if so, why? For ransom? It seemed unlikely, and we'd received no message. As part of some other mad scheme – but if so, what and who? I remembered with horror those stories of kidnap and chains, where sadism and torture seemed to be ends in themselves. My mind refused to focus, because it was insane to wonder whether I hoped for that rather than some lonely killing. And Estelle put her arms round and kissed me.

'Forgive me,' she said.

'What the hell has been going on?'

Her throat pulsed as she shook her head. 'Nothing. Nothing. There is no more to know. You must be brave.'

In French it sounded strong. I knew I had to deny her. It was time to go back to Emma.

13

Emma was sitting in the shade of the plane trees on a wooden seat. She did not see us at first, but appeared to be lost in thought, staring ahead, oblivious of the bustle, the prosperity of new cars and well-dressed shoppers. It was as if she was mourning the very things we had come for with such high hopes, at the start of the holiday: the rebuilding of our relationship, and a whole run of new pleasures. As we walked across to her she looked up suspiciously and I feared for her peace of mind. Something inside her had awoken in response to an unspoken threat. The other woman disturbed her. Estelle had brought her to life.

Emma was very subdued. Perhaps the drugs were telling, perhaps she was reaching decisions. She looked very English as she put away her paper and smoothed down the Marks & Spencer sundress.

'Hullo.'

Estelle had regained her composure. She smiled. 'I think we have found out something. Let us go and have a drink.'

Emma, unmollified, at least consented to listen and we went in search of coffee in one of the café-restaurants scattered down by the river. Sitting at white tables under a striped awning, the nightmare might never have happened. Our children were a past life on which a door had shut. I struggled against the warmth of the day and the murmur of talk mingling with the sounds of the weir, where the water tumbled into trapped pools of foam. Still pondering those deaths in the woods, and the toys stolen only last night.

When Estelle repeated what we had learned that morning, and what she had told me, Emma was quiet for a long time. She played with a coffee spoon, a disarranged look on her face. I put out my hand to her and the skin of her bare arm seemed dry and snake-like. The sedatives were taking their toll.

'How far have you gone back in time?' she suddenly asked.

Surprised, Estelle said, 'Thirty-seven years.'

'I mean right back to find out why the Soult children acted like that?'

'They were strange children. In a strange family.'

'Ah!' Emma began to smile, a faint, curving, almost insolent smile. Before we married she had had a brief affair with a psychiatrist and something of his cynicism at human nature had stuck to her. 'I don't think they start like that. Not children from that kind of family. What makes them mad?'

Estelle frowned, those sparrow creases in the forehead.

'Weren't the Soults in the war?' Emma persisted.

I realized how sharp the needle was by the way Estelle reacted. The war was still a raw nerve.

'Of course.'

'The factories were in the south?'

'In Toulouse and Marseilles.'

'So what happened to aircraft production?' Emma asked quietly.

Estelle began to prevaricate. 'I would have to check on that . . .'

'Let's have another coffee,' I said. We could sense Estelle's discomfort, but she tried to answer our questions. The old Anglophobic uncertainties came between the two women.

Who were the Soults? A dynasty founded by Marcel's father, a pioneer who flew with Blériot and Grahame-White. In 1940 the patron had handed over to Marcel and the family fortunes had foundered. The Toulouse factory had been producing Faucon fighters when the collapse came, and Pétain ordered it to stop. What do you do with a war-plant when your government loses and neutralizes the country, Vichy France? Switch into saucepans and light-bulbs? No, sir. It wasn't so easy in the circumstances of the time but the retooling had just begun when the Germans got tired of Vichy and marched in. Soon afterwards my old man in Pittsburgh had to evade the draft.

'What sort of business?' Emma pressed.

'Well . . .' Estelle was flustered under her suntan. 'They . . . we . . . made things again for the war.'

'For the Germans?'

She nodded. Not exactly a chapter of glory.

'Ah.' Emma sighed, as if she had proved a point and scored a bull. She drank the fresh coffee as if for once she enjoyed it.

'What sort of things? War planes?'

Slowly, Estelle admitted the fact of collaboration. 'No, no. Components. Not complete planes. The Toulouse plant switched to rocket parts, for the V1 and V2.'

Emma leaned back, finished the coffee, began to collect her bag. 'And you say the children went bad: Marcel's children? How old were they?'

'They were born during the war . . .'

Emma gathered herself. 'I'm tired. You must take me back, Jim.' Then, as a parting shot, 'What happened to the family at the end of the war?'

'I do not know,' Estelle admitted.

Emma asked me to settle the bill. She held out her hand to Estelle.

'Goodbye,' she said.

We left Estelle in Pontauban and drove back to the gîte. Emma lolled in the seat as if the morning had exhausted her as much as it had unnerved me.

'I'm going to check it out,' I said. 'What happened to Soult Engineering during and after the war to produce two crazy kids . . .'

'I don't know and I don't care,' she said. 'You do what you like. You brought me here.'

'Honey . . . please. It could throw light on what happened to ours.'

'They're as dead as the Soult children,' she whispered. 'Don't try and tell me otherwise.'

I looked across at her. The colour had drained from her face. I knew she was doing no good staying on in that place, with the heat and the memories.

'Why don't you go home, honey?'

She roused herself as if she suspected a plot. 'Why me? What about you, and the job?'

'Me?' I hadn't even considered it, since everything I had striven for had gone out the window.

'You'd better ring the office.'

'I rang Bob a couple of times when you were sick. And John Simpson. Bob said they could carry on.'

I used to be a six-day-week man, but what did it matter now when the chips were down?

Acres of disused fields, and crumbling walls. A disused country. And yet I could not leave it.

'I'll stay. But, honey, you'd be better at home.'

'What are you staying for?' Again that sharp stare of suspicion, as if I had arranged things.

'I still think I ought to be here. To help the police.'

'What about your design work?'

'Fuck the work, darling.'

We came in sight of Chenoncey, then the lane to the house, buried in uncut grass. In the distance the line of hills where the storms had formed up, in the foreground the pastures where the cows chewed a meadow a day.

'Honey, there's really no need for you to stay.'

'I'll think about it.'

'OK.'

'What happens if I go? Will you see that woman again?'

'I doubt it,' I said.

But like Emma I could not help staring at the mixed belt of oak and ash and walnut where the Soult children were found. The house had been built to face that scene, yet it gave no hint of the tragedy. Apart from the parked police car it was the rural escape that I had set out to find. Its stonework gleamed in the sunshine, a creamy white, the bougainvillaea was blooming, pinned out along the eaves.

The duty gendarme saluted as our car swept in. We might have been M. le President. He was a familiar face, and I stopped the Ford.

'What happened to the guy who ran away last night?'

This one was young and fair, with brown cropped hair, like a well-clipped hedge. 'He was not well, I think. He returned a little early.'

'Well, he scared the shit out of me.' And maybe Clerrard was lying about him chasing a car.

'You heard about the break-in here? My kids' toys stolen?'

A stony look. 'That is for the Chief Inspector.'

Le Brève again, though he was nowhere around. I hoped Emma would realize there was no point in her clinging on, just waiting for news. These people had failed us but I wanted to try on my own.

Grim-faced, my wife stared out of the kitchen window towards those sinister trees. A shudder ran through her. 'Jim. Perhaps I should go home. That's what you want, isn't it?'

She said it as a challenge: a statement of fact. There was a chill between us, however much I half denied it. She thought I had gone there on purpose, because I had business there. Unfinished business.

'Darling, it's not what I want. You do what you think best.' I held her hand, feeling guilty.

'Maybe I'll go . . .'

'Think about it, honey. When?'

'In a day or two. If there is no more news.'

I hesitated. 'Do you want me to come too?'

'Not unless Bob Dorcas needs you . . .'

'I don't think that he does.' That was another home truth. Emma and I had each other now, and that was all. And not enough.

'Suit yourself.'

We were staring at each other, unable to break through.

'Where will you stay?'

'I'll go back to our house.'

Our house in suburban Richmond. A distant castle from which we had sallied forth. The job, even the current project for the Bristol hospital, now held no interest for me. Loss took us different ways. Looking at Emma, I wanted to give her time, time to be her old, strong self.

'Darling, I miss them too,' I said. 'Terribly. But I'm going to stay on a while, Em. In case the police want me. I've got some things to check out.'

Emma shifted the items on the kitchen table as if they'd been pieces of chess: salt, pepper, plates and cutlery. Peaches and nectarines tipped from a paper bag.

'As you like.'

I spent a miserable afternoon going over old ground, even walking up to the woods. There was no one around, yet I had the feeling of eyes in the shadows. The gendarme watched from the gate, but when I tried to ask him what had happened to his pal he said he had no idea. He'd only been drafted in from Marseilles, for special duty.

That evening I persuaded Emma to venture out again for a meal, driving the other way, in less haunted country, to a crossroads on the Route Nationale where there was an auberge. In the restaurant she was silent, forking her food as if she was scarcely tasting it. A good meal that passed us by, two people peeling apart, and nothing the wine could do, or coffee and brandy for me, could repair the bridge between us. As we drove back under a clear sky where the stars were diamond-hard, I was seized by the desire to hold her and take comfort between us. But she stared ahead through the windscreen up the long dark road, with the white splashes marking the middle, a tunnel that had no ending.

In bed I felt her warmth. She lay on her back in a shift, like a small girl again, and said neither yes nor no. I sensed her tiredness, the drifting replies to my questions. When my hand touched her she lay there unmoving.

I realized she was crying without tears.

I swore that I would find out. Softly: a kind of incantation.

'Don't, don't, don't,' she said.

Our bodies collided, hip to hip, and there was a moment when she might have relented. But then she submerged again in those private griefs. We lay there together yet apart, waiting for things to unfold. But nothing came. At last I went to the window and opened the shutters to see

126

if the police car was there. It was parked in the drive: this cop preferred to stay outside, half asleep in the seat.

What did they expect to happen now, to keep a gendarme on duty? Was it just reassurance, or a sense of atonement, or was there an unknown threat from the thief in the night?

The porch light had been left on, and the air was full of shadows.

When I came back to the bed, Emma had removed her slip and was lying there naked. Humidity bathed her in sweat.

'I think I'll go home now,' she said.

14

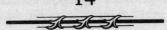

We had been there eleven days when Emma returned. Days that seemed like a lifetime. I managed to book her on a flight from Toulouse, which meant a two-hour drive winding down through the hills, then hitting the N88.

Le Brève was there watching us pack. 'Where are you going, monsieur?'

'I'm not going anywhere, Inspector. But my wife's going home . . .'

'Ah. I think it is best,' he said.

I turned on him when we were alone in the living room. 'You haven't helped,' I said. 'She's been waiting for news, and you've come up with damn all.'

He ran his fingers over his chin.

'Investigations take time.'

'Like hell they do. For God's sake what is going on here? How did the Soult kids die?'

Le Brève reacted sharply. 'Who told you who they were?'

'Let's just say I found out.'

'It is no business of yours.'

'Then why show me the spot?'

He stared at the trees in the distance and then at me. 'I thought it might worry you,' he said. 'I see it did. Where did you hear the story?'

'It's in the records,' I said.

He continued polishing his chin. 'Ah. So you read in French?'

'Not much. But I have some help.'

'You should not bother,' he replied. 'It is nothing for you.'

And that was all he would say.

I took Emma's case to the car. She had only packed one

bag: the rest of the things were with me. When the end of the two weeks ran out Clerrard had promised to book me into some local hotel, and I would take our stuff there. The kids' stuff, except the toy dog. Even as Emma left we still relived the horror of those two nights: first when the kids had gone, then when we lost that pooch.

I had pressed le Brève about the vanishing gendarme, but he had the same story as Clerrard. 'He followed a car, monsieur. Someone came for a theft.'

'A theft!' Not Chocolate Dog and comic books.

'It is likely, monsieur. The duty man said he saw a figure. Then you confused him. He ran outside and and saw a car. He jumped in his and gave chase. But in the end he lost it.'

'He blew it, huh?'

'If you like, monsieur.'

'That's crap,' I said. 'The guy was petrified. I smelt his fear.'

'Oh come. It is better that you leave this place. It is too full of memories. Then we withdraw the guard.'

'I don't want a guard,' I said. 'He didn't come for us. You know something: he didn't even come for clothes, he came for a cuddly toy and a few books. What do you make of that?'

'It is possible, monsieur, that he was disturbed before he got any further.'

'Huh. So he took a woolly dog . . . ?'

'Perhaps as a souvenir. In the dark, monsieur.'

I must have shown what I thought. I distrusted him and he had me tagged. He reckoned I was involved. This little bantam was bugging me.

Now, as I slammed the car door, I saw him still watching from the window, and had the feeling he might tail us. Instead he waved his hand as I shot through the gates.

Emma took it internally, not even glancing back. 'They won't be found,' she said.

'They will. They will.' But whether alive or dead I could not say. I forced myself to go on. I was not prepared to give in, but to Emma they were lost already.

On the drive to the airport she hardly said a word. I had at last called her parents, and heard the shock wave.

'Oh my God. We saw something in the papers, but we didn't dream it was you. You never do. It just said two children were missing, but didn't say where or who.'

I arranged for Emma's father to meet her at Heathrow, and pictured the stiff-backed Gerald receiving her with open arms, and bearing her off to Hampshire.

'Sure you'll be OK?'

She was walking with me to the departure gate. People were staring at us in that provincial way, as if we had just quarrelled.

'Emma, I'm going to miss you.'

She looked at me as if I was lying, and made no attempt to kiss me. 'Do you want me to phone Bob Dorcas when I get back?'

'You can call him if you like. He knows the worst. Tell him I'm staying on until the police find something. Anything,' I added desperately.

'All right.'

'And, honey—'

'Yes?'

'I loved them just as much as you . . .' I choked. In twelve years Susie and Martin had been built into our lives, spin-offs of our own existence. We had watched the tiny resemblances, in a grin or a flicker of anger. There would be no more games. I had to wipe tears from my eyes.

'I'm going,' she said.

'Kiss me.'

She hesitated, as if we were on display, then gave me a peck, and moved through the barrier.

'Emma. I'll telephone. Give them my love . . .' But she had gone.

I was desolate as I drove back, to begin to clear up in the house. As I returned via Pontauban and St Maxime they seemed no more than normal towns: the shops open and well stocked, the girls in their summer kit, kids running after balls, but inside me was a fear, a fear that I'd lost our children, Emma's and mine, without ever knowing why. I wasn't getting anywhere with le Brève but I wanted to work on Clerrard. It defeated reason that the police should really believe our thief in the night was simply a casual intruder.

OK. So I needed to nail them. The police as much as anyone, but suddenly with Emma gone the house was besieged. Neither le Brève nor Clerrard showed up again on that day or the next. I was going to chase them in Pontauban but events intervened, for by now the story of the lost children had reached the national news. It had taken a while but it made it, which was how Emma's parents knew, when the reports reached London. The first newshounds from the Paris weeklies arrived that afternoon, then in the next couple of days the house seemed full of the stringers for the British and American press. Unlikely characters festooned with cameras and flash guns, turning up at the gîte in a collection of vehicles, hire cars and station wagons. The shirtsleeved brigade, guys with a nose for a story and women in tight pants. The duty cop was impressed, and I didn't feel lonely. I could have been Frank Sinatra, but they wanted to see where it happened, and photographs of the kids. And Emma too. They seemed to find it amusing when they met with each other, one of them driving in as another one reversed away.

One by one I took them into the kitchen, showed them the children's bedrooms, pointed to the clump of trees. I wanted them all to see, to feel sick at what had happened, wanted the facts written up, featured in the French press in the hope that someone came forward, someone who had noticed something.

For a few days we hit the front pages and were featured in the TV news slots. A counsellor arrived from Paris on behalf of the US Embassy: condolences and concern. I was photographed from every angle, inside and outside that house, and they took away my snaps of the kids.

I had warned Emma's mother by telephone that they would be at her door too, and her parents had gone to ground. I telephoned from Les Trois Oranges to let them know the story had broken.

'I know. It's in the *Daily Telegraph*.'

'Don't let them worry you.'

131

'There's no need to call,' Emma said, 'unless you've got some real news.'

It was as if I was already irrelevant, or had chosen a trial separation, there was now so little we could say to each other.

Instead I had to cope with the French. One of them was Charles Lucas, an elderly newspaper guy with a ragged moustache who wanted an illustrated piece, and spoke pretty good English. He came with a petite woman, Augustina something, who knew about the place in the woods. They freelanced for a Marseilles syndicate and I screamed at them for help.

'You say that the police have no clue? Even when a toy is stolen?'

'So they tell me. Why don't you ask Chief Inspector le Brève?'

'I have tried,' the woman said. 'But he has gone away.'

Was this a copybook killing, a replay of two young lives lost thirty-seven years before? They shook their heads in turn. No way. Impossible. But what had happened then: and why had le Brève bothered to establish the connection? What was the earlier story in which he and Elorean had been involved? It was enough to make those two journalists dredge into their memories.

'You must go back to the war,' Lucas said, scratching his crotch with a hand dipped in his trousers, a large, bespectacled man. He remembered hidden passions. Old man Soult, the aircraft pioneer, had handed over to his son who made a living from wars, first on one side and then the next, the Pétainists. The Toulouse factory had resumed production of the casings and warheads for flying bombs, and the rumour was the old man rather approved. There had been sabotage and savage reprisals. One day there had been a shoot-out in the works which had taken a force of Germans twenty-four hours to put down.

After that Soult was co-operative, to save his plant.

'Where will I find this written down?'

Lucas smiled sourly. 'You won't. In France we don't record those things. There is no market for them, it hurts too much.'

'So what happened?' We were sitting over a glass of wine, on my last evening in the cottage. I was packed to move out and fixed up with a small hotel in St Maxime.

'They took him away for a while, some said to Berlin, but he managed to get back, about a year before the end of the war. In time to safeguard the factory, on the grounds that it was productive, right up to the great retreat after the Normandy landings.'

'I thought the Germans blew up everything as they pulled out to the north?'

Grimly, Lucas said, 'That's right. Mostly, they did. The bridges and factories. Only the churches were left, and things like bottling plants.'

'Then why weren't the Soult factories . . . ?'

Lucas seemed embarrassed, looking round to make sure that he was not overheard. 'You shouldn't ask me that. But since you do . . .' He spoke in a whisper. 'It was said that the Germans respected a collaborator, up to the end.'

I remember getting up, staring out of that damned window towards the clump of trees.

Slowly. 'But . . . if they . . . did, what about . . . the . . . reaction? Retribution? The price paid when the Germans left?'

Lucas scratched his balls again, an uncouth giraffe of a man who bit the ends of his nails. 'Soult was powerful. It was said he tried to buy them off. But . . .' He stopped.

I remember pouring more wine and pressing him. 'Well? But what?'

'There was a story, it's in the back of my mind, but it's so long ago. Something about his family being raped.'

'Raped?'

But he would not enlarge. There were bad memories. For him as for so many of the older French generation the embarrassing question was what happened during the war. Doubts were running through Lucas, for he suddenly turned towards me, head lowered like a bull.

'Listen. Past history is no good. We don't rake things up round here. Not if you want press coverage.'

'There's something going on,' I said.

He belched. 'Monsieur. Like you I have a living to earn.

133

There has been . . . what should I say . . . a contemporary crime. The disappearance of two children, English children who have come over on holiday. That is of concern to people.' He swept his arm round as if Augustina was answering for his fellow hacks, an edge in his voice. 'But when you start asking about what happened over forty years ago, about what happened here in nineteen forty-four, you won't find many will talk.'

What did that mean? I enquired.

He shrugged, and clamped his lips with his fingers.

When the second week was over I moved into the cheap hotel, not much more than a pension, the Levant, in St Maxime itself. I telephoned Emma but she was unavailable, and then I set about tracking the Chief Inspector.

He proved elusive. At the local gendarmerie which had been made the enquiry headquarters even Inspector Clerrard, behind a plywood desk with timetables on the wall, professed not to know where the Chief was. Nor did the Commissariat in Pontauban. No, he was not on holiday, nor on another assignment. Why did I want le Brève: had I got some new facts? If that was not so, would it not be better, Clerrard suggested sadly, if I returned to England like my wife and awaited their further enquires. Surely I should be with Emma? It was a pat routine, solicitously murmured above the coffee cups.

'No, sir,' I said. I was hanging on by my fingernails until there was some progress. I demanded to see le Brève, but it was almost as if he was hiding.

Clerrard rubbed his hands softly, like rustling paper. He switched on his desk fan, then switched it off again, took off his glasses and polished them with a silk square.

'I'm sorry. I cannot help. We are not responsible for the movements of the Chief Inspector. Try Pontauban again. Perhaps you should stay there.'

Christ Almighty. Susie and Martin had now been missing for two weeks, and time must be running out if there was any chance, any lingering possibility, of finding them alive. And we had heard nothing: no note, no clue, no discovery.

They seemed to have vanished in air, with no more effort than a puff of smoke. But it also appeared to me that I came up against barriers of policing which concealed not so much indifference as something they dared not uncover, some ancient or ritual secret connected with the place at which we had booked our holiday. I hated them for it, despair boiling to bitterness as my hopes were driven into the ground.

'Where is the gendarme who left his post that night?'

Clerrard smiled. 'He is on other duties.'

'I would like to talk with him.'

'Monsieur, you do not speak French. And anyway, he is in Marseilles.'

I was troubled by many thoughts, a haunting and a tiredness which seemed to drain my energy.

I called London daily, Bob Dorcas and the solicitor, Emma's folks in the New Forest, even the Paris embassy. None of them had anything to say, and Emma seemed to be there rarely. I feared I stood to lose a marriage.

Trying to rest on my bed in the poky hotel room, I was in a state of turmoil. I wondered if I should ring Emma again, and decided against it. What could we say to each other? I showered and changed my clothes, while all the time in my mind's eye I saw the sinister figure of that pocket Svengali, Chief Inspector le Brève.

Why had that damned man shown me the site in the woods, the morning when the kids went missing? So much had flowed from that, not least meeting Estelle and learning of the buried facts about the Soults. I thought back to our second encounter when Estelle had seen me on that seat in the public garden. She had been commissioned to find me, so she said, but she also knew le Brève. She would have been in the Commissariat and no doubt they had told her – the desk officer perhaps – that I had been in there asking for the Chief Inspector.

Waiting made me feel uneasy.

I went downstairs and looked at the newspapers on sale

in the rack in the foyer, along with the Paris magazines and a selection of porn in cellophane.

'Monsieur?'

The woman behind the tabac bar was watching me: a red mouth with a mole just above the cupid lipstick, hennaed hair and dark eyes. Perspiration stained her black dress.

I bought a copy of *L'Horizon* with its shrieking blue headlines. It consisted of sensational stories, murders, accidents, drug raids, picked up from police reports throughout the south; but one of them was more to the point. I spelled out the headlines laboriously with the help of a pocket dictionary.

'Why do they disappear?' I read, by Charles Lucas. 'Links between the present and the past?'

'It's rubbish, monsieur,' the tabac woman said, watching me devour it. She had seen my passport and was anxious to practise her English.

'What do you mean?

'The press, all filth and lies.' She pointed to the headline. 'They print anything.' She said she had lived in London, years ago as an au pair.

'This says that there are a lot of unexplained disappearances, mysteries still to be solved, in this part of the country . . .'

'Pah. They say anything.' She heaved her bosom from the counter in the little kiosk and came to stand beside me. Business in the Hotel Levant was hardly booming, and there were no other customers. 'Look at that . . .' She pointed to Lucas's article.

'You've read it then?'

'Of course. I look at all the crap in the stands, except the dirty pictures. That sort of muck should be banned. Monsieur, what I can't stand is people who make a living out of other people's misfortunes.'

Her fluency improved as she spoke. She said that she liked to meet tourists. Otherwise life was dull.

'You don't believe in coincidence?'

'Monsieur?'

'Coincidences at Chenoncey?'

'Not with sex crimes, monsieur.'

'Sex crimes?'

'Two children stolen or killed. What else?'

'I don't follow you, madame.'

The tabac woman sniffed. 'Somebody wanted to play with them. Sexual games, monsieur . . .' I must have shuddered. 'The Soult crimes were different, monsieur,' she said. 'I grant you that.'

Again I did not understand.

'Believe me, if you'd been brought up in these parts, you'd know the Soult family passions. Obsessions. What's left of them that is.'

'Is there anyone left?'

She laughed. 'Well, old Madame Soult is still alive they say. The old girl's ga-ga. She wouldn't run to murder.'

'All the same,' I said, 'there are unexplained facts. The disappearance of two more children in the same place.'

'Don't be taken in, monsieur. For a start there were not two deaths. Not two Soult deaths, I mean.'

I stopped in my tracks. Le Brève had told me two. 'What?'

She sucked her carmine lips, and began to sort the papers, unaware of the significance.

'What do you mean? Not two deaths, when the Soult children were burned? I've just read it in the paper. Two of them.'

'Ha.' She finished with the rack of tit magazines and took a duster to the counter, going back inside. I could see the hall porter, equally bored, picking his nose by the doors. 'I tell you not to believe all that you read in the press.'

I leaned on the counter and forced her to concentrate. 'What do you know about it?'

Something about my manner made her step back in alarm. She peered at me more closely, then scratched her head as the light dawned. The roots of her hair were silver. 'You're not connected with those poor English children?'

'I am their father.'

'Oh, Mary. Mary, Mother of God. Please forgive me, monsieur. I wish the ground could swallow me.'

'What do you know about Chenoncey?'

They were all watching me now, the porter, a maid who

137

had come from the lift, a couple who had strolled in. I banged the counter with my fist. 'For God's sake, what do you know about the deaths of the Soult children?'

'I'm sorry, monsieur, so sorry. I shouldn't have mentioned it.'

'For Christ's sake, what do you know?'

'Know?' She suddenly became obtuse.

'What happened at Chenoncey? In the woods?'

She stared at me, mouth puckered. 'In the woods? It wasn't children, monsieur. There were never two of them. Only one child died. Everybody says that.'

'One child?' Could it be that le Brève was lying, in spite of what the papers reported.

'Yes. So they say.'

'They. Who's they?' I hammered on the counter.

'People round here.'

'How many children did Madame Soult have?'

'Two, monsieur, but only one was . . . killed.'

'The police told me two. The paper reports say so.'

'Well, monsieur, they would, wouldn't they?'

'What the hell do you mean?'

A slow smile ran across her heavy face. 'The Soults were a wealthy family. They knew how to hush things up.'

I remember standing there, trying to persuade her to talk, if she knew something; if she knew something, that was, other than small-town gossip, and handed-down rumours.

She shrugged.

'All right,' I said. 'If there was only one, what happened to the other child?'

The tabac woman shook her head. 'Don't ask me, monsieur. You'd better ask madame's lover.' And she burst into cackles of laughter, inane, stupid and empty-headed.

'Whose lover?'

'Madame Soult's.' She grinned.

'Is Madame Soult still living in France?'

She tapped her nose. '*Bien sûr.*'

I stared and stared. 'And she had a lover who is still around?'

'*Bien sûr,*' she said again. 'Old Dr Raymonde in Pontauban.'

15

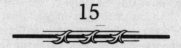

I telephoned through to Ringwood, where Emma had gone to stay. She seemed reluctant to talk.

'How do you feel, honey?'

'All right. Have you got any news?'

'Not yet, darling. I'm waiting to see le Brève.'

'What are you up to?' she said.

'Emma, please. I just want to find out what happened.'

'Are you still seeing that woman?'

'What woman?'

'That journalist.'

There was already a wedge, a tension. 'No. Emma, listen. I'm sure our kids' disappearance is connected with the Soult story.'

'What story?'

'I'm not certain, but there's something. People are covering things up.'

'That Chief Inspector is a poseur,' she said.

'It seems he's lying.'

'But it won't help to bring them back.' I heard the catch in her voice.

'Please, Emma, darling. I want proof of what happened. And I'm staying here till I find it.'

I now had something to go on, while the police hunt continued. Clerrard observed to me gloomily that they were ending the road checks, but hunting door to door. And he repeated the line that the past was totally irrelevant. But in my mind I thought otherwise, especially if there was someone else living in Pontauban who knew the Soult story. Dr Raymonde should be traceable, but I would need to call up Estelle, and that made me uneasy after our visit to Elorean. The Lord helps them that helps themselves, as Mom would say. Anyhow I couldn't just sit there.

It occurred to me then that maybe there were other records back there in the cabinet where Emma had found the press cuttings. We had been too disturbed to make a systematic search: she had just pulled out that book, *The Story of a Soul*, and there they were. What about the other books, three great shelves of the things? Why not go back and check through, give them another look? Anyway, it was something to do. It got me out of that damned hotel, it stopped me thinking about the kids or worrying about going home. Clerrard kept coming back to that, when I went to the enquiry room in the St Maxime gendarmerie.

'Why do you bother to stay, monsieur? There is nothing you can do.'

'I guess I'm the judge of that.'

He seemed surprised, then put out. 'Then I can only assume, monsieur, that you have some other motive of your own.' A look of cunning, almost of satisfaction, came into his eyes.

'I'll go in my own good time.'

'I'm sure that is . . . most wise.' He rose to his feet and held out his hand. Two other men rose with him. 'If there is anything more . . . any news. We will not abandon our efforts. Police work is like that, monsieur. It goes on when the world has forgotten. And sooner or later, who knows . . .' he stared at me '. . . there will be a break-through. It may not be the news you hope for, but sooner or later, we will find something.'

That afternoon I drove back to the gîte. It remained empty now, but I hoped the police would let me in. Instead, the shutters were closed and the place was deserted. Unguarded. There was no one about and the sun beat down out of a cloudless sky. Cattle clustered under the shade of the oak trees in the opposite field. The house seemed small

and remote, and the marigolds along the borders had withered and died.

The road into Chenoncey was empty, the hedges dry and
unclipped, and it seemed as if no one had been there since
I had left on the Saturday. I stopped the car, unlatched the
gate and drove in, tyres crunching over the gravel as they
had on that fateful first evening, over two weeks before.
Cicadas were whirring in the long grasses as I walked up
and tried the door. Our door, the one that we had opened
so excitedly, surveying the dark, boxed-up interior. Now it
was firmly locked and I had no means of access. I walked
round to the side and tried the shutters, but they were all
fastened. There were fresh molehills like small graves in
the untended grass, but that was the only change. The
washing line hung limply between two concrete posts, and
I saw the plastic top of a ball-point pen like a red bullet in
the grass. Martin's pen. As I bent to pick it up, I heard the
noise of a car, cruising down the narrow road, and something made me stay concealed at the back of the house.

It was an old-style Citroën, one of those torpedo shapes
with flashers at the corners of a curved roof, that seemed
to have been designed for French films. I don't know why
I expected it to stop, but somehow I knew it would, a
conspicuous noise in the silence of the afternoon. I saw
two men inside, examining the white shell of the house
and the GB-registered Ford parked just inside the gate. I
had felt eyes on my back before, but now I knew. I was
being tailed.

I froze in the shadows. They were in front of the gîte now
and I could no longer see the car, but I listened, wondering
whether they would get out. No fresh noises, no banging
of doors. They would be sitting there talking, smoking,
watching; and although they must have deduced from the
Sierra that I would be nearby, they made no move. After,
I suppose, three minutes I heard the engine restart and they
drove on.

I walked round the house remembering Martin and Susie
running around outside in the yard, letting off steam after
the long car journey, on the evening of our arrival. Shouting
at the start of things, exploring the geography, the little

clump of birch trees by the barbecue pit, the stretch of rough lawn where Martin wanted to play cricket. In my mind, going back to why that car had stopped, I saw le Brève's cunning face, and the dark wood opposite, to which he had taken me.

I was sweating: the temperature must have touched ninety and the sun stood high above the house. I completed the circuit and walked back up the front gravel, through the little gates and into the opposite field. Up the track where le Brève had taken me that morning. I remembered the police car bumping up the path by the side of the hedge where the cows had sheltered. And the dead black mound in the middle, the beast struck by lightning. The soil had been sodden then, just as it was bone-dry now, in this country of extremes. I walked up that side track in the blazing afternoon, an insignificant dot in the landscape, empty at heart. Two hundred metres of rutted ground, scored by tractor wheels, grooves in the dried mud, which led to the woods. I remembered le Brève unlatching this loop on the fence and ushering me through, into the trees.

It drew me back like a magnet, the trail to that lost clearing, to the hump in the soil, sprouting with weeds, where he said the bodies were found. It was just inside there, through the trees, and I needed one more look.

I plunged on through the undergrowth, aware of nothing except thoughts of my kids.

There. Just there at the end of the trail was the clearing to which he had led me. The mound that he said marked the tragedy. Where one if not two Soult children, the same ages as my own, had been discovered. Dead.

There. A slight mound in the earth, a large molehill.

All around the lozenge shape, rose bushes had been freshly planted.

Next minute I wasn't alone, as figures came towards me: I knew they were the ones in the car although I had never seen them. Men in their middle twenties, flat-haired, dark-eyed, tough and fit. They came at me before I could run. I simply stood there and waited, for this was something tangible at last.

'What do you want?'

They gave me no clue. One of them went for my neck, the other one for my knees in a quarter-back tackle. They had me by the legs and the three of us fell to the ground. I smelt alcoholic breath as the stockier of the two squirmed on top of me, then I got my fist on his mouth and saw the blood spurt, but number two went for my crotch. He doubled me up in agony, and as I tried to stop him number one hit the side of my head.

The pain came and went, a balloon-shaped headache. The first guy was spitting blood, but I was crocked. One of them hit me again and I kicked out so hard that it floored him. On my knees, then my feet, but they regrouped and came at me. I was scared they were going to kill me.

'Jesus!' I looked for escape, then for some kind of weapon, but they were on me again. I could see them coming and attempted to block. Next minute all three of us were ducking, running, weaving. The worst thing was their silence, only the grunts of effort. We rolled among the newly planted rose bushes and I began to shout. In English. Absurdly. 'Help. Help.' I saw the trees going round. Then I was up and running, but they were fitter and faster. They recovered and caught me, hanging on. I was pitched on my back. One of them straddled my chest, holding my arms. The other one stood over me and began to kick steadily. My ribs and legs.

The face on top of me was angry now, bruised and vicious, and swaying dangerously.

Another jab in my ribs, just short of cracking them.

I tried to get a hand to my face, but the guy on top prised it away. I photographed him in my mind: short hair, single furrow between black eyebrows, small scar on his right cheek. My ribs were getting the worst of it, until I got one hand loose and grabbed at the guy who was kicking. But in pulling him over I left myself wide open to the stocky bastard who was on top of me. He started to pummel my head. Then he stopped. The other guy shouted something. Both of them stopped. And signed off.

*

When I looked round they were gone. I shifted on to my side and rolled over under the trees, picking myself out of the earth, hearing the silence. I felt as if I'd collided with a dumper-truck but all my ribs seemed intact. It was just that they hurt like hell. They had made sure I was alive, left me alone and vanished. I sat up and tried to be sick, but my head was spinning too much. My body ached all over but the key bits still seemed connected. It was stifling and eerie in the woods and I saw no point in waiting. No one would see or care. Those bastards had been watching me. Somebody didn't want me around. I clawed my way out of the terrible clearing where we had fought – the rose bushes trampled and flattened – along the path through the trees, and across the open field. I reached the road. The hammers stopped in my head, replaced by a roaring thirst. I was scared they would come back, I was concerned about dehydration, I knew someone was warning me. The gîte was still there, shuttered and deserted on the other side of the road. I must have sat for some time on the grass verge, hoping someone would come by. My body slowly stopped shaking. Nothing stirred on the road, not even a murmur of traffic.

I realized I still had my car keys. They had not bothered to search me, or take my papers and money, which were still in my pocket. I staggered across the road to the Sierra. The car was where I had parked it, just inside the gates to the house, its window open. I slid in and started the engine.

Once on the road I felt better. Safer, more alert. I covered the three kilometres to Chenoncey, gradually feeling more confident, wondering about going to the police. There was no sign of the Citroën. I needed attention but by now I did not trust anyone. I was in too big a mess to go back to the hotel. The car stalled at the junction of the main route to St Maxime and the cross-country road to Pontauban, as if making up its mind. To report to Clerrard in St Maxime meant disclosing where I'd been. I winced with effort, restarted the car and kept on. I felt I could last out an hour.

The Sierra careered across country as if I had the devil behind me. Hard, impoverished countryside littered with megaliths. I do not remember much about that journey, swerving round corners, running more than once on the left as if I was back in England, sweeping past tractors and farmyards and leaving peasants gaping behind me, but somehow I made Pontauban. I was driving through the tree-lined avenues and over the bridge, up into the old town. I wanted to talk to Estelle.

16

I traced the pain in my ribs and a cut on my right cheek. There was a cream sheet in a cream room, late sunshine, as I woke up.

It took me half a minute to remember what had happened, just as Estelle came in. She wore a floral dress and her hair shone like silver. I recalled it all now: remembered arriving at the newspaper offices, the *Sud Journal-Express*, and somehow calling out. Then Estelle's gasp of horror as she saw the shape I was in. Afterwards was a daze, as she bundled me back to the car and told me to drive to her place. I had collapsed on a couch.

I was in Estelle's bed. She had washed and undressed me.

'Christ. What's the time?'

'Seven o'clock.'

I had slept for four hours.

'You'll be OK,' she said. 'You switched off like a lamp. Drink this.'

All I wanted was water. I was as tender as a rare steak.

'I don't think anything is broken.' She came and sat on the bed, feeling my face and ribs, then peeled back the coverlet to look at the darkening bruises. 'What happened?'

I told her. Told her how I'd gone back to the place in the woods, and found the rose bushes. Then how I'd been attacked.

'I can't believe it,' she said. 'You must inform the police.'

I sat up and groaned. The room was bathed in that elusive personality that was so curiously attractive, at once hard-edged and vulnerable. A feminine room, but not excessively so: there were few signs of prettiness in the furnishings and soft fabrics. Estelle herself was the flame warming the neutral surroundings.

'They might have been involved,' I said, remembering those two cropped heads. Powerfully built young men.

Estelle shook her head.

'Le Brève doesn't trust me,' I said. 'Those two guys were following me. Things got a bit out of hand, but they could have worked me over to order.'

Her fingers traced the line of my bruises, then gently pulled up the sheet. 'I don't think so. You must trust the Chief Inspector.'

'No way. I think he's a liar.'

She reacted sharply. 'You should not say that.'

I told her what the tabac woman had said, about Madame Soult and her lover, still somewhere alive.

'Ask Inspector Clerrard.'

'Clerrard won't tell me. He backs up le Brève.'

Again she said, 'Go to the police,' as if she refused to believe me.

'The roses,' I said. 'Who planted the roses?'

'Perhaps someone from the village?'

'Don't give me that. Why after all those years? The kids weren't even buried there. Only one body found there . . .'

She stroked my hair. 'You should not have gone back . . .'

'Who is it wants to stop me: the same guy that stole Chocolate Dog?'

That fragile frown-line appeared. 'Stole what?'

I reminded her about the caller in the night, another cock-up by the police.

'It's crazy,' she said.

'Those bastards who jumped me weren't crazy. Somebody stole a toy dog. And somebody planted the roses.'

'I cannot understand . . .'

'I can. Somebody who knows I'm on to something. And a guy who feels guilty about the original death.'

'Jim. You are tired. These are nonsenses.'

There had been too many nonsenses in that remote corner of France.

'My kids disappeared for a reason. I'm going to find out why.'

'There are strange people about.'

'Not in a case like this. There's a method to it somewhere.'

'Forget about it now,' she said. 'All that matters is that you are here.' She kissed my forehead.

I swung my legs over the side of the bed, feeling rough but alive. In underpants. Estelle wanted to rub some lotion into the raw bruises but I waved her away.

'Why don't you trust le Brève?'

'How can I trust him? I've spoilt his roses,' I said.

And at this time, if I had only known it, they were trying to contact me from Paris. The fellow in the British Embassy was ringing the empty hotel room in St Maxime, anxious for news having read up the papers. Emma told me later that when she informed le Brève that they couldn't find me, his office assured her that I was safe in Pontauban. As if he knew where I was.

Perhaps it was the telepathy of those enquiries that solved the problem of Estelle. I felt my strength come back, and took a few tottery steps across the room.

'Jim. Please don't try to walk . . . Stay here.'

'Don't worry. I'll be OK. I've got unfinished business.'

We disengaged and she drew back from the bed, her mouth turned down in sadness. 'Jim,' she whispered. 'Your clothes are over there. I washed your shirt. It was a mess.'

I went through to the bathroom. It was tiled in aquamarine with light green curtains giving it a submarine feeling, but there were no unguents, no fancy soaps and potions, only a small shelf with toothbrush, some powder, a razor.

Estelle began to fill the bath, which was deep and slippery. I stripped off my pants and stepped in. As I relaxed we talked about our pasts in broken sentences. Her marriage had not worked out, leaving her with Jeanne, seventeen now and in Paris. Her husband had simply walked out on her twelve years before, and she had let him go. In her way she had loved him, been attracted to him, submitted to a great deal, but it had never worked, and she had faced the mistake. He'd been a petroleum engineer and gone abroad. Though she could have traced him she never felt the need. If he wanted her he would contact, but the letter

148

or call never came, and she had turned to journalism, at first a few small pieces, then as a general reporter. I told her about Emma, my hopes for the family, my fear that the kids were dead.

'What do you mean? What makes you say that?' She looked at me in the water, and her eyes were startled.

She was silent for a while and then suddenly asked, 'How much do you love your wife?'

'Very much.'

She remained there standing beside me. The water was easing my aches. 'I don't understand,' she said, 'why you do not go to her.' She stood back, and handed me a bath towel. She seemed diminished, infinitely sad.

Estelle made no further reference to what had passed between us as the evening drew on and we had a meal together, in her kitchen. She rustled up a cheese fondue which we ate with little prongs from a heated dish, a candle-lit supper. She wiped her lips with her fingers and smiled that secret, almost disembodied smile.

'Jim, stay the night,' she said.

I paused, looking at her. 'No, I can't.'

'I shall be civilized. You must not condemn me. I can't help what I am.' She slipped her fingers through the candle flame.

I was aware of her power, but something held me back, a sense of shame, of guilt. In the flickering lights, with the warm air and the wine, I fought against Estelle becoming more than a helper. The urge to love, like hunger, is among the strongest there is. With her it seemed a struggle for survival, as drowning kittens try to swim. Old women in the streets of Pontauban searched in the waste bins. Estelle was searching for love.

I tried to find safer ground. 'Tell me about Jeanne.'

She hesitated. 'She is away in Paris. At the Sorbonne.'

Her daughter was an unknown person. Apart from the photographs of the fair-haired girl on the mantelpiece, there were no intimate signs; but perhaps she had a room else-where, a place I had not seen.

'Does she come back here? In the vacations?'

Estelle nodded. 'Naturally, she sees me.'

I walked through to the living room and came back with Jeanne's portrait in a silver frame. A girl with bold eyes and short fine hair: the nose and mouth were chiselled and firm, perhaps like her mother's, perhaps not, it was difficult to be sure.

'So you had to bring her up?'

Estelle shrugged. 'Inevitably.'

'And then she left home?'

I sensed an emptiness there, a loneliness.

'We all do.'

'Does she come back often?'

Estelle did not want to talk about herself. The subject seemed to embarrass her, and I found myself edged away.

'She comes. She stays. She goes. It is the same with all children.'

I turned back to my own problems. She touched my hands over the table and inspected my bruises again. 'They do not look so bad now.'

'Estelle. You helped me once. When we visited Elorean. Will you come with me again?'

'Where?'

'To get the truth from le Brève.'

'I don't think I can.'

I stopped drinking, slid the glasses away and climbed to my feet. I felt that I wanted out, that I was strong enough to leave. It was eleven o'clock.

'Where are you going?' she asked in alarm.

'Back to St Maxime.'

'Jim, please stay with me. You cannot drive there tonight, in that condition.'

It was a tempting offer. We were two anxious people and we could have given and taken, but the desire had gone. Not this time, not now.

'Why not?'

'I have to think,' I said.

'Don't go now. Please.'

I was fighting for my marriage. The easiest thing in the world would have been to forget who I was, why I was there. To persuade myself that I could help her. But I had been beaten up by professionals who had been trailing me.

Somebody was feeling guilty and someone else was warning me off. I could not trust little le Brève, so why should I trust her? Doubts were sown in my mind, a gut feeling that if I gave in, and stayed the night, I would be more than compromised, I would be overwhelmed.

'Estelle, my dear, I'm sorry. It would be better not.'

In a voice that was no more than a whisper she said huskily, 'What do you want me to do?'

'Help me to find out about the Soult children.'

Frustration, unhappiness, fear were in her eyes. She held me tight. 'No.'

'Why not? Why not?'

'Stay the night with me first.'

But if I did Emma would know. She would know as soon as she spoke to me. Emma. Martin. Susie. They were the reasons I was there, still struggling on.

'Estelle, my dear, I must go.'

She was in tears. 'What about the police? Will you report the attack?'

I was feeling pretty good by then. 'I'll let it ride,' I replied. 'Estelle. Will you still help me?'

'I'll think about it,' she said.

17

Le Brève seemed to have left the case. I made repeated enquiries, but he failed to show up.

Clerrard noticed I had a bruise on the side of my face.

'That's right,' I said. 'I ran into a couple of things.'

'You should be careful, monsieur.'

'Don't worry, I will.'

I felt his eyes watching me all the way to the door.

I rang Estelle the next day, but there was no reply. I drove to Pontauban in the Sierra still loaded with the kids' stuff, and left a note, telling her to call me. As I walked back down the cobbled streets of the old town in which her flat was tucked away I seemed to feel eyes on my skull, behind the curtains, in doorways.

It was now steadily hot, an electric-blue sky day after day, cloudless and enervating. I found it increasingly hard to explain why I was staying there, but some kind of cussedness stopped me giving up. At least I could try to keep going, and possibly stumble on something as I careered like a madman in the family car between St Maxime and Pontauban, with the windows open and gear fluttering in the back.

Emma's number in Hampshire was unobtainable. God damn them, didn't they understand at the Commissariat either? I insisted on another interview with the Chief Inspector in charge of enquiries, the man who had posted gendarmes, hinted to me of past horrors, and promised every effort. The man who suspected me.

They shook their heads. He had gone on leave, they thought, for a few days. Or possibly to Paris. Why that should be they did not know. But I still had the addresses from the telephone book that I'd found when investigating the garage: just as well, for the police said he was now ex-directory and they did not pass on the private addresses of officers. I needed Estelle's help. I settled down to wait till I found her: it was as if she was avoiding me too.

I telephoned every hour, throughout the evening, sure that she would come back . . . 8, 9, 10, 11, 12. Still no reply, and yet the phone was ringing in the Pontauban apartment where the press boys said she still was.

Then, at one o'clock in the morning, I heard her lift the receiver. In a tired voice she said, 'Hullo?'

'Estelle, listen. It's me. I've got some addresses to check on. One of them could be le Brève's home. Will you come with me. Please?'

I heard her draw in breath. 'I'm tired and terribly busy . . .' she said. 'Do you know what time it is – the middle of the night?'

'Please. I must have some help, Estelle.' I pushed and pushed at her.

'All right,' she answered reluctantly. 'I'll do what I can.'

I read over the two addresses in the name of le Brève and asked her to check. In the morning she rang me back, at the hotel. The first house had long since gone, pulled down in demolition, but the other in the Boulevard Gambetta was the house of a Madame le Brève. A long pause, then Estelle said, 'What do you want me to do?'

'Just come there with me,' I shouted. She must have thought I was mad.

We found the place, with a small name-tag on the gate, in the fashionable part of Pontauban, a suburb along the river. It was a big house, two-storey with wrought-iron balconies on the bedroom floor, a double garage, a row of young cypresses as a screen from the road. One of those French front gardens that belong to Jacques Tati, with a pond and a metal sculpture. A large dog started barking as the little green Citroën drove up and we rang the bell.

She was not what I expected, but then I was not clear what I had hoped for. Le Brève himself, perhaps, some proof that he was a twister, pretending to be in Paris, his face surprised as he saw us there. Instead she was petite and charming, a dark-haired girl in her mid-thirties who peeped round the door like an elf.

I asked if Monsieur l'Inspecteur was available, or failing that, Madame.

'I am Madame le Brève.'

We must have looked a bit strange, this tall, thin guy with a bruise on his cheek, and the slender, silver-haired woman, but she expressed no surprise. She might have been a daughter, instead she was le Brève's wife, twenty-odd years his junior, a pretty little dark-eyed piece in a jumper and tight pants. She had been painting some window boxes and apologized as she stood in the doorway with a small brush in her hand, which she put down carefully. And sensing my disappointment she promptly asked us in.

Evidently le Brève confided. She knew all about the children, my children, because he had told her, and her gamine face filled with concern. She offered us a drink and we all sat down to Cinzanos in the front room, which had one thing in common with that lonely house in the hills to which Estelle had driven me, Elorean's place: it was a well-heeled residence. There were fittings and furniture that would not have disgraced a château: First Empire candy-striped chairs that looked suspiciously original in a determinedly French way, a battery of expensive hi-fi and a flat-screen TV, a bronze statuette of a torso, an air of calm money.

It seemed more than a coincidence that the two policemen connected with the Soults in the past had both done well for themselves, one inside, one outside the force. It was not quite enough, I thought, to tell me he'd inherited wealth, or married it.

His wife's name was Ninette, and she seemed almost eager to talk, as if le Brève's detective duties left her too much alone. I wondered what she saw in him, this girl from Nîmes, who had married someone so different and apparently had no children. There had been a previous madame, and a divorce. She had moved into the house.

It was not my business to quiz her but I wanted her on my side, now that le Brève was away, and she gave me the feeling that she had nothing to hide. Perhaps she just liked

154

being married to a man in authority with a smart house to offer, and maybe the age gap did not matter. I sensed a sexual chemistry and a girl who liked money, as Estelle tipped back her head and began to translate my questions.

'Your husband forgot to tell me who the children were that he found, close to where mine disappeared, thirty-seven years ago,' I said.

Ninette le Brève raised her charming eyebrows. Something she didn't or couldn't understand, and I explained what he had shown me, the little mound in the woods. Then what happened there recently.

'Oh my God,' Ninette gasped. 'Can that be true? It can't be the same place where the Soults were found?'

'He didn't tell you – where it was? Chenoncey?'

'Yes.' Hands over mouth. 'But not that the Soults were found there.' There were tears in her eyes, as if she also feared something, a truth or a recollection.

'The kids of Marcel Soult, the aircraft company boss. My children may have been the victims of some kind of ritual.'

'Mother of God. No.' She drew back in a way that showed she knew much more, real horror in her face. I wondered again what kind of relationship there was between her and le Brève.

'Listen to me, madame. What can you tell us?'

And then she opened up. Sitting in that polished drawing room with the half-open shutters, Estelle seemed to drag out from her the secrets of the past.

'She says she knows all about the Soults. Her mother was a good Catholic and believed in original sin. I am a little less certain.' Estelle paused. 'We should not be asking her . . .'

'She wants to talk. Let her go on.'

Estelle looked at me. I turned again to Ninette. 'I want to know. And nobody else will tell me. How many Soult children died?'

'Two, monsieur.'

'How?'

'There was a fire.'

'Deliberate?' I feared some terrible crime, some abomin-

155

ation in those woods, that had enmeshed my own children. 'Estelle, please ask her.'

'She says it was a straightforward case of accidental death. They played with fire and they were burnt. It was quoted to her as an example, when she was small: never play with matches.'

'How does she know?'

'Le Brève investigated the case.'

Le Brève must have talked his past over with his young second wife; or he was gossiping and she had wheedled it out. It didn't matter, the fact was, she was ready to speak. I could get the story from her, so long as she didn't dissemble. There was something doll-like about her, sitting head on one side, legs crossed, high heels even indoors. A gold-digger of a kind, but a charming one.

Her face had straightened out, after the first revelation. She said she asked about his cases, because she wanted to know. That was how she knew about me, almost as if she expected I would come to her door.

Maurice had told her about the missing children, English children, but somehow she had never connected them with the Soult case that haunted her childhood.

'What exactly was the Soult case?' I asked through Estelle.

'It was ten years before I was born, monsieur.'

Slowly, sentence by sentence, Ninette and Estelle unfolded it. We were going back to the August of 1944, when the Panzers had pulled out, leaving the Toulouse factory with a stock of spare V2 parts, and Marcel Soult still in charge. Years later Ninette's mother, who had worked for the Soult family, had recounted what she saw to the little girl in Nîmes.

The Soult mansion was in the country, in the Forêt de Bouconne outside the city, and half-starving slave-workers had gone there baying for blood, when the Wehrmacht left. In a convoy of vehicles scraped from the debris of war and the run-down streets of Toulouse: an ancient bus, four or five horse-drawn carts, a commandeered police van. They had found several *flics* trying to guard the estate, and one of them had attempted to stop the frenzied mob. The

156

country girl Maria, who later gave birth to Ninette, had seen him go down in the dust, that gendarme, and lose his gun to a madman who put him to sleep like a dog. It was the first of the shootings, as they broke through the gates and swept up the curving drive to the big house. Maria had always remembered men falling under the cart wheels and the shouting and screaming. A maid had tried to run away, a red stain on the white of her pinafore, but the main rabble rushed the steps and forced the heavy doors. All the bitterness of five years of war spilled out. They were breaking and looting, revenge for the sweated labour in the machine shops, and the labour camps. There was no holding them. A staircase of marble and carved wood, and frightened rabbits at the top.

'Soult! Soult!' They had been whipped to madness, and they took Marcel as he stood there, trapped, in the double-breasted blue pinstripe of the man of property. They had taken him and torn him to pieces, obsessed with bloodlust, literally (so Ninette whispered) pulled him limb from limb, four ways, at the foot of the stairs, until he lay there a dislocated, twitching bundle. One of the gang had urinated on him as he died; then they shot him five times, with the gendarme's pistol.

There had been no justice, only retribution. The factory had been confiscated, along with the house and lands, as part of the price. The vision of it stunned everyone.

Ninette was tearful, Estelle's face intense and moved.

'My mother never forgot it . . . because of the tiny children,' Ninette said.

'The children? What does she mean?'

'She says the Soult children saw it all, from the first-floor landing that looked down to the hall.'

At last, perhaps, I began to understand a few things.

'Then they came for the mother,' Ninette recounted, her fingers twisting the crucifix on her breast.

It did not take much to imagine the brutalizing obscenity.

'What happened?'

'Apparently Madame Soult tried to protect the children. They were no more than two or three. She begged the mob

157

to stop, but they were crazy by now and had emptied the Soult cellar. The whole house stank of broken bottles. People made love in the grand rooms and copulated in the beds.'

'It is true, monsieur,' Ninette said in English. She dried her tears.

Estelle shuddered and clenched her fists. 'The children were ripped from her arms and Madame Soult was stripped naked. You know what happened to collaborators, she says? Her head was shaved, even her eyebrows. And then they raped her. One by one in her own bedroom.'

'How does Ninette know?'

'Her mother was marked for life by that experience. When she came back to Nîmes she tried to blot it out, but she never forgot.'

And yet Ninette had married le Brève. I wondered again what combination of stars had pulled her to him, and saw the query flash to her.

'You're surprised that I married Maurice, and settled here?'

'In a way,' I admitted. I sensed that she wanted to explain, a kind of self-justification for a marriage that must often have been questioned.

'Her father was a policeman,' Estelle relayed. 'In Nîmes and Arles. She has her roots in the south. The Inspector came there on duty, after his divorce. They met at a police dance. He can be very charming, and she felt sorry for him.'

'Thank you,' I said.

'Married four years,' Ninette smiled. 'Another drink, monsieur?' I realized why she felt so isolated in that big house. I asked how long he would be away. She thought no more than three days. He was still on the enquiry, but wanted to check with Interpol. Yes, in Paris. Did I believe it or not? I was not sure.

'Yet you did not know that the Soult children were found at Chenoncey?'

Her fingers were gripping the glass as if she was holding a rail, white at the knuckles. 'No, monsieur,' she said.

I turned to Estelle again. 'What happened after the looting?'

158

'Afterwards they burnt the house. The Soult château. Poured petrol on to the furniture and threw in lighted rags. Some say several people were trapped there and burnt alive: their screaming could be heard. She says it burned like a box of matches.'

'And Madame Soult?'

'Somehow she saved the children. Some basic instinct. Her mother never saw that: but they survived.'

18

Estelle seemed too upset to talk. We carried away the memory of those crying children, the naked, cowering mother, and the bloodlust of the mob. It haunted us as we drove back into Pontauban and I dropped her off at the offices of the *Journal-Express*.

I wanted to discuss things with her, to get her view on Ninette, to find out how much of the Soult story she accepted. The Soult kids had been saved, but what kind of future was theirs, to make them into little arsonists? Had one or both died in the woods? And what were the connections with Chenoncey today that might point to a reason for losing Martin and Susie? But Estelle only said she was tired. She had her living to make, she added crossly.

I suggested we meet for dinner.

'I'm busy, monsieur,' she said. Monsieur!

'Estelle, don't be ridiculous. You can't work all the time. I tried that once.'

'I work at night . . . Jim.'

'But not tonight surely?' This was a woman who had tried to seduce me. I wanted to take advantage.

'It would be unwise,' she said.

'It would be a recognition of your help.'

'No.' But she hesitated, legs half out of the car. Traffic piled up behind us in the narrow street.

'Please, Estelle.'

She seemed both sad and reluctant, as if she wanted to run. The traffic was impatient, and we were holding it up.

'Tonight,' I said.

'Well . . . perhaps.' She frowned, then smiled. I said I would call at eight.

I went back to the Hotel Levant and tried to make calls from the stuffy little bedroom. One was to Bob in the office.

'Jim,' he said. 'What are you doing out there? Why didn't you come back with Emma?' It was almost as if staying on was now a suspicious act, as if he thought I wanted to be there.

' "Helping the police with their enquiries", is how you guys would put it.'

'Any news, Jim?'

'Nothing definite, Bob. I'm getting to grips with the past.'

'You're what?'

'It doesn't matter, Bob. You want me back?'

He was a pretty good fellow, underneath, and I think he had seen in my family something he would have liked.

'No. We can cope. We've finished the Bristol job.'

I had forgotten it existed. 'That's great,' I said. 'Maybe I'll be back soon.'

'You take as long as you need.'

'Thanks, Bob.'

I walked downstairs to find the tabac woman, but the kiosk was shut. The hotel was one of those places where strangers met in the lobby like lost souls. It smelt of stale cigarettes and slightly uncertain plumbing, but I was kept hanging about because they were trying to ring Emma at her parents' address. I knew that they would not have left there without letting me know, and yet throughout yesterday and today there had been no reply. I rang on the hour every hour, from one o'clock through to six, and it was therefore with some relief that I heard the bedside phone ring.

'It is England, monsieur.' She said it as if it was Mongolia.

'OK. Great. Thanks. Hullo?'

It was Emma's father, the Colonel, in that pepper-pot voice that always sounded as if he was trying to stop sneezing.

'James?'

'Hi. Is Emma around?'

'Where are you?'

'St Maxime le Grand. Just up the road from Chenoncey. Is Emma there?'

A pause. A kind of sniffing noise, like he was wiping the receiver. 'Emma's not very well.'

'Gerald. What's the problem? I was hoping she'd pick up now . . . Can you get her to the phone?'

Another pause.

'She doesn't want to talk to you right now.'

Oh Jesus. My heart sank. 'What's the matter with her, Gerald?'

He countered with, 'Is there any news, James?'

'Well. Nothing to go on so far, but I'm working on it. Is Emma in bed?'

'No . . . she's resting.'

'Then can I speak to her?'

'Not at the moment.'

I lost my temper. That didn't help Anglo–US relations. 'For Christ's sake man—'

'She's gone away,' he said. 'Gone away to a friend.'

'Where? Who?' I shouted down the wire.

The old man was equally huffy and we were yelling at each other. 'Leave her alone, James. She wants to work things out on her own.'

'What?'

'You heard. She doesn't want to speak to you right now. She's gone off with some friends.'

'Who?'

'Jennie Macomber,' he said.

The Macombers. The fucking Macombers from Sunbury, Emma's old University College, London, pals, whom we were supposed to be dining with before all this began. Emma had cancelled it then because I was too damned busy. I felt they were getting their own back.

'How long for?'

'I don't know. A few days.'

'In Sunbury? Do you have the number?'

'I'm sorry. She said you were not to call her. Any news, you phone me here.'

Emma was avoiding me. Perhaps she had decided I did it. Perhaps she thought I was staying there to have it off with Estelle Devereau. I was furious.

'Don't play games with me, Gerald. I might just do the same.'

That was a stupid remark, forced out of me under pressure, and I regretted it. I could sense his prejudices being confirmed. But I was very angry, feeling that the poisonous suspicions encouraged by le Brève and others had eaten into her mind.

'Ring when you want to speak sensibly' was all he would say.

'I'm sorry. Forgive me.'

He calmed down a little too. He was ambivalent. 'It's all very difficult,' he said. 'Very unfortunate.'

'I'm here because I'm looking for the kids, man. No other reason. OK?'

'I appreciate that.'

He appreciated it, did he? Well, that was good of him. She was the mother of my kids, and I had things I wanted to tell her, about the strange deaths in the past, but hell, no, I had to communicate with that half-pay, half-embarrassed father, while she went off with her friends to sort out what she thought about me. And left me with no choice.

'OK, OK, Gerald, you'd better tell her I called.'

Instead, I told Estelle, when she came to the door that night. She looked stunning in deep cherry-red, a simple dress which showed off her supple figure. For the first time she seemed exotic, her hair washed and gleaming like a waterfall. I had reserved a table in a restaurant in Pontauban down by the bridge, under the rustling trees, with flags strung out between the branches. The Croque d'Or had tables outside by the river, and a pianist playing on the dining floor. In the evening air it had an intimate feel: a place for assignations.

'You are better?' she said.

'Much better.'

We smiled across the glasses, as if we knew what we were doing.

'Except that my wife won't speak to me ...'

Estelle's face clouded, then seemed to relax. 'Jim. What is the matter?'

I told her about Emma's elusiveness, as if she, like le Brève, was avoiding me.

'It will be all right soon,' she suggested. 'Jim, I feel sure it will . . .'

'What makes you so sure? All I find is half-truths, and more and more uncertainties.'

She stroked that moon-coloured hair. 'Such as?'

'Well, such as how many Soult kids died up there in the woods. And what exactly the police are covering up.'

'One or two, does it matter?'

'I don't know. But unless I find some other motive, suspicion still points at me. Even my own wife . . .

She reached out and stroked my face. 'Don't think about it, Jim.'

But I reflected on what I had found. 'It begins to look like a conspiracy. We may have a deception embracing le Brève and Elorean, the two men who investigated the Soult children.'

'It's impossible,' she said.

'Is it? Why? You saw Elorean's place. Neither he nor le Brève made that kind of money from police work.'

She paused in the act of dismembering a chicken breast, and drank another glass of Chablis. I longed to smooth that frown-line between the exquisite eyes.

'What do you want from me?'

'I still need your help.'

'But I can't bring your children back.' Her features were troubled.

'We can find out what might have happened.'

'Sometimes I hate myself.'

'Don't say that, Estelle.'

She was leaning towards me. I saw the blue eyes misting, as if she fought back tears.

'It is no good. I can't.' She shook her head. 'Go back to Emma, Jim.'

'When I've got news, honey. Why cry about it?' In a clumsy way I sought to help her.

She was staring at me with moist eyes, her voice falter-

164

ing. 'You know why I cry. You know why you brought me here.'

I tried to deny it, explained that when I set up the meeting I did not know Emma was rejecting me, that we were working together, that was all.

I saw her sit very still. 'We make a professional team.'

'Very professional.'

'Oh, for Christ's sake.' I was driven, I was naïve. The music wafted over us, sweet and sentimental, and blood pounded through my veins. I had lost two children and was confused by grief. My wife had gone back to England half thinking that I was responsible. And Estelle was waiting here.

We had liqueurs and afterwards walked by the river which swung round a bend and eddied under the bridge. She put her hand through my arm. The restaurant had lit a path, a shingle track through the plane trees down to the water's edge, where lovers strolled. I had no time to think about Emma brooding at home. I shut the door on my fears. It mattered more at that moment that Estelle chose to stroll there with me. Her warmth was a part of me, her perfume musky.

'Where does this path go?' I asked.

She shrugged. 'As far as you like.'

Under the shadow of the trees, the music a distant tinkle, I stopped and took her in my arms. Our lips met and she collapsed against me.

'No. Jim, no. It must not be—' she whispered.

'Don't talk.'

'I'm so sorry. For the children. For everything.'

The evening was not over as I took her back to my car and drove to her apartment. The boulevards were full of strollers, and car headlights blazed behind us. In the edge of my mind, I wondered if we were observed.

'I feel so much for you,' she said.

We walked up the cobbled street, into the little white-washed courtyard to her apartment. 'Three weeks ago,' she said 'we had not met.'

'Three weeks ago, I was driving down through France, a happy man with a family.'

She fumbled for her keys. 'You must not say that.'

In the passage of the apartment, we kissed behind her front door. Inside the flat her chaos of books had been tidied, as if she was half expecting me. She wanted me. I needed her. The sense of assignation was overpowering as she closed the door.

We were tearing our souls, as the red dress slipped from her shoulders. In the hot little passage for those few minutes she made me forget my grief. We felt our bodies respond. I was my unique self again, one person and not four.

Estelle shuddered and cried.

I could see the bedroom beyond, the pillows and coverlet through the open door; she had left the lights burning. There was a double bed with a brass headrail, similar to the one in the gîte.

My desire died. Lust choked in my throat and I released her.

'What is the matter?' she asked.

I could not explain or tell her. I wanted to get away, to stop us exploring each other as if sex itself was new, unique and untried.

'Please, Jim. Please don't feel guilty,' she said.

'I am.'

She began to refasten the dress. 'What do you mean?' she asked sadly. 'You cannot be.'

But in my mind I was less sure. What might have happened then, as we huddled together, I could not say. The time was already late but she was a night bird, and we were hesitating. We both heard the ring on the bell.

Estelle put a hand to her mouth. 'Wait,' she said. 'Go through and wait in there.' The living room. She disappeared into the passage, leaving me wondering how easy it was to be unfaithful. No question of falling: it needed a kind of commitment. In accepting the help she gave me I was creating a secret life. Secret from Emma in England, and a marriage close to exhaustion.

I heard Estelle unlock the door and begin talking. Stupidly I straightened my clothes, with drifting, unfocused thoughts.

She returned with a white jacket over her bare shoulders as if she was cold, the same white linen coat she had worn when we met in the park. It emphasized her slim figure in the red summer dress. Behind her was a thin young man, dark-haired, designer-stubbled. He wore a green jacket and jeans, and Estelle introduced him as Jules.

Jules was a cub reporter on the *Sud Journal-Express*, who had contacts at police headquarters, and had heard a fresh rumour. From Estelle's hesitancy I saw she was afraid.

'Jim. They have found a body,' she whispered. 'Inspector le Brève is coming back and they would like to see you tomorrow about identification.' She stopped, pressed her hands on her heart and then held me. 'Oh Jim, it can't be true.'

I felt expectation drain away. I didn't know what I hoped for now. All my suspended ambitions had been for the kids, and the children would not return. Not come back, ever. The most I could expect now was to know what had happened. I found myself gripping Estelle's hands like a drowning man, while Jules was mumbling platitudes.

'Where? Where?'

A long way away, it appeared, in some sandpit further south, near Carcassonne. The Commissariat had given no details, merely implied a lead. Le Brève would be back to investigate.

We crowded into the kitchen while Estelle made coffee. Then Jules was despatched and we stared at each other.

'I'm sorry . . .'

'No need . . .'

'I mean about tonight.'

'Forget it,' I said.

She shook her head. 'I never will.'

'Nor me.'

'What will you do if it's true? If they have found them?'

I considered. It was the sort of question you never ask yourself until the disaster happens. Is that what they are for, those traumas no one can duck, illness and loss and death, that catch up with us all? Soul-searching? Would even a body help Emma and me?

'I don't know,' I replied. We sat at her kitchen table, under the hanging lamp.

'There are two sorts of tragedy in life,' Estelle said. 'One is to find what you dread. The other is not to find it.'

19

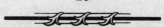

A gendarme called in the morning at the hotel in St Maxime. He asked me to go immediately to the enquiry room in the gendarmerie, where le Brève turned up a couple of hours later.

I was sitting in the waiting room overlooking the court-yard and watched his blue Citroën sweep in. He jumped out and ran across the cobbles, eager and bouncy. As if he found life exciting.

I could hear him talking animatedly to Clerrard in the corridor, then the door banged open and he stood there smiling. 'Monsieur Freeling.'

'What now?'

'I am sorry. It is not very pleasant news, but at least it is something. They have told you?'

'They tell me you have found a body . . .'

'We have uncovered a boy's body. A gravel pit near Carcassonne. A hundred kilometres south of here.' He shrugged. 'Maybe a little more . . . I would like . . . I want you to come and see.'

'You mean identify?'

'If you like.'

I saw Clerrard observing me, but le Brève commanded my attention. In a brown double-breasted jacket with semi-official gold buttons and tight fawn trousers, he was dressed like a theatrical manager, or an expense-account bookie. To cap it all, he wore a bright blue tie. How could I trust the guy, any guy who appeared like that?

I said I would go.

'We leave at once,' le Brève commanded. 'Let us try and get things over with.'

I squeezed into the car with le Brève and his deputy, a morose and silent man in his mid-thirties, introduced as Constant. Two uniformed men sat in front, alongside the driver. A grumbling, sticky carload which shot out into the traffic and picked up the autoroute to Toulouse. We cracked on through high, dry country, fields of ripe corn and wheat, vineyards, orchards of hard old fruit trees, heading south-east along dusty ribbons of road.

'Do you want anything to eat?' le Brève hissed in my ear. 'A stop for lunch?'

I told him that I had no appetite.

My stomach was cold and empty but not hungry. I also felt guilty for being tempted by Estelle, when Emma was sick at home. I was exhausted, pumped dry.

'Compose yourself,' le Brève said.

I told him to drive straight there.

More hot country where sunshine blanched the farm-houses, and dogs sprawled in the shade. Le Brève took off his coat and pushed it on to the rear window ledge. He was wearing blue braces and there were wet patches under his arms.

Some thirty kilometres north of the old walled city of Carcassonne the car pulled off the main road and headed across country. We wound up into hills where the villages were sleepier, emptier. The earth was bone-hard and baked and the vineyards raked in terraces.

Le Brève watched me watching it.

'Sometimes they kill each other from boredom in these parts. There have been many stories.'

'Who do you think you have found?' In the end I summoned the courage to ask him.

'It is a boy. Mutilated. The legs are missing,' he said.

'Missing?'

He said yes, they had found only a torso, nearly naked. Dead about two weeks. A boy of eleven or twelve, according to the pathologist.

'Where are we going now?'

'To show you where we found him.'

'But is the body still there?'

'No. Of course not.'

'Then why bother?'

He smiled thinly, his skin shiny with sweat. Le Brève must have gone round in circles and come out where he started, with a finger pointing at me.

'In case you are reminded of anything.'

We arrived at an excavation, where bulldozers had cut furrows across the soil, churning it into powder.

The car bumped over ruts and followed a makeshift road of steel webbing, down to the edge of a quarry. Below us, dumpers and earth movers were tearing out a giant hole as le Brève hopped out and began a conversation with the men who were waiting, standing by some parked cars.

I was introduced to the manager, an Italian engineer employed by a sand and gravel business, who explained that they had the concession. He shook my hand – his own stained yellow by sand – and led the way in a scramble down the cliffs, which had been sliced into layers like an enormous cake.

'Anyone can walk in here,' le Brève explained. 'It is too big to fence off. There is no chance of stopping them.' He pointed to the series of ledges.

Someone had driven through the fire paths in the plantation surrounding the quarry, through the acres of pine trees, right to the edge, and dug a shallow grave. They showed me where it was: a pit in the gravelly soil, thinly covered with branches. It had been found by chance when two of the workers had gone to search for a dog. Le Brève was standing beside me. I was looking at an empty trench, in which they had found a body, decomposing, on its back.

As I stared at the rough grave I faced the end of my hopes and realized how little now mattered. It all ended in this, somewhere, somehow. An unendurable horror overwhelmed me.

I found le Brève plucking my arm. 'What do you think?'

'Nothing.' I was numb. 'I think nothing.'

'It does not remind you of anything?'

'Why should it?'

He stooped and picked up a handful of earth, letting it trickle through his fingers. 'Another place. A mound in the woods? Where other children were killed?'

His face loomed up at me, dark and suspicious. I hated him. Standing there in the ring of police, with the cars semi-circled behind us, on the path to the grave, I gave way to basic fears of something black and terrible which had happened at Chenoncey. In my mind it was Martin, poor helpless Martin and the nameless things that I tried not to see.

I remember croaking, 'What the hell do you mean?'

'Nothing.' Le Brève echoed my own words. 'I wanted to see how you felt.'

How I reacted: whether there was any tremor of contrition or guilt, a trick which I should have realized when I discovered where they were taking me. Le Brève still suspected me, although he could find no evidence. I could see the way his mind was working: what if I had a motive? How could he know our relations with the children, Emma's and mine? I suddenly realized that he had been talking to Emma before she left, when she was in the gîte alone. And Emma had been so confused, so sick with worry, that she might have said anything. Hadn't I been resentful when they smashed up the Buddha? Hadn't I shouted at them when they burst in as we made love? Had she remembered these things, and told them all to le Brève? Hadn't I said I could have killed them when they saw us in bed? Hadn't I been seeing Estelle? Suppose, in short, they had concluded between them that I had had it in mind from the start?

Le Brève looked at me, birdlike, head tilted on one side, The police stood around watching.

'OK, OK. We go.' He nodded towards the cars.

The trick had failed. Whatever he was fishing for, some clue or motivation, it had not emerged, and he set about the next stage. He led the way back. 'I will show you the boy.'

We drove in convoy to the city of Carcassonne, through the Ville Basse, along the shady boulevards lined with municipal offices. Le Brève's car turned off into a narrow gateway where an old grey building baked in the sun. A notice said 'Morgue Municipale'.

I hoped against hope that it would not be Martin, this

thing that he wanted to show me. I saw something lying in a zinc bath, flesh the colour of fish skin, purple in places, dark hair caked with soil. 'Look at the neck,' le Brève said softly, 'the evidence of asphyxia: haemorrhages of the face and scalp.'

I forced myself to see blue mottled marks on the windpipe, an ugly bruise on the chest bone and what looked like a bruise on the forehead.

'How long?'

Le Brève shrugged. 'Two, maybe three weeks. We have not yet had a full autopsy.'

'It's not my son,' I said. 'Thank God.' Some other poor mother's boy. My stomach heaved.

'Put it away,' le Brève commanded to the white-coated attendant. I was thankful as the drawer slid back.

'These are police procedures,' he added, half apologetically. 'I have to establish . . .'

'Look. This is a hundred-odd kilometres from where my kids disappeared. What makes you think that there's a link?'

'I do not think,' he said. 'I only observe; I see if the evidence fits.'

'And does it?'

He squeezed my arm, as I remembered him doing when he first showed me that place in the woods, and elbowed me outside into the sunshine.

'Let us go and have a drink. It is time we discussed things.'

'Too right,' I said, remembering the fight in the clearing.

We were driven to the local police headquarters, a stone-fronted nineteenth-century building with the tricolour flying. Le Brève seemed to be at home there, and effected introductions to plain-clothes men standing around.

'Now.' He clapped his hands and led me into a panelled room with shuttered windows and three or four little tables scattered across it. 'Please – ' indicating a chair – 'you deserve coffee and cognac. It is time we had a talk.'

I accepted the brandy and swallowed it gratefully: my nerves felt as if they'd been scraped with broken glass.

'Well?'

Le Brève rubbed his hands together and leaned forward conspiratorially. 'Why did you go back to the woods in Chenoncey?'

I showed him the bruise on my cheek. 'Ah. So you know?'

'I regret that you – how you say – obstructed my men.'

'Obstructed? The bastards tried to kill me.'

He shook his head. 'No. No. They exceeded their duty, but you caused them to panic. Remember we are all nervous about what happened there. I'm sorry,' he added.

'I could get you for assault.'

He smiled. 'I do not think you would have evidence . . . Now. Let me ask you a question. Why do you see that woman?'

'What do you mean?'

'Don't try to fool me, monsieur. I know you went back to Madame Devereau, and visited her last night.' He shrugged. 'It is of no importance who you sleep with, when your wife is away, but in police terms it may be significant, eh?'

'We have not—' I began. 'You're talking rubbish.'

He grinned, and poured another generous helping from the bottle of Bisquit. 'My friend, your wife would be interested, would she not?'

'What are you suggesting?'

'Ah. You see. You do not deny it.' He ran a finger across his lips. There were gold rings on both hands.

I studied him. I distrusted him. He was only doing his job, but he represented to me different cultural values deep in the subconscious: a touch of mystery.

He inspected the moons of his nails. 'I think that you may not be so sorry that your wife is gone away.'

'Listen. I love her. We have lost two children. For Christ's sake you can't expect me to be entirely sane.'

'Sane?'

It was a bad choice of words, and I regretted it. I wanted the past back, a country for which there are no visas.

'Have you spoken with her recently? On the telephone?'

'I can't get through.' It was almost as if he knew.

Le Brève suddenly jabbed a finger in my direction. 'Why did you decide to come to this part of France?' We were going round the track again.

'You know why. A chance booking.'

'When did you last come to France?'

'Seven or eight years ago. To Normandy.'

'Ha. So you suddenly decide to come south to Chenoncey?'

'For God's sake—'

'And then you find the children missing, on your first night?'

'Yes. Please stop trying to make me guilty.'

'Don't be difficult, monsieur,' he said. 'More cognac?'

I shook my head. 'No.'

'So. You come, and the children disappear. And you know nothing about it. You only wake up, you say, because of the storm. You get your pyjamas soaked without going outside.' He paused. 'Now, does that seem very likely? Is it true, I say?'

'Of course it's true, and you bloody well know it.' It was my turn to attack. 'And since you want to question me, let me ask a few of you. What you have done about it? How many men have been searching? What the hell have they found, apart from that poor little wretch in the quarry?'

'We have searched every building within twenty kilometres.'

'They could have been taken anywhere.'

'Monsieur, I am more interested in your motivation.'

'Motivation.' I remember banging the table. 'Don't give me that crap.' I was shouting at him. 'Hear me, Inspector. I could accuse you—'

'Of what, monsieur?'

'Of failing to protect the gîte, when we had the second break-in. Of knowing about the attack on me in the woods.'

'You have no means of proving it, monsieur.'

'All right.' Suddenly I pitched a different ball. 'Why didn't you tell me who the babes in the woods were?'

'Which babes?'

'You know which ones. The kids that were found there thirty-seven years ago, opposite that damned gîte.'

'What do you mean?' His voice had gone flat, hard.

'How come that even your wife didn't know? How come that you didn't tell her?'

'Tell her what?' he almost hissed.

'That they were the Soult children. The heirs to a fortune.'

He seemed to jump, sitting erect, small-backed. 'It is no business of yours.'

'I'm telling you. The children of Marcel Soult were playing with fire there and you found them. You and Elorean. And got rich on it.'

He eyed me with a basilisk stare. 'You have talked to my wife, Ninette. Is that so?'

'Yes.'

'You went to my home . . .' he mused.

'I presume she tells you more than you tell her.'

A white line of spittle or froth seemed to form for a moment in the corner of his mouth, and then he licked it away. He seized the brandy bottle and poured two more drinks. His attempt to incriminate me was promptly abandoned.

'You should not have done that,' he whispered.

'Why not? You were away. I was trying to find you.'

'Because . . . because it was not wise. Not sensible. She should be left alone.'

'Not sensible?' I thought again of the lonely young woman in that big house. 'Why didn't you tell me who those children were?'

'What children?'

'Don't prevaricate, Chief Inspector,' I said quietly. 'You deliberately showed me where they had been found, on the morning that Martin and Susie disappeared.'

He paused, drumming his fingernails against the table. I was conscious of someone coming into the room disturbing our tête-à-tête, speaking rapidly in French.

'A minute.' La Brève waved the uniformed officer away and turned to me, his eyes like berries. 'What are you saying?'

'I'm saying that the disappearance of my two children might be a form of ritual, a replaying of the fate of the two Soult children.'

He laughed tunelessly. 'Oh no, no, monsieur. That is not so.'

I snapped at him, getting up to end the discussion. 'OK. So why didn't you come clean with me?'

Le Brève rose too. 'Because there were not two children found there.'

'You said there were.'

'I said that to try you, to test you.'

'Like today, I suppose.'

'Yes. Like today.'

The tabac woman had been right. 'Are you telling me that what your wife told me, about the two Soult children, and what the papers said at the time, was all a myth?'

Again that flicker of spittle at the edge of his mouth. He licked his lips. 'No. Since you ask, I will tell you. There were two Soult children, certainly. They were born during the war and they were discovered later as – what you say – arsonists.'

'Yes. So I've heard. And you've investigated them, as a young detective?'

'And what did you hear next?'

'That they were killed in a fire. In some construction that they set alight. Near our cottage. On that site in the woods.'

Le Brève shook his grey head. 'Nearly, but not quite, my friend. There were not two children there, if you must know.'

'Then you have lied to me, Inspector.'

'Marginally, I confess.'

'And what does that mean?'

Icily, he said, 'Only one body was found.'

20

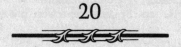

The police drove me back to St Maxime, and dropped me off at the hotel. Le Brève was going on to the Commissariat in Pontauban. On the journey we said very little, as if pondering our exchanges, but as he left me outside the Levant, he advised me again to go home.

'Have you not got a job?'

'I guess so. What about you?'

He stared at me, stony-faced.

'Do not be clever, monsieur. We will contact you if there is news. There is no point in staying on here . . . unless you have a reason.'

'Reason,' I snapped. 'There's been a crime committed. Against me, against my kids. I want to know why.'

He sighed. 'I told you, on the first day. Sometimes there are mysteries that can never be solved.'

'But you're a smart cop. You know that.'

He sighed. 'I do not know all the answers.'

'OK. So I'll try to find them.'

I stood there in the street and watched his departing car, then went inside the lobby. The kiosk was closed again. Upstairs, from my bedroom, I put through a call to Emma, but again it was her father who answered.

'Gerald? I've been to see a body. In Carcassonne. But it wasn't one of our kids.'

'Thank God for that,' he said.

'How is Emma? When is she coming back to Ringwood?'

'Emma is all right,' he said crisply. 'We don't know when she'll be back. She was very insistent that you were not to phone.'

'Jesus Christ. She's my wife.'

'I should do what she says. She knows her own mind.'

I rang off. I called Estelle at the newspaper. She was equally cold. I tried to give her a list of the things on which I wanted some more research: the Soults during the war, the fires in 1953, whether there were more recent disappearances of children in the same area. I said that I still needed help.

'I'm sorry, Jim . . .'

'Don't you want me to find them?'

'Of course, Jim. But there is really nothing more I can do.'

I suppose things might have ended there. I might even have given up, if Lucas had not come back to me. Old Charles Lucas of the ragged moustache and shiny trousers, who had come out to the gîte that day with the petite woman called Augustina, and first told me about the Soults. About the way they had played the war years, and what had happened to the family, confirming Emma's own sharp suspicions, soon after we had talked to Elorean. Lucas had not wanted to follow up the Soult lead then, but now he got in touch and suggested we met for a drink, at a café in a local square.

We rendezvoused on the next afternoon. An ordinary café with tables in the street and an awning against the sun. Lucas came ambling across, his shirt bulging out from his belt, a big, rather awkward man who had told me he freelanced for papers based in Marseilles. He said he had driven up from there because he had something to tell me, and I could see by his face that he was excited. He shook hands and settled heavily in one of the basket-weave chairs, which creaked under his weight. In the square people lounged past us; I bought him a Stella Artois beer; someone came round selling tickets for a charity raffle. Like some reminder of the land I had left behind me I saw a Chevy with a New York registration roll in, driven by a guy in Bermudas. He glanced in our direction as if looking for someone who could understand the language, then marched into a restaurant. Charles Lucas swallowed the beer and wiped his moustache.

'Well,' he said, in his competent English, 'I have been

doing homework since you linked the Soults to the place where your children disappeared. On the court reports, and records in the press.' He tapped the table. A curious enthusiasm began to take hold of him. 'Then I went back to the war. I told you, monsieur, that those are the years we forget, but there is an official history.' He pulled out a paperback book which explained about the great Soult factories in Marseilles and Toulouse, confiscated after the war, with sparse references to the reprisals in 1944. The book said only that there had been 'disturbances' when the Germans withdrew, and the family were branded as collaborators. The factories had been nationalized in 1946.

I had by now heard three accounts of that time, each of them slightly different, from Estelle, Ninette and Charles Lucas. I bought him a second drink.

'You have no more news, monsieur?'

'No news,' I said.

'So. Listen to this. Please, I will try to translate.' He opened a canvas bag and extracted a series of photocopies from the files of the post-war newspapers. Descriptions of horrors uncovered, in pits by the side of the road, where summary executions had been carried out as the Panzers left. And tales of heroism by the Maquis, of sabotage and bridge-blowing to try to delay their retreat, among which was an account of the ambush of a convoy of machinery leaving the Toulouse factory. Components and rocket stabilizers, gyros and timing mechanisms, had not got back to the Reich even though, Marcel Soult claimed, they were paid for under contract. 'It had enraged the workforce,' Lucas read from the *Sud Presse*, 'that such a claim should be made and they determined to show their anger.' A party of workers had secured the main assembly plant while 'another group of workers and relatives' had marched on the Soult estate. That had been the party that Ninette's mother had described, where the ringleaders had raided the house and raped Soult's wife. There was a blurred picture of women being led away, and another of roadside corpses.

But what had all this history to do with me?

'Wait a minute, monsieur,' he said.

'The revolutionary blood of their forebears,' he translated, 'inspired by the sense of a new dawning, a fresh release from chains, seemed to burn in their veins as they surrounded the château in the forest. At a sign the people moved forward, an irresistible tide shouting "Traitors, traitors." M. Soult tried to restrain them but they were the rulers of his property and no force on earth could oppose them. "Justice," they cried, "and vengeance, in the name of France." Marcel Soult himself lay dead at the foot of the staircase.'

I looked at Lucas over the blur of people moving around us. The accounts were very similar in three papers of that time, 1 September 1944, as if there was a common source.

He twisted his glass in the sunlight. 'You want to know what happened next?' I nodded. 'It seems that Madame Soult went into exile somewhere, with the two children. There is reference to her living at Chenoncey for several years.'

'Ah!' It was coming together. That would be when the gîte was built, and would account for the books in the cabinet.

'Listen. Listen. Madame Soult is still alive.'

'Yeah. I found that one out too.' From the tabac woman.

Lucas was disappointed, but he ploughed on. 'Also I have found out where. I've checked it out. The confirmation came through yesterday. Would you like to know that? Buy me another beer and I'll tell you.'

'OK.' I hustled up the waiter.

Lucas grinned. 'A place called Gourdon-sur-Loup. About thirty-five kilometres north of Pontauban, in the hills.' He rubbed his hands together. 'A bad country,' he said.

'Why?'

'It is like a desert, monsieur.'

'Then why should she want to live there?'

'Maybe you should find out.'

But again the question recurred, what did it matter to me?

'You see, the old woman left Chenoncey when her children were burned.'

'Children, or child?' I said. 'Le Brève now says only one.'

181

He looked puzzled. 'All the accounts say two. I checked those as well, monsieur, in writing up my story.'

'I know.'

He leaned over the table towards me, perspiring and breathy. 'There is one brief reference,' he said, 'after the account of the fires and the loss of the Soult children, to a scandal involving the widow. She had an affair with a doctor called Raymonde to whom she had gone with the children, because they were very disturbed. Some say half mad. After the children died Madame Soult was still wealthy, but she lived as a recluse.'

'What kind of man was Raymonde?'

Lucas shrugged. 'I do not know. I've told you what I established.'

'But Christ, man, all this was nearly forty years ago. How can it affect the disappearance of my two kids?'

'I don't know,' Lucas said slowly, 'but yours were the same ages, and the same sexes as the Soult children when they died.'

'When one of them died—'

'OK. If you like . . .' He stared round the café. 'Why don't you visit Madame Soult? Or better still visit her doctor, who is still living in Pontauban.'

Just as the woman in the hotel kiosk had said. She had also implied that the doctor and Madame Soult had had some kind of affair. Maybe there was something there . . . just maybe. I was clutching at any straw. I looked at Lucas.

'Why are you telling me this?'

He lowered his head. 'I am ashamed for France that we cannot find your children. I have given you what help I can.'

'You think I should talk to this old lady?'

'Certainly, monsieur. But first I would talk to the doctor. Ask him about the children after the war.'

He stood up and held out his hand. 'Good luck, monsieur.' The handshake was firm and convincing.

We walked from the café together, into the sunshine, the normality of that square. Traffic and noise and people.

'But surely a doctor will not talk about one of his old patients?' Especially a lover, I thought.

Lucas scratched his groin. 'This is southern France, monsieur. You tell him you have lost two children in the same place.'

I walked back to the hotel, and was told there was a message. A lady. She would ring back.

Estelle. Perhaps Estelle with some news. I could ask her to come with me when I visited Dr Raymonde.

'Did she say when?' I enquired at the desk.

'No, monsieur. And she did not leave a name, but I do not think she was French.'

'Emma?' My heart jumped. Emma was returning my call. Inside me that terrible fear that if I lost the kids I might lose Emma too began to be less real. I took an indifferent meal in the hotel restaurant, and sat in my room, waiting.

The call came at nine o'clock. A guarded 'Hullo?'

'Emma! Darling, where have you been?'

'About this . . . body?' she said. 'What does it mean?'

So Gerald had been in touch. 'It wasn't our kids,' I said. 'Don't worry, honey.'

'I've got to worry,' she said.

'Honey, where are you?'

She hesitated. 'With Jennie Macomber.'

'Why did you tell me not to call?'

'I . . . wanted some time . . . to think.'

'Emma, I love you. For God's sake don't shut me out.'

'I'm not,' she said, but she didn't sound convinced. 'Why don't you come home?'

'Where to?' I asked. 'Jennie Macomber? I haven't given up yet.' I told her what Lucas had dug up, about the war and the Soults.

'That's just an excuse,' Emma said. 'An excuse for you to stay there.'

'For me to what?'

'Stay out there, away from me.'

'What the hell do you mean, honey? Don't you want to find out what happened to Susie and Martin?'

'I'm not sure you're helping that, obsessed with some forty-year-old scandal.'

183

The gibe went deep. But if I went back then what would we ever know? Nothing. Except the little that emerged from the half-baked enquiries of the Pontauban police. I was not prepared to give up, and told her so.

'Who is helping you?'

'Chief Inspector le Brève.'

'I mean apart from the police?'

'A guy called Charles Lucas. Works for a Marseilles syndicate.'

'Who else?'

'What do you mean, who else?'

'The woman who took us to Pontauban? Estelle someone?'

So that was it. I was appalled that she should trust me so little.

'Listen, honey . . .'

'Are you still seeing her?' Emma asked sharply.

'No,' I lied, and knew she did not believe me. 'Honey, I'll call you tomorrow. After I've seen this Dr Raymonde fellow, who may be able to give me some kind of lead. What is the Macombers' number?'

'There's no need for you to telephone me. In future I'll call you.'

21

All the same, I thought about calling Estelle, because I persuaded myself that I needed her to translate. But Emma had warned me off, and I had the unhealthy feeling that somehow she was sitting there watching, like a fly on the wall.

Once I actually dialled the extension at the *Sud Journal-Express* and then put the phone down quickly before anyone responded. I decided to visit Raymonde on my own and hope that the guy spoke English. At least he wasn't difficult to find. Like the others, he was in the address books, and living in the Rue Bartholdi, one of the radial roads leading to the Cours Verdun on the outskirts of Pontauban.

I drove there on the following day, after a sleepless night trying to think what I would say. The familiar townscape of shuttered houses and courtyards now seemed part of the nightmare in my dreams, beyond which, somewhere, someone had claimed my children. Searching for a lost logic I parked under the plane trees and saw the neat brass tablet on the wall with his name: *Le Docteur Anton Raymonde*, it read, *Philosophe; Vénéréologue; Spéléologue*.

I climbed three steps and rang the old-fashioned doorbell in a grey façade.

An elderly woman ushered me into an apartment at the rear of the building. A window on the stairwell showed washing drying in the garden. A cement-coloured door and more steps leading to a second-floor room cluttered with papers. She gabbled at me in French, and indicated I should wait. Although the doctor must have been long retired it

was clear that he still took patients. There were some
ancient chairs and copies of recent magazines.

The old woman returned, and nodded me through to a
study.

The room was dark and shabby, full of papers and furniture. A table, two chairs and a large, flat-topped desk,
behind which sat an elderly man as craggy as an alp. A
lined and perplexed face, as if he'd seen a great deal that
he'd been unable to cure. It was hard to imagine him a
lover, as he shuffled erect. He'd been pouring a saucer of
milk from a cardboard carton for a couple of cats, which
he now shooed away.

'Monsieur?' he said cautiously, holding out his hand. A
survivor in a stained cardigan and crumpled shirt.

I asked him if he spoke English. He hesitated, coughed
and considered. Then suddenly he smiled.

'A leetle,' he said slowly. 'Sit down. Sit down.' It was a
one-room empire, an old man's consulting room with a
coffee machine on the table and a surfeit of notebooks.
'What is the problem?'

It took me some time to establish that I wasn't there for
VD, but trying to investigate the fate of two missing
children. He sighed and commiserated, said he had heard
the story. These things were terrible. He was a father-
figure, a confessor. Even so, looking at his bottle-green
cardigan held together by wooden buttons, his shapeless
trousers and slippers, as he ran a hand through white hair
and hoisted on tortoiseshell glasses, I had little expectation
that he would tell me anything.

'Monsieur, I treated Madame Soult,' he said. 'It was a
long time ago.' He seemed to search his memory. A shaky
hand offered coffee, and biscuits from a Peek Frean tin. The
cats were scratching at the door and he let them back
in. One of them jumped on his lap and sat there purring
aggressively.

I told him about Chenoncey, and the place in the woods.
'How many children died there?'

'Two, monsieur.'

'I believe you knew Madame Soult well. Can you tell me
what happened?'

Immediately he began to close up. 'I am a doctor. You have heard of the Hippocratic oath. I cannot discuss relations with patients, past or present. But . . . I will advise you this . . .' he began stroking the cat, a black and white animal with big golden eyes, as if he were polishing shoes, and the cat purred like a small generator '. . . the children were brought into – what do you say – an abnormal world. You know what happened at the end of the war?'

'I have heard.'

'And at the château?'

'Yes. I have spoken to people.'

He stared into some distant past. 'A pack of wolves.'

'What does that mean?'

He clenched his hands. 'To see your husband destroyed, your home wrecked. To be raped, monsieur. Humiliated. Dispossessed. She turned to me for comfort. You understand?'

Sure. I understood.

Dr Raymonde was now a fidget. Having wound up the cat, he put it down again and urged it to drink more milk. I had a chance to look at the room: as with so much in France there was something marginally strange, familiar yet different, which I could not immediately identify. My eye ranged over bookcases, three wicker wastepaper baskets stuffed with cartons from pre-packed meals, a plethora of framed certificates, the armchairs, a tallboy, a washstand, an empty grate. And then I looked at the books, many of them in English, glancing at the nearest row. Tier on tier, they dealt with sexual practices: *The Elements of Sexuality*; *Deviation*; *Sexual Guilt and Repression*; *Forms of Sexual Conduct*; *Initiation*; *The Mating Urge*; the catalogue went on and on, and I understood now the tablet on the wall outside.

He noticed my discovery and pushed the cat away. He rubbed his eyes behind the pebble glasses.

'What happened to Madame Soult?'

'So. You want to know what happened to Madame Soult? She became a recluse.'

'And then the children died in a fire?'

187

He began to examine some papers on the desk. 'That is so, monsieur.'

'And did she have any more children?'

Raymonde shook his head. 'Impossible, monsieur.'

'But you attended her?'

'I was called. I had some expertise . . . an expertise, that is, in the problems of children. Certain parts of the human relationship.' He waved his hand at the library. 'Monsieur, I am busy. This is not a consultation.'

He did not look very busy, just old and tired. I pressed on to win his confidence. Told him about the circumstances in which we had hired the cottage, the way that le Brève had turned up and shown me the site in the woods, the facts that I had discovered about his ex-companion Elorean, the scenes witnessed by Ninette's mother when the Soult mansion was sacked.

Raymonde listened carefully, head on one side like a watchful hound, then murmured slowly, 'I do not know if the past is relevant.'

'But it might be?'

'Monsieur, who knows?'

'Did the Soult children die accidentally?'

'It is not for me to say, but something I will tell you – those children were very disturbed. They were *isolé*. Isolated.'

'They did not go to school? No private tutor?'

He shook his head. 'Nothing. Only madame. The three of them.' He hesitated as if he would say something more and then decided against. 'It was – how you say – a mare's nest. They were not . . . normal.'

'So how did they die?'

'Who knows, monsieur?' He smiled thinly. 'You must remember that they were only ten and twelve at the time.'

'The same age as my two children.'

Raymonde seemed not to notice. 'I think you must go, monsieur. I am sorry.'

'But I am told, by Chief Inspector le Brève, that only one child died.'

He stiffened. 'I believe two, monsieur.'

'Believe what you like, but le Brève has changed his story.'

He pursed his lips. 'It is of no importance. I do not know. I did not see madame for some years after the fire. She withdrew from the world.'

'But that was thirty-seven years ago.'

He seemed to reflect on time past with those fading eyes. 'Exactly so.'

'Why? Why did she withdraw?'

'Please go.' He began to show me the door.

'Why?'

He hesitated. 'Madame Soult was obsessed. They were her only possessions. They lived very close. Very close, you understand. Intimate. The mother and the children.'

'In the house at Chenoncey?'

'For a time, monsieur.'

'How were they abnormal?' I asked. 'Why did she keep them apart?'

He was now irritated, trying to get rid of me. 'I am a doctor. I cannot answer that question.' He rang the bell for the old woman.

'Were they subnormal? Idiots?'

Raymonde shook his head. 'On the contrary, they were clever.'

'OK,' I said. 'I know where she is living, so I can ask her myself.'

He caught at my arm in the doorway. 'Do not go there, monsieur.'

I teased him. 'Gourdon-sur-Loup? Why not?'

'Leave her in peace, I beg you.'

'Madame Soult. Why?'

'Human life, the end of a life, is a very sad thing. You are a professional man?' He raised his eyebrow in query.

'An architect.'

'Ah. An architect. You may think the world is straight lines. Measured quantities. My friend, it is not.'

'No way. What are you telling me?'

'Monsieur, I must warn you. Madame Soult is old and frail and ill. We all grow old, it is a fact of nature.' He held out his hand again.

'I would like—'

'But you should be warned. She is old and frail. A victim. And she is also mad.'

Mad? Which of us was sane, I wondered, least of all me for being there, still hoping to uncover things that had defeated the police? In the afternoon, when I drove back to the Pontauban Commissariat, one of those ghastly French buildings with caryatids and round windows under a mansard roof, like a small railway station, to ask again about progress, I found le Brève on the steps, on the way to his car. He nodded and came across, shining with perspiration, anticipating my questions.

'No, monsieur. No more news.'

Looking into his face, I knew better than to tell him about my latest researches into the earlier deaths. Instead he mopped his brow and added, 'The enquiries are not yet complete . . . not at all.'

People went past us in the courtyard. 'Meaning?'

'Meaning, monsieur, that I have not finished with you, or anyone. You stay on at the hotel in St-Maxime?'

I nodded. The bastard had still not ruled out that I had somehow killed them. I could see it in his eyes. Those crumpled wet pyjamas on the night of the storm, and perhaps something Emma had said before she left, had confirmed his suspicions when no other motive appeared. He was looking at me as if I was a criminal, and I did not have the means to refute him. Yet.

We do not know the moments at which our fates are sealed, except much later. I came away from that meeting on the steps of the Commissariat, after my talk with Raymonde, and ran straight into Estelle. She was hurrying to her car, across the narrow street, and no doubt had been there on business.

I shouted to her, and at first it seemed that she did not want to see me.

'Estelle!'

She turned, in the little white jacket and yellow slacks,

a sling bag across her shoulder. A bronze skin like toasted marshmallow set off by the ash-blonde hair.

'Estelle. Listen.'

She shook her head. 'It is no good. I can't help.'

Emma had warned me off with her call the day before, but Emma was a long way away. Estelle was there in the sunshine and I had news to impart.

'Estelle. I've seen the old doctor who treated the Soult kids. Dr Raymonde.'

'What did he tell you?' she asked tensely. I rattled off what he had said about the isolated family who had lived in the gîte at Chenoncey.

She shrugged. 'So? It is all in the past.'

'Estelle, I'm going to make sure. I'm going to see Madame Soult.' And, whatever Emma might feel, I needed some help for that. 'At Gourdon-sur-Loup.' I told her about Lucas's visit, and my discovery of her whereabouts.

'I know,' she said.

'You knew?' I stared at her. 'For Christ's sake why didn't you say?'

Her blue eyes smiled at me. 'It is no secret where the old lady lives. She bought an estate in the hills when the courts awarded compensation, after big legal battles in the sixties, for the confiscation of the Soult business. Now she lives there alone. She talks to no one.'

'She must talk to me. And I need you to make sure. Please come, Estelle.'

I remember us standing together in the busy street as if the world had stopped. Her figure beneath the jacket, and the look in her eyes.

'Let's go back to my apartment,' she said.

I should have drawn back then, conscious that I was pulled between two women, one who was there, one not. But grief, and the search for the children, somehow caught up with the exile in a foreign country.

I found myself swallowing. She put a hand to her hair and I saw the invitation in her eyes.

'Jim, please come.' She slipped a hand through my arm.

The loss of two children could have happened anywhere,

any time; but it had happened to me. I had fought it and lived with it and now was offered release.

'Estelle . . .'

We climbed into the little CV and rattled back to her flat, up the cobbled streets of the old quarter. I remember Estelle running up the stairs ahead of me.

Inside, she took me straight to the cluttered bedroom where bits and pieces hung over the bedrail and books were scattered on chairs. Her last change of clothes was still lying there, and she now cast off the jacket and held me. If she had planned to seduce me she would not have been in such disarray.

'Come to bed,' she whispered.

She received me like a goddess, her eyelids lowered, the bedside light switched on. I felt the softness and ripeness, and even as we joined I feared the journey started, the guilt and the anxiety. It was not me, this naked back, but some half-crazy impostor between her sheets.

Afterwards we sat together in the bed, and drank Perrier water.

'Is that better?' she asked, quite calmly.

It hadn't brought them back, or repainted the past, but like a toothache tincture it had relieved the pain. 'I don't know.'

'Don't be hard on me.'

'Estelle . . .'

She sighed, covered her breasts, but I pushed the clothes aside. 'Honey. Help me.' Short-term or long-term, I could not have said.

Estelle began to cry. Full and bitter tears. 'It is impossible. You must go home.'

And I knew that 'home' was Emma. Yet in those limited moments the circles overlapped, Estelle's and mine, blotting out the rest. Then, as the storm passed, she rolled away from me. I kissed the nape of her neck, the salty moisture.

'My darling Jim.'

She lay very quiet. She was still crying. What were we doing to each other: were we totally stupid? I had lost my family and in the ruins found Estelle, but what did she really mean . . . who was she really inside?

It was some kind of need that I could not control. A temporary passion. I could not explain to her that I was emotionally confused, and still loved Emma. I was exhausted and dazed.

Estelle now lay there, hands on her breasts, the damsel who had eaten St George.

Then she sat up. 'Would you like a stronger drink?' The room was stiflingly hot.

'Tea,' I said. 'Do you have tea?'

She laughed. 'We make love and you want a cup of tea?'

'Acquired old British habit.' Some kind of gesture to Emma, but I felt a shit all the same.

Estelle simply stroked her hair. 'All right. You stay there.'

I saw her brown body, trim buttocks and long legs, disappearing into the kitchen. She was still naked.

When she came back, carrying two cups of lemon tea, she had a wrap on and I had nearly dressed.

She came and perched beside me on the bed. 'Why did you dress so soon? It is too hot,' she said.

'I am ashamed.'

'Ashamed?' She seemed truly astonished.

'To have compromised you. To have used you . . .' I hesitated, unsure what I was saying. Not standards, but instincts. I had a watered-down code of conduct, but still one I tried to fulfil. And a picture in my mind of Emma, small and tight, sitting with the Macombers, or maybe back at Ringwood, or maybe . . . where?

In fact I did not know. I realized that I had stayed in France, and persuaded Emma to leave. Stayed on a hopeless goose-chase, which Emma had come to suspect. Something of my resentment, my bafflement, seemed to convey itself. Estelle leaned over and kissed me.

'Where are you going?' A note of alarm.

I had resumed my search, and a normal life. My shirt had fallen on to the floor and I picked it up.

'I want to see the old woman, Madame Soult.'

She stood up, began to dress, fumbling for the slacks and top discarded when she stripped.

'No, Jim. Don't go there.' Her voice was urgent, pulling at me.

'Why not?'

'Because no good can come of it, raking over the past.'

'What does that mean?'

She was white-faced, combing her hands through her hair. 'All you care about is yourself. That is what matters, not me.'

I recognized a cry of despair: finding what had happened to my children, and keeping the marriage intact, were still of overriding importance, and Estelle knew it.

'I like you very much.'

'Like? Like?' Her eyes were full of tears. 'Is that all?'

'Will you please come and help me?'

She mopped her face with a towel as she tried to decide. Then she slipped on her shoes. 'Perhaps. I don't know.'

'Look. You don't have to.'

'Jim. Why ask me? Why visit an old woman? A recluse.' She paused and sighed, trying to make up her mind. Then she said slowly, 'It will not be good.'

'I'm going to see her, whether you come or not.'

She put her arms round my neck.

Somehow I had the sensation that Emma would know, and that one of us would not survive the double entanglement. Where were the smug little standards, Mom's guiding principles, now?

'You are sorry because of this?'

I felt her very close, against my body as if we were dancing together, her head on my shoulder.

'Not sorry. Worried.'

'That is absurd. Listen.' She pushed me away a little, but her face seemed magnified. I saw the wide eyes and mouth, framed by that mane of hair. 'Jim. I do not want to hurt you. You should know that there have been other men, from time to time.' She smiled.

I thought of her tanned body, some place south in the sun. And of Emma and me, doing the Saturday shopping, collecting the kids from school, driving down to the awkward parents. Worlds apart.

I could not rescue her, and yet I owed her something, for rescuing me.

'Oh Christ. It's a mess.'

'What is, please, Jim?'

'This. Us. My kids, don't you understand? At least you still have Jeanne.' I began to fumble with the French, which could not keep pace.

She shrugged. 'Forget it. Forget, darling. All this is temporary. Life itself.'

'No. It isn't.' I didn't like that philosophy. 'What happens, matters.'

'Not in the long run.'

Two conflicting philosophies, but hers was not possible for me. 'I've got to continue searching. Hoping. I must talk to Madame Soult.'

'Then I will come with you.' I could see the strain of the decision.

There was a silence between us. I heard the noises outside again, through the shutters: children shouting and a screech of car brakes. Superficial sounds in the air.

'I think I'd better leave you.'

She took it calmly now. 'When will you go?'

'I'll drive there tomorrow,' I said.

Her face was blank as a wall. She walked over to the window and peered between the slats. No one was watching us.

'Poor Madame Soult,' she whispered.

22

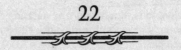

As long as I live I shall remember the morning that we drove to the village of Gourdon-sur-Loup. It was one of those summer days when the promise of heat hangs in the air from first light, bleaching the earth and buildings until they are warm to the touch.

Emma had telephoned several times on the previous evening, so the hotel said, only to find me out. Hanging on there in St Maxime, with the cries of children echoing in my mind. Before this course of events I would not have said that I ran scared: I wouldn't have thought in such terms; but now circling round in my brain were a series of pictures and noises. I was embroidering, making up, but my imagination alarmed me, the force that controlled the image, for what I saw in my mind's eye were two monstrous black figures who came into the gîte during those frightening thunderstorms, silhouetted against the lightning. They walked out of the night through the garage side door, and they were built like Samson, superhuman black figures stalking through that dreadful house, silently, in rubber shoes, their faces indistinct but menacing. The same image in my mind again and again, as they crept past the car and sneaked into the children's rooms, Susie's first, then Martin's. What did they want? What did they do? In my dreams they seemed to carry the sleeping children, drugged and inert. Sometimes they came back for the toys.

I sat eating food that had no flavour, no meaning, in a crowded restaurant, as this illusion faded, only to be replaced by another: this time the children were naked, bound together, in a dark room with hooded men. A smell of burning flesh. One of the supermen was heating a branding iron . . . I pushed away an untouched dish and settled the bill. Unspeakable fears.

I went back to find Emma's messages. They only made me feel worse. In spite of what she had said I put a call through to Ringwood.

Gerald answered.

'Is Emma there?'

'No,' he said. 'I don't think so.'

'You don't think so? Gerald, she's been trying to call me from England.'

'Has she?' He didn't seem to know anything. What you might call the cold shoulder.

'OK. Straight. Is it the Macombers again, or is she some place else?'

'Don't ask me, old boy,' he said in that clipped let-the-natives-have-it voice.

I wondered about trying Bob Dorcas, but it was too late, and why the hell should he know?

'All right, Gerald. If she calls tell her that I rang back.'

And in the end I left it, then and on the following morning because I was picking up Estelle. As I drove into Pontauban I had wondered if she would come, whether she would have changed her mind, but she walked down to meet me seemingly without a care in the world. She looked a million dollars in a lime-coloured dress that set off her tanned skin. She looked cool.

'Hullo, Jim.' She smiled.

'Hi.' Neither of us made reference to what had happened yesterday as if for different reasons we both wanted to forget. Or to ignore it. This was a business assignment, she seemed to say.

The road up to the village of Gourdon-sur-Loup ran north out of Pontauban by way of the Cours Verdun, gradually widening into a surreal landscape of hard, cracked rocks, like the background to a medieval painting. In the harsh sunshine of mid-morning the rocks seemed as old as time. St Jerome-in-the-wilderness country, crowned by the crumbling remnants of ancient castles and chapels, an abandoned and desolate region where crows picked at dust in the fields.

'It's different,' I commented.

'It has always been known as the *pays maudit*, bad country,' she said. 'The people who live here in-breed. A kind of gypsy. You understand? They intermarry. They have too many children.'

It was a thoughtless remark, and I wondered at her heartlessness. Then she seemed to realize she'd hurt me.

'Jim. Forgive me.'

I told her about my dreams. This seemed the moonscape for them. We watched without speaking, as the Ford climbed higher, twisting and turning up the edge of an escarpment where the vineyards ceased, and we saw the plain below, a patchwork of field and farm stretching to the horizon, a blue inland sea. Here and there were small plantations of pines, clinging to the side of the hills, and the abandoned workings of a quarry. We saw hawks in the sky, drifting and curling, and once a rabbit bounded away up the bank, but the country seemed rock and scrub. Rough scrub that even the goats had left untouched. Fierce patches of yellow furze. There was no water.

'For God's sake why should anyone come here to retire?'

'Ask Madame Soult,' she said.

The empty landscape glared back at us, the hills more and more precipitous as we neared the crest, the rocks blasted into huge pieces where the road was marked '*Dangereux*'. Uninhabited farms, the sun a red-hot coin high in a paper-thin sky without a whisper of air. Far behind us the flash of a windscreen, like a heliograph.

Estelle was silent. Her hair was like tumbled ice in the slipstream from the open windows. I was sweating, but she had a frightening ability to become a different person, and now she was distant and poised.

'Why are you so quiet?' I asked.

She looked at me and smiled.

All the old uncertainties were still there, but the bubble between us had burst. You could never put it together again as it once was. In the heat I saw mirages, barriers in the shimmer of the road, and tried to concentrate on what I was going to do. I had to ask about deaths in the past. I had to ask if my children were some part in a ritual.

We came to a bend in the road where the houses began; stone clusters on the side of the hill. I looked for the river that had given the gorge its name, but there was only a bed where water had once run, as dry now as the rocks. A cleavage of broken earth, lined with a few huge boulders, ochre-red and purple, and patches of what looked like heather, between two cliff faces at the end of which was a village perched like a bandit's lair. Two rows of houses crowded a pebbled street which twisted and turned towards a small church in the square.

'This is Gourdon-sur-Loup,' Estelle said. She asked me to stop by the church. As we did so a blue and white police car came up the road behind us, almost as if it was following, but drove straight on.

'Have you been here before?'

'Oh yes,' she said. 'Several times.'

'Where's the Loup?'

'It dried up many years ago. The village was more or less abandoned. Then a few families moved back. Scavengers, tinkers, squatters.'

We parked and surveyed the square. It was nearly midday and the sun was like a hot plate. There were no trees, no screen.

'I think they cut them down for firewood, one bad winter.'

'You don't like this place?'

'I hate it,' she said.

A thin dog slunk inside a doorway. All round the square I could see shuttered houses with scarcely a sign of life. A general store with a tattered awning, a shop selling clothes and shoes, to God knew what kind of custom, and on the other side a grocery with vegetables drying in the sun, which advertised hardware as well, drums of kerosene, forks, spades and shears, plastic bowls and containers.

As we got out and stretched our legs, I seemed to feel prying eyes behind the shutters. Two staring women emerged from the store; the driver of a Renault van was eating a brioche in the cab. Somnolence settled on the square, and we seemed to be walking through an oven as she led the way to the little Romanesque church.

Like the village, the church had seen better times. In its day it might have been attractive, when the stonework was new, clean-cut, and the lines of Roman tile-work had stitched it together. Now it was crumbling, with a moth-eaten, disused air, though there was still a board proclaiming daily Mass. The tower with its squat spire was the stub of a building once intended to be larger, too broad for its height and inset with niches, one or two of which had weathered figures of saints and animals. Over the portico was a strange, headless figure of a man on a horse, the carving erased and scored, and pitted with what looked like bullet marks.

Looking around the square, sheltering from the sun under the shade of the porch, I realized what had seemed most odd about that little piazza. It was not just the lack of trees, or cars, or people, it was the fact that the houses, though shuttered and faded, were, unlike the church, too regular. Small peasant cottages typical of the region but, unlike the ones on the road leading into the centre, these were not patched and rickety, these were . . . almost new. They had been repaired, I thought, and then I examined them more closely, squinting against the light.

'They are all new,' I said.

Estelle nodded. 'Come inside,' she said, and pushed open the heavy door, where the wood had been splintered and smashed, and carefully repaired.

We found ourselves in the nave, blinking to adjust to the gloom. A round window cast strong light at the end of the chancel. The glass was plain, blood-coloured, filtered by the sun into a stain of red which washed over the floor. The altar was stone, with a simple brass cross. On one side was a sedilia, on the other a lamp hanging empty over a big carved pulpit. The nave and the single aisle were wrapped in chilly darkness. The place felt unhappy and dank, as if generations of blankets had been left to dry out inside it. Why should it be so musty, I wondered, on such a bone-baked hilltop where there seemed to be no water? I could see no mould on the stonework, no mildew inside or out.

As my eyes adjusted I realized that the plain interior was very bare. Not even a stall in the vestibule selling postcards, or a 5-franc history. Events seemed to have passed by the little church of Notre-Dame, leaving a handful of rush-seated chairs on the stone floor, and three or four monuments. And then, as I looked at these, I realized that one was bigger, newer than the rest: a copper plate set in the wall.

I crossed over to read it, followed by Estelle, and saw that it was a tablet to the village of Gourdon-sur-Loup. The words were chiselled roughly into the burnished metal, as if deliberately miming a shaky hand; or perhaps a peasant had punched them. *To the memory of the dead of Gourdon-sur-Loup*, it said. *Mort pour la Patrie, 30 Août 1944.*

Underneath was a list of fifty-seven names.

Very quietly Estelle said, 'The Germans destroyed this place. There was a German column, retreating north from Toulouse . . .'

'But this is miles out of the way.'

'The Maquis caught them on a detour. They mined and blew up the leading vehicles and then boxed them in behind. It was to be a bloodbath. But there was a second column, following the first, because they were warned of an ambush; and this second column surprised the Resistance before they could escape to the hills. They caught most of them and shot them.'

'Were they all from here?'

'Three or four, I believe. Probably not any more. But they brought them back here to execute them, as an example, in the square. Then they shot the villagers in the surrounding houses, and blew up the buildings. Only the church was spared.'

'So, who rebuilt the houses? The government? Is that why it was resettled?'

She placed a hand on my arm. 'Jim. Not exactly. It was rebuilt by Soult money.'

'Soult money?'

'Yes.' She ran through the names alphabetically. One of them, I saw, was Marcel Soult.

'Marcel Soult? The head of the aircraft firm? But he was supposed to have died when the mob broke into the château outside Toulouse. Killed on his own estate . . . literally ripped to pieces. For God's sake, what really happened?'

She stood before the tablet, a tall slim figure lost in thought. 'I do not know what is truth concerning the Soults. Not any more. It is said that there was an SS unit bent on hostages, which arrived before the mob. They took Marcel Soult away, then later they shot him here as a reprisal.'

I stared at her in the vault of the empty church where our voices echoed.

'But Ninette said her mother was there. That she saw him torn limb from limb. And those accounts in the newspapers that Lucas found . . .'

'In those times many stories went around. Fantasy fed on rumour. People heard stories and wanted to believe they were there. They had been so quiet in the war when the Soults were preserving jobs that they wanted to claim some glory when it was over. The march on the Soult house became a kind of myth . . . like the fall of the Bastille. Pah! It could fit anyone's heroics, those who claimed they were brave.'

Stunned, I whispered, 'So, what do you think happened?'

She pointed to the tablet. 'It is better to believe the memorial.'

The letters were scored on the metal. 'Marcel Soult'.

'Why didn't you tell me before?'

She shrugged. 'There was nothing to gain. Your researches kept you alive.'

In the darkness of the church I felt myself shivering. I felt that she had deceived me. I began to wonder if she also suspected that I could have killed and hidden my own children. Even whether she had been planted on me by le Brève, to see how I would react. And where I would not look.

'Estelle, don't you trust me?'

'That is a matter for the Chief Inspector.'

'He still suspects me,' I said. Le Brève. Emma. And now perhaps Estelle.

'He is only doing his duty.'

'Let's go back into the air.'

We had forgotten how hot it was in the square. The heat hit us as if we had left a house and found the ground on fire: it reflected from the sunbaked stones, fried our exposed limbs and burned the tops of our heads. It must have been 100 degrees, possibly more, in the noonday glare, enervating, emptying thought.

Standing in that dried-up square, where even the Renault van had disappeared for siesta, and nothing moved, it was easy to picture the scene at the end of the war that Estelle now described, when the retreating Totemtoft SS had clattered up the hill to destroy the heart of the village. A mixture of tanks and half-tracks and a couple of trucks into which the French were crammed, prisoners and hostages together, making that last journey up to Gourdon-sur-Loup.

'Why here?' I asked.

'The ringleader and several of his men – a unit called le Loup – had come from here. In those days it was remote, nobody thought that the Germans would come, and so it became a hideout for the Maquis. But the SS came, on their way north to Normandy.'

I understood a little more clearly the story of the shuttered houses. As if they were living with a nightmare, just like me.

'They didn't blow up the church?'

'No. They were in a hurry. They shot their prisoners in the centre of the square, then dynamited the houses. The church was left.'

In spite of the sun I felt chilled.

'And then Madame Soult went mad?'

'No. Not then. Not until the time of the fires, nine years later,' she said. 'Like you I have done some research. The stories do not always tally, but what is certain is that there was a massacre in this village . . . and that Marcel Soult died here.'

'So Madame Soult had a double tragedy? First the death of her husband, shot up here; and then later the children? Even so, she came to live here. Why didn't you tell me?'

She did not reply, only shrugged. And I accused her.

'You didn't trust me . . . You have been spying on me. You . . . think I did it?'

'No. No. No. I just want you to go away. Go away.'

'Go away. What the hell for?'

We were shouting at each other in the square.

'Leave me alone. Haven't you seen enough? Why don't you believe le Brève? There are mysteries here.'

'Shut up.' She was hysterical. 'Go back if you want to,' I said.

But that would mean my taking her.

'Jim.' She calmed a little. 'What are you going to do?' There was fear in her eyes.

'I'm going on,' I said.

23

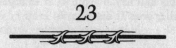

The mansion was outside the village. The road from the square continued over the hill, where the houses ended abruptly, and corkscrewed through the barren, stone-walled fields. Apart from one patch of shrivelled corn, nothing seemed to be growing there except thistles, bindweed and brambles. The sun beat down on the sides of the car.

Far off on the hillside we could now see a château, a plain white mansion, regular and pitch-roofed, standing at the end of a drive lined with straggling pines. It lay well back from the road inside a wild estate of wind-blown trees and self-seeded bushes and shrubs. Even from a distance there was something forbidding about the big old house, a long façade of shuttered windows, with two wings at the sides, at right angles, forming a yard at the rear closed off by a collection of outbuildings. It was set up on the hill like a child's model dropped by mistake.

And then we came to a wall. When the estate was established someone had taken trouble, for the wall was a huge construction, winding round the grounds in an unbroken line as far as the eye could see. It must have been twelve foot high, solidly built in stone and capped with a line of cement. In places the mortar was new, indicating that it was kept in repair. There were no signs of weakness. It was a strong stone wall, making the house a prison, topped by a course of broken glass and what looked like an alarm wire, running along its length.

A place for a recluse. A place for someone to hide in.

We had to drive a long way: it was a big estate, parallel with the road for two or three kilometres before the wall turned off to circle the house at the rear. One small door, barricaded, must have led to a path in the grounds, but I saw nothing more until, on a curve in the road, we suddenly came to the entrance to the main drag. It would have been imposing once, four massive pillars with central iron gates and two smaller ones at the side, all in rusty wrought iron, through which I could see a weed-grown path to the house, out of sight because the drive curved round. Inside the gates were twin lodges of lemon-coloured stucco, in good condition, again as if someone took care, although they must have been old. Doric columns and architraves, I put them in the 1840s, though in these parts you could never be sure, for the style might have flourished much later. It wasn't Richmond Park. Through the bars of the gates, which were handsomely worked, two large German shepherd dogs started barking. To my surprise a police car was parked inside, and I recalled the one that had passed us earlier.

A guy came from one of the lodges and ambled forward, tucking his shirt into his trousers. One of those faces you see in old TV films, pushed in, stubby and jowled, with a cigarette in his mouth.

'*Avanti*,' he waved, a Mafioso Italian.

I got out and strolled up to the gates. The lodge keeper picked up a stick and threw it at the dogs. Peering through the bars, he might have been in a zoo.

'Madame Soult?' I shouted. Estelle was beside me now, trying him in rapid French.

He shook his head, and sniffed, as if he was clearing his sinuses. She turned to me.

'No. She doesn't speak.'

'What do you mean?'

'He says she doesn't see anyone.'

'Why?'

Another burst of questions, and a dismissive reply.

'He says because she's too old.'

'Tell him it's very important.'

'Jim. Let's go.'

'No.'

I began to rattle the gates, which were fastened by a thick

206

padlock on a length of chain. The guard glared back. He was a tough-looking bastard.

'Is there anyone else here? An estate manager?' Somebody else who can understand, instead of this Italian moron.

We stood sweating in the heat. I suppose I might have turned away, maybe given it up and written off Madame Soult, simply classed her as a wealthy lunatic, had it not been for the police car.

'Ask him what that is doing here?'

This time he did not reply. He simply cursed and waved. He stood there angrily, in a collarless shirt and reach-me-down trousers.

'It's no good,' she said. 'Let's go.'

Obstinately, I stood my ground.

'Oh come on. We won't get inside.' Estelle was anxious to leave.

And then we had a diversion. From the second lodge, on the other side of the gateway, two uniformed gendarmes emerged, buttoning tunics as if disturbed from siesta. In khaki drill, with kepis, buckling on side-arm belts. They marched up to the bars, and made clear their support for the lodge guy.

'OK. What's he saying?'

One of them was a corporal, who adjusted his jacket, clipped on a leather belt.

'He wants us to move on.'

'Why should we?' I asked. 'I want to see Madame Soult.'

'Madame Soult is not available. No one is allowed inside,' the corporal said to Estelle. He was young, red-faced, and sure of himself.

I planted myself in front of the gates and confronted them. They looked quite nasty now, lining up with the Italian on the other side, a kind of hit squad.

'Why not? I want to request an interview.'

'Papers?'

I passed my US passport through the gate. He glanced at it and handed it back.

'He says we've got to go.' The others murmured in support.

Their whole manner annoyed me. Off the top of my head I said, 'Ask them where their orders come from.' After all it was a strange phenomenon, finding fully armed policemen hanging round the entrance of this isolated estate, guarding a single old woman.

'Nobody sees Madame Soult,' one of them said half apologetically. Even I understood the finality of that statement. The widow of an aircraft manufacturer, who'd been the wife of one of the richest men in France, a collaborator shot by the SS in this remote landscape, a place she had chosen for widowhood, grieving for the loss of her child or children, and now at over eighty she was guarded by a special police squad, effectively incommunicado. It did not make sense, and I was ready to argue.

'Estelle, ask him how anybody knows that she is still alive.'

'Madame is alive,' the corporal said. 'I'm telling you to drive on.'

'Whose orders?' I repeated.

'Mind your own business.'

'Look. Say that I want to know his authority. Otherwise I shall file a complaint.'

Reluctantly she fed the questions. That seemed to quieten them. The corporal hovered uneasily, weighing up how far he could go.

'The Commissariat, Pontauban.'

'Inspector le Brève?'

He cursed fluently.

'Is he keeping us out or Madame Soult in?'

'Jim. Don't . . .'

'What are they going to do, then?' I said to her. 'Come outside and arrest us?' I appealed to her. 'Tell him I'm looking for two children who have disappeared.' Every cop in the neighbourhood must know that story.

She relayed the information, speaking softly. They nodded and understood.

'Ask them if they've noticed anything strange.'

'Strange?' she said. 'What makes you think that someone brought the children here?'

'Ask them.'

So she put the last question.

They shook their heads. Nobody had come here.

There was little point in arguing further. But I strongly suspected that whatever secrets Madame Soult held were not unknown to le Brève.

We climbed back into the Sierra and drove away, past the end of the wall, across the stony plateau and down to the fertile plain basking in the sun below.

'You should not have gone,' she said.

'Why not?'

'I don't know what you want.' Her lips tightened, but she would not explain.

I concentrated on driving, but glancing at her face I seemed to see anxiety underneath the suntan. 'What the hell is going on?'

'Ask the Chief Inspector, not me.'

'Don't worry, I will,' I answered grimly.

We came to another village clinging to the side of the hills, prettier and less abandoned. There was a restaurant – The Red Hat – and we stopped for lunch, but I was unable to eat much and Estelle was distracted. Several times she seemed on the point of talking, and then pulled back, lost in some private uncertainty.

'Go home to London,' she said.

I wondered about that. There could be only two reasons why le Brève was required to put the old woman under police protection, one more remote than the other. He was protecting her from someone else, or he was stopping her from talking: either way the question was why.

We ate largely in silence, in a pretty room with pot plants and flowers. Estelle was looking at me over the red and white tablecloth. The windows were open to catch any breath of air.

'Will you come back to the flat?'

I shook my head. It was an invitation, and had to be rejected. The bond between us had broken and even the extent of her help had now diminished. Estelle was strained, almost irritable, and yesterday's affair was dead.

She had not wanted to come on this excursion to Gourdon, and perhaps it was better left there. The ash-blonde hair and tanned skin were as beautiful as ever, but she was not mine. Not any more, not again.

'I can't.'

She waved her hands helplessly. She had good hands, long slim fingers, carefully manicured. She raised her glass and looked through the wine to the light.

'You don't want me . . . ?'

We touched glasses and I saw a distorted image of her face. 'It's impossible, Estelle. All I want to do is to find out why my kids disappeared.' Not whether they were alive, I found myself noticing, but why they had gone. The terrible loss resurfaced as I mentioned them. I could not speak.

'What will you do?' she asked after a pause. 'Go home to Emma soon?'

Home was further away than a couple of hours flying time, and she knew it. It conjured up visions of Emma being brave, trimming bushes in the garden, with her parents offering that middle-class solidarity best called Backs to the Wall. It would be tea on the lawn, and come and help with the flower beds, and there was something touching about it.

I wanted to hold Emma again.

Estelle saw that. My vows had been made. Martin and Susie were kids fresh out of school, running to meet me six or seven years ago, at the start of their summer holidays. The year that we went to Greece. 'Daddy,' Susie had asked, 'can we stay together for ever?' 'It can't be like that,' I'd said.

Instead I went to see le Brève, or tried to. I dropped her off in Pontauban, where I had first met her, three weeks before.

'Goodbye, my darling,' Estelle whispered. She kissed me and walked away. I caught the despair in her eyes. Looking back in the mirror, I could see that she watched me until I was lost to sight.

*

I drove down the road to the Commissariat and cursed them all, these hopeless provincial police who had done nothing to help me. Nothing. Their dragnets and their road blocks, their house searches and enquiries had found fuck all. My children had disappeared like the crew of the *Marie Celeste*, and I was bitter. The heat had built up to a point where another thunderstorm seemed possible, like the storms of the first few days. The flags on the castle by the river clung limply to their poles and an air of inertia seemed to blanket the town. I hated Pontauban and St Maxime, hated that house in Chenoncey, and wanted to scream it aloud. The police had come and gone, the press had run their little stories, a team had come down from Paris on behalf of RTF. It had been a five-minute wonder, a couple more missing persons, interesting because they were children, tourists on holiday, but nothing more. Add them to the list of unknowns: cyclists, lonely young women, sexually ambivalent men, found buried or mutilated in plastic bags.

It was in that black mood that I walked up the steps of the Commissariat and asked for the Chief Inspector.

'We are sorry, but he is not here.'

'Then where the hell is he? When can I see him?'

They knew me and felt sensitive; I could tell by the way they looked away and hovered uneasily.

'He is investigating a case.'

'What case? My case?'

The sergeant shook his head. He could not say, but Inspector Clerrard was available. I went into Clerrard's room and confronted his sad face again, grey with some stomach ulcer, his body slumped over the desk. He shook my hand, and his was as squashy as a warm rubber glove.

'I'm sorry. There is no news. We are still trying. You should go home and wait. What about your occupation?'

We went through it all again. Bob Dorcas had said I could have as long as I needed; certainly another week. I found I no longer cared: any ambition had died. But they seemed to think I was staying there because I liked it, and I wondered how much they knew about my trips with Estelle.

'Listen,' I told them. 'Your enquiries have turned up

nothing. A blank. Even the popular papers have given up. What kind of detection is that?'

Clerrard wrung his hands, an empty gesture, as if he was warming them. 'Monsieur, we are doing everything that we can.'

I sat down and glared at him. 'Why is the Chief Inspector sending a police guard to seal off the Soult château, in Gourdon-sur-Loup?'

Clerrard raised his eyebrows. 'You have been there?'

'I've just come from there. Why? Why are armed police there?'

'Madame Soult,' he said slowly, 'is a very wealthy old lady.'

'Then she can afford her own security. Not the gendarmerie.'

Clerrard shrugged. 'It is not my decision.'

'Look,' I said, 'just tell me what is going on.'

The creases on the side of his face seemed to drag themselves down, sadder than ever.

'Nothing is going on, monsieur. It is just a matter of protection.'

Clerrard knew all about it but he wasn't saying, that was for sure; whether he knew why was another matter. For me, getting to the heart of the past was now the central issue.

'I want the truth,' I told him. 'I want to know if there is some connection between my children and those two tragedies in the woods.'

'The Soult children were not lost, monsieur. They were found.'

'Dead.'

'Please be calm.' He winced at the pains in his stomach. 'You are jumping to conclusions . . .'

'Am I? Am I? Why did they both occur there? To kids of the same age? Tell me that!' That haunted, horrible spot that Emma and I had picked. And then I remembered how: through the local agency, the Relais Départemental des Gîtes de France, which had an office in that very town. The booking had been made from London, and I had signed a contract. Why had they selected us, a family with two children of ten and twelve? Who owned the house now?

Clerrard was looking at me blankly, as if he had nothing to say. Perhaps he didn't know, only that le Brève had duty men out there on the Soult estate. I wondered if they stayed all night, and concluded that they probably did. Clerrard wanted me to leave.

'All right,' I said. 'I'll make my own enquiries.'

It was surprisingly easy. The booking agency was still open in the Tourist Centre, a modern shop-front selling posters and bits and pieces, tourist tat, and handouts for museums and galleries. A thin girl smiled nervously, her nipples showing through a sweater.

Perhaps she had heard of me? I had reserved the gîte, and my children had disappeared. There were other people in the centre buying bric-à-brac, but it became quickly silent as they tuned in.

'You understand? At Chenoncey.'

'Yes,' she said. She knew, and offered her deep regrets.

'Just one thing I want to know.'

'Monsieur?'

'Who owns it now?'

You could have heard a stamp flutter to the ground. Everybody pretended not to listen, fascinated by brochures as she said, 'Excuse me, please, I check.'

There was a microfile and a card index, and she flicked through them rapidly.

'A Madame Soult,' she said.

I should have realized earlier, but I felt the thrill of new certainty.

I smiled at her. 'And how many gîtes were on offer in the area around Chenoncey?'

She told me at once. 'None, monsieur. Yours was the only one.' She seemed to colour. 'It is not – ah – a popular area.'

'So you couldn't offer much choice?'

'That's right, monsieur. Most of the accommodation has gone by May. Except the rural locations, away from the towns.'

I remembered telling Emma, when I had made the booking, that there were two other places nearer Albi, but this one seemed what we wanted.

I peered at the poor girl's card index. 'Were there any conditions, any requirements that the owner asked about the gîte?'

She looked again, and struggled with her English. 'Two children would be welcomed.'

Welcomed!

And that, of course, had appealed to me.

'Anything else?'

She frowned. 'Strange, monsieur. They mention ages. That is unusual.'

'What does it say?'

Someone asked for 'service' and no one noticed.

'Ages ten to twelve,' she read. 'But we do not ask for ages in our information sheet.'

'What information sheet?'

'The one we send to the owner, asking for details.'

Later that evening Emma phoned me, loud and clear.

There seemed a new composure in her voice as she asked, 'Any news?'

'Not yet.' I decided not to unsettle her with the story of Gourdon-sur-Loup.

'There never will be.'

'You mustn't say that. Not yet.'

'What are the police doing?'

'Still looking.'

'Do you think they are trying?'

'Yes.' I wondered if the phone was tapped.

'I don't trust them,' she said. 'Come home, Jim. Promise me you'll come home soon.'

'Where are you, honey? Your father didn't seem to know.'

'I'm going back to Ringwood in a day or two.'

'Great.'

'What about you? Are you still seeing that woman?' Her voice was sharp with anxiety.

'Estelle? No.'

'Why did you talk to her?'

It was almost as if she knew. 'She's a reporter.'

'Hasn't she got any other stories?'

'I needed her to translate.'

'Perhaps.' And then, 'Oh Jim. Be careful.'

'Careful?'

'For us both. I'm worried out of my wits. They are dead, Jim, and it's no good pretending. Or seeking comfoi . The terrible thing is that we may never know why. Or who.'

'Don't give up, honey.' There were no props to hang on to, so far as I was concerned, except my gut feelings.

'I love you, Em.'

'Goodnight, Jim,' she said.

It was almost a reconciliation, after what we had been through. If I had only recognized it for that before what was to come.

24

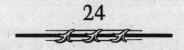

The thunderstorms returned that night, not so violent as before but rolling round the hills of St Maxime. My mind went back to the empty gîte, and the cows in the sodden fields. I lay in bed sweating, listening to the rain beating patterns on the windows of the hotel, overflowing the guttering and eddying down the plastic corrugations of the lean-to in the yard. The storm raged for half an hour, pestilential and persistent rain, creaking with stabs of lightning, and then it stopped, as suddenly as it began. In the silence I seemed to hear their voices, Susie and Martin. And Emma saying they were dead: a statement as definite as a death certificate. I fought against despair like an alcoholic avoiding drink.

In my book you don't cry. But I did then: I hammered my fists on the wall and I shouted out, 'Why? Why me? Why does it have to be me?'

I rolled on my side in that stifling room, threw back the thin quilt and tried to control myself. Where the hell was Emma? I wondered. Why was she so elusive, between the Macombers and Ringwood? She had gone back to England hardly able to speak to me, in a cloud of despair, but that should be over by now. What was she hiding from me, she and Gerald, almost as if she had gone missing too? Well, Emma was on the end of a telephone line. Tomorrow I would track her down, tell her I was coming home, or ask her to come out and join me. We needed to meet again, as soon as my business was over.

*

In the morning I hired a car: my GB plates were too obvious. Immediately after breakfast I found a hire-firm from the yellow pages and ordered a Renault 5, inconspicuous enough for what I wanted. It was another of those sunflower days when unbroken heat bathed buildings and people, washing over everyday life in the small town of St Maxime. I picked up the Renault and parked near the weekly market, where stallholders shouted their wares, and housewives with varicose legs hidden beneath black stockings bargained for beans and cabbage, fish and pork cutlets, ripe figs and cannon-ball melons. As I elbowed my way through the square towards the gendarmerie, enclosed by its spear-topped railings halfway down the hill, I could hear the raw music of a street singer, over the babble of voices. It was some kind of lament, but I could not understand the song.

A hard chorus on a sunny morning, as I walked in and asked where le Brève was.

In the enquiry room it was almost as if I was expected. He was relaxing in the Superintendent's office, marked *Privé*, reading a file of papers. Two uniformed men were sitting with him, but he was bouncy as ever, wearing an open-necked shirt and navy-blue trousers. He looked at me, head on one side, as if I was some kind of object that he was pricing. I half expected him to voice some fresh suspicions about my trip to Gourdon, but instead he came forward with his square hand outstretched, this jockey-sized Maigret. The room was half in sun and half in shadow, patterned in black and gold, with the policemen sitting in the darkened part as if they had turned on a spotlight.

Le Brève shook hands and I felt his dry palm.

'Monsieur. It is a pleasure to see you. I am so glad you called. I can bring you up to date on our efforts.'

I saw one of the gendarmes reaching for a pile of message slips, telling of more abortive searches, pointless interviews, false messages, and cut him short.

'Don't bother.'

He waved his hands disconsolately. His palms were pale, almost beige. 'Please don't distress yourself . . .'

'I haven't come for sympathy.'

He retreated behind the desk, flanked by his two custodians, and I couldn't help thinking that he felt more secure there.

'I've come for an explanation.'

His eyebrows contracted, two grey tufts of hair. 'Monsieur? An explanation?'

I stared back at him, into the rock-pool eyes.

'Chief Inspector. Why are your men guarding Madame Soult? Night and day, in the grounds of her estate?'

'You must be mistaken.'

'Hell. Don't fool me around. I've been there and seen for myself. I've talked to Inspector Clerrard, in Pontauban yesterday.'

He tried to bluff his way through. 'Ah well, then you don't need me.'

'I'm asking for an explanation. Why do you have a police guard on an elderly widow? Madame Soult?'

He pretended to struggle to understand my English, then shrugged his shoulders, implying it was of no consequence. I caught just a whiff of petulance at the same time, but he decided to play it cool.

'Because, monsieur? Because she asks me.'

'Why?'

'Why? That is a police matter.' His mouth set into a thin slit. 'She is a rich woman: entitled to ask for protection. That is all that I am prepared to disclose.' He glared at me as if to say 'I'm sorry you've had a personal problem, but don't push me too far.'

I remember looking at those three blank faces. They could have been a court of enquiry, rejecting a plea of insanity.

'Chief Inspector, one more thing. Are you aware that Madame Soult is still the owner of the gîte from which my children disappeared? What do you think is the significance of that?'

He made a circle on the desk in front of him with his index finger, as if he was rubbing out a sign.

'Significance? I see no significance. It is a coincidence.'

'And yet you guard her?'

'That is a separate matter. A police matter. It has nothing

to do with the gîte. She owns, let me say, several properties.'

'But one happens to be the place where her children were . . . found. In the woods. You told me first two, then one. You lied to me, Inspector, and did not say who they were.'

He cleared his throat. 'You must not confuse fact and fiction.'

'Fact? What kind of facts have you given me, since my children were taken? Nothing. Not even a single sighting, except that poor kid in the quarry, miles away. All your searches and checkpoints, the newspaper enquiries and the appeals for witnesses—'

'Please—'

'What have they given anyone by way of information, or clues? Fuck all,' I said. 'So you end up suspecting me.'

'That suspicion must still remain, monsieur. Until we can prove otherwise,' he said curtly.

'Look. You showed me that place. That dreadful place in the woods. Why did you do it?'

'That is a police matter also,' he said. Some cockiness, perhaps, or some attempt to incriminate me. In an odd way I was grateful, for if he had not done so I might never have known or suspected the underlying currents.

But le Brève was anxious to humour me.

'There is no mystery about Madame Soult. She is old and frightened. She asks the police to help. She pays for protection. That is one fact. In the past she had children who went, how you say, amok. One of them burned himself to death. That is another fact. She grieved for him: it turned her mind. The accident occurred near the house where you were staying, and afterwards she could not or would not sell it. Fact three: she could not bear to go there afterwards. So it became a holiday place. Many people have stayed there. You understand?' As if he was underlining his own words, he said slowly, 'These things are not connected.'

And I did not believe him.

His eyes seemed to recess into the small head. 'I hope you will not do anything stupid.' His two sidekicks were smiling as if to say 'Don't try some crass Yankee move: we'll never trust you.'

'What can I do?' I said blandly. 'I've lost my kids. I've got to clear up the suspicions on me.'

'No one is accusing you, monsieur. The matter is still open.'

Looking at him I read both cunning and resentment into those dark features, before they shifted away from me as if I was not really there. His fingers were tapping the desk and I found my prejudices rising. He was, at the very least, a man prepared to lie and conceal. And the common factor, I realized, between the original death or deaths and my children's disappearance, between the gîte and the secluded mansion at Gourdon-sur-Loup, between le Brève and his old colleague Elorean, the common factor was the old woman whom I had never seen.

I went back to the dark bedroom in the little hotel, half expecting there would be some messages, from Emma, from Estelle, from someone. But there was nothing, and I felt so weary that I kicked off my shoes and lay down on the bed, shunting this debris of knowledge to and fro in my mind. Why had le Brève first shown me the grave where the body was found, and lied and said it was two? Why had he concealed the story of the Soults? Was he still tailing me now? Had the assault in the woods been a mistake or a warning? Was he in league with Estelle in some unspecified way? Who had planted those roses? The questions came and went, and Madame Soult might hold the answers.

First, there were things I wanted, and one by one I bought them, at small and dusty hardware stores on the outskirts of the town. I wondered what le Brève was up to, but I was reasonably sure that no one was shadowing me, although I had that feeling, as on the road to Gourdon, that I was being observed. I took the anonymous Renault on a series of expeditions to acquire a variety of tools from the list in my mind: a pair of wire-cutters with pointed ends and a plastic grip, a small blanket of thick coarse weave, gardening gloves and a tiny torch. I wasn't sure what sort I wanted but I looked for a pencil beam and finally settled for a pen-torch, one of those schoolboy gadgets that clips into Scouts' pockets.

My last item was the most difficult, and one for which I had to make certain no one was following the car. When I had identified the hardware store I drove round and past it three times, just to establish that I was unnoticed in the rather shabby side street of the suburb over the bridge.

The bell rang in the emporium and a woman emerged from somewhere clad in a fluorescent pink nylon apron.

'Monsieur?'

'I would like a collapsible ladder.'

She nodded as I selected the one that I had seen: light aluminium steps that folded into four-foot lengths. It was not very strong, but easy enough to carry, and extended over twelve feet, with small rubber hooks on the top.

'Monsieur is buying a fire-escape?' the woman joked.

That night I ate a good meal for the first time in four days. I tried to telephone Emma, to find, as I expected, that she was not around. Gerald still did not know her whereabouts. As I sat there in St Maxime I felt a sudden confidence in what I was going to do. I drank my coffee with relish, on my own, knowing that outside in the car I was equipped like a cracksman.

Driving back to the hotel, the clouds were thick in the sky, blacking out the stars, and the air was humid. As I closed the lobby door behind me, I caught a glimpse of a woman in the shadows across the street. She was sheltering behind a car and loitering almost like a hooker. I could not be sure, and of course it was absurd, but I felt that she was waiting for me.

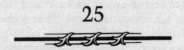

25

It was dark when I went out again, driving up into the hills to the village of Gourdon-sur-Loup, and so cloudy that I seemed to be moving through a cavity cut by the headlights. Stone cottages and witch-like trees reflected briefly in the yellow beams as I slipped past, and then were gone, lost in a world of half-shapes. I could have been on the moon for all the life that I saw as the road twisted upwards, climbing through that desolate valley. It was a buried land, cowering away with its secrets, and two of them were my children.

I turned the corner into the central square of the village at 11.30 p.m. It was still warm, but the place was dead. A single suspended street bulb cast a feeble light on the boule pitch and outlined the three wooden benches with not a soul in sight. The store and *alimentation* were shuttered and deserted, the church spire seemed an alien spacecraft poised on the end of a launch pad. I noted the parked Renault van, a couple of stray cars, an unsatisfactory silence behind which it was easy to imagine lingering eyes and ears. But I neither waited nor cared, driving straight through, on the road out to the château.

I remembered what Estelle had told me about the ambush, the bloody fight somewhere along here when the Maquis had caught the Germans and been captured in their turn. Easy to imagine it now, isolated in the night, to picture the screaming and burning as the SS set about the village, systematically, on the following day. Leaving only the church with its plaque on the wall, and the memories shut in behind those rebuilt, secretive façades. And Madame Soult.

I was coming to the wall now, the long white perimeter of her estate, and somewhere inside the grounds there would be the gendarmes. The wall was a challenge, a parcel I had to open, unwrapping the unknown: the same sort of gruesome excitement as landing through fog in some aircraft.

There was a gap in the roadside opposite the wall, maybe two hundred metres beyond the padlocked and darkened gates. I coasted the car and parked in what seemed a road bay. With the headlights out it was difficult to tell, but some whitened oil drums gave off a faint reflection against the rocks. All I had now was the pocket torch. The night was black as tar as I pulled out the folding ladder and left the car.

I froze as a vehicle went by, the only one I'd seen that night. Then in the darkness I crossed the road and followed the line of the estate. The blood was singing in my head as I extended the ladder and found the trip wire at the top of the wall, above two strands of barbed wire, together with a ridge of bottle glass. This was something I had thought through, with the blanket, the pliers and the gloves. I was taking a chance with the lodge but my guess was they would not expect prowlers at that time of night. Even if the alarm went they might well think it a fault, or something triggered accidentally.

Nevertheless I was shit-scared as I pulled out the pliers and made a single snip in the alarm, then edged the blanket over the strands of razor wire that topped the stonework. Sitting astride the wall I listened anxiously for movements. Voices? Barking? But nothing came out of the dark, so I hoisted up the ladder and repositioned it, clean on the other side. I didn't particularly fancy a twelve-foot leap into space. It slid down against the stonework, and after a moment I followed it, carrying the rolled-up blanket.

It was now 12.14, and I was on the ground. Inside. Above me the alarm wire was broken, which could trigger a search, and I moved to hide my tracks. For a few seconds I risked a beam from the torch, which showed a wood of thin trees, probably self-sown, in the area beyond the wall.

I could not tell how far they went: the immediate need was concealment, in case the bastards came running.

The ladder refolded neatly into its four-foot lengths, but the aluminium was shiny. I cursed myself for not having painted it, and decided to carry it with me, further into the trees.

12.19 already: beginning to waste time, as I stumbled on through high bracken, moving away from the wall. Somewhere up there was the house.

Pausing. Listening. Nothing to be heard or seen. It seemed there had been no alarm, the trip wire might have been dead, or the guards fast asleep. I felt I had called their bluff.

I found I was convincing myself: go on, Jim, fuck the lot of them. They would never think I could break in. But that was why I had come: to find out what was going on.

Humping the ladder and blanket, I pushed my way through the trees, now growing thicker and taller, as if the ground was more fertile further up the side of the hill. Better cover but slower, a mini-forest.

Suddenly, there was the road, the tarmacked driveway up to the front porch, glimmering faintly.

Waiting. Listening again. No sound of voices or vehicles: fingers crossed, I was in luck. Keeping to the grass verge, close enough to the trees to merge into them if need be, I followed the drive as it curved in a semi-circle towards the shuttered house. My whole body had tensed. That house was the bottom line.

A château that no one visited, with le Brève's troops in the grounds, though as yet I could see nothing. I fumbled my way through the grass that ran by the side of the tarmac, slowly and carefully, stray branches stretching as if they were trying to stop me. An eerie, formidable blackness, things rustling in the shadows.

I must have walked for fifteen minutes, still carrying the ladder, trying not to make a sound, before I saw the house appear as a blur at the end of the drive, closed up and unlit. It was hard to believe that anyone could be living inside there: a white portico glowing against the dark. I halted inside the trees. The size of the mansion was visible now, a long two-storeyed building with a classical porch supported by four pillars. Each of the shutters was closed. 12.39 by the watch, and the night was velvety.

When I saw it I was struck by a sudden chill. What in God's name was I doing here, a guy who had lost two kids and refused to go home, reconnoitering in the grounds of a recluse, heiress to the Soult fortune, simply because she owned the place that we had once hired, Emma and I? Or was that all? What about her own lost children, I asked myself, and why was she guarded like this?

I had promised Emma that I was going home, but not before I knew.

I decided to junk the ladder and the other gear, at a spot four trees in, about a hundred metres from the front of the house. A mad old tree, a silver birch with an amputated branch, would serve as a marker. I concealed the ladder beside it, with a blanket on top, and covered them both with bracken.

I was sweating. When I had finished I straightened up again to listen. Nothing moved in the blackness, in that sticky air which promised heat in the morning and more storms in the hills.

With the ladder disposed of I moved up to the château itself. The white columns of the portico shimmered like candles, as I slipped in and out of the shadows. The silence was complete, as if the place was abandoned and the world had shut down, and yet I knew it was not so.

I reached the house, my heart thumping like old machinery. Still nobody came. I made a run across the grass and skidded, panting, close by the steps. The tapering columns were really only painted wood, at the top of shallow steps to the entrance, which had shuttered windows on either side. Only the thought of my kids stopped me from chickening out, but I forced myself to go on, creeping along the façade. Every window was fastened. Someone must close them nightly and pull them back in the morning: old-fashioned wooden louvres like scrubbing boards.

Four high windows on either side of the doorway, without a chink of light.

It was 12.52.

What did I expect to find? Evidence? Black magic? Or police guarding the old woman? I wasn't sure. I reached the corner, where rainpipes ran down the façade like cracks in a rock, and continued round the flank. When I drove past with Estelle I remembered noticing these side wings, with outbuildings at the rear, across a courtyard. I turned the corner of the house: four more rectangular windows and a door in the middle, then the west wing stopped, uncompleted.

Three of the windows were blank. The fourth window held a light, a chink of light through the shutters. My heart revs increased.

I began to edge towards the light. The bottom of the window was about four feet from the ground, so that had it been open I could have looked in easily. As it was I could see only the thin slivers of light escaping through the shutters. But I could hear. This one room was alive; indistinctly through the shutters I listened to a voice. An old woman's voice, weeping and crying and moaning. Madame Soult.

Madame Soult, the mother whose own children had been lost. Soult, the widow. Soult, the grieving recluse. Soult, the owner of our hired gîte, who had specified the children's ages.

I tried the handle of the side door, but of course it was bolted, and I had no means of forcing it. Heavy, panelled wood that would need an army to shift it. The only tool I carried was the small pair of pliers that I had bought in St Maxime.

I searched for another solution, moving on past the lighted room, past the adjoining door until I came to the end of the wing. What seemed like a temporary wall was shored up by a wooden buttress as if the intention at one time had been to extend the house. I was looking at an amputation, an unfinished extension ending in timber struts. Then a gap across the yard to the outhouses at the rear. All as silent as the grave.

I knew that I had to break in, as if my children were urging me, small voices in my head.

At the end of the building, between the scaffolding, I

found another door, no doubt to allow access from a kitchen to the yard. I tried that door handle too. It was either locked or bolted but I took the thin-nosed pliers from my pocket and inserted them as a probe. Maybe the door wasn't locked, or maybe I touched a tumbler; certainly I heard a click. When I tried the handle again, it moved gently in the lock box.

I eased the handle, and felt the door give.

A breath of festering air, as if from a long-shut interior. The door was opening into a black passage, and a smell came at me in the dark.

I had an impulse to run. It was a primeval smell, a whiff of earth and mould, an odour of unwashed flesh, dampness and faeces, and behind it another essence that I could not for the moment define. Was it my straining senses, or was there a whisper of burning?

The door had been only half locked with an old mortice key, and the pliers had dislodged it: I heard the tumbler click into the offset position and the heavy key fall on a carpet. I hesitated in the doorway, confused by the sickening smell, which clearly came from the room where the light had been. And then I stepped inside, shutting the door behind me. A tunnel of darkness, the sensation of being locked in a vault. I gripped the little pocket torch and fumbled to switch it on. I saw the dislodged key on a strip of carpet, and the unfastened bolts at the top of the door. The pencil of light ran ahead of me, along the shadowy passage where nothing moved, but now I could make out doors on either side of the corridor, high doors to big rooms. The first one on my left was ajar and I peered in: an empty scullery or washroom, stone-flagged with heavy sinks and zinc-coated tubs on tables. The strange geriatric stink, mixed with the smell of burning, was coming from elsewhere.

I fought to steady my nerves and moved cautiously along the corridor, past other closed doors. On the floor was a brown carpet, and the walls were the same sludge colour, but the light did not reach very far. I crept along yard by yard, disturbed by that fetid atmosphere, that odour of age and decay. Could it be that my children's disappearance was somehow linked to this morgue? To that sickly, burnt smell?

At the end of the silent corridor I reached the room with the light. The door was heavy, oak, with an ancient brass doorknob, while a second door, immediately opposite, was painted white, as if there might be a nurse, something hygienic there. I paused. The smell now was stronger than ever, a compound of ancient flesh, and burnt paper, and that peculiar stench that I realized came from stale chamber-pots. From the other side of the brown door, faintly but distinctly, there also came a sound of rustling, and a sliver of light. I looked at my watch and saw it was now one o'clock. As I switched off my torch I stood enveloped in a dark and overpowering mystery.

Inside the room the faint noise continued, the sound of mice or paper. And then that wavering threnody that I had heard outside, through the closed shutters, the cracked sound of an old woman singing or moaning to herself.

'Oh, ah, we, wey, ah, so, me, wey . . .'

The sounds had no sense, no cohesion, but they were there as if something she could not articulate pressed to be said.

Very gently, I turned the handle and inched open the door.

It shifted, fraction by fraction, and I heard the lock spring free.

The murmuring continued and as the door moved the stench from the room intensified, the same smell that I had sensed in the passage, magnified now into a smell of decay, of shit and unwashed body, confused by expensive scents which sat on top of the human odours like a spray in a latrine, compounded all the time by burning, that smell of charred paper.

I pushed open the door and looked in.

It was a big square room, almost empty of furniture. High up in the ceiling a single bulb burnt in a light fitting protected by a wire grille. The floor was uncarpeted boards, blackened and trodden with burnt paper, some of it sodden with urine. But my eyes were drawn to the corner, by the outside wall, where a figure with fluttering hands lay in a big iron bed, one of those ancient iron bedsteads constructed like a prison gate. At first I hardly knew that she was there, except for the praying hands climbing up and down invisible ladders. or silently counting time, but as I stood in the doorway she recognized my presence and the cackling increased.

'Ah, we, wey, tor . . .'

Inarticulate sounds, inviting me across to the frail figure prone on the bed under a weight of blankets, and a filthy embossed coverlet. She was a pitiable sight, a head from the cupboard of my nightmares with wide, staring eyes, a thin covering of off-white hair through which the ancient scalp showed, a cadaverous and scabbed face with purple-brown fleck-marks of age and dried sores which she had picked with those long, uncut claws, like the talons of a bird. The overwhelming impression was a sense of decay, in that fierce, wrinkling stench of decrepitude, which caught at my nostrils and throat, and a body past care.

As I stared at her, one skeletal hand seemed to rise from the clothes and beckon me to study her, waving to show me the room, as I looked from her to her circumstances. For this, I had no doubt, was the legendary Madame Soult, the woman le Brève was guarding, the survivor of those traumas of the Liberation over forty-five years before, when she had clung to her children as the mob stormed the house, her house, that other and grander château that had once been a home.

'Ha . . . ha . . .' A rattle in her throat told me that she was aware. Given the state of my nerves, the stench of the room shut around me until I thought I might choke, an overpowering smell of decay, of something out of control. I would have gone back if I could. This was no basilisk who had turned me to stone but a fragile old woman on the fringes of human care, of life itself . . . and yet . . . and yet. As I glanced round the room, standing transfixed in the doorway, I seemed to have heightened senses of my own, as if every detail was being pinned in my mind: the paint flaking from the iron bedstead, the slip rug on the floor by the bed, the only covering over those blackened boards, the one wooden chair, the light shining from the ceiling, a bare bulb in a cage, a grotesque kind of cell with the old woman inside it whose nails were as curving and long as chicken's feet. She hunched there under the coverlet with two mad old eyes watching me, and moaned softly in some private language. I would have gone, and run away for ever from the room and the house, but for one thing.

At first it was a pile of clothes, dumped on that filthy floor as if in some old rag-and-bone shop; I could see her soiled day clothes and a pair of woman's shoes, so perhaps she was sometimes dressed. But there was more. There were two more pairs of shoes that brought a blind rage to my mind. I was sure that I knew them. The trainers that Martin had been wearing, and a pair of girl's sandals that must have belonged to Susie. They lay there now, lined up neatly beside the untidy pile of the old woman's garments. And almost as if she understood, her cackling rose to a new and shriller note.

'Ha ... ha ... heh heh.'

I walked over to inspect the shoes, to touch them and to believe, in spite of the stink from the bed, and as I did so the door behind me opened. I turned but he was too quick for me, a dark figure, the bodyguard or nightnurse who had been aroused at last. And what a nurse! As I tried to side-step, the big fellow lunged towards me with a kitchen knife, one of those square-bladed hatchets made for ama-teur butchers. If he shrieked I do not remember, only the thrash of air as the blade whistled past my head. I ducked and ran. The figure seemed gigantic, dressed entirely in black, a rollneck sweater and trousers, moving formidably. He came at me across the room. I caught the heat of his breath, a leatheriness, but it was the terrible features that etched themselves on my mind. The face, the features, or lack of them: for a moment I did not understand, too busy saving my skin as the figure crashed past me and turned again with the knife. He wound up to come back at me, six feet of darkened muscle, broad, thickset and lethal. The face was aquiline, yellow, Chinese-eyed, unemotional and unreal, and in that half-second before I escaped I was not looking at a human being but at someone in a mask. A painted skin that concealed his nose and mouth, and behind which glittered the eyes of some caged animal.

I yelled and hurled myself through the door left open behind him. He turned to pursue me, chanting like the old woman, but I managed to slam it behind me. The light, the room, the stench, the threat was all forgotten in a rush for survival down that unlit passage. I could hear the monster shouting in the bedroom, but I made the end of the tunnel quicker than an express train. 'Wa . . . heh . . . wey . . .' The madman behind intoned the sounds like a chant in the sickroom, with the old woman responding.

These were the people, I knew, who had taken my children.

I ran as if hell was behind me, slammed the loose key in the outer door and locked it from the outside. I could feel the panels shudder as he tried the handle in frustration and then banged them with his fists. Nothing in my life had prepared me for the hopelessness of the old woman, the madness that lay in the knife-edge and the menacing giant.

Outside, I breathed in the night air in great gulps, then ran and ran through the trees, leaving a nightmare behind me, the terror of an old woman, her crazy, murderous keeper and the sight of my children's shoes.

'Le voilà!' I heard them shout as they saw me. The guys out there.

There was a vehicle somewhere at the front of the house as I tore across the yard and tried to find cover. The car came screeching round the side of the building, spraying its headlights. I caught a glimpse of police markings, saw a jumble of garages and brick outhouses, padlocked and empty, then I was running like a lunatic for the gap between them and the trees beyond.

Somehow they lost the sighting as I slipped through. I could hear them blundering and shouting in all directions: le Brève's boys. Three or four of them, judging by the noise they made, but they weren't sure which way I'd gone, and stumbled over holes in the yard.

The police, sealing off that house. That's what they were, le Brève's men. Why in God's name was I running: shouldn't I give myself up? But they had beaten me up once, and now it was me they were after, not the creature in the mask. A thief in the night, like the one I'd reported in Chenoncey.

I steadied inside the trees, gasping for breath, my heart pounding. The noises were less audible now, as if the pursuit had calmed down. The car drove off: I could hear voices out there, but nothing more.

Exhausted, I began to grope through the trees, from one to the next. The ground now was a tangle of brambles and broken branches, as if the surrounding woodland, like the house itself, was trying to stop me. It was rough going but things seemed to have quietened down, as if they had lost the trail. I wondered who they thought they'd seen.

I decided not to risk the torch, which made the going slower, feeling from tree to tree. As I recovered breath a whole series of questions was flashing around in my brain. If the old woman was mad, why were they taking such trouble to keep her shut up? And if she was rich, why was she kept in conditions that would have disgraced a political prisoner? As for that bloated black figure in the face mask, who in God's name was he, and why did he act as a nursemaid? But, above all, hammering into my mind, why were my children's shoes there? Susie's and Martin's shoes.

I didn't yet know the answers, but I saw that things had been kept from me by le Brève and his boys. My view of le Brève was full of bitterness, but there was no time to consider that. I had to bale out of the grounds.

An evil place. When I stopped running I could feel myself shaking. Somewhere there – perhaps in those rooms that I had run from – Susanna and Martin, Susie and Mart, had died. I clenched my fists, determined they should not get me.

Monstrous trees seemed to be blocking my escape. I was badly disturbed, at the end of my tether, not knowing which way to go, confused by sudden black shapes. They pressed against me under a leaden sky as a breeze began to stir the branches, and I realized that I was lost.

I decided to move to my left. The big drive was on that side, and somewhere there I had hidden the ladder. Still no sounds of pursuit as I trod carefully, trying not to trip on branches, looking for my exit route.

It was then that I heard the dogs: the yelping of the two German shepherds.

The Alsatians I had seen at the lodge gates were getting excited. I began to run again, floundering almost at once into an unseen ditch. The earth slid under my feet.

'Voilà. Hey.' I heard them again, much nearer, coming in my direction, the dogs straining on leads.

Somehow I picked myself up and began to stumble on blindly, stupidly, anywhere to get away, panicking into roots and bushes, falling over.

They were almost on top of me.

'Les chiens. Les chiens. Ici. Ici.'

I knew they were coming up behind me. A blind panic now, to find somewhere and hide. These weren't ordinary police, they might be madmen, killers. I had to survive or else be another victim of that dreadful house.

I blundered into a hole and the dogs heard me again. The barking was ferocious; I imagined them leaping at me, tearing into the flesh.

I pressed flat against the earth. Please God, no. They seemed to be wavering. I decided to move: just what they wanted. I panicked again. I ran like a hare, my lungs bursting and my heart pounding. All I could think of was to get the hell out.

There was a gap in the trees and I made for it. It was the main drag. I caught a last glimpse of the house, like a ghost in the night.

'Voilà.'

Flickering lights through the trees. They had caught a scent of something. The shouting was hysterical.

'Cochon!'

The men at my back came through the wood like tanks. Two of them with two dogs, which flew at my chest, and locked their teeth on my arm. I tried to knock them off, but was dragged over, fighting to cover my face. I heard the men kick the dogs off, then I was hauled to my feet as the police car came shooting up beside us. Two of them grabbed me. I got a crack on the neck, then a blanket over my head, as they pushed me inside.

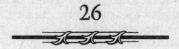

26

It seemed for ever in the car, in practice maybe an hour, suffocating under the blanket. They had handcuffed my wrists, and no way could I slide them off. Disorientated; treated like some kind of criminal. I heard the two-way radio going, but could not understand what they said. The car slowed and manoeuvred; we were coming into streets. It stopped and I was bundled out, across some uneven paving into a warm building. Somebody opened a door. Then they unlocked the cuffs and I was inside a room. The blanket fell off at my feet as the door closed behind me. I saw a bed. Two beds.

It was a light room, with a window showing fair sky, an early-morning sky somewhere. A wooden locker by the head of the bed had my wristwatch and wallet on top of it. I had worked that much out before the door reopened.

It was an armed gendarme, accompanying a dark-haired nurse.

'Where the hell am I?'

It was a small twin-bedded room, white-painted with blue curtains, but the other bed was empty.

'Pontauban. The hospital,' she said in English.

'The hospital? Why?'

'The Chief Inspector asked us,' she said, 'because of the dog bite.'

I sat down on a bed and felt the gash on my arm. The nurse slipped in a jab, dressed it and began to fuss. She took my pulse and pushed a thermometer inside my mouth. Jesus, perhaps I had rabies, just like Emma feared when Susie found that kitten, the first day out. Susie! Susie's shoes!

'Mmmm . . . I want to go . . . Mmmmmm . . .'

The nurse shook the thermometer and tried again. 'Don't talk,' she ordered. 'Monsieur – a bad arm.'

But not so bad I couldn't think. Maybe they didn't realize. There was nothing wrong with my reasoning, sitting there on the bed, remembering what I had seen.

'Look . . . Christ . . .'

The temperature was OK apparently, and the nurse seemed pleased, telling me to sit still. The gendarme perched on a chair by the door. I closed my eyes and listened to the squeak of her rubber soles on the linoleum.

No, there was nothing wrong with my mind. I probed the arm gingerly. Not too bad. Just a bit torn and bruised. I wasn't foaming at the mouth, except when I remembered those shoes. I needed to get out of here. I needed to go back.

Then the door opened again.

'Emma!'

The blonde hair was a little longer, framing the bones of her face. She was wearing a long-sleeved dress, straight from an English summer, and I felt a huge sense of relief, almost childishly happy, at seeing her there.

'Emma?' I found my tongue and my senses.

She sat on the other bed and touched my arm, then ran her fingers over my head, as if she doubted I was real. I held out my arms to kiss her but something drew her back.

'Emma,' I croaked. 'Darling, how did you know? How did you get here, honey?'

'Inspector le Brève,' she said. 'He came to see me. In England.'

'In England?' I knew now why le Brève had gone missing, and why she was hard to trace.

She nodded, grimly. My euphoria vanished: something was wrong.

'Emma, what's the matter?'

My wife, everything that I wanted, my home and my adopted country, everything I had worked and tried for, had come to me by courtesy of Maurice le Brève. I sat there cold.

'You were a fool,' she said. 'I warned you not to be stupid.'

'Emma, for Christ's sake, what is going on?'

'That woman,' she said. 'She told you to go there.'

'Emma. I've found the children.'

'Don't lie to me,' she said. 'They're dead.' Le Brève must have poured his suspicions into her mind, and brought her back to spy on me. The bastard.

'Emma. Listen. I've found two pairs of their shoes.'

'What have you done with them?' she said.

I was appalled. 'Done with them?'

'You know where they are . . .'

'Of course I know where they are.'

'You've killed them,' she said. 'You hated them. You wanted to kill them. To go and live with that . . . woman . . . that whore.'

'Emma, you're mad—'

'No. You are.'

'Honey, you must believe me. I've been up to the Soult château—'

'With that woman. I saw you in the car.'

'I went back again last night. I broke in and found their shoes. That's how this happened.' I pointed to the arm.

'I don't believe it. Where are they? Where are the shoes?'

I tried to explain but her mind had been pre-set. How could she believe a story about that house in the hills that she had never seen, the old woman and the masked figure? All Emma knew was that I'd been there with Estelle, and then been brought in here with a dog bite in the arm, like some criminal, after a break-in.

'I tell you I saw their shoes.'

'You're a liar.' There were tears in her eyes. 'Stay away from me. I hate you. Hate you.'

'Emma! Honey!'

'Don't ever call me honey. We're washed up. We're through,' she said.

'No. Emma, darling, I'm going to find them. Listen to me.'

I suddenly realized – I should have known – that the gendarme was taping us. I did not care.

'You made arrangements to have the children abducted . . .'

'They were taken to the Soult château—'

'You arranged it. That's why you went back there. You secreted them. And they were killed.'

'No. No. No.' I shook my head till it hurt. 'I've been up there to *find* them.'

Emma sat rigid, saying almost automatically, like a lesson learned from le Brève, 'You wanted to stay in France, with that woman, so you had to get rid of them. And then send me home.'

'Emma. That's absurd. I stayed here to search for them.'

'You stayed here because she led you on.'

'No.'

'Oh yes,' Emma said. 'I saw you coming away from that whore's apartment. The police have been watching you for days.'

That bastard, that shit le Brève. I remembered half seeing the woman who had reminded me of Emma last night, loitering outside the hotel, before I set off for Gourdon.

'Emma, how long have you been here?'

'Four days,' she said.

'Four days! And you didn't let me know?'

Four days. She had watched when Estelle had taken me back to her apartment in the rue des Escaliers, after I had talked to old Dr Raymonde, and picked up the first clue about Madame Soult's state of mind. Planted there by le Brève.

'You slept with that woman! Do you deny it?'

I couldn't and wouldn't, but how could I explain not just a momentary passion, but the sexuality Estelle had used to try to stop me visiting the old woman at Gourdon-sur-Loup?

Le Brève was trying to catch me, using my wife as bait. Something to confirm his suspicions. I paced the room. Emma saw the look in my eyes and the gendarme's hand moved to his side-arm.

'Emma. You can't think . . . ?'

'You slept with her.'

'Emma, give me one more chance. Come back with me to find the kids.' I begged and pleaded with her.

Emma had a stunned expression. In a voice scarcely more

238

than a whisper but hoarse with effort she said, 'I don't know any more. Inspector le Brève says that you are implicated. He asks me why you went outside, why your pyjamas were soaked, on the night that . . . it happened. And he asks me why you stay on, when there is nothing to see . . . except . . . that woman.'

'Emma, you can't believe—'

She blew her nose to stop herself crying. We seemed the only two people left, isolated, shipwrecked in a white plaster box in the hospital.

'Why go with that woman? What do you see in her?'

Her lonely words dropped into the gulf between us. There are times when the truth is unfaceable.

'I had to have help . . .' I mumbled.

But Emma was ruthless. 'Why sleep with her?'

I remembered Estelle's simple offer of love, when I recovered in her apartment, after being pummelled by le Brève's thugs. I had been lonely too, and ready to take advantage.

I looked into Emma's eyes, which were troubled by her own self-doubt.

'I don't know,' I said. 'Forgive me, Em. For God's sake forgive me.'

'Forgive? And forget what you've done with the children?' Emma's lip curled in contempt.

'Emma! We're going to find them. You and me.'

'Find their bodies.'

'I don't know. But they're at the old woman's château.'

'Impossible.'

'Emma. Come with me.'

She looked away, her eyes on some distant view. I wondered what she was feeling, whether she really believed that I would abandon her for some woman in France.

'Emma,' I begged. 'Darling, I love you.'

'Prove it,' she said.

'Emma, listen. For Christ's sake. I broke into the place. I saw their shoes.'

She seemed to be rehearsing a speech. 'Inspector le Brève suspects you may have been involved. We saw you go out last night . . . His people arrested you.'

'There was a crazy guy with a knife who tried to kill me. With a face mask of yellow plastic.'

'I don't believe it. You're making it up. You're trying to confuse me.'

'Em. I was nearly ripped to pieces inside the Soult estate. Look at this arm.'

She stared at me again as if trying to make up her mind which story she believed, mine or le Brève's.

'The Chief Inspector tells me they picked you up after you broke into the house. Is that right?'

'They had a pack of guard dogs.'

'Dogs?'

'German shepherds. Alsatians.' I could feel the sting from the bites.

'What were you really doing there?'

'Emma, you've got to trust me. I've been trying to find the children.'

She got up and walked to the window. 'Trying to find them, or sleeping with that woman? That bitch.'

'For God's sake, it's not like that. It never has been.'

'You've wrecked our marriage,' she said. 'Wrecked our love.'

'Please, Em. It's not true. Listen. The children have been there. Taken inside that house.'

She still did not believe me. 'So many lies. It's got to end.'

'Emma, this is insane. I love you. I love the kids. I've been trying to find them, and got beaten up for my pains. All you've done is go back to your bloody parents.'

'You shit.'

'Emma. I didn't mean it like that. I meant that I had to stay. I had to find them. Let's go to Gourdon together.'

'You'd better tell the police.'

'Don't trust le Brève,' I said. 'He's in this up to the neck. All of the local police.' Let them have that on the record.

Emma frowned. 'Then why would he bring you here?'

It was true. The guards could have cut my throat and thrown my bits in the pigswill. But they were still the police. Someone had not followed through during the attack in the woods, and had hauled off last night. Le Brève

240

had a kind of duty, warped and crude though it was, to guard a mad old woman.

I tried to explain to Emma, and told her all that I knew about the children of Madame Soult. The tablet to Marcel and others in the church. The whole bloodlust story, leading to that shuttered mansion.

'Come with me now to find them.'

I put my arm gently around her as we stood together, observed only by the gendarme, staring out of the window into the hospital courtyard. A truck was offloading linen.

'Emma. For the kids' sake let's give it one more try. Come back to the house with me.'

I saw that she was crying. 'If they're not there,' she finally said, 'it's all over between us.'

'Ahem!' The little black-stockinged nurse had returned with another policeman in uniform. 'If monsieur is rested, the Chief Inspector wishes to see you.'

Emma was now holding on to me as if she dared not trust her own legs.

'The Chief Inspector is waiting,' the prim nurse insisted.

I was too busy kissing Emma, in spite of the pain in my arm. Finally Emma released me and stood back. 'He brought me here to see you. Le Brève. He's in a car outside. He asked me to come to you first.'

On condition we were taped, I thought. How could he both condemn and help me? I wondered, and shut out the thought that I was still a suspect.

'He might have done it himself . . . for all I know.'

'Jim, you've got to work with him. You can't afford to be bitter.'

'Bitter? Do you expect me to condone a policeman who seems to be guarding the place where my kids have disappeared? Probably where they are buried.'

'Don't say that.' She caught her breath, but she was changing sides now, bit by bit.

I felt the tug in my arm, through the bandage, where the big dogs had caught me.

'Tell him to go to hell.'

She shook her head. 'Jim, you must talk to him.'

The new policeman was still waiting, twisting his cap in

241

his hands. A smart young fellow with white piping under his shoulder-tab, a kind of aide-de-camp.

Emma's hand found mine again. 'OK,' I said reluctantly. 'Show the bastard in.'

'Monsieur, I am so glad to know you are OK.' He swept in and bowed towards Emma. 'Your lady has worked the miracle.'

'I didn't need a miracle. I didn't need a dog bite or a blanket over my head.'

'Tut, tut. Dog bite most regrettable, so I thought it wise to send you straight to the hospital.'

'Listen. I'm here because your trigger-happy half-wits with the guard dogs assaulted me. What the hell for?'

He flashed his teeth, each shining molar a tribute to diet or capping. 'Why did you run, monsieur? You entered private property. You set off an alarm. And then when they found you breaking into the house, you ran away. What were they to think?' He rubbed his nose. 'Also, we have found a ladder concealed under the trees. What were they to do? You might have been armed. Dangerous.'

'Why are you guarding Madame Soult?'

He looked for a moment taken aback, almost as if he had expected me to understand. His sigh was a trifle weary.

'Surely, I have explained? She asked us to. She pays for protection.'

'She pays,' I said. 'Jesus, I can believe it. Enough to have men on duty round the clock with guard dogs. What is she frightened of?'

'I think you saw her,' he said quietly, striving to find some sympathy. 'She is a frail old woman. *Folle. Folle furieuse.*'

'What the hell does that mean?'

'Mad. Mad as a hatter, I think you say.'

'OK. So you play games with her?'

'I do not understand?'

'Conjuring tricks,' I said, the pain shooting when I moved my arm. I saw the young nurse and gendarme worried that I might flatten him, but I simply stared.

'Why are my children's shoes in that château?'

Le Brève put his hand up, as if he could not believe what I was saying. I felt him touch my sleeve.

'I'm sorry, monsieur?'

Emma stood beside me, her eyes fixed on my face. The little room was crowded with people as a white-coated doctor arrived.

'Their shoes were in the old woman's room. Together with a madman in a mask.'

'Are you all right, monsieur?'

'*Très agité*,' the little nurse intervened.

'Agitated! Chickenshit, Inspector. I climbed over that wall and found out more about my kids in half an hour than you have in a month.'

He took it in slowly, apparently confused. 'What do you mean?'

'Man, they've been taken there. I saw their shoes,' I yelled.

He seemed to freeze into a block of wood. The head and torso rigid, the small feet glued to the floor.

'What do you say?'

'I saw shoes belonging to my children in the old woman's bedroom. That old mad woman that you're so keen to guard. Madame Soult.'

'You . . . saw . . . their shoes?'

'Shoes. That's right, Inspector. Their goddam shoes.'

'How can you be sure?' It was a good piece of acting, it seemed to me. A slow and careful query.

'Of course I'm sure. I know what my kids wore.'

He stood there bemused, his face as blank as a statue. 'You are certain?'

I picked up my wallet and wristwatch from the locker and straightened my clothes. 'I'm sure. And I'm going back.'

Were those eyes cynical or puzzled or just plain devious? I could not decide. Le Brève waved the doctor away and next moment Emma weighed in.

'I want to go with him,' she said.

Something stirred le Brève's mind. He shrugged. 'As you wish.' He motioned to the tape recorder. 'But first I want to hear the tape.' The gendarme nodded, then le Brève turned to me. 'All right. Now, what did you see?' His eyes seemed to glitter.

I told them again. The old woman in the bed. The shoes. The creature in that yellow face mask, who rushed at me with a knife.

Le Brève, like Emma, at first accused me of lying. 'It can't be true. Madame Soult lives alone.'

'Alone! Who in God's name looks after her? How does she get her food?'

'There is a nurse,' he answered unconvincingly. 'A trained woman.'

'A six-foot nurse in a mask, running round with a kitchen knife? Don't give me that crap.'

'Monsieur, you invent stories,' he said flatly. 'This is another fabrication. A false trail.' He turned to Emma. 'You see, madame, why I asked you to come?'

'Will you come out there with me?'

Le Brève looked from Emma to me. 'You are not fit to go anywhere. Please wait until you are recovered. Until you are fully better.'

'No way. I'm going straight back.'

He did not like that: resentment flared between us. Resentment and suspicion.

'Monsieur, I could charge you with breaking into private property—'

'What about charging her for stealing my kids' shoes?'

'Shoes? Don't be a fool. What does an old woman want with your children's shoes?'

'I don't know,' I said. 'But I'm going to find out.'

Those brown eyes got the message. He stood upright, light on his feet as a dancer, paused, then came to a decision.

'Monsieur. So be it. I will escort you back there with a warrant. Under police protection. Tomorrow. We shall pay an official visit. But I warn you, monsieur, if you play the fool . . .'

I was both surprised and angry. Surprised that he was willing to go, angry that he still disbelieved me.

I reached for Emma's hand. 'It's our kids I'm looking for, Inspector. Somewhere inside there. I'm going back today.

Whether you take me or not. And no one on earth will stop me, until I know the truth.'

He rubbed his brow; every gesture seemed artificial. 'Don't try and fool me, monsieur.'

'Jim, what does he mean?'

'I'm going back,' I shouted. 'I want the whole fucking place searched.'

Le Brève was obdurate. 'I have decided. I take you back tomorrow. I must have authority to search the house and grounds. And I must warn you, monsieur, that you are still a suspect. But if . . . a big if . . . what you say is true, you must be prepared for the worst. Please understand that.'

In the excitement, and in that claustrophobic room, I had tried to turn my mind away from the implications of the discovery. 'OK. Let's go.' I was not prepared to wait.

'Jim . . . show me where they are,' Emma said.

Slowly and deliberately, le Brève crossed to the window and opened it, as if to let in air.

'You must be prepared,' he said, 'to face a terrible possibility . . .'

'What possibility?'

'That we shall find their bodies.'

27

No point in life is darker than the heart's despair. Absolute and total despair. I blamed le Brève for not tracing the children, for not saving them. And I feared that I would lose Emma if I did not find evidence about them in the château.

'I will do everything that I can,' le Brève said coolly. 'It will be done properly. Rest assured. You can both accompany the police. But first you should rest. I shall need time for arrangements.'

His glance flickered over my face. I could see he was asking himself whether I had planted those shoes, and what I really wanted.

'Goddammit, Inspector. Doesn't time matter? If my kids are there, I want to find them now. Today, not tomorrow. Don't you understand, man – today.'

His eyes surveyed me as if I was something he would like to break up. And then he nodded. He went outside to consult, and I felt Emma's uncertainty, a mix of suspicion and fear.

'Honey, you've got to believe me.'

She did not respond. She stood there bleakly, while the nurse brought in glasses of orange juice. I tried to think of my responsibilities, back in England, to Emma, to Bob Dorcas, to what remained in our marriage. I looked at her and hoped.

Le Brève returned, and the gendarmes withdrew.

'The doctor says it's up to you, monsieur. Do you feel fit enough to go this afternoon, if I can so arrange things?'

'Give me an hour,' I said.

He inclined his head. 'I will leave an escort outside.'

246

That next hour was full of pain, physical and mental.
The effort of moving my arm at first made my head giddy,
but I washed and shaved, and they supplied coffee and rolls,
which we ate on the side of the bed. We tried to talk of
different things, but always came back to the children.

'I'm scared,' she said. 'The way le Brève looks at you.
The way you look at him.'

'I think he's in this somewhere.'

'Don't say that.'

I pushed away the empty tray, and stood up.

'What are you going to do?'

'Telephone Ringwood.'

'What for?'

'To let them know you're here. And tell Gerald where
we're going. Just in case.'

'In case of what?'

I smiled at her. In case of the unknown? In case le Brève
tried to silence us, for good and all? I wasn't sure.

'My father knows I'm here.'

'Sure.' I'd just about worked that out, but I still wanted
him advised. 'I'll tell him I've found some evidence, at the
Soult château.'

'No. Don't do that—'

'Why not, honey?'

'Because . . .' Her words trailed off. What she meant was
because she didn't believe me.

'I'll phone him,' I said.

I found the dark-haired nurse outside in the corridor. 'Is
there a telephone?'

They showed us an empty office littered with box files
and cabinets. The blinds were pulled against the sun and
my first act was to release them. Mid-morning light flooded
in.

We got Gerald on the line. I told him about the shoes.

'Really?' he said. 'Extra-ordinary.' Jesus Christ, these
Brits.

A long silence while he thought.

'This . . . er . . . château place. How did you come to find
it?'

'It's a long story,' I said, 'but in the end I broke in.'

247

'I say . . .'

'Listen, man. The kids have been there. We're going back with the cops. I just wanted you to know.'

'And Emma's going too?'

'She wants to come.'

In that half-strangled voice he said, 'Take good care of her.'

'I will, Gerald.' I looked at her standing there with me. 'I love her.'

I rang off and we walked down the corridor towards the hospital entrance where le Brève said the escort would be. Emma had that English reluctance to declare too much devotion in public.

'Why did you tell him that?'

'I meant it.'

'No. I mean about the visit to this place. It only builds up false hopes.'

'Perhaps. It's also a safeguard,' I said.

Emma stood silently with me, no emotion on her face, looking out at the forecourt. 'Oh fuck them,' she said. 'Why should we be scared?'

I wanted to grab her and kiss her, if she would have allowed it. This was my true Emma, the little vixen I'd fallen for, no longer the sad woman who had come into the hospital. And, as we waited, Clerrard drove up in a car. 'Ah, monsieur, madame. We have been looking for you.' He beamed. 'We have the necessary authority. In a few hours we are ready.'

Emma was very pale.

'Madame Freeling still wishes to come?'

I looked at Emma and saw there all the hopes that we had had, between us, of cheating mortality. And all our fears. Fears that in finding our children, or what had happened to them, we might still lose each other.

28

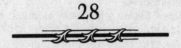

We drove there in a convoy of vehicles, in the evening of that same day. Le Brève, Emma and I were in the first car. The others contained Clerrard and le Brève's deputy, Constant, with a supporting cast. In procession we turned out of the flagstoned courtyard of the Commissariat and headed north towards the hills. The sun was still fierce in the sky. We moved off rapidly, le Brève's whirly-whirly lights clearing a way through the streets, out into that dry, sand-coloured country.

I had to admit that le Brève was an organizer. The support group in the Renault van had picks and shovels and plastic bags, and were kitted up in polyester track suits. We were like a small army, an expeditionary force weaving our way to explore the château at Gourdon-sur-Loup.

Emma herself was nervous, as if she was not quite sure which of us was a liar, or even a murderer, le Brève or me. My call to her father had worried her, in spite of her apparent calm. As I sat in the back beside her she bit her lip and did not want to be touched. I saw le Brève watching us through the rear-view mirror, just as he watched everyone all the time, picking up moves and mistakes.

Le Brève turned round. 'What kind of man did you see, in the mask? Big or small?'

'Tall,' I said.

'And you say he did not speak?'

'Only a kind of shriek.'

'But he rushed at you with a knife?'

'Right. A kitchen knife.'

'And then stayed with the old woman?'

'Yup, like I said. The guy talked to her, then he chased me.'

'Monsieur, I can't believe it,' he said, continuing to stare at me. 'It is incredible.'

'It is horrible,' Emma whispered, as much to herself as to me.

'We shall see,' the Inspector muttered.

The little convoy began its climb into the bleak, surrealistic hills, where the scattered farms scratched a living. She saw the terraced vineyards and small, indeterminate plots. We toiled, with the windows open and the cars accelerating, up the side of the valley which led to Gourdon itself, a country of dust and lizards.

Le Brève shouted over his shoulder. 'This is bad country.'

'I know. Especially in the war.'

'You know that too? The village was almost destroyed.'

Emma glanced at me. I helped her to pull on a jacket, as if she was feeling cold. 'I saw the plaque in the church,' I said.

'Ah!' He scratched his wire-wool head. 'Those were bad times.'

'Especially for the Soults.'

We drove into the square at Gourdon, hooting imperiously. A scatter of people, a couple of cars under the shade of the houses, women in darkened doorways who watched us with stolid faces. We saw the tower of the church which Estelle and I had explored, standing like a Roman castle among the rebuilt houses, its wartime scars still visible on the puny spire. Then we were out of the village, running through that lunar landscape of stone walls and empty fields full of rocks until habitation stopped, and the walls of the estate began.

Le Brève became agitated. He gesticulated at the view. 'Who would want to live here? It is a cemetery.'

'You tell me.'

He became cunning again, twisted round to confront us. 'All right. I tell you, my friend. You live here because you are mad. Old and wealthy and insane, and you shut yourself up in a box because you feel persecuted. That makes sense, eh?'

'And pay the police to guard you? Stick things over people's heads?'

Again that fleeting, sour smile as he turned to look at us. 'Of course. Why not?'

We came to the big rusting gates with their twin stucco lodges. Le Brève must have forewarned them and they were expecting us. A uniformed man on duty just inside saluted and hurried to open them. From the way that the heavy ironwork moved they were quite used to cars.

I tapped le Brève on the shoulder. 'The last time I came through here your boys were trying to suffocate me.'

'I regret the blanket, monsieur. They had orders to be discreet.'

Why? I wondered again. What was so secret about this place where an old woman lived with a madman? Surely the police must know.

We were driving now up the curving path that I had followed through the trees on the previous night. It seemed like a lifetime ago. The ache in my arm had vanished in the excitement of returning, the hope and fear that I would at last discover what had happened to the kids, after so much and so long. Le Brève seemed to catch the mood and waved the warrant that he said he had obtained from the Préfecture.

'They will have to let us search everywhere.'

We saw the colonnades of the house, the blistered paint peeling in the sun like some old southern mansion, as the convoy stopped in front of the steps. Le Brève's men began to fan out, round the sides and rear, as if he expected the mystery man to come running out, but the house stayed silent and unwelcoming. I saw that the shutters of the lower windows had now been drawn back, but curtains concealed the interiors.

Le Brève trotted up the steps, which I realized to my surprise were wooden. There was a temporariness about the embellishments, the portico with its steps and pillars, that gave it the appearance of cheapness, as if they had been stuck on. I wondered again at the house, and why the old woman would have chosen it in the days when she was sane. The effort to make it seem grand, this mansion which

251

petered out in the outbuildings and shacks at the back, might also have been an illusion, an attempt to pretend.

The Inspector rang the bell, which echoed inside the hall, a part that I had not seen. 'We shall go through room by room,' he said, while his men finished unloading their tools.

The woman who came to the door was dressed in widow's black and down-at-heel carpet slippers. She had one of those remote faces that we had seen in the square, peasant-like, bleak-eyed and suspicious.

'Police,' le Brève said. 'I have a full warrant. I wish to see Madame Soult.'

She stared at us: le Brève dapper in a light blue suit, Constant holding a notebook and looking beefy, the slow-moving sallow Clerrard, Emma and me.

'You can't. She is asleep,' she said sourly. 'She always sleeps in the day.'

'And wakes at night,' I added.

'It doesn't matter.' Le Brève pouted and pushed out his chest. 'I will see her. Show me to her room.'

The woman shrugged.

'Are you the nurse?' Emma asked.

'I look after her as is necessary.'

We straggled across a hall that had seen better days, the entrance to a one-time farmhouse, resurfaced to give it airs. A dusty chandelier shaped like a cut-glass pendant hung at the foot of a staircase of polished wood. Arches at either side led through to the wings, but the décor was grey and empty. Our footsteps echoed dully on tessellated mosaics of reproduction classics: fairies and seahorses. Perhaps they were goddesses, I didn't care. All I wanted now was to get this thing over.

'Where is she?' le Brève asked as the woman followed us.

She pointed along the corridor which I had entered from the other end and we marched down it in procession, led by le Brève. As we turned the corner and made for the bedroom where I had found the old woman, I could see the Inspector's nostrils twitching. There was the smell again, but not as overpoweringly nauseating as my first visit; it was remoter, washed down, mildly disinfected. Not the experience that had confronted me.

'Here?' He pointed to the door I had found.

The village woman protested. 'But Madame is asleep.'

'It is of no consequence,' he said. He turned the handle roughly, and we entered.

The bed was still in the corner, with the old frail figure huddled under a counterpane, but the sheets had been changed and the room was clean. There were fresh carpets, good-quality rectangular strips across the floor and the smell of burning had vanished. The floorboards which had been blackened by a charcoal of burnt paper were newly polished and waxed. The room was a sanitized version of the indignity I had seen, and the old woman lay still. I heard Emma's intake of breath.

I went across and peered down, wondering for a moment if this was another charade, some different cadaver, but it was the same old face, blue-veined with age, the cap of the skull covered by that wispy hair, the eyelids stretched like thin parchment over the huge eyeballs. Madame Soult was on her back, like a monument, a sentry guarding the ceiling, and only the shallow rasping of her chest told us that she was alive.

Le Brève stood with hands on hips. 'Well?'

'You must not disturb her,' the woman admonished.

'Shut up. Where are the shoes?'

'What shoes?'

'God damn you,' I said, 'my children's shoes.'

The face was the face of a pumpkin, a turnip, as she responded dumbly. 'There are no children here.'

I began to prowl the room, desperately, looking out of the windows, at the corners, the single wooden chair, the one skimpy chest of drawers, the unlit fireplace. I tapped the heating pipes and they echoed dully. It was an empty place.

'No children, ever? Not in the last three weeks?'

She shook her head. 'Not since Madame has lived here.'

'How many staff are there?' Emma asked.

'Just me and my husband to look after Madame; and Lisette from the village who cleans.'

'For this huge house?' I could see the disbelief in her face, and wanted to shout out that there was something wrong. There must be. There must be.

'Yes, madame.' She twisted her hands together as if she wanted to curtsy.

'And no one else? Then what are all your guards for?' I asked, through Emma.

'Because she pays for them. She wants to be alone.'

Emma was looking at the head on the bed, and she was clearly shaken. She stood there pitying the old woman. 'God help us,' she whispered.

The companion began to fuss. 'If you please you must go.'

'Not before I have searched this house from top to bottom,' le Brève asserted.

She threw up her hands in despair. 'Madame would never permit—'

'Madame has no choice,' le Brève said. 'Come on, let us begin.'

We started on the ground floor, room by room. It was a large house with four front rooms on either side of the hall, shabbily furnished, and forbidding. A home under dust covers, where armchairs and settees of faded chintz were preserved for hospitality to visitors who never came, but who if they did would have been left to confront bookcases of bound editions of Zola, Balzac and Maupassant, or to stare at ormolu clocks on marble tables. The rooms had an air of fatigue, and the wall pictures hung awry: landscapes of distant mountains, shepherds in unidentifiable hills. What struck me about the whole place was the way it had run down. These decaying furnishings at one time had been much prized: the veneered woods of the tables, the inlay work on the cabinets, the gilt of the stained mirrors and tarnished clocks, the faded rugs. Room by room we examined, with le Brève's men tapping the walls, opening cupboards and boxes. The sense of a life forgone tumbled out at us, as if Madame Soult's existence had stopped like the clocks twenty or thirty years before. We came across nothing modern, no artifact that seemed recent; these were museum rooms, a shrine to a life in the past, and that past already old when Madame had been a young mother. No personal mementoes either: we searched in vain for the family photographs, albums of snapshots, pictures of children, toys or souvenirs from younger and happier times. But there was nothing: only the hostile house resentful of intruders and everywhere weeping dust, as if its spirit had gone, leaving the bones of the past. And in this vast ramshackle warren, only three people were living, the servants, whose name was Challendar, and Madame Soult herself.

The front rooms were drained of interest: a shrouded library, two drawing rooms, one that was apparently for dining. On the other side, facing the rear, the spaces were largely empty, half-furnished accommodation that once might have been a nursery, a sitting room, day room, sewing room with its treadle machine, and a bathroom, garden room, billiard room. The billiard table was covered with a grey apron, stained with the rings from coffee cups, and the cues had been broken. In every case the shutters were fixed and bare bulbs provided the light.

Emma shuddered. 'This is an awful place, a mausoleum.'

But le Brève bustled about as if he knew what he was doing, shouting out clipped orders to his little band of police in their green search overalls, as they dived into corners, rummaged in bins of old clothes and pulled out the contents of boxes.

'Remember that we are looking for evidence that children were brought here. Shoes or other items.'

'Maybe some books and toys. A little stuffed dog,' I said. They nodded and continued probing.

We combed the eight rooms upstairs. The bathroom was hors-de-combat and five of the bedrooms were empty. In the others the beds stood stripped: old-fashioned iron bedsteads with mouldering horsehair mattresses and washstands with pitchers and ewers. Again nothing seemed changed, not just since Madame's youth, but stretching back another generation to the youth of Marcel Soult's parents, around the turn of the century. That sense of wasted time pervaded everything, as if they had given up, sold out and gone away long, long ago.

There were cupboards in two of the bedrooms full of Madame Soult's dresses: fox furs and cloche hats, silk cocktail gowns and lamé evening robes, none of them, I guessed, post-war. It was a museum of memories which had not been disturbed for years, with only the moths as curators. The dustiness made us sneeze and it was a relief to return downstairs, to the wing where the old woman was still sleeping. We bypassed her room now and took in the others, one by one. The high-ceilinged kitchen at the end, where I first smelt decay, had been cleaned like the rest, and now had some pots and pans that had seen recent use: an empty milk skillet, dirty plates in the sink, a saucepan of nearly cold *potage* on the solid-fuel cooker.

Emma picked up the used plates. They had a kind of grey rind, a gravy smelling vaguely of meat, lodged on their rims.

'What is this?'

The village woman shuffled resentfully forward. 'Madame's food.'

'And what is that?' An elegant finger, flicking at the encrustation. 'It looks like a child's purée.'

'She eats like a child. Madame has no teeth. We prepare baby food. Meat and potatoes, and she sucks a little.'

The remaining rooms were as bleak as charity, on either side of the passage. Several were abandoned, the others mainly filled with rubbish: suitcases and trunks from the past, a junk shop of mementoes which the police squad pulled open and scattered on the floor while Madame Challendar protested with a series of squawks. Again we were looking at history, tea chests and boxes of memory, packed up and wrapped in old newsprint from 1945.

'Why does she live here?' I asked.

'Madame came here to escape.'

'What did she do,' Emma said, 'before she became ill?'

'She has always been ill.'

'But not like this. Not in bed?'

'Madame did not do anything. She grieves.'

The Challendars' own rooms were on the other side, a

small, self-contained flat which at least showed signs of life: a television and newspapers, cheap pieces of modern furniture.

'Where is your husband?' le Brève challenged.

'He has taken the car to go into the village. He will be back soon.'

When he arrived, le Brève's men picked him up and marched him in like a prisoner. I knew at once that he was not the man in the yellow face mask. He could not be. He was a small, stupid-looking peasant with glasses and protruding ears, white-haired and into his sixties. There was a dimness about him, as if he had been brain-damaged, and he spoke with a hesitant slowness.

Le Brève began to bully him. 'Don't try and lie to me. Who is it that you have brought here?'

The man's oxlike eyes blinked. 'No one has come here.'

'Of course someone has come. Don't lie, I say. We have the evidence.' Le Brève strutted like a cock chicken, walking up and down the room while Challendar sat on a chair.

Challendar looked at him dumbly. 'I don't understand, monsieur.'

'Don't understand, you idiot? Unless you tell us the truth, I will have you put inside,' le Brève shouted. 'Don't play with me. Children's shoes. Two pairs of children's shoes. We know that they have been seen here.'

The potato face was unmoved. 'I don't understand. Your policemen are on the gates. No one has come here.'

We left them, the Challendars, staring blankly at each other in their cluttered living room where at least a clock was ticking and a green-winged canary fluttered about in a cage.

29

'All right,' le Brève said at last, standing in the hall. 'You want me to go on?'

He pushed his chin towards me. 'No shoes? No madman with a knife?'

'I saw them both.'

'When you are under strain, all kinds of illusions . . .' He looked at Emma. 'What do you say, madame?'

But I was as obstinate as old Challendar. 'Listen. Hell, I tell you I saw them. Two pairs of shoes. My children's shoes.'

Le Brève wiped his hands carefully on a spotted bandana. His men stood around waiting.

'What about the grounds?' Emma said.

'Very well. We will search the outbuildings and cellars, and the grounds.'

There were refreshments in the police van, flasks of coffee and packaged biscuits, and we paused before starting. Somehow the house was choking us and even le Brève, it seemed, wanted to get some fresh air. He came and stood with me on the wooden steps outside, morose and suspicious as ever, when Emma was elsewhere.

'Monsieur, I warn you. I have not abandoned my suspicions.'

'I tell you I saw their shoes here. I swear to God.'

He shrugged. 'It is easy to say so.'

'The search is only half done.'

'I would have grounds for stopping, for calling it off,' he muttered.

Emma returned and caught the conversation. 'That would be stupid,' she said.

'Why, madame?'

I saw that she was shivering, in spite of the linen jacket over her summer dress, and the warm air.

'I don't know. It is just a feeling.'

'I am a policeman, not a medium.'

But I saw from his eyes, the cloud of unease that passed through them, that she had hit a mark. His dark face puckered, he rose to his feet and shouted for his crony Clerrard.

'We'd better restart. Before it gets dark. The outbuildings and the yard. Get the boys together, and ask the lodges to help.'

'But Madame is paying them . . .'

'Damn Madame,' he cursed, his voice suffused with annoyance.

We began with the cellars, which were entered from a wooden staircase at the back of the house. They were brick-built and dry and empty, storing a few old planks and a series of broken bottle racks. Perhaps when the house was first built this had been a cold larder, storage for dried meats and fruit away from the fierce southern sun, and then made into a wine vault in more prosperous days; but now it was a brick cave where huge spiders scuttled in corners, a subterranean crypt of old wood and empty bottles. I picked one up and tried to read the label: a long-vanished Château Lafitte of 1953.

There were no footsteps. No shoes.

We came back to the surface and made our way across the yard to the tumbledown outbuildings. Some of them were wooden stables converted into primitive garages, where oil drums had leaked on the floor. The harnesses were still hanging like so many warped tyres with the horses' names inscribed: Cha Cha, Rouget, Belle. Long gone to the knackers. Le Brève picked over the details and told his men to make notes of anything that seemed recent, or used: an aerosol spray of disinfectant, a large drum of weedkiller, a fork with the label still on it and gleaming silver.

'I will ask Challendar to say why he bought those,' the Inspector said.

But it was no use pretending that we had found my

children, and I faced a sound barrier of bleak and sickening despair.

Emma did not leave my side. 'Are you still sure ... ?' she whispered.

'I'm sure.'

She pressed my arm, fingers digging into the bruised flesh. 'Then tell them to carry on.'

I found le Brève still watching us, standing a little back as his men opened the doors: none of the buildings were locked. 'Police work is nine-tenths routine,' he said. 'Checking. Recording. And that takes time.'

She nodded at him, and a tiny flicker of gratitude seemed to cross his face.

He rapped out further commands. 'Come on, boys, all the rest still to do.' I understood, but he turned and explained. 'I am encouraging them.'

As the evening drew on they climbed on the roofs of the buildings, where they would bear weight, and probed with sticks down a well, discovered in the far corner. It was filled in with bricks and must have been an old cesspool, murky with ancient rubbish.

Still le Brève was not satisfied. 'Get down there and pick it out.'

It took them a couple of hours to get to the bottom of the well, digging and cursing. They brought up layers of detritus from the history of the house, sandwiched between the rubble: leather cases stained black by water, rusted pieces of iron, bicycle wheels, bedsprings, axles, a series of smashed chamber-pots, assorted pieces of wood, decaying cloth, a broken rifle, bleached and dried-out ox bones, the skull of a cat, a single and sad golden ring that turned out to be from a curtain rod, a milk churn, a starting handle, the parts of a broken mower.

Spread out on the dry ground it looked like an archaeological dig, ticketed and described, but none of it was recent or useful.

'Damn her,' le Brève said again, and called for powerful torches as the dusk came on.

'Go on,' Emma said.

He requested the Challendars to come back. The elderly

couple, the woman in black, Challendar himself in a battered grey suit, stood awkwardly in front of the busy little Inspector, twisting their hands together.

'When does the old lady stop sleeping?' he demanded.

'Any time, monsieur. Often when it gets dark.'

It was as if Madame Soult inhabited a twilight world where the day never came, and woke up when she need not face it.

'She's not awake yet?'

'No, monsieur.'

'All right. Stay with her. Let me know if she revives.'

Madame Challendar made a face and limped away on her husband's arm. They were a close-knit, secretive pair.

Emma said at last, 'This is no good. I can't see any sign. I don't feel them.'

'We find no shoes,' le Brève said.

'Shoes are easy to hide,' Emma replied.

'Or bury. Like bodies,' I added.

'Oh Jim. Don't say that.' Emma's face was white. 'Let's go,' she urged. 'This place unnerves me.'

But I held back. 'I'm staying until we've looked everywhere.'

That seemed le Brève's ambition too. His squad were getting tired, and two of the men from the lodges had to be returned for the night guard, but he pressed on doggedly.

'Le Brève doesn't give up,' he declared, 'until we've been in, on and under every available space.'

For once I felt like cheering him, but the rest of the outbuildings yielded as little as the well. In a potting shed we found an old bicycle, rusted solid, and garden tools left to rot. They had no garden to keep now, Challendar said, not for some twenty years, since Madame stopped going out.

'You mean that Madame Soult has not left the house in that time?'

Challendar shrugged. 'At least that time.'

The range of sheds was a junk yard, remnants of the old farm. We peered into derelict barns, and le Brève's men climbed to the rafters. They took a series of incinerators apart brick by brick, but nothing had burnt there for years.

Even the old presses for olives and wine had no traces of past harvests. The whole place was abandoned and dead, and the final range of lean-tos yielded no more than a button, green with verdigris, from some *poilou*'s coat.

Le Brève turned it over in his hand. 'Did the Germans ever come here?' he asked old Challendar.

Emma translated. 'He says that he wasn't here in the war. He was in Toulouse. But he doesn't think so.'

Le Brève threw it into the trees beyond the range of buildings, and shone his torch along the roofs. The deputy, Constant, told him the men were exhausted.

'*D'accord. D'accord.*' Like Napoleon he was less concerned for his troops than his own ego, and we could see it dented. He stuck out his chin and glared at me. 'Tomorrow,' he said at last, 'we shall start in the woods.'

They gathered their tools together and tramped back to the cars. A single light was on in the house, in the corridor to Madame Soult's room, but we chose not to go back there. Something about the old woman in that cheerless room seemed to make us all prefer the scented night air outside, where cicadas were whirring and moths came to chase the torch beams.

At the entrance to the house, the bottom of the steps, le Brève paused, with the vehicles drawn up in line.

'Aren't you going to wait?' I asked. 'Until she wakes?'

The dogged face looked at me. I saw the whites of his eyes. Scared. He could have waited, or asked Clerrard to wait, and hoped to unravel from her mumbling some grain of truth or sense; but I saw fear in those eyes, the vulnerability that I had noticed before. He was shit-scared.

'I do not think it will help,' he snapped. 'Do you think she will tell me about a man with a knife?'

'You could ask what happened to the shoes,' I said. Even Emma would begin to doubt me and slip back to le Brève's side.

His mouth was set. 'I will come back tomorrow. We will find nothing tonight . . .'

'You don't believe me, Inspector, do you?'

'I only know what you tell me, monsieur. Tomorrow we will make an end to it.' He gave a slight nod of dismissal and turned away, leaving me standing with Emma. I made a snap decision.

'Honey, go back with him,' I said. 'I want to stay.' My mind was made up there and then. If there was anything in that place left to find, now that I was inside, I was hanging on till I found it.

'No, Jim. No.' Emma's voice quavered. 'It's dangerous. Please don't do that,' she pleaded. 'In any case, they won't let you.'

'Dangerous?'

I called to the police, 'I'm staying.'

Le Brève and Clerrard turned back. 'I'm ready to depart, monsieur.'

'I'm not.'

His even teeth shone in the dusk. 'Perhaps you would like to remain here overnight?'

'Exactly, Inspector. I'm staying.'

As he came up to me, I saw the tired faces of his police squad peering from the Renault minibus. Old Challendar was standing there too, waiting to see us off.

'I don't think you have Madame's permission,' le Brève sneered.

'I didn't have it last night, but she did not object. Only your strong-arm boys.'

He laughed uneasily. 'They have their orders.'

'OK. I stay here until the old lady awakes.'

'You can't, Jim, please.' Emma was pulling my sleeve. 'Let's go from this place. Please.'

'Darling, I'm staying,' I said.

'There is no bed, monsieur. And no food,' Challendar announced. But he did not object.

'I'm sure there will be some coffee. There always is,' I said. He stared at me, then his old face cracked as if I had made a joke, but le Brève found it less funny.

'Don't be a fool. No doubt you are tired. Upset. Perhaps it is the injection to your arm. I understand, but I cannot leave you here, monsieur.' He held out his hand.

'No.' I dug my heels in.

'Monsieur. Please. Come on now, in the car.'

'I'm staying.'

He recognized the tone in my voice, and suddenly gave up. He shrugged. 'All right. You stay. Your problem. We will come back tomorrow.'

'Good.'

'Where will you sleep?' he asked.

'It doesn't matter. I just want to talk to the old woman.'

Le Brève turned to Challendar. 'You hear that? Tell him it's not permitted.' Challendar waggled his head.

Suddenly Emma was beside me, exerting her charm on him. 'He says that it doesn't bother him.'

'But his wife is nursing Madame.'

I heard Challendar's cynical tone. 'He says that you're welcome if you can get any sense from her. She's deaf and mad.'

I turned to le Brève in triumph, knowing that what I wanted now was a further session in that sickroom, one last chance.

But it needed all Emma's courage, I could see, before she herself could face the dark rooms of that house. In a small voice she whispered, 'If you stay, Jim . . . I will too.'

'Madame, I do not advise . . .' le Brève began, and thought better of it. He kicked at the gravel with his shoes, petulantly.

'Honey, there's no need,' I told her. 'It could be frightening. And there is nowhere to sleep.'

'There are plenty of empty beds in all those rooms upstairs,' she said.

'And stained mattresses.'

'What does that matter?' she replied.

'All right. All right.' Le Brève seemed to relent. 'It's your funeral; I'll tell the boys on the gate. If you change your mind you will have to telephone. Understood?'

'Understood.'

'And if anything goes wrong—' He bunched his fists at me.

'Why should it? Why say that?'

He shrugged and turned on his heel, as quick on his feet as a boxer. We watched him, Emma and I, take his place in the first car, where Clerrard joined them. He did not look at us again, as the vehicles started and rapidly drove out of sight. It was so quiet that we heard the iron gates shut, on the other side of the trees. We were alone.

Emma caught hold of my arm. Her lips moved in a kind of prayer. 'Oh Jim. God help us now.'

I pulled her to me and kissed the top of her head. 'It's all right, honey, I love you.' But she was trembling. 'Emma, darling, what's wrong?'

'I can't explain.'

'Tell me . . .'

'Not now. Not here. Let's go indoors,' she said.

The light had gone. That night, past ten o'clock, there was a coolness in the air, as we stood together on the steps, facing the park. A treacherous moon, three-quarters full, cast patterns across the trees, and as I watched the darkness I feared that Susie and Martin were lying out there somewhere. Beyond help, their graves unmarked.

Beside me, Emma was breathing heavily. 'This place is haunted . . . I'm terrified.'

I put my arm round her and realized her body was chilled. 'There's no need to be frightened. I've seen the worst that can happen.' But I was less sure than I admitted.

'Where are the Challendars?' she asked.

'I imagine the old woman is looking after Madame Soult. Challendar disappeared when the cars left.'

'Why do those policemen always stay down at the gates? I would prefer them up here.'

'Because the old woman says so. They must not come to the house unless Madame requests it. Le Brève told me so.'

'That's weird,' she said. 'That's crazy.'

'There's usually a method in madness.'

She hesitated. 'Do you believe that?'

'In this case, yes. Let's find old Challendar.'

The front door had been left open and we entered the hall, the overblown marbled space where I switched on the lights, including the chandelier.

'It doesn't look real,' she said.

The place might have been an opera set. It looked phoney. A staircase with a balustrade curved to the first-floor landing, a grand staircase, designed for ballgowned ladies. You half expected to see faces peering over, but there was no one there. We stood in an empty shell, with the arches stage left and right to the two wings of the house, Madame Soult on the left and the Challendars on the right.

As we stood there the lights went out.

I heard Emma scream and clutch at me. 'It's all right. Some fool has switched them off.'

We saw the skull then, coming through the right-hand arch, a disembodied head, highlighted, the cheeks sucked hollow. Challendar's skull, and I realized he was holding a torch, deliberately or not, underneath his chin, so that it picked out his head like some monstrous Halloween.

'Challendar!'

'Monsieur?' The old man's voice was obsequious as he shuffled closer.

'What the hell are you playing at? You frightened the lady.'

'*Comment, monsieur?*'

Emma had recovered her wits. 'He says he is sorry if he frightened us. He was coming to escort us upstairs.'

As he drew nearer I could see he was carrying candles, and soap and hand towels. But we were so tensed up that any move pumped the adrenalin.

'Why did he switch off the light?' I was now relying on Emma, and it brought us closer together.

'Madame Soult's orders, monsieur. The big light is never to go on, unless she says so. So we use torches, madame, and the little bulbs in the corridor.'

The small naked bulbs that I'd seen.

'Does she ever say so?'

'No, monsieur.'

'Well, you could have warned us.'

'I'm sorry, sir.' He stood complacently before us, a squat and dull-witted figure. A peasant who lived in the twilight of that gloomy place. 'Now, please, I will show you your bedrooms.'

'Where is Madame Challendar?' I asked.

'She is preparing Madame's evening meal. For when she wakens.'

'And when will that be?'

'About midnight, monsieur.' He seemed to relax now that we were speaking to him out of his wife's earshot. 'We keep strange hours here, monsieur. This way, please.'

As we followed him up the staircase, I enquired, 'Ask him why he stays on here?'

He turned, and peered at me quizzically in the torchlight, then at Emma, as if the thought was a novel one. 'Because she pays me.'

'Well?'

'Enough, monsieur.'

It was as far as he was going, before showing us to one of the rooms which we had inspected with le Brève. Each of them had a brass bedstead from an earlier era, and he excavated blankets from the closets. 'There are no sheets available, monsieur, but as this is your choice . . .'

'We understand.'

'The mattresses are old, but good. And firm.' He pulled the dust cover from a double bed and thumped it until it squeaked.

'Thank you.' He chose the end room, and we watched him lighting the candles, which stood in cheap tin candlesticks, like illustrations from *A Christmas Carol*. The uncertain light flickered over the pitcher and ewer on the washstand, where he laid soap and towels, a tallboy and wardrobe of ancient mahogany and the small strip of carpet on the floor.

'There is a bathroom along the corridor, monsieur.'

'I know. Thank you.'

He hesitated. 'I'm sorry there is no meal. But I could bring coffee and rolls.'

'That's all right,' Emma said. She shut her eyes and seemed exhausted. 'It is too late to be hungry.'

'If Madame and I had known earlier that you were staying . . .' He gave an oblique kind of nod.

When he had gone we stood and looked at each other. 'What am I doing here?' Emma said weakly. 'What have you brought me to?'

I took her hand in mine. It was cold. In the half-light her fair hair seemed coloured by the moon. 'I didn't expect you to stay, honey. All I can say is I love you very much.'

She did not reply for a while, but her eyes burned into me. 'This place is full of ghosts. Ghosts that come in the night. I sense them.'

I thought I knew what I was doing. I was looking for a madman. And for two bodies. I knew and I denied it. I could not tell her. For a moment we clung to each other, listening to the sound of the old man's footsteps dying away down the stairs, then a door closing. We were alone.

The urge to have and hold Emma that I had been suppressing all through that fearful search took hold of me then. I crushed her in my arms as she shuddered and cried.

'Jim. No. Don't touch me.'

'Honey. It's going to be OK. Between us. Between us two.'

'Jim. What do you know?'

'Nothing, honey, nothing, except that something happened here . . .' She was shivering, and I draped one of the blankets round her shoulders. 'Why don't you lie on the bed?'

'No.' She sat on the side and put her head in her hands.

'Emma, you mustn't get cold.'

'Jim. Tell me what went on here. In this terrible place. Tell me the truth, Jim.'

'Em, I wish to God I knew,' I began.

She rose from the bed and walked over to her handbag on the washstand. And then as I stared at her, the moon drifted out of the clouds, clearer and more intense. I saw her head against the window, with the light in her hair. But it wasn't her hair I was looking at in the moonlight but the paler ash-blonde of another woman. I saw sudden similarities that had not been evident before. I realized what I'd seen in Estelle, but I also realized far more. As Emma moved her head I saw the skeleton beneath the skin.

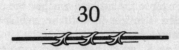
'Emma. Wait here,' I shouted. I replaced the blanket round her shoulders and led her back to the bed.

'Where are you going, Jim?'

'Madame Soult.'

She made no attempt to stop me. As I scrambled and sweated she stood there immobile. 'I'll come,' she said.

'No, darling. Not this time.' I thought of that hideous room, and what could happen there. I was prepared now. 'Wait here. I won't be long.'

This was the time at which he'd come to the old woman the night before, the madman they had not found.

I left Emma with the candles and raced down the creaking stairs, nothing stopping me now, no dark, no dust, no magic, as I tore across the hallway and along the corridor to Madame's room. The bare bulb shone on the strip of carpet, and the smell was there again: not quite the same, but similar, the smell of old flesh and decay, urine and faeces.

A light under the same dark-painted door and a muttering and rustling told me that the old lady was awake. I turned the handle and burst in.

She was sitting up in the bed, dressed in a clean pink nightgown, evidently just changed, for the soiled one was thrown on the floor. Madame Challendar had just finished bedwashing the old woman, and part of the stench came from her sore and emaciated body. The head with its wisps of hair was like a worn-out child's doll, with great staring blue eyes, wide open this time.

The nurse turned in anger, as if she had not realized that I was staying. She screamed at me in French.

The smell was also something shut up, like veal calves that have not seen daylight.

She screamed again, 'Get out.'

But I went over to the bed and touched the old woman's gaunt shoulders. She was in a flimsy nightdress, a nightdress that might have looked attractive on a younger woman. Her neck turned like an old tortoise, the skull already withering, a head staked on a post, but the eyes were no longer crazy. She clapped her hands and I heard the bones clicking.

Madame Challendar had come up behind me, trying to pull me away, but I pushed her back.

'Shut up.'

The smell. A stink of chamber-pots in a crowded space, of defecations. Madame's commode, with the cover off, was unused in the corner.

As I felt the bones of the old woman's shoulders and looked into that sunken face, the tiny pinched-in nostrils of old age, the dry blue lips with their stubble of moustache and the emergent cheekbones of the skull, I saw it larger and firmer, as it might have been in her youth. I saw, as if reconstructed, the clear blue eyes and pale hair that must have made her, when young, a woman to admire. The same high forehead, the same wide oval face, the same fiercely independent eyes.

I was looking at Estelle's mother.

I shook her, feeling the dry skin slide over the withered flesh. 'Where are they? What have you done with them?'

She gave me a lopsided smile as if she was preparing an answer in the inarticulate rage of her brain, but another figure was closing on me, from the half-open door, a figure which had come from the kitchen where Madame Challendar had been preparing the slop that kept the old woman alive.

This time I was ready for him. He came at my back again, the kitchen knife in his right hand, a hideous bulk in black, a strong, heavy man in a sweater and dark trousers, wearing the yellow mask. But he had lost the edge of surprise. As he lunged at me, clumsily, I grabbed the knife-hand and smashed my fist into that Chinese face. His head snapped back on his neck and I knew that the blow had gone home. The pain jolted through my arm, but his was worse, much worse, as I kicked at his groin.

'Awrrgh.' He was in trouble now, and I twisted the knife-arm to try to break his shoulder.

The knife clattered to the floor and out of the corner of my eye I saw old Madame Challendar bending to pick it up.

'Leave it!' I shouted.

Then we were rolling on the floor, where the horror tried to use his weight to get on top of me. But he was hurt from that kick and the fight seemed to go out of him as I rammed his head on to the floorboards.

He levered me away and scrambled to his feet. At first I thought he was going for the knife again but then I saw that he wanted to run.

'Wait a minute—' All the time consciously in my mind I saw the old lady sitting bolt upright in bed in that bare cage of a sickroom, and the potato face of Madame Challendar cowering on the floor where the carpets had been rucked and scattered as we fought.

The mask half turned. He heard me all right, and hesitated, his chest heaving, then made a bolt for the door. I saw that the mask was a fine skin of yellowish plastic, fitting closely over the face, and fastened behind his head. He moved to escape through the door as the old lady cackled and clapped her thin hands together in excitement, but he was too late. I closed with him and pulled him back, but this time he offered no rèsistance, only an eel-like squirming to get away, as my hand tore at the covering on his face.

It was a flimsy thing, little thicker than skin. I heard him squeal in pain, but I didn't let him go, and as I pulled, the mask ripped away in my hand.

There was a face: just. One side had been burnt out of recognition, the other was scarred red and yellow with untreated burns. He cringed and tried to run away, half human, half thing, a mind turned by suffering beyond my comprehension. One eye socket had gone, collapsed into scar tissue, and the nose had been eviscerated, leaving fragments of discoloured bone. The teeth poked through what once had been a mouth but there were no lips, only a macabre gap like the jaws of a skeleton. Instinctively I drew away, but I had seen too much and once again had no doubts that this was the other Soult child, the second of the children that the papers had said were buried in that wood opposite our cottage. Henri Soult was one of the living dead, with a burn mark for a face on one side of his skull, and the skull itself on the other, an impacted mass of tissue. Somehow he had lived on, half blind and tormented for life by that inferno.

Now, as she cackled behind me, I saw why Madame was mad.

As I drew back he escaped like a wild animal, and the shriek was the closest I have come to hearing the truly insane.

'Aee . . . ei, arr . . .'

It trailed away as he rushed through the door, and I recovered myself to see the old woman rocking in bed from side to side, her sticklike hands on her breasts like some mummified doll, while Madame Challendar still crouched in the corner, covering her face.

The room had been disrupted by our fight and the carpets rolled back from the boards. The smell, that putrefying, rotten smell, had come up from beneath them.

But I had no time to investigate as I ran after Henri Soult. For a heavy man in his late forties he was agile and fast, as if he was used to running, to hiding from the light. I caught sight of him turning the corner and sprinting towards the hall as if he was escaping outwards, into the grounds, but under the unlit chandelier, in the darkness of that space, I lost him. I stopped on the edge, listening. Somewhere inside there he was breathing and shuffling; I could hear him moving round in the shadows, the only light coming through a crack in the shutters.

I wanted to get my bearings and tried the light button, but Challendar must have controlled it from a master switch elsewhere.

'I'm here, Henri Soult,' I shouted. 'What have you done with my children?'

My voice echoed round the hall. No reply. Only the soft pattering of his feet in some kind of sneakers.

And then he ran for the stairs. I heard him bolting up the staircase and realized that Emma was there.

'Wait for me, Henri. Wait.'

But he was running from everything, from me, from retribution, just as he had run from the world, and I chased him as if my life depended on it, my heart hammering my ribs.

In the darkness I missed a step and slipped, which gave him precious seconds. I heard him opening doors, and shouting and crying in that agonized subhuman voice, looking for someone.

The doors slammed in succession as he rushed along the upstairs corridor and then I knew he had found and entered Emma's room. A lock clicked on the inside. Sick at heart I threw myself at the panelling but the door was solid oak and would not give.

I stopped in my tracks and listened. He was rampaging round the room. I heard Emma scream. I heard the furniture breaking, the creak of the bedsprings as he jumped on them and then seemed to turn the bed over in a crash of iron that shook the floor I was standing on.

'Don't do it, Henri,' I yelled. 'Leave her alone.' My shoulders hit the door as I tried to smash it open, but it was solid as rock and I fell back numbed. 'Henri, for God's sake. Don't touch her.'

But the crashes and splinterings continued as if he wanted to tear every item apart, to break into tiny pieces anything that remained, while a wild howl of despair, a growl like some caged animal, echoed round in the room and etched itself into my mind.

I made one last desperate lunge against the door, and fell back helpless as the noises suddenly stopped. 'Emma!' I screamed.

And then I charged next door, partly to find a weapon, partly to see if there was any way that I could get in from outside, stretching from window to window.

'Challendar!' I roared for help. But the old house had resumed its silence, sinister and closed in. Yet down there over the trees which I could see from the window, down there by the lodge gates was a party of le Brève's police. It did not begin to make sense as I tried to stop Henri Soult from committing another killing.

'Henri, where are you?'

He was silent now, and I imagined him inside there with Emma, listening, puzzling. What was I going to do?

'Emma! Are you all right?'

A low moan that might have been her, or Soult himself. Another one, half animal, half human.

'Emma! Answer me!' I shouted into the dark.

But nothing came back. Thirty feet above the flagstones I smashed the window open and pushed the shutters apart, but I could hear and see nothing. The next room was another world. A taste of hell. I blundered back inside, catching at a chest of drawers and the marble top of a washstand.

The washstand had knobs sticking out, and as I grasped at them the drawer came away in my hand. The nearest I could get to a weapon. I picked up the drawer and splintered it against the iron edge of the bed. The wood disintegrated, leaving me with the two parallels of the oblong drawer. I pulled them apart and armed myself with a three-foot bar of wood.

I hammered on Emma's door again, trying to break through a panel. The din that I was making ought to have wakened the dead but in the house there was tomblike silence. I wondered if they could hear at the gatehouse half a mile away beyond the trees. Perhaps they had grown used to noises in the night. Not even the dogs barked.

'Emma! Henri! For God's sake, don't . . .'

Don't what? Don't strangle her? Don't beat her to death to add to the other killings? What did I know of Henri and his relationship with Estelle, this brother-and-sister act, so private and so disguised?

'Don't touch my wife,' I screamed.

And then I heard a single shot, a final shattering of wood and the breaking of glass as someone fell through the window.

*

I roared out again for Challendar, but he could not or would not come. My voice shook, and the old house seemed to sway with the echo, but inside the room where I had left Emma there was only silence.

'Emma? Henri?' The words spun round in the air, as I raced downstairs and burst on to the portico.

He was lying there spread-eagled, his head cracked open on the flagstones, blood seeping from a wound on his temple. His neck was probably broken and he lay like a straw man, his raw face turned to the sky, the one eye and the lipless teeth grinning at me. Henri Soult made no sound. I rushed back inside again, and up the stairs to Emma. The bedroom door was open and she was standing there, ashen-faced but alive.

'Thank God. Thank God.'

I clasped her in my arms. 'Are you OK?'

She was trembling but unharmed. 'It's all right, Jim,' she whispered. 'He was mad but he didn't touch me.'

I held her as if I would never let her go again. 'What happened?'

'He came in and locked the door. I think he was looking for someone. When he saw it was me he seemed to go berserk. He didn't lay a finger on me and I ran to a corner. He just smashed everything up. He had a pistol and shot himself. Then he fell out of the window, and I unlocked the door.'

'Jesus Christ. He didn't hurt you?'

'He was looking for someone else.'

The truth struck home. I kicked myself for not seeing it.

'Yes, honey. Come on!'

I think she understood instinctively. Hand in hand we ran down the blacked-out stairs and along that dimly lit corridor to the prison-like bedroom where Henri and I had fought.

The old lady was sitting in the bed, clasped in the Challendar woman's arms, and as I turned towards her she smiled, the empty and pointless smile of someone completely insane and someone at last at ease.

I knew I had made a mistake in thinking that Estelle might be there, and in doing so had lost precious time.

'Come on,' I said again, and we began to run, pounding down that curving avenue between the trees to the gates. They fled past us like masts, a fleet that watched us go and swayed indifferently. We needed help and there were police inside the lodge who lived in comfort, playing cards. We ran and ran, my bad arm now hurting like hell, until I saw the lodges. The gates to a prison.

As we rushed up the dogs started barking. They kept them inside for company.

I battered on the door and heard the first sane voice. *'Hola? Qui va là?'*

I screamed that we needed help. We were staring at one of the gendarmes who had taken part in the afternoon search. He was in shirtsleeves, buckling on his gunbelt.

'Oh, it's you. The old woman get too much?'

'There's been a shooting up there.'

To his credit he snapped to at once and called out to his companion. There were two of them there, one on duty, one off.

'Let's get moving,' I said. 'I want torches and a first-aid kit, a fire axe and a stretcher.'

We piled them into their car and rocketed back up the drive. Henri Soult lay there in the headlights like an abandoned toy. He had not moved.

'Mon Dieu,' the young gendarme said. He pointed at the face.

'Cover it up,' Emma said.

He shifted the body gently, to examine the wound in the head. Henri's one eye stared at the moon. The other gendarme was quietly sick on the grass.

'Put a blanket over him. We'll telephone for a doctor, and the Inspector. The Challendars must have a phone.'

One of the gendarmes stayed. Emma and I, together with the second man, ran up those wooden steps and raced along the other corridor to the Challendars' flat. I pounded on the door.

We heard the distant voice of the old man as he roused himself from sleep and pulled back a chain. He swayed and blinked in the doorway as the uniformed man went in, and I caught the smell of his breath. Challendar drank.

I took him by the shirt and rocked him. 'Has Estelle Devereau been here?'

He shook his head without knowing. His puzzled frown must have been genuine as he blinked in the torchlight. He saw Emma behind me. 'I do not understand, monsieur?'

'Switch these damn lights on.'

'Madame says we must economize. She does not like too much light.'

'Switch them on!'

Reluctantly he complied, fumbling with a master switch on the kitchen wall. The yellow light flooded our faces, leaving Challendar smaller and shabbier, his forehead wrinkled with effort.

'Telephone?' I said. 'Where is the telephone?'

He pointed dumbly through to the living room behind him where the debris of an evening meal, soup dishes and a wine bottle, still littered the table.

The gendarme pushed through to the telephone while Emma and I confronted Challendar. 'Madame's daughter? Was she called Estelle?'

He shook his head again, his face crumbling.

'Who is she? Who is she?' I banged his back against the wall until his eyes popped.

'Hélène . . .' he mumbled.

'OK.' I looked into his frightened eyes. 'Has Hélène Soult been here?'

He swallowed. He hung his head. 'Two days ago, monsieur.'

'Two days?'

'Yes, monsieur.' He seemed to have no trouble remembering. 'In the evening.'

'Jesus Christ!' She must have gone there as soon as she left me, after our trip to the château, when we got only as far as the gates. When she said goodbye in Pontauban she must have driven straight back. Challendar had let her in, down at the gates, driving a borrowed saloon car. A big car, he said, not like the little green Citroën that she usually used. But had she come for the kids, and were they still alive?

As I released my hold he collapsed in a chair and buried his head in his hands.

'What did she want?'

'I do not know, monsieur.'

She must have known the game was up as soon as I visited Gourdon. And what a game: to conspire with that half-mad brother to steal two children. Then the shock of meeting me, of being told to interview me, of having me ask for help.

The questions reeled in our minds. But why, why, why?

I stood there stunned by the double revelation of who she was and what she had done, sure now that I would find something, the bodies, the evidence, my children. But where?

The young gendarme returned. 'The Inspector is coming at once. With an ambulance.'

I remember nodding distractedly but the sequence of events eludes me. We must have continued talking, trying to cross-question Challendar. The gendarme remembered too: the silver-haired woman who had driven up in a Peugeot 604. Challendar had asked them to let her through. She had seemed very calm as she drove away an hour later with a load in the back.

'A load?'

'Under blankets, monsieur.' Just like me. Nobody was allowed to pry into what went in or out of the Soult estate. That was a standing order, from Madame herself.

They had saluted and opened the gates.

'Dead or alive?'

He shrugged.

Jesus Christ. 'How long will the Inspector be?'

'Maybe an hour. Perhaps a little more.'

Even so I could not wait, whatever lay in store. I turned to the gendarme. 'Will you come with me?'

He was a tough young man with a cowpat of cropped hair, but I could see him blench at the thought of that skeleton head and the old woman. His stomach had already thrown up but he was game. 'Yes, sir,' he said.

We left Challendar sitting there and switched on all the lights so that the mansion blazed. It was comforting to see the ghosts recede into the shadows as we crossed the echoing hall under the big chandelier. The staircase looked somehow smaller, less ominous.

We went back to the old woman's room, without another glance at the body lying under its blanket. As we came closer the familiar smell returned, wafting along the corridor towards us, that stench of putrefaction.

'Hurry!' Emma urged.

'My God,' the young man said, holding his nose with one hand and his pistol in the other.

'Nothing to be scared of,' I reassured him. I knew what it was now, or at least what I thought it was: the smell of every concentration camp in the world, of old shit and blocked drains and human degradation. The smell of an underground, airless, unlit prison.

The policeman kicked open the door and we entered the old woman's room.

Madame Soult was lying on the bed, apparently asleep, as if she'd fallen back exhausted. The nurse had pulled up the bedclothes and sat there on the only chair, an elderly, broken-backed figure holding her charge's scrawny hand. She scarcely moved as we came in, and the only sound was the rasping of the patient's breath in her chest.

It was of no consequence now, and we did not even look at them. What caught the eye were the rugs that my fight with Henri Soult had scattered. The rugs so carefully placed on that newly polished floor which had been covered with burnt and blackened paper the first time I had seen it. Now I understood why: both the carpets and the paper served to conceal the floorboards. On my first visit the charred fragments had been burnt to reduce the stench, perhaps to give an impression of pyromania. Tonight they would have known that le Brève was coming, and cleaned the bare boards. On top of them were fresh rugs.

But the rugs had been displaced by our struggle. Close by Madame Soult's bed, where no one would want to look, was the square cover of a trapdoor.

31

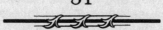

I was on my knees like a madman, Emma screaming 'What's down there?' as we pulled at the flap in the floor, while old Madame Challendar crouched on the chair, like some ancient tricoteuse.

'Monsieur, perhaps we should wait . . .' the young gendarme said, panic-stricken, 'for the Inspector?'

'They were my children.'

The flap slipped upwards easily, and the smell poured out again, but it was almost as if my senses were attuned. I scarcely noticed, though the gendarme held back. Emma was strong now. 'I want to know,' she cried.

We peered into a small pit, like an inspection chamber, with wooden steps running down, into the darkness. 'Give me your torch,' she said to the gendarme.

We were terrified of what we should find but we could not stop. As she flashed the light to the bottom I saw a brick tunnel, ten or twelve feet below, sloping inwards.

I slipped my legs over and began to climb down.

I was shaking as I touched the bottom and found impacted earth, cold and dry. Emma was right behind me. We were under the foundations of the original farmhouse: a series of interconnecting chambers. As the torch beam shifted along them, I saw that they were wired, that there were bulbs and a light switch, high up on the crude brickwork. Whoever had been shut down there at least had not been in the dark, and I thanked God for that.

As the lights came on we realized that there were several rooms, without doors, constructed from timber supports, and simply furnished. The smell was the smell of confinement, of defecation and urine for which there had been no outlet.

We walked through from room to room, four rooms in all. In the first were the beds, nearest to the ladder and air: two camp beds strewn with an assortment of clothes, blankets and unwashed sheets. But no sign of the children.

The two beds lined the alcoves on either side of a passage that connected all four rooms. They fitted like bunks in a cabin, but there were no windows: only the single light of a low-powered bulb.

We walked through to the second room: a living space with a table on one side and three chairs on the other. On the table a television set and a few books. Children's books in French and English, recent comics, a copy of the *Sud Journal-Express*. And Chocolate Dog. The detritus of living: an empty cereal packet, a ball-point pen and scribbles on paper. As I picked up the paper I recognized Susie's writing.

Emma screamed and picked up the woolly toy, hugging it to her.

But the children had gone.

The third room had been a kitchen, with a small electric oven, enough to heat up a meal, but it was cold, and there was no sign of food. Cheap china plates and a series of mugs, all of them washed and clean. In a small cupboard I found salt and pepper, a bag of sugar and a jar of instant coffee, along with a kettle, a bowl, and a container for water. There was no sink or taps.

And then, inexorably, I was drawn to the final room, where the brickwork stopped at a wall that glistened green with damp, seeping through from the earth outside. The place smelt like a sewer, the rank stink of defecation in a confined space. Airless. A pair of wooden latrines, buckets on the earth floor, covered with pieces of paper. A quagmire of sewage, concealed behind a blanket. There was no door and the smell wafted through. Whoever had been shut up there had had to live with the stench that crept its way up the stairs and into the mad woman's room, no matter how much they disguised it with burning paper.

The underground prison was empty. If they had ever

been there they were gone: our keepsakes remained, those scribbled-on sheets of paper, and Chocolate Dog.

The young gendarme had followed us along the passage. 'Mon Dieu. C'est impossible,' he kept muttering.

'It is an underground prison. And worse, a shit-house.' They had burnt paper to hide it, in memory of some past horror, or in retribution.

'You find something?' His face was the colour of chalk as he looked at Emma, still clutching the dog. She nodded, speechless.

'No,' I said. 'Not what we want. She's taken them away.' Or killed them, I dared not add.

'Monsieur, do not touch,' he said, his police training reasserting itself. 'You must come upstairs and wait. We'll take this place apart now.'

Slowly we retraced our steps, from the latrines and the kitchen through to the living space and the bunks in the bedroom. A kind of air-raid shelter. When we emerged the nurse had gone, leaving the old woman wheezing away on the bed. I suppose the Challendars knew that when Madame Soult went to sleep it was over for the time being, that terrible haunting laugh and the mindless chatter.

We left the sickroom as it was, the entrance flap closed, the carpet pushed over it and the naked light in its cage above the old woman.

Le Brève arrived as we tried to question the Challendars. I did not want to lose any time, but they were confused and obdurate, and also scared. The Chief Inspector wore a rollneck sweater of thin black cotton that seemed to have been pulled on in a hurry over a beach shirt and trousers. His brown face was set hard.

'I've found the gun,' he said. 'Suicide or murder?' He stared at me. 'And a broken neck it seems. Where is the old woman?'

'Where she always is.'

We were crowded into the Challendars' apartment, with the two old peasants placed under close arrest.

'The body. What happened?' le Brève asked.

'We had a fight. He came at me with a knife, just as he did before, but when I pulled off the mask he ran away.'

He nodded. 'A terrible face.'

'It was no reason for stealing my children,' I said. 'And in God's name why?'

'What happened then?'

'He ran upstairs to find his sister, Estelle or Hélène.'

I heard le Brève inhale. Then he said slowly, 'How much do you know?'

I swore at him. 'Jesus Christ. How much do you know, Inspector?'

He seemed to be fighting for calm, his dark eyes flickering over me, bleakly aware of the Challendars sitting there listening and half understanding.

'Monsieur, madame, a word outside,' he said.

We walked again down that corridor and into the hall. 'I do not know where your children are,' he said quietly. 'I did not know of this place underground. I do not know where they are now. You must believe me.'

I wondered if I did.

'But you knew most of the rest.'

'No, monsieur, only parts of it.'

'You knew about the madman here. You knew about the two children, the Soult children. You lied to me. And tried to fool me.'

Le Brève whispered into the night. 'Monsieur, please understand. I told you that I would search, everywhere, and I have. Now we will take this house apart, and tomorrow we will search in the woods. But you must steel yourself.'

'She's already taken the kids. In a big car.'

'Then we will trace it, monsieur. We will arrest her.'

'How much are they paying you?' I accused him.

'Monsieur, how do I know you are not in league with her?'

'For God's sake, don't wait. Just find them.'

We could have argued for ever, but Emma slipped her hand through my arm. 'Inspector, if we trust you, you must also trust us.'

Le Brève's career must have been finished, but he gave no sign of nerves. We stood underneath the chandelier and he looked up to the ceiling. I followed his eyes. It shone and twinkled, now it was fully lit, an expensive piece of equipment, surviving from grander days. From the original house. 'I agree. I accept,' he said.

'Inspector, we must find Estelle.' I still thought of her by that name. 'The car was a big Peugeot—'

'I want to see the room first, and the old woman.'

'I want to know the truth.'

He stared at me as if truth did not exist. 'I must see Madame Soult first.'

I was not going to let him out of my sight: I stuck to him like a leech as he walked to Madame's room and peered in at the lonely figure in the bed, and opened the trapdoor.

'Did you suspect?' I asked. 'Did you think that they might be there, in this secluded house? A house she paid you to guard?'

He rounded on me, his lips lined with white spittle. 'God damn you. How the hell could I know? Do you think I would have left them here?'

'You had men on the gate. Cars have gone in and out. Didn't they know her? Didn't they inspect the load?'

'They only knew the cars, monsieur. The little Citroën. The Peugeot. They had orders to respect the privacy of a figure under a blanket.'

'Henri Soult?'

He nodded.

'You let them imprison my kids.'

He was smouldering with resentment. 'That is a lie. Men were on the gate because Madame Soult asked me. She wanted to keep Henri secure. No one must know.'

'She can't have been sane for years.'

'She treated him like a child because he was one,' he mused. 'We knew that she kept him inside here, instead of committing him to care. I did not know of the prison. He was insane, but Madame would never believe it.'

'And so she paid for guards?'

'Yes, monsieur.'

'And you knew about the daughter? You knew about Estelle Devereau?' I challenged.

He shook his head slowly. 'I knew her as a woman trying

to live her own life. A new life. I did not interfere. I tried to warn you. Stupidly you became involved.'

We looked at the frail old woman, who had woven the web around us. She might have been a wisp of cloth, a tiny bird in the blankets, and yet she had taken my children, and nearly destroyed our marriage. She was a flimsy monster, an attenuated ghost, whose breath rattled like an old refrigerator.

'She is surreal,' le Brève said.

'Find my children!' Emma cried.

'Everybody here may be an accessory to murder,' I stormed. He was a Caliban, and he knew it, from the sweat of his brow to the bloodshot whites of his eyes.

'There are no bodies, monsieur.'

'For God's sake, man, where are they?' I shouted at him, my nerves shredded. 'It's your responsibility.' He must have suspected some link by taking me to that bleak wood on the first day.

'I wanted to explain, monsieur, that when children vanish it is unwise to have too much hope.'

'I'll find them,' I swore at him. 'And I'll have you for negligence.'

'That is a threat, monsieur. You must first be sure of your facts. This part of France has long memories,' he said, licking his lips.

'You knew about Estelle Soult. You knew, and you did not tell me.'

'You would not have believed me,' he said. He glanced at Emma. 'Perhaps he would not have listened.' He turned on his heel and closed the door to that room. 'Let us leave her alone. There is not much we can do until I can question her.'

I waited for him outside as he gave orders for two of his men to search the basement prison, then photograph and wait by the body.

'Now. If you would permit me, I will attend to certain other duties . . .' He began to walk back to the Challendars' wing.

'Find her,' I yelled.

In the atmosphere of that house every noise seemed to

285

whisper their names, Martin and Susie. Emma and I stood on the steps holding on to each other. It would be first light soon. The moon went skidding through cloud. After two long nights I was drained and exhausted, and I feared that some further secrets would slip away. One of the police team brought us two cups of coffee. Tomorrow would soon be a fact, and with it the harsh truth that I had really found nothing except a crazy old woman, a crippled son and a conspiracy. I passed each fact through my mind, examining le Brève's explanation, desperate to discover what had happened. This whole estate was the graveyard of my hopes. Were our children now here, or elsewhere, dead or alive? And why . . . and where . . . now that Henri was dead?

Perhaps we were all insane, in our different ways. Le Brève, the little underdog who had bought his way to the top on Madame Soult's money, like his former colleague Elorean. Old Madame Soult herself, corrupted first by the war and then by the loss of her son. Henri Soult, who had played with fire and been burnt, burnt to the bone and the soul, twisted out of humankind. And in the process his sister . . . Estelle. Hélène. Estelle who surely was not mad? Estelle who had been married and lived with the family secret and produced a child of her own. Estelle who in the end had come for them.

Estelle who knew the answers. Hélène. Between the death of the brother, the shock of the old witch-woman, the Challendars' obtuseness and the discovery of that underground prison I had been too slow.

I ran back inside to find le Brève, in the Challendars' room, drinking a glass of cognac.

'Are you arresting Hélène?'

'I have given orders, monsieur, to pick her up.'

'Where?'

'Who knows?'

'I want a car. Now.'

'Why, monsieur?'

'She may have gone to her flat. In Pontauban. I want to see her.'

'We will soon check, monsieur. She is not escaping.'

'Not escaping? What has she done with the kids?'

286

He raised his eyebrows. 'If she has taken them, monsieur . . . Leave it to my officers.'

'She must know where they are. Martin and Susie. She must.'

'I think they are buried up here, monsieur. It is more likely. We will dig in the morning. As soon as it is light. I have a professional team, and sniffer dogs. Do not worry: we will soon find them.'

I was torn with uncertainty. Emma said, 'Find that woman!' We needed to question le Brève, who could be implicated up to his neck. We also wanted to be there if and when the bodies were found: it would be a part of our lives dug up for inspection. But we needed to act.

Le Brève seemed to hesitate. Then he handed over the interrogation of the sullen Challendars and stood up. The canary chirped in its cage, its routine disturbed.

'I suggest you go back and rest. In a day or two it will be all over, your nightmare.'

'Inspector! We need a car.'

He did not answer but stood there with me in the numb hours of the early morning, before the dawn broke. We wandered like lost souls through to the hall which seemed somehow greyer and shabbier in spite of the blazing lights.

We followed him out to the portico, where he summoned his big blue police Citroën. It braked at the foot of the steps, just short of Henri's body, now lying under a sheet. Inspector Clerrard emerged. 'He will take you back,' he said.

I ran down the steps, away from that grim house for the last time, with Emma beside me. It was only then that I realized she was still holding the little toy dog.

32

We ran down the steps together as if we were prisoners escaping, Emma's hand bunched in mine. I jumped in the back of the Citroën and told them to go, go, go: down that curving avenue of trees where I had first been hunted and then come back to search. A gendarme pulled back the gates and we roared out on to the road, our headlights picking up the white stones of the wall and the rocks marking the ditches. We hurtled through the village, Gourdon-sur-Loup, where the houses were closed up like tombstones in a huge graveyard. The church tower loomed in the night and I tried to tell Emma of the things that had taken place there, concealed now but not forgotten, at least by the old woman.

'Emma,' I whispered, as the car swept past, 'Emma, will you ever forgive me?'

She clutched the inside strap. 'Let's find them first.'

The car wound round the square, disturbing the feral cats whose eyes glowed in the dark, and out on the other side, the valley where nothing grew. I opened the window a little and we caught the scent of eucalyptus. Emma's fingers sought mine and she breathed in deeply.

'I'm glad to get out of that place,' Clerrard muttered, his long face staring at the roadside.

'I think she's still got the children,' Emma said.

If only thinking were fact. I feared that if they had been taken they would not be left to give evidence.

Clerrard was silent. We accelerated through the night, while faint streaks of light appeared in the eastern sky. 'O God, our help in ages past, our hope for years to come . . .' Once again, lines from the old hymn came to my mind.

We were coming into better country, flatter and more prosperous as we drove out of the gorge. A village with street lights, houses with lights behind curtains. Gourdon had been shuttered and dead, as if guarding its secrets. Now there were dry-stone walls alongside the road, marking out the vineyards, occasional farms, a criss-cross of power cables on the posts zapping past. The pink lines of pre-dawn.

'I'm sorry,' Emma said suddenly. 'I'm sorry I doubted you.'

'Love you, my darling.'

'What happened to us, Jim?'

She swayed against me in the car, a small bundle in the cotton jacket, her hair mussed. I told her about my searches and the way I had called on Estelle. I had been blind. I begged her to put from her mind that afternoon when I'd been seduced. In the final analysis there are some things that must be forgiven.

'Is that all?'

'Yes.'

Emma did not respond. I told her how I had seen the skull beneath the skin, as we prepared to spend that last night in the house.

Emma leaned forward and urged on the driver. 'Hurry,' she said.

That cluster of lights was Pontauban in its pre-dawn glory. I recognized the landmarks and realized how much of myself was grafted there, indelibly, in three and a half grim weeks. We fled past the river at the bottom of the hill and up into the main square, passing the newspaper offices where I had first seen Estelle. The park where she later met me. Empty spaces waiting for daybreak.

'Where to?' the driver asked.

'Rue des Escaliers,' I said.

The car followed a boulevard towards the old town, where the houses were pushed together, shoulder to shoulder.

The driver nodded. '*Cq va.*' We bumped up the narrow street where Estelle had brought me, high on the hill near the old church of Mary Magdalene. Cobbles shiny as grease, only just room to park by pulling up on the sidewalk. I was looking for another car, the one she had used for them. A number of small Renaults or Fiats were scattered about, but no big Peugeots. I pointed out the gate to the courtyard with the broken fountain, where she had once taken me. Was it really less than four weeks ago? It was already four lifetimes, Emma's and mine and the kids'. The gate was closed but unlocked. In the first light the birds started singing somewhere up on the rooftops as we ran across and up the stairs, Clerrard, Emma and I, racing up to Estelle's apartment on the second floor. The half-wild cats scattered, the uncollected washing still flapped on the balconies like babies hanging out to dry. Other police had already arrived and were fanned out around the building. Clerrard had drawn his gun. Estelle had ridden the tiger and the tiger was coming to get her.

We hammered on the door. There was no response. We stood outside on the landing, then Clerrard forced the lock and we burst in. This was the place I remembered, the passage past the bedrooms to the living room and kitchen beyond. It looked smaller and shabbier now as he switched on the lights. The hatred had gone from my mind, leaving only a stark reminder of what she had done, amid that nondescript furniture, and the clutter of pictures and books.

'Madame Devereau—'

'Estelle—'

Clerrard ran through the rooms, kicking open the door to the bedroom that we had used — Estelle and me, that bed with the clothes hanging over it as if she had forgotten them, panties, and bra and a skirt — then the kitchen and bathroom. I saw again the aquamarine tiles and the patterned soapdish and remembered her watching me there, when I had sought her help after the attack in the clearing.

The clearing where she had planted four new bushes of roses in some small act of contrition.

'Where are they?' Emma called. But Estelle had gone.

We were ransacking the place now, in our turn pulling out drawers and cupboards, tipping boxes on to the floor. The typewriter in the study was plugged in and switched on, but we could find no message. The documents were neatly filed, and entirely domestic. In a drawer was her purse and cheque book, a passport and 2,000 francs. Only the handbag was missing. In the kitchen the coffee pot was warm. Estelle had been there only an hour or two ago, and then vanished again.

'She can't have gone far,' Emma said.

Clerrard fingered the passport and gave his weary shrug. 'The whole of France—'

But Emma turned to me. 'Where else would she go? Somebody else who knows?'

And it was clear enough.

'Come on,' I said to Clerrard. 'Let's move, man, move.'

We left a gendarme on guard and raced back to the cars. The old town was ablaze with lights now, people disturbed by the sirens as our little convoy of cars hit the long tree-lined avenue to the outskirts of Pontauban.

'Rue Bartholdi,' I said.

'Why there?' Emma shouted, over the shriek of alarms.

'The one guy who understands her. Old Doc Raymonde,' I said.

'Who?'

'The family physician. Philosopher, sex expert and speleo-logist.'

'What's that?' Emma asked.

We skidded round a corner, across the medieval bridge and into the Cours Verdun.

'Speleology. The study of caves,' I said, and I knew now that the old man was dealing in codes. The caves of the mind, the black holes of human conduct.

It was only five minutes away, that drab building in the suburbs just over the bridge with the brass plate on the door. 'Le Docteur Anton Raymonde'.

No lights were showing as the police cars switched off and began to stake out the building, front and rear. 'You think she might come here?' Clerrard asked.

I remembered the day I had gone there, after the tabac woman had first given me the name. It was there that I had learned the extent of Madame Soult's madness: Raymonde was in it too, this closed-circle conspiracy that had kept hold of its secrets for nearly forty years, while the old woman became finally and totally insane. Raymonde who had warned me not to go to Gourdon-sur-Loup. Small wonder that afterwards, when I told Estelle, she had been so fearful that he might have given her secret away. That had been the day she had taken me, on that brass bed in the apartment, the time that she had made love.

'Jesus Christ,' I said. 'I'm sure that she'll come here.'

'Perhaps she will resist arrest?'

'God knows—'

'Just find her,' Emma said.

The main door was open, almost as if they expected us. We plunged up the stairs and I led the way to his apartment. The bell jangled in the hall.

It was five o'clock in the morning but we could hear him coming, flip-flop down the passage. The bolts were drawn back and Dr Raymonde peered out, a frost of white stubble on his chin, wearing pyjamas, a faded dressing gown tied by a cord round his middle.

'Police,' Clerrard said.

The old man sighed, and pulled the door open.

'I understand. Come in.'

33

I brushed past Raymonde and walked into his consulting room. She was waiting for me inside the door in a scarlet dress like the whore of Babylon. As I burst in I saw the book-lined room, the room where he had once talked to me, in disarray. And Estelle. Smaller and older than I remembered, the bloom seemed to have faded and the silver-blonde hair had dulled. A room that had not recovered from her sudden arrival, when she rushed there in the night and they had confronted each other. The old man's eyes were disturbed: I could see that his hands shook. Now she awaited us, an abductress in a red dress. The dress was as tight as a sheath, but her face was haggard.

'Where are they?' Emma said. Clerrard, entering behind us, had pulled out the pistol from the waistband of his blue suit.

'Put it away,' Estelle said. 'It won't be necessary.' I was conscious of gendarmes crowding us.

'Jim,' she whispered.

We confronted each other across the room. The remaining child of Madame Soult.

'I'm charging you with abduction and concealment. Suspected murder,' Clerrard intoned.

She smiled, as if her thoughts were far away in her own private world.

I found a small voice inside me. 'Henri is dead.'

Estelle shrieked, and I thought she would collapse. She pointed a finger at me. 'You've killed him,' she cried. 'You went there and you've killed him. Why can't you leave us alone?'

'Estelle, he shot himself.'

'The children?' Emma screamed at her. 'What have you done with our children?'

'Done with them?'

'You took my children. Our children. You had it planned from the start. Someone came in the night,' I said.

'I borrowed them.'

'Borrowed?'

'Where are they?' Emma howled at her.

Estelle looked at her for the first time, a look of contempt and envy. 'Listen.'

I started across the room to the door beyond, which led to the bedroom. It was closed, with a key in the lock, but the handle was rattling. We heard them. We heard them.

Nothing mattered any more. We pushed Estelle aside and charged at the door. The key turned in the lock and they were suddenly there, thin and pale and exhausted. They had come back from the dead.

'Susie! Martin!' We blurted out their names between the tears and could think of nothing more. Nothing but snatching them to us, almost too painful to hold, instantly real. Flesh and blood and not illusion. Emma pulled them into her arms and crushed them as if she was terrified that they would disappear again. But they were alive, survivors of an ordeal, dressed in unrecognized clothes. Martin's thin face was contorted with happiness, and all he could say was 'Dad, take us away!' Susie had lost less weight and seemed almost old, mature. Although she was two years younger she would survive it better. But all I could do was thank my new-found God that they had been found . . . alive.

We hugged and kissed in that room, while Clerrard and my temptress stood there watching. 'It will be necessary to see . . . if anything has happened . . .' the Inspector said. 'A medical check.'

'Daddy, Daddy, they haven't touched us,' Susanna volunteered.

'But we were shut up in a really dreadful place . . .' Martin shuddered at the recall, 'and paraded for an old witch.'

Emma's arms encircled the kids. 'I know. I know,' I said. 'I've seen her . . . But it's all over now.'

I kissed them both to make sure they would not go away. These were my children returned, and I found myself saying, 'Jesus. Oh sweet Jesus.' Susie seemed newly grown-up, her hair scraped back in a ponytail, held by an elastic band, her pallid face alive with happiness. And Martin, the elder, more vulnerable, was only a twelve-year-old kid who needed a haircut, dressed in some new French casuals.

'Oh Dad. Oh Dad. They came on the night of the storm. That terrible man in the mask. And took us away. We couldn't cry out or anything: he put something over our mouths. When we woke up we were sick, and locked in a barn of a house.'

'I've been there too.'

'They kept us underground so that no one could see us, and then each night we had to come out of this trapdoor to talk to the mad old woman. She was horrible. A dragon.'

'Don't talk about it,' I said.

They were only kids, why in God's name should it have been them? Why them, why us? I hugged them to me again and saw the flaws in my own character that had brought us to this. And standing there in the corner, in that dress as sharp as a flame, was the woman who had taken advantage. I felt I had betrayed myself, and betrayed Emma. I hated them all, Estelle, Raymonde and the old woman in the madhouse protected by le Brève.

Our eyes met. Estelle's were that cold blue of frosty skies, and I saw that they were empty.

Clerrard moved across, talking about charges and custody. It was a warning from the sidelines, the formalities clicking into place. A babble of French voices. More police arriving, and the stocky figure of le Brève pushing his way inside.

'Why? Why did you do it?' I asked her.

In a murmur that was scarcely audible, Estelle said, 'I wanted to borrow the children – only borrow them – for my mother's sake. And then . . . and then . . . she would not let me return them . . .'

I comforted Susie and Martin, who were beginning to cry. 'It's all right now. It's going to be all over. Just let me see this through. Wait . . . just for a moment . . . in the other room. You're quite safe now.'

But they would not go. They clung to my arms, and as the room filled up we were in a theatre where Estelle commanded the stage.

'You led me on, you bitch. Why didn't you stop it?'

'You kept asking my help. Why didn't you see? As soon as you had gone home I would have released them and no one would ever know where they had been.'

'Liar.'

Her figure was slim as a girl's; now it seemed statuesque. 'You had your family. I wanted to help mine.' She placed her hands on her hips, fingers clenched, while flash bulbs began to go off, and the police recorded every agony.

'But when we began to search . . . ? When I went up to Gourdon?'

She shook her head. 'I hoped you would give up when you couldn't get in to the château.'

'Knowing my kids were inside there – in that unspeakable place?'

'I wanted to explain to you,' she said. 'I really wanted to, Jim.' The name came out quietly.

'Don't say that word. Don't call me that any more.'

But she ignored me. 'I should never have become involved, but the past catches up. My brother asked me to do it. Then I fell . . . in love with you, Jim.'

I heard le Brève sucking his teeth, but the room had gone silent. Somewhere outside that building other people were living, sleeping, but at that moment the only real world was there, sealed off like a disease by a ring of police cars.

'Henri? How often did you see him?'

'I was his point of contact with the outside world. He was hidden in the house. After what happened to us when we were the same age as your children now. The cellar was his hiding place.'

'Who built it?'

'My mother had it made for him, before she lost her mind.'

Very quietly, Emma said, 'What did Henri ask you to do?'

Estelle looked at her rival, the woman she had dispossessed. 'Mama was suffering, having delusions. She could not even remember who Henri was, and that hurt him terribly. She kept demanding the children – calling for us as children. And Henri said if we found some it might restore her peace of mind.'

'You hoped to cure her?' Emma asked in disbelief.

'No. Just to give her some happiness in her last days. You witnessed how she lives, not even facing the daylight.'

My own children were listening, and I saw that they had to know if they were ever to wash away the experience of those few weeks.

'So. How did it come about?'

'I was responsible for running Mama's estate, including the hire of the gîte. Henri suggested that we should find some children by stipulating ages in the advertisement. When you replied it seemed ideal. A late booking by an English couple with two children. A boy and girl, just the right ages. I thought . . . I hoped . . . it would be easier with them. They would not understand the language when we took them there to see her, and then brought them back.'

'You kidnapped them.'

'Henri was with me,' she said. 'We came in the night and borrowed them.'

'Borrowed? It was a murder hunt. They have been missing for over three weeks. And you went back and stole their toys.'

'Henri. To keep them happy.' She spoke like an automaton. 'When my mother saw them she seemed to rally. She wanted them to stay, so that she could always see them. And Henri begged me to keep them, or else he would kill himself.'

'So you just agreed and kept them,' I said bitterly.

The old man Raymonde began to intervene. 'She came to me. Her mental state shows a deteriorating sexual psychosis . . . she is a schizoid persona . . .'

'But you didn't care about us?'

'I wanted to tell you, I swear,' Estelle said.

'You knew where they were all the time?'

'I thought they were free in the house. Not in the cellar.'

297

'Lies.'

'No. Mother of God, it's the truth. I only saw them at night. We would play games in the house. Ask them. Ask them.'

'Games?' I remembered how erratic her hours were, how late she was coming home. But how much was truth or fiction, in her own mind, I wondered, looking from Estelle to le Brève and then to Emma and our wide-eyed kids.

'It's true,' Susie suddenly said. 'We played Monopoly. And we had television, but it was all in French.'

'I swear to you I never expected it would end as it did. I did not ask you to come to the newspaper offices. Or want to interview you.' That ominous day in Pontauban, when she had sat in the sunshine, and I had asked her to help me.

Le Brève asserted himself. 'All right. Enough. We shall have a prosecutor's interrogation. Not here.'

But I accused her. 'You kept my children . . . like animals.'

And then at last she cried. She sobbed into her hands, her body shaking. 'I did not intend to hurt them, but Henri demanded loyalty. My mother and my brother were as dear to me as your family.'

'You took them there and left them and then heard that we were searching.'

'I did not know how to stop you.'

'How did you get them from the gîte?' I held them tightly again, Martin and Susie, those two underground faces returned from hell.

Raymonde said, 'She came to me . . . for drugs.'

I turned to le Brève. 'Did you help?'

In a distant voice Estelle said, 'Chief Inspector le Brève knew nothing.'

'But you suspected something,' I told him. 'You took me to the clearing: to the place where the fire occurred.'

Le Brève said, 'Estelle Devereau, I am arresting you. I warn you to say no more.' One of his men produced handcuffs which swung from his wrist like small gallows. I watched them pinion her.

*

The Inspector bowed his head, birdlike, as she was led away, but the part that he had played also mattered to me. I turned on him angrily as soon as Estelle had gone. 'You knew about the Soults. We interviewed your friend Elorean, who was paid off by them. You lied to me that two children had been burned in the woods.' I blazed across and stared down at his compact little figure.

He waited, listening to their footsteps down the stairs, the doors shutting outside. A sound of departing cars. Then we were alone, le Brève, Emma, the children and me. Old Raymonde had collapsed in one of his frayed leather armchairs.

Le Brève turned for a moment to Emma. 'Madame, may I ask you to walk the children downstairs? We will join you in a few minutes.'

I nodded to the kids and they agreed. 'All right,' she said. 'Don't be long, Daddy. I want to go home.'

We confronted each other, le Brève and I, the once-cocky little Inspector and the man who had drawn the short straw in a lottery. He seemed smaller and darker, diminished.

'Monsieur, you must understand that being black is never easy. Always there is an extra hurdle to jump. And prejudice. You are aware of that?'

I understood, but made no comment.

'So. I wanted to get on. In the police force. My father was in the police,' he said proudly. 'In Toulouse, before the war.'

'I know. I talked to your wife, Ninette.'

He smiled. 'When you stayed on to investigate I thought you were laying false trails.'

'I found that you lived in style.'

He grew agitated, then angry. 'Listen, monsieur. Do you know what I am paid? Three hundred thousand francs a year. Do you think I want to live on that? Do you think I keep Ninette on money like that?' He laughed in my face. 'No, sir.'

'So you resort to blackmail?'

'Blackmail?' Again he laughed. 'Don't be so stupid. I have done nothing wrong, except a little dissembling. Nothing illegal. When we were young policemen, Elorean and I, like

299

the ones you saw here, we investigated a child who was burned to death in the woods. That would be in nineteen fifty-three: thirty-seven years ago.'

'I know. Who was he?'

He shrugged. 'How you say: a gypsy. A Romany. Poor people's children were rounded up by the Soults, Henri and Hélène, for sadistic games. One summer they were staying at the place you rented. They made a house in the woods, and tied these children up and set fire to it. One of them was burned to death. There was a mad streak to Henri even then. It was said that he tried to rescue him and fell into the flames.'

'You said two, at first. The papers reported two.'

'Of course. To protect the Soults. The Soult boy Henri, who was terribly disfigured, and his sister. Madame Soult wanted to protect them both. And she was prepared to pay. They were given different identities. The boy's death was then concealed. The roses were on a real grave.' He pointed to the exhausted Raymonde. 'The old man here can confirm it.'

'Henri Soult was deranged,' the doctor said. 'A sado-masochist.'

'Are you sure?'

'Yes. The evidence was quite clear. Even in those days Henri had to be kept apart. Isolated, and dangerous. Like Madame, he never recovered from the war.'

'Is that true?'

'I swear it is, monsieur,' Raymonde said. 'She paid the price.'

The room seemed to be stifling us, hemming us in in spite of the growing daylight. I wanted to get out, pick up Em and the kids and run, never see them again, any of them or any part of that countryside, but I held on.

I turned to le Brève. 'And you?'

'I was the investigating officer. A young black policeman with a career to make. Can you understand that?'

'A little, perhaps.'

'The Soults were a wealthy family. Once they had been the richest in southern France. But of course the war, the confiscations, the destruction of their château . . . Madame

Soult was still rich, and she adored the children. Unfortunately they had been left in that isolated house at Chenoncey while she was away in Paris. And then it happened. The fire and the death, and the injury to Henri.'

'What did they ask you to do?'

He squared his shoulders and seemed to stick out his jaw. He was not apologizing.

'You can guess, monsieur. Someone was burned to death in a tragedy in the woods. By wealthy children, one of them already half crazy, who was then hideously injured. Madame came to see me. She came to see me,' he repeated.

'And made you an offer?' I said.

He shrugged. 'Put it that way if you like.'

My eyes wandered round Raymonde's apartment: the rows of medical books in the disordered room, the coffee machine and the desk, with its endless notes for the book that would never be written. I had a panicky feeling that they might have disappeared again, Emma and the kids. Vanished into the night. I needed them.

'So you took the pieces of silver?'

Le Brève put his head on one side. 'If you like. For the old woman's sake.'

'And your own.'

'Sometimes, monsieur, people's lives coincide. Like yours and Estelle Devereau's. What do you think she could do, Madame Soult, with a son so deformed and both children suspects for murder?'

'Murder?'

'He was tied up, monsieur, the little boy. Assaulted and tied up. Both the Soult children were sadists.'

The revelations were sickening. I remembered Estelle's bronzed body, the games she had offered to play. And le Brève had been part of a cover-up.

'It allowed her daughter to live a normal life, and Henri to stay concealed.'

'And you and your friend Elorean to live in luxury?'

Le Brève's face was impassive.

'Perhaps,' he said, 'but not in peace.'

34

I left him there, with the old physician, in the chaos of the apartment. No doubt he would grill the doctor about the extent of his role in the whole shabby affair, starting with his liaison with Madame Soult. There would be fresh locks on the doors, the usual police procedures, but I was finished with them. I was free of suspicion and guilt. I wanted out.

Dawn was breaking, and my family were waiting below, with the gendarmes le Brève had left on duty and the cadaverous Clerrard. The Inspector saw me emerge from the doorway and offered us one of the police cars, but I waved him away. Where could we go with the children at that hour in the morning? Anyway we were too happy, too excited to sleep. Instead we walked hand in hand along the cobbled streets, not caring where we were heading so long as we were there together, making up for stolen time. It was half past five in the morning but the air was heady as champagne.

Susie was skipping beside me; Emma held Martin's hand. We were a unit again, but Emma's face was troubled.

'I want to go home,' Martin said.

Home? Where was home now unless there was trust between us? My hand gripped Emma's. 'Ring your parents,' I said. 'And then we'll go. We'll drive all day.'

A shudder ran through her. Memories of pressure, pressure that had driven us here.

Jesus. As if we would ever forget that endless drive to the sun, with the kids and the gear in the back.

Now there would be the statements, the press stories, and the charges. Nothing was ever solved quickly. I needed to call Bob Dorcas, tell him when we'd be back, and Simpson in London, and the guy in the Paris embassy. The future was piling up.

I noted the police car shadowing, with Clerrard inside waiting to take us somewhere, to some hotel for breakfast.

'We'll fly back as soon as the statements are made,' I promised her. 'The car can come by rail.'

'You said we could go to the sea,' Martin cried. He was becoming alive, more like his old self; the past was a door that had shut, I hoped without scars.

I tried to joke with him. 'No more holidays. Ever.'

Emma shot me a look, as if to say 'No more obsession with work: if we hadn't drifted apart—' Then she smiled.

'She was kind to us in a way, the woman in red,' Susie whispered.

'You must forget her completely. Forget that it ever happened. Just like a dream,' Emma said. I tightened my grip on her hand, too full of emotions to talk. All of us had picked up the tab for my lack of understanding.

Emma disengaged, then slipped her hand through my arm. 'Ow. You're hurting,' I said.

We were walking over the pavé, between the parked cars, across the road, down the hill to the river. The town was very quiet and the air was still, promising another day of heat when the mist cleared. There was the old stone bridge, and the church of Saint Sepulchre on the far side, hemmed in by pollarded trees. Its stonework glistened against the pearly sky. I wanted to pray but the right words would not come. Instead Emma clung to my arm, with Susie on the other side.

We scarcely knew where we were heading. Cars began to flow past us and I felt in some kind of slow motion, watching what might have been lost: a family gathered together, the street lights on the bridge, the green water underneath, the white tower of the church on the other side. A family that was still in being.

The pressure of Emma's body showed that she felt it too.

Clerrard's car nosed past and waited at the end of the bridge, ready to take us somewhere.

I held Emma in my arms in the middle of the bridge and

kissed her. In the middle of France. In the middle of our lives. The kids were there, looking and giggling.

'Honey?'

'Yes?'

'Next time it's a family holiday.'

'Just let me know first,' she said.

Only the nightmares remained.